S0-BSQ-857

Love and the Single Heiress

By Jacquie D'Alessandro

Love and the Single Heiress
Who Will Take This Man?

Jacquie D'Alessandro

Love and the Single Heiress

AVON BOOKS
An Imprint of HarperCollins*Publishers*

This is a work of fiction. Names, characters, places, and incidents are products of the author's imagination or are used fictitiously and are not to be construed as real. Any resemblance to actual events, locales, organizations, or persons, living or dead, is entirely coincidental.

AVON BOOKS
An Imprint of HarperCollins*Publishers*
10 East 53rd Street
New York, New York 10022-5299

ISBN: 0-7394-4540-5

Printed in the U.S.A.

This book is dedicated with my gratitude to John Hensley for all his kindness, support, and hard work on my behalf. My heartfelt thanks also to his top-notch team for making me feel so welcome: Dawn Doud, DeeAnn Kline, Pam Manley, Bev Martin, Carrie Murakami, Tracey Neel, Anna Shea-Nicholls, George Scott, and Susie Straussberger. Thank you all for showing me the Power of One.

And, as always, to my incredible husband Joe, for his steadfast love, patience, and support, and for always saying "you can do it" exactly when I need to hear it; and my wonderful, makes-me-so-proud son Christopher, "you can do it" Junior. I love you best!

Acknowledgments

I would like to thank the following people for their invaluable help and support:

My editors, Carrie Feron and Erika Tsang, for their kindness, cheerleading, and wonderful ideas.

My agent, Damaris Rowland, for her faith and wisdom.

Martha Kirkland, for always knowing the answers to my research questions.

Jenni Grizzle and Wendy Etherington for keeping me going and always being up for champagne and cheesecake.

Brenda D'Alessandro, for being lots of fun, the world's best shopper, and for walking three hundred city blocks without complaining (sort of).

Thanks also to Kay and Jim Johnson, Kathy and Dick Guse, Lea and Art D'Alessandro, JoBeth Beard, Ann Wonycott, and Michelle, Steve, and Lindsey Grossman.

A cyberhug to my Looney Loopies Connie Brockway, Marsha Canham, Virginia Henley, Jill Gregory, Sandy Hingston, Julia London, Kathleen Givens, Sherri Browning, and Julie Ortolon, and also to the Temptresses.

A very special thank-you to the members of Georgia

Romance Writers, JoBeth Beard, Ana Payne, Judy Wilson, and Jeannie Pierannunzi.

And finally, thank you to all the wonderful readers who have taken the time to write or e-mail me. I love hearing from you!

Chapter 1

Today's Modern Woman should strive for personal enlightenment, independence, and forthrightness. The perfect place to begin this quest for assertiveness is in the bedchamber . . .

A Ladies' Guide to the Pursuit of
Personal Happiness and Intimate Fulfillment
by Charles Brightmore

"Scandalous, that's what it is," came an outraged male whisper. "My wife has somehow secured a copy of that deuced *Ladies' Guide*."

"How do you know?" came another gruff male whisper.

"Damned obvious, what with the way she's been acting. Been spewing out nonsense about 'today's modern woman' and 'independence' like a steaming teakettle. ust yesterday she marched into my private study and oceeded to question me regarding my gambling mark- and the amount of time I spend at White's!"

harp intakes of breath followed. "Outrageous," mut- the gruff whisperer.

ecisely what I told her."

"What did you do?"

"Why, I marched her right out of my study, called for a carriage, and sent her to Asprey's to pick out a new bauble to occupy her mind."

"Excellent. I assume your strategy worked?"

"Unfortunately not as well as I'd hoped. Last night I found her awaiting me *in my bedchamber*. Gave me quite a turn, I tell you. Especially as I'd just left my mistress and was thoroughly worn-out. Bloody hell, a wife's not supposed to make such demands, or have such expectations."

"My wife did the same thing just last week," came a third aggrieved whisper. "Entered my bedchamber, bold as you please, pushed me onto the mattress, then . . . well, I can only describe it as to say she *jumped* upon me. Completely deflated my lungs and damn near crushed me. As I lie there, immobile with shock, fighting for my very breath, *she* says in a most impatient tone, 'Bump your arse a bit.' Can you *imagine* such undignified goings-on? *Then,* just when I thought I couldn't be more astonished, she demanded to know why I'd never . . ."

The voice lowered further and Lady Catherine Ashfield, Viscountess Bickley, leaned closer to the Oriental screen that secreted her presence from the gentlemen on the other side.

". . . This Charles Brightmore must be stopped," whispered one of the gentlemen.

"I agree. A disaster of gargantuan proportions, that's what he's brought upon us. Why, if my daughter reads that cursed *Guide*, I'll never marry off the foolish chit. In dependence, indeed. Completely insupportable. Th *Guide* could well prove even worse than the uproar cited by that Wollstonecraft woman's writings. Not but ridiculous reformists' balderdash."

Murmurs of agreement followed that pronounc

Then the whisperer continued, "And as for the bedchamber, women are demanding enough creatures as it is, always wanting a new gown or earbobs or carriage or the like. 'Tis outrageous that their expectations should extend to *that*. Especially a woman of my wife's age, who is the mother of two grown children. Unseemly, that's what it is."

"Couldn't agree more. Should I ever find myself in the company of this Brightmore bastard, I'll personally wring his bloody neck. Tarring and feathering is too good for him. Everyone I've spoken to feels certain that 'Charles Brightmore' is a pseudonym, and coward that he is, he's refused to step forward and identify himself. The betting book at White's is a frenzy of wagers on the subject of his identity. Damn it all, what sort of man would think, let alone write, such unseemly ideas?"

"Well, I stopped at White's just before coming here, and the latest theory proposes the possibility that Charles Brightmore is in fact a *woman*. Indeed, I heard . . ."

The gentleman's low-pitched words were drowned out by a trill of nearby feminine laughter. Catherine inched closer, all but pressing her ear to the screen.

". . . and if it's true, it would be the scandal of the century . . ." She heard some more unintelligible mumbling, then, ". . . hired an investigator two days ago to get to the bottom of this. He comes highly recommended . . . ruthless, and will ferret out the truth. In fact—oh, bloody hell, my wife's caught sight of me. Hang it, look at her, fluttering her eyelashes at me. Shocking, that's what it is. Appalling. And altogether frightening."

Catherine peeked around the edge of the screen. Lady Markingworth stood at the edge of the dance floor, her rotund proportions ensconced in an unfortunate shade of yellowish green satin that cast her complexion with a distinctly jaundiced hue, her brown hair arranged in a complicated coiffure involving sausage curls, ribbons, and peacock feathers. With her attention fixed on the opposite side of the screen, Lady Markingworth was batting her eyes as one might if caught in a dust-ridden windstorm. Then, with an air of determination, she marched toward the screen.

"Egad," came a horrified, panic-filled whisper that Catherine assumed belonged to Lord Markingworth. "She's got that damnable gleam in her eye."

"And it's too late to escape, old man."

"Bloody hell. A plague on that bastard Charles Brightmore's house. I'm going to find out who this person is, then kill him—or her. Slowly."

"*There* you are, Ephraim," said Lady Markingworth, her greeting followed by a girlish giggle. "I've been searching for you everywhere. The waltz is about to start. And how fortunate that Lords Whitly and Carweather are with you. Your wives anxiously await you near the dance floor, my lords."

Throat clearing and several harrumphs followed this announcement, then the scuffle of shoes upon the parquet floor as the group moved away.

Catherine leaned against the oak-paneled wall and drew a shaky breath, pressing her hands to her midsection. Slipping behind the screen in search of a moment of sanctuary from the hordes of party guests had taken a very unexpected turn. All she'd wanted was to avoid the approaching Lords Avenbury and Ferrymouth, both of whom had dogged her footsteps since the moment she'd arrived at her father's birthday party and separately attempted to maneuver her into a tête-à-tête. Lords Avenbury and Ferrymouth had been followed closely by Sir Percy Whitenall and several others whose names escaped her, all of whom bore unmistakable—and unwanted—

gleams of interest in their eyes. Good heavens, her official mourning period for her husband had ended only days ago. She could almost hear her dear friend Genevieve's voice warning her just last week, *The men will come out of every nook and crevice. Such is the fate of a single heiress.*

Damnation, she wasn't single—she was a *widow*. With a nearly grown child. She had not believed she would generate such male . . . enthusiasm so quickly. If she'd suspected, she might well have been tempted to continue wearing her widow's weeds.

Yet by avoiding her unexpected suitors, she'd inadvertently eavesdropped upon a conversation far more disturbing than the male attention. Lord Markingworth's angry words echoed through her mind. *The possibility that Charles Brightmore is a woman . . . if it's true, it would be the scandal of the century.*

What had he said that she'd missed? And what of this ruthless investigator hired to ferret out the details? Who was he? And how close was he to discovering the truth?

. . . I'm going to find out who this person is, then kill him—or her. Slowly.

A foreboding chill snaked down her spine. Good Lord, what had she done?

Chapter 2

Today's Modern Woman should know that a gentleman hoping to entice her will employ one of two methods: either a straightforward, direct approach, or a more subtle, gentle wooing. Sadly, as with most matters, few gentlemen consider which method the lady might actually prefer—until it's too late.

A Ladies' Guide to the Pursuit of
Personal Happiness and Intimate Fulfillment
by Charles Brightmore

Tonight he would begin his subtle, gentle wooing.

Andrew Stanton stood in a shadowed corner of Lord Ravensly's elegant drawing room, feeling very much the way he imagined a soldier on the brink of battle might feel—anxious, focused, and very much praying for a hopeful outcome.

His gaze skimmed restlessly over the formally attired guests. Lavishly gowned and bejeweled ladies swirled around the dance floor in the arms of their perfectly turned-out escorts to the lilting strains of the string trio.

But none of the waltzing ladies was the one he sought. Where was Lady Catherine?

He sipped his brandy, his fingers clenched around the cut glass snifter in an attempt to stem the urge to toss back the potent drink in a single gulp. Damn it all, he hadn't felt this nervous and unsettled since . . . never. Well, not counting the handful of times over the past fourteen months he'd spent in Lady Catherine's company. Ridiculous how the mere thought of the woman, how simply being in the same room with her affected his ability to breathe straight and think properly . . . er, think straight and breathe properly.

His efforts to seek out Lady Catherine this evening had already been interrupted three times by people with whom he had no desire to speak. He feared one more such interruption would cause him to grind his teeth down to stubs.

Again he scanned the room, and his jaw tightened. Blast. After being forced to wait for what felt like an eternity finally to court her, why couldn't Lady Catherine—albeit unknowingly—at least soothe his anxiety by showing herself?

The hum of conversation surrounded him, marked by peals of laughter and the chime of fine crystal goblet rims touching in congratulatory toasts. Prisms of light reflected off the highly polished parquet floor from the dozens of candles glowing in the sparkling crystal chandeliers, casting the room in a warm, golden glow. Over one hundred of Society's finest had turned out for Lord Ravensly's sixtieth birthday party. *Society's finest and . . . me.*

He reached up and tugged at his carefully tied cravat. "Damned uncomfortable neckwear," he muttered. Whoever had invented the constraining blight on fashion should be tossed in the Thames. Although his expertly tailored formal black cutaway rivaled that of any noble gentleman in the room, part of him still felt like a weed amongst the hothouse flowers. Uncomfortable. Out of his element. And painfully aware that he stood far outside the lofty social strata in which he currently found himself—certainly much further than anyone present would ever have expected. His long-standing friendship with Lord Ravensly's son Philip, and growing friendship with Lord Ravensly himself, as well as Lady Catherine, had secured Andrew an invitation to this evening's elegant birthday celebration. Too bad Philip himself wasn't here. With Meredith soon to give birth, Philip hadn't wanted to venture far from his wife's side.

Although perhaps it was just as well that Philip wasn't in attendance. When he had given Andrew his blessing to court Lady Catherine, he'd warned Andrew that his sister wouldn't be eager to marry again, given her disastrous first marriage. The last thing Andrew needed was to have Philip nearby, muttering words of doom.

He drew a deep breath and forced himself to focus on the positive. His frustrating failure to locate Lady Catherine in the crowd *had* afforded him the opportunity to converse with numerous investors who had already committed funds to Andrew and Philip's museum venture. Lords Avenbury and Ferrymouth were eager to know how things were progressing, as were Lords Markingworth, Whitly, and Carweather, all of whom had invested funds. Mrs. Warrenfield appeared anxious to invest a healthy amount, as did Lord Kingsly. Lord Borthrasher who'd already made a sizable investment, seemed interested in investing more. After speaking with them, Andrew had also made some discreet inquiries regarding the matter he'd recently been commissioned to look into.

But with the business talk now completed, he'd retreated to this quiet corner to gather his thoughts, much as he did before preparing for a pugilistic bout at Gentleman Jackson's Emporium. His gaze continued to pan over the guests, halting abruptly when he caught sight of Lady Catherine, exiting from behind an Oriental silk screen near the French doors.

He stilled at the sight of her bronze gown. Every time he'd seen her during the past year, her widow's weeds had engulfed her like a dark, heavy rain cloud. Now officially out of mourning, she resembled a golden bronze sun setting over the Nile, gilding the landscape with slanting rays of warmth.

She paused to exchange a few words with a gentleman, and Andrew's avid gaze noted the way the vivid material of her gown contrasted with her pale shoulders and complemented her shiny chestnut curls gathered into a Grecian knot. The becoming coiffure left the vulnerable curve of her nape bare . . .

He blew out a long breath and raked his free hand through his hair. How many times had he imagined skimming his fingers, his mouth, over that soft, silky skin? More than he cared to admit. She was all things lovely and good. A perfect lady. Indeed, she was perfect in every way.

He knew damn well he wasn't good enough for her. In spite of his financial successes, socially he felt like a beggar with his nose pressed to the glass at the confectioner's shop. But neither his mind nor his common sense were in charge any longer. She was free. And while he cherished the platonic relationship that had blossomed between them over the past fourteen months, his feelings ran far deeper than mere friendship, and his heart would not be denied. His sullied past, her noble lineage, his lack of lineage—all be damned.

His gaze tracked her slim, regal form as she made her way around the perimeter of the room, and his heart executed the same erratic hop it performed every time he looked at her. If he'd been capable of laughter, he would have chuckled at himself and his gut-level reaction to her. He felt like a tongue-tied, green schoolboy—quite deflating as he normally considered himself a man of at least *some* finesse.

Rolling his shoulders to loosen his tense muscles, he pulled in a lungful of air and prepared to step from the shadows. A firm hand grasped him by the shoulder.

"You might want to straighten your cravat before heading into the fray, old man."

Andrew turned swiftly and found himself staring into Philip's amused, bespectacled brown eyes. Frustration instantly gave way to concern. "What are *you* doing here? Is Meredith all right?"

"My wife is fine, thank you, or at least as fine as a woman in the final weeks of pregnancy can be. As to why I am here, for reasons I cannot fathom, Meredith *insisted* I make an appearance at Father's birthday celebration." He shook his head, clearly bemused. "I did not want to leave her, but if there's one thing I've learned over the past few months, it is that only a fool argues with an expectant mother. So I reluctantly left her side and suffered the three-hour journey to London to bestow my felicitations upon Father. Meredith suggested I remain here overnight, but I flatly refused. My coach is being brought 'round even as we speak. However, I couldn't leave without talking to you. How goes the progress on the museum?"

"Very well. Hiring Simon Wentworth as our steward was one of the smartest things we've done. He's extremely organized and keeps the workmen on schedule."

"Excellent." Philip's voice dropped to a near whisper. "How goes the Charles Brightmore investigation?"

Andrew blew out a sigh. "The bastard doesn't appear to exist, except on paper as the author of the *Guide*, but that only serves to intrigue me further. Trust me, I have every intention of collecting the impressive sum Lord Markingworth and his friends have promised me for identifying the author."

"Yes, well, that's why I recommended you. You're tenacious and unrelenting when it comes to ferreting out the truth. And thanks to your ties to the museum and your association with the, *ahem*, exalted likes of me, you have access to both Society's finest and persons of, shall we say, more humble origins. People would be far more inclined to confide in you than a Runner, and your presence at these types of soirees doesn't raise a brow, as a stranger's or a Runner's would."

"Yes, that is to my advantage," Andrew agreed. "It has been my experience that clues are often inadvertently revealed during casual conversations."

"Well, I've no doubt of your success. I only hope that revealing this Charles Brightmore's identity puts a stop to this damnable *Ladies' Guide*. I want that book pulled from the shelves before Meredith manages to secure a copy. My lovely wife is by far too independent as it is. Keeping her in check already requires nearly more energy than I can muster."

"Yes, I'm certain that it's your beautiful wife's *independence* that drains your energy." His gaze skimmed over Philip in a pointed fashion. "You do not appear to be suffering overmuch at her hands. But fear not—I intend to unmask this Brightmore person. I'll not only have the pleasure of exposing the charlatan, but the money I'll earn doing so will help further my campaign with regard to your sister. I have every intention of giving Lady Catherine the luxury to which she is accustomed."

"Ah. Speaking of which—how goes the courting of my sister?"

Andrew looked toward the ceiling. "Rather slowly, I'm afraid."

"Well, quit dawdling about. I've never known you to be anything less than relentless when you wanted something. Why are you dilly-dallying?"

"I'm not dilly—"

"And for God's sake, quit tugging at your hair. You look as if a lightning bolt struck you."

Andrew scraped a hasty hand through his apparently lightning-struck hair and frowned. "You're a fine one to talk. Have you consulted a mirror lately? Your manner can only be described as harried, and your own hair looks as if you were caught in sudden freakish storm."

"I *am* harried, but considering that my first child is soon to be born, I at least have a valid excuse for yanking at my hair and behaving oddly. What the devil is wrong with *you*?"

"There is nothing *wrong* with me, other than frustration. I haven't had an opportunity even to speak with Lady Catherine. Every time I finally spot her in the crowd, another museum investor or potential investor claims my attention." He shot Philip a pointed stare. "I was attempting to approach her for the *fourth* time this evening when I was again waylaid—this time by *you*."

"And you should be glad you were. If she'd seen that mess of a coiffure, she would have run screaming from the room."

"Thank you. Your encouragement warms my heart. Truly. Although I find it difficult to take fashion advice from someone whose own attire and coiffure most often resemble a squirrel's nest."

Instead of taking offense, Philip smiled. "True. However, *I* am not attempting to court a lady this evening. *I* have already succeeded in winning the woman I love."

"Yes, and almost in spite of yourself, I might add. If not for my advice on how to woo and win Meredith . . ." Andrew shook his head sadly. "Well, let us just say that the outcome of your courting was highly questionable."

A rude sound escaped Philip. "Is that so? If you are such an expert, then why haven't you yet succeeded with Catherine?"

"Because I've yet to *start* with her—thanks, most recently, to you. Tell me, is there not some other house in Mayfair you can haunt?"

"Fear not, I'm on my way out the door. However, if I leave now, I won't be able to tell you about the two very interesting conversations I had this evening. One was with a Mr. Sidney Carmichael. Have you met him yet?"

Andrew shook his head. "The name is not familiar to me."

"He was introduced to me by Mrs. Warrenfield, the wealthy American widow." Philip lowered his voice. "If you happen to speak with her, be prepared to listen to her describe, in detail, her plethora of aches and pains."

"Thank you for the warning. If only you'd told me an hour ago."

"Ah. Something struck me as rather odd about the lady, but I cannot put my finger on it," Philip said, frowning. "Did you notice anything?"

Andrew considered a moment. "I admit I was preoccupied when I spoke to her, but now that you mention it, yes.

I think it's her voice. It's unusually deep and raspy for a lady. Combined with the veiled, black hat she wears, which obscures half her face, it's a bit disconcerting to speak with her."

"Yes, that must be it. Well, back to Mr. Carmichael. He's interested in making a *very* sizable investment in the museum."

"How sizable?"

"Five thousand pounds."

Andrew's brows shot upward. "Impressive."

"Yes. He was most anxious to meet my American partner as he spent a number of years living in your country. I'm certain he'll seek you out before the evening is over."

"I suppose for five thousand pounds I can work up a bit of enthusiasm."

"Excellent. Your tone, however, and the fact that you keep looking about indicates a decided lack of curiosity about my other conversation, which was with Catherine." Philip heaved a long sigh and flicked a bit of lint from his dark blue jacket sleeve. "Pity, as the conversation concerned you."

"And naturally you'll tell me, in recompense for saving your life."

Philip's face screwed up into a confused scowl. "If you're referring to that incident in Egypt, I thought *I'd* saved *your* life. When did you save mine?"

"Just now. By not tossing you out headfirst through the French doors into the thorny hedges. What did Lady Catherine say?"

Philip cast a surreptitious glance around. Once assured that they weren't in danger of being overheard, he said, "It appears you have competition."

Andrew blinked. "I beg your pardon?"

"You're not the only man attempting to win my sister's favor. Apparently other men are showing interest in her."

Andrew stared, feeling as if he'd just been slapped. Then a humorless sound pushed past his lips at his own conceit. Why hadn't he anticipated this turn of events? Of course other men would cast their lures in Lady Catherine's direction. He cleared his throat to locate his voice. "What sort of interest?"

"Surely an expert such as yourself should know. The usual romantic gestures. Flowers, invitations, trinkets. That sort of thing."

Annoyance, along with a hefty dose of jealousy, smacked Andrew. "Did she indicate that she enjoyed these attentions?"

"On the contrary, she indicated that she found these gentlemen bothersome, for she has, and I quote, 'no intention of ever compromising my independence by leg-shackling myself to another man.' I must say, my sister has become startlingly blunt of late. That, added to the headstrong streak I've detected in her manner lately *and* these other suitors . . ." A sympathy-filled wince pinched Philip's features. "Not a stellar start to your wooing campaign, my friend, although I did try to warn you of that."

Andrew brushed aside the vaguely uncomplimentary description of Lady Catherine as being blunt and headstrong. Didn't sisters always seem that way to their brothers? However, there was no ignoring the rest, and his eyes narrowed to slits. "Who are these men?"

"Egad, Andrew, that frigid tone doesn't bode well for the fellows, and I don't believe I've ever seen that particular glare in your eyes before. Hope I'm never on the receiving end of it." He considered for several seconds, then said, "She mentioned some village doctor. Then of course there's the Duke of Kelby whose country estate is near her home in Little Longstone. And then there was an assortment of earls, viscounts, and the like, a few of whom are here this evening."

"Here? This evening?"

"When did you develop this troubling habit of repeating everything I say? Yes. Here. This evening. For example, Lords Avenbury and Ferrymouth."

"Our investors?"

"The very ones. I ask that you please remember they would no doubt withdraw their funding if you bloodied their noble noses."

"I suppose that means knocking them onto their noble asses is also out of the question."

"I'm afraid so, although that would make for a fine evening's entertainment. Apparently Kingsly also made an overture toward Catherine."

"He's *married*."

"Yes. *And* has a mistress. Then there's Lord Darnell." Philip jerked his head toward the punch bowl. "Note his besotted expression."

Andrew turned, and his jaw clenched. Lord Darnell was handing Catherine a glass of punch and looking at her as if she were a delectable morsel from which he longed to take a nice, big bite. Several other gentlemen, Andrew noted grimly, hovered about, all wearing similar expressions.

"Looks like I'm going to need to purchase myself a broom," Andrew muttered.

"A broom? Why is that?"

"To sweep that bastard Darnell and his friends off Lady Catherine's porch."

"Excellent idea. As her brother, I can't say I like the way Darnell is looking at her."

Andrew forced his gaze away from the group surrounding the punch bowl and looked at Philip. "Can't say I like it myself."

"Well then, since you're quite capable of handling yourself, I'll take myself off so you can proceed. I'll send a letter once I'm a papa to let you know if the tyke is a boy or girl."

Andrew smiled. "Please do. I'll be anxious to know if I'm an aunt or an uncle."

Philip laughed. "Good luck in your quest to win my doesn't-care-to-be-won sister." Amusement flashed in Philip's eyes as he glanced toward the group at the punch bowl. "I'm sorry I won't be able to witness the wooing as I'm certain it will prove very entertaining. And may the best man win."

After seeing Philip off, Andrew started up the brick walkway to reenter the town house, anticipating finding Catherine. He hoped there would be no further interruptions—

The front door opened and a group of gentlemen exited the town house. His jaw clenched as he recognized Lords Avenbury and Ferrymouth. Both young lords were impeccably dressed, complicated cravat knots adorning their throats, their coifs artful arrangements of careless, rakish curls. Each wore large jeweled rings that glistened in the moonlight as they indulged in a bit of snuff. Andrew decided they would not look quite so well turned-out sporting swollen jaws and blackened eyes.

And that reprobate Kingsly was with them. With his paunch, puckered lips, and beady eyes, Kingsly was already a remarkably unattractive fellow, but Andrew would be more than happy to make him even uglier if he continued his pursuit of Lady Catherine.

The thin, bespectacled Lord Borthrasher looked at Andrew down his long nose. With his pointed chin and sharp eyes with their unwavering, cold stare, he reminded Andrew of a vulture. Two gentlemen Andrew did not recognize rounded out the group. The last thing Andrew wanted was to speak to any of them, but unfortunately there was no way to avoid them.

"Ah, Stanton, care to join us for a smoke?" asked Lord Kingsly, his beady eyes raking over Andrew in a way that set his teeth on edge.

"I don't smoke."

"Stanton, did you say?" One of the gentlemen Andrew didn't know raised a quizzing glass and stared at him. Like his peers, this man wore perfectly tailored evening clothes, a complicated cravat and a jeweled ring. Although he was clearly older than his companions, he was surprisingly well built and broad-shouldered, leading Andrew to wonder if the man's physique was enhanced with padding. "Been wanting to meet you, Stanton. Heard a great deal about this museum."

"May I present his grace, the Duke of Kelby," said Kingsly.

Ah, the suitor whose estate was near Catherine's. Andrew offered a brief nod, only partially mollified by the fact that the duke, hearty though he appeared, resembled a carp.

"I'd hoped to meet you as well." The other gentleman unknown to Andrew stepped forward and extended his hand. "Sidney Carmichael."

Andrew recognized the name that Philip had mentioned as the potential investor of five thousand pounds. Of average height and build, he judged Carmichael to be in his late fifties and wearily wondered if he was but yet another suitor. He shook the man's hand, noting the firm grip that pressed the ring he wore against Andrew's fingers.

"I understand from Lord Greybourne that you're American," Mr. Carmichael said, his assessing gaze clearly taking Andrew's measure, a favor Andrew returned.

"The instant he opens his mouth 'tis obvious he's from the bloody colonies," Lord Kingsly said with a loud guffaw, which drew laughs from the group. "Not that he says a lot. Man of few words, eh, Stanton?"

Ignoring Kingsly, he said, "Yes, I'm American."

"Spent some time in your country during my travels," Carmichael said. "Mostly in the Boston area. Where are you from?"

Andrew hesitated only half a beat. He didn't care for answering questions about himself. "Philadelphia."

"Never visited there," Carmichael said with a regretful air. "I'm a lover of antiquities. Avenbury, Ferrymouth, and Borthrasher have been singing the praises of your and Lord Greybourne's museum. I'd like to discuss an investment with you." He pulled a card from his waistcoat pocket and handed it to Andrew. "My direction. I hope you'll call upon me soon."

Andrew slipped the card into his pocket and nodded. "I will."

"I'd like to discuss investing with you as well, Stanton," chimed in the duke. "Always looking for a good opportunity."

"Always looking for investors," Andrew said, hoping his smile was not as tight as it felt. "If you gentlemen will excuse me . . ." He nodded and made his way around them.

As he passed Lord Avenbury, the young lord said to the group, "Ferrymouth and I are off to the gaming tables. I'd wanted an opportunity to dance with Lady Catherine, but I suppose there's always next time."

Andrew froze and glared at the young man's profile.

"Delectable tidbit, she is," Lord Avenbury said. He licked his lips, and the group laughed. Andrew had to clench his hands to keep from discovering how Avenbury would look without any lips at all.

"Her estate is close to mine, you know," the duke said, lifting his quizzing glass, jeweled ring flashing. "Very convenient."

"Really?" Lord Kingsly said, a distinctly lecherous gleam in his beady eyes. "I might need to pry an invitation from you, Kelby. Yes, I believe I feel a sudden urge to visit your place and take the waters."

"Excellent notion," seconded Lord Ferrymouth. "Borthrasher, don't you suffer the occasional bout of the gout? The waters would do you wonders, I'm certain." Borthrasher nodded, and Ferrymouth beamed at the duke. "I believe a gathering at your home is in order, Kelby." His sweeping hand encompassed the group. "We'd all love to come. A few days of hunting, soaking in the springs"—he waggled his brows—"visiting the neighbors."

"Might provide an enjoyable break from the usual boring rounds of fetes," the duke agreed. "Let us take to the gaming tables and discuss it."

They moved down the walkway, laughing, pulling out cheroots and snuffboxes. His jaw tightened to the point of pain, Andrew turned and strode into the house. Damn it to hell, this evening was not going at *all* the way he'd envisioned it. But at least with that group now departed, things could not get worse.

Standing in the shadows of the far corner of the drawing room, Catherine drew in a long breath, relieved finally to find herself alone for a moment to calm her turbulent thoughts. Knowing this haven would offer only a short respite from the crowd, she cast her gaze about the room in search of another sanctuary.

"For whom are you looking so intently, Lady Catherine?" asked a deep voice from directly behind her.

Her breath caught, and she turned swiftly to find herself staring into Mr. Stanton's familiar dark eyes. Steady eyes. Friendly eyes. Relief rippled through her. Here, at last, was a friend she could talk to. An ally who meant her no harm. A gentleman not intent upon courting her.

"Mr. Stanton. You startled me."

"Forgive me. I noticed you standing here, and I wanted to say hello." He made her a formal bow, then smiled. "Hello."

She forcibly pushed aside her worries and smiled in return, knowing that he would notice any discomfiture on her part. "And hello to you, too. I haven't seen you since I last ventured to London two months ago. I trust you've been well—and busy with the museum?"

"Yes, on both accounts. And I can see that you've been well." His gaze dipped briefly to her gown. "You look lovely."

"Thank you." She was tempted to admit to him her relief at finally packing away her mourning clothes, but wisely held her tongue. To do so might lead to another discussion of Bertrand—as her appearance this evening already had with other guests—and she had no desire to speak of her deceased husband.

"May I help you locate someone, Lady Catherine?"

"As a matter of fact, I was looking for you." Not strictly the truth, but he did represent what she'd been searching for—a safe cove amongst the choppy waters.

Unmistakable pleasure flashed in his eyes. "How convenient, as here I am."

"Yes. Here you . . . are." Looking strong and solid, familiar yet imposing—the perfect candidate to distract her attention from her worries and discourage the bothersome gentlemen who had buzzed around her all evening like hovering insects.

His lips twitched. "Do you plan to tell me *why* you were searching for me, or are we to play charades?"

"Charades?"

" 'Tis an amusing game where one person acts out words, in a pantomime fashion, while others guess what he is trying to say."

"I see." She pursed her lips and made an exaggerated show of studying him. "Hmmm. Your clearly tugged-upon cravat, combined with that hint of furrow between your brows indicates you are trying to say that you wish Philip had remained to chat with all these potential museum investors."

"A very astute observation, Lady Catherine. Philip is much more adept at navigating these waters than I. I can only hope I do not frighten off any of our financial backing before Meredith gives birth and Philip returns to London."

"I saw you speaking with several people this evening, and none appeared *overly* frightened. As for Philip, I was pleased he came to the party, albeit for a short time."

"He told me Meredith insisted he come to the party, in spite of his objections."

"I'm certain she did."

"Rather odd, considering her delicate condition, don't you think?"

"Not at all." Catherine grinned. "I received a letter yesterday from Meredith in which she wrote that my normally calm and collected brother has taken to alternating between frantic pacing and croaking, 'is it time yet?' After a fortnight of such behavior, she was ready to cosh him. Rather than risk injuring the father of her child, she instead grasped upon the excuse of this party to push him literally out the door."

Mr. Stanton chuckled. "Ah, now I understand. Yes, I can picture Philip, hovering over Meredith, his hair standing up on end, cravat undone—"

"—cravat missing altogether," Catherine corrected with a laugh.

"Spectacles askew."

"Shirt horribly wrinkled—"

"—with his sleeves rolled up." Andrew shook his head. "I can only sympathize with poor Meredith. Makes me wish I was at the Greybourne country estate to enjoy the show."

She waved her hand in a dismissive gesture. "Pshaw. You simply wish you were anywhere but here, attempting to entice investors."

Something flashed in his eyes, then an engaging grin spread over his face—a grin that coaxed twin dimples to crease his cheeks. A grin she found impossible not to respond to in kind. He leaned toward her, and she caught a pleasing whiff of sandalwood. An inexplicable tingle shivered down her spine, surprising her, as it was quite warm in the room.

"I must admit that soliciting funds is not my favorite pastime, Lady Catherine. I owe you a boon for affording me this moment of sanctuary."

She was tempted to tell him that she owed him a boon for a similar reason, but refrained. "I noticed you speaking to Lords Borthrasher and Kingsly, and also Mrs. Warrenfield," she said. "Were your efforts successful?"

"I believe so, especially in Mrs. Warrenfield's case. Her husband left her a sizable fortune, and she possesses a love of antiquities. A good combination as far as Philip and I are concerned."

She smiled, and Andrew's breath hitched. Damn but she was lovely. The entire thread of their conversation disintegrated from his mind as he continued to look at her. Finally his inner voice coughed to life. *Cease gawking at her and speak, you nodcock. Before Lord What's-His-Name comes back, no doubt bearing a huge bouquet and spouting sonnets.*

He cleared his throat. "And how is your son, Lady Catherine?"

A combination of pride and sadness flitted across her face. "Spencer's overall health is fine, thank you, but his foot and leg do pain him."

"He did not travel with you to London?"

"No." Her gaze flicked over the assembled guests, and her expression chilled. "He dislikes traveling, and he especially dislikes London, a sentiment I equally share. Nor is he fond of parties. If not for my father's birthday celebration, I would not have ventured to Town. I plan to depart for Little Longstone directly after breakfast tomorrow."

Disappointment coursed through him. He'd hoped she might remain in London at least a few days, to afford him the opportunity to spend time with her. Invite her to the opera. Show her the progress on the museum. Ride in Hyde Park and stroll through Vauxhall. Damn it all, how was he to launch his campaign to court the woman if she insisted on hiding out in the country? Clearly a visit to Little Longstone was in order, yet as she hadn't issued him an invitation, he'd have to think up some plausible excuse to venture there. But in the meanwhile, he needed to stop wasting precious time and make the most of his present opportunity. The strains of a waltz floated on the air, and his entire body quickened at the prospect of dancing with her, of holding her in his arms for the first time.

Just as he opened his mouth to ask her to dance, she leaned closer, and whispered, "Oh, dear. Look at that. He's going about it all wrong."

"I beg your pardon?"

She nodded toward the punch bowl. "Lord Nordnick. He's trying to entice Lady Ophelia, and he's making a complete muck of it."

Andrew turned his attention to the couple standing next to the ornate silver punch bowl. An eager-looking young man, presumably Lord Nordnick, was handing an attractive young lady, presumably Lady Ophelia, a cup of punch.

"Er, there is a wrong way to hand a woman a beverage?" Andrew asked.

"He is not merely handing her a drink, Mr. Stanton. He is *courting* her. And doing a very poor job of it, I'm afraid."

Andrew studied the couple for several more seconds, then shook his head in bewilderment. "I don't see anything wrong."

She leaned a fraction closer. The intoxicating scent of flowers filled his head, and he had to grit his teeth to remained focused on her words. "Note his overeager manner."

"Overeager? 'Tis clear he is smitten and wishes to please her. Surely you don't think he should have allowed Lady Ophelia to fetch her own punch?"

"No, but he clearly didn't ask her preference. From her expression it is obvious that Lady Ophelia did not desire a glass of punch—no doubt because he'd already handed her one not five minutes ago."

"Perhaps Lord Nordnick is merely nervous. I believe it

is common for sanity to flee a man's head when he's in the company of a lady he finds attractive."

She made a *tsk*ing sound. "That is indeed unfortunate. Observe how bored she clearly is with his inept attentions."

Hmmm. Lady Ophelia did indeed look bored. Blast. When had courting become so bloody complicated? Hoping he sounded like a coconspirator rather than an information seeker, he asked, "What *should* Lord Nordnick do?"

"He should shower her with *romance*. Find out her favorite flower. Her favorite food."

"So he should send her roses and confections?"

"As your friend, Mr. Stanton, I must point out that that is a sadly typical male assumption. Perhaps Lady Ophelia prefers pork chops to confections. And how do you know her favorite flower is a rose?"

"As *your* friend, Lady Catherine, I must point out that it would be very odd for a suitor to come calling with a gift box filled with pork chops. And don't all women love roses?"

"I couldn't say. *I* like them. However, they aren't my favorite."

"And what is?"

"*Dicentra spectabilis*."

"I fear Latin is not my strong suit."

"You see?"

"Actually, no—"

"That's but yet another problem with Lord Nordnick's unoriginal methods. He should recite something romantic to her in another language. But I digress. *Dicentra spectabilis* means 'bleeding heart.' "

He pulled his gaze from the couple and turned his head to stare at her. "Something called *bleeding heart* is your favorite flower? *That* hardly rings of romance."

"Nevertheless, it is my favorite, and *that's* what makes

it romantic. I happen to know that Lady Ophelia is especially fond of tulips. But do you suppose Lord Nordnick will bother to discover that? I think not. Based on his fetching of numerous glasses of unwanted punch, I'm certain he'll send Lady Ophelia roses because that's what *he* thinks she should like. And because of that, he is doomed to failure."

"All because he fetched punch and would send the wrong flowers?" Andrew turned back to the couple, and a wave of pity for Lord Nordnick engulfed him. Poor bastard. He made a mental note to pass along the tulip information to the hapless fellow. In these perilous courting endeavors, men needed to stick together.

"Perhaps such clumsy attempts would have gained a lady's favor in the past, but no longer. Today's Modern Woman prefers a gentleman who takes into consideration *her* preferences, as opposed to a gentleman who arrogantly believes he knows what is best for her."

Andrew chuckled. "Today's Modern Woman? That sounds like something out of that ridiculous *Ladies' Guide* everyone is talking about."

"Why do you say 'ridiculous'?"

"Hmm, yes, perhaps that was a poor choice of word. 'Scandalous, appalling, trash-filled balderdash' is closer to what I meant."

Andrew studied the couple for several more seconds, trying to decipher the apparently misguided Lord Nornick's errors so as not to make them himself, but in truth he couldn't figure out what the man was doing wrong. He was being polite and attentive—two strategies Andrew himself had deemed important in his own wooing campaign.

He turned back toward Lady Catherine. "I'm afraid I don't see—"

His words cut off when he noted she was regarding him with raised brows and a noticeably cool expression. "Is something amiss?"

"I wasn't aware you'd read *A Ladies' Guide to the Pursuit of Personal Happiness and Intimate Fulfillment,* Mr. Stanton."

"*Me? A ladies*' guide?" He chuckled, torn whether he was more astonished or amused by her words. "Of course I haven't read it."

"Then how can you possibly call it 'scandalous, appalling, trash-filled balderdash'?"

"I don't need to read the actual words to know the content. That *Guide* has become the main topic of conversation in the city." He smiled, but her expression did not change. "As you've spent the past two months in Little Longstone, you couldn't know the stir that book has caused with the nonsensical ideas put forth by the author. You've only to listen to the gentlemen in this very room to realize that not only is the book filled with idiotic notions, but apparently it is poorly written as well. Charles Brightmore is a renegade, and possesses little, if any, literary talent."

Twin flags of color rose on her cheeks, and her narrowed gaze grew positively frosty. Warning bells rang in Andrew's mind, suggesting—unfortunately a few words too late—that he'd committed a grave tactical error. She lifted her chin and shot him a look that somehow managed to appear as if she were looking down her nose at him, quite a feat, considering he stood a good six inches taller than she.

"I must say that I'm surprised, not to mention disappointed, to discover that you hold such narrow views, Mr. Stanton. I would have thought that a man of your vast traveling experience would be more open to new, modern ideas. And that at the very least, you were a man who would take the time to examine all the facts and form your *own* opinions on a topic, rather than relying on hearsay from others—especially others who most likely also have not read the book."

Andrew's brows rose at her tone. "I do not hold narrow ideas at all, Lady Catherine. However, I don't believe it is necessary to experience something to know it is not to my liking or does not mesh with my beliefs," he said mildly, wondering how their conversation had veered onto this out-of-the-way path. "If someone tells me that rotten fish smells bad, I am perfectly content to take their word for it—I do not feel the need to stick my nose in the barrel to sniff for myself." He chuckled. "It almost sounds as if you've read this *Guide*—and found favor with its far-fetched ideals."

"If it only *almost* sounds as if I've read the *Guide*, then I don't believe you are listening closely enough, Mr. Stanton, an affliction I fear you share with most men."

Certain his hearing had indeed become afflicted, Andrew said slowly, "Don't tell me you've read that book."

"Very well, I won't tell you that."

"But you . . . have?" His words sounded more like an accusation than a question.

"Yes." She shot him an unmistakably challenging glare. "Numerous times, in fact. And I did not find the ideals it put forth the least bit far-fetched. Quite the opposite in fact."

Andrew could only stare. Lady Catherine had read that scandalous rag? Numerous times? Had embraced its precepts? Impossible. Lady Catherine was a paragon. The epitome of a perfect, gently bred, sedate lady. But clearly she *had* read it, for there was no mistaking her words or obstinate expression.

"You appear quite stunned, Mr. Stanton."

"In truth, I am."

"Why? By your own admission, nearly every woman in London has read the *Guide*. Why should it surprise you so that I would read it?"

Because you are not every woman. Because I don't want you to be "independent" and "modern." I want you to need me. Want me. Love me. As I need and want and love you. Good God, if that bastard Brightmore's drivel had turned Lady Catherine into some sort of upstart bluestocking, the man would pay dearly. All this bloody nonsense about "today's modern woman" certainly wouldn't help Andrew in his quest to court her. Based on what she'd said about Lord Nordnick, he already ran the risk of distancing Lady Catherine by the simple act of fetching her a glass of punch.

"The book just doesn't seem like the sort of thing a lady such as you would read."

"And precisely what sort of lady am I, Mr. Stanton? The sort who is unable to read?"

"Of course not—"

"The sort who is not intelligent enough to understand words containing more than one syllable?"

"Certainly not—"

"The sort who is incapable of forming her own opinions?"

"No." He raked a hand through his hair. "'Tis abundantly clear that you're fully capable of that." *How* had this conversation gone so wrong so quickly? "I meant that it did not seem the sort of reading material for a *proper* lady."

"I see." She gave him a cool, detached look that tightened his jaw. Definitely not the way he'd hoped to have her looking at him by the end of this evening. "Well, perhaps the *Guide* is not as scandalous as you've been led to believe, Mr. Stanton. Perhaps the *Guide* could be better described as scintillating. Provocative. Intelligent. But of course, you wouldn't know as you haven't read it. Perhaps you *should* read it."

He raised his brows at the unmistakable challenge shining in her eyes. "You must be joking."

"I'm not. In fact, I'd be happy to lend you my copy."

"Why on earth would I want to read a ladies' guide?"

She offered him a smile that appeared just a bit too sweet. "Why, so that you could offer an *informed, intelligent* opinion when next you discussed the work. And besides, you might actually learn something."

Good God, the woman was daft. Perhaps the victim of too much wine. He took a discreet sniff, but smelled only alluring flowers. "What on earth could I possibly learn from a ladies' guide?"

"What women like, for one thing. And do not like. And why Lord Nordnick's wooing attempts directed at Lady Ophelia are bound for failure. Just to name a few."

Andrew's jaw tightened. He knew what women liked . . . didn't he? He couldn't recall hearing any complaints in the past. But his inner voice was warning him that maybe he didn't know quite as much about what *Lady Catherine* liked as he'd thought. Actually, maybe he didn't know *Lady Catherine* as well as he'd thought—a notion that simultaneously unsettled and intrigued him. God knows she'd revealed an unexpected side of herself this evening. He recalled Philip's warning about her newfound headstrong, blunt behavior. He'd put no stock in Philip's comment at the time, but it appeared his friend was correct. And it further appeared that the blame for this change rested on the *Ladies' Guide*'s shoulders.

Damn you, Charles Brightmore. You and your foolish book have made courting the woman I want—an already Herculean task—even more difficult. I'll relish exposing you and putting an end to your writing career.

Yes, more difficult indeed, for not only had the *Guide* clearly filled Lady Catherine's head with ideas of independence, but this discussion, which was supposed to lead to him asking her to dance and the start of his courting campaign, had turned contentious—a turn of events he needed to correct immediately. No, this meeting was not going at all the way he'd envisioned. According to his plans, Lady Catherine should be in his arms, gazing up at him with warmth and affection. Instead, she'd backed away from him and was glaring at him with annoyance, a feeling he shared, as he was more than a little irritated himself.

He pressed his lips together to keep from arguing further. Indeed, arguing was the last thing he wished to do, especially tonight, when they had so little time together. His wooing campaign was off to a disastrous start. Retreat and regroup was definitely his best alternative.

Raising his hands in a show of acquiescence, he smiled. "As much as I appreciate the offer to read your copy, I believe I'll decline. As for the likes and dislikes of Today's Modern Woman, I bow to your superior knowledge on the subject, madam."

She did not return his smile; rather, she lifted a single brow. "You continue to surprise me, Mr. Stanton."

A humorless laugh escaped him. "*I* continue to surprise *you*? In what way?"

"I hadn't taken you for a coward."

Her words stilled him. Damn it, this had gone far enough. "Most likely because I am not one. And I hadn't taken you for an instigator, yet you appear to be deliberately baiting me, Lady Catherine. I wonder why?"

Another layer of crimson deepened her flushed cheeks. She drew a deep breath, then emitted a nervous-sounding laugh. "Yes, it seems I am. Forgive me. I'm afraid I've had a rather difficult evening and—"

Her words were cut off by a loud cracking sound and the crash of breaking glass. Gasps and cries of stunned fright rose from the party guests. Andrew turned swiftly, sickening dread oozing down his spine as he recognized the first sound as being that of a pistol report. Shards of glass sprayed across the floor beneath the now-broken windowpanes. In the space of a heartbeat, a myriad of tormenting images he'd believed buried flashed through his mind with a streak of vivid anguish. A ringing commenced in his ears, drowning out the sounds around him, and he bludgeoned back the unwanted reminders of the past.

"Dear God, she's hurt!"

The frightened cry from directly behind him jerked his head around, and everything inside him froze.

Lady Catherine, a trickle of blood oozing from between her lips, lay sprawled on the floor at his feet.

Chapter 3

There comes a time in the relationship between a man and a woman when they notice each other in that *way. Many times this notice manifests itself with either an inexplicable tingle or a clenching of the stomach. Unfortunately, the feeling is therefore often mistaken for a fever or indigestion.*

A Ladies' Guide to the Pursuit of Personal Happiness and Intimate Fulfillment
by Charles Brightmore

Voices, jagged and disjointed, echoed through Catherine's mind, along with a myriad of inexplicable, contradictory sensations. Her head ached as if someone had smashed it with a rock. But that discomfort was nothing compared to the hellfire burning in her shoulder. And who precisely had set the swarm of angry bees upon her bottom lip? Yet she somehow felt as if she were floating, engulfed in a strong, comforting embrace that suffused her with warmth, like being wrapped in her favorite velvety blanket. Her cheek rested against something warm and solid. She inhaled, filling her aching head with the scent of clean linen, sandalwood, and something else . . . a delightful aroma she couldn't define, other than to know she liked it.

She became aware of the hum of voices. One voice, low, deep, and fervent, and very close to her ear infiltrated past the noise of the others. *Please wake up . . . God, please.*

Something jounced her, shooting pain through her, and she groaned.

"Hold on," the voice next to her ear whispered. "We're almost there."

There? Forcing her eyelids open, she found herself looking up at Mr. Stanton's profile. His face appeared pale, his jaw tight, his rugged features stark with some unreadable emotion. A breeze dislodged a curl of her hair, blowing it across her cheek, and she realized that she was moving swiftly down a corridor . . . a corridor in her father's town house, cradled tightly against Mr. Stanton's chest, her knees draped over his one arm, his other arm supporting her back.

He glanced down, and she found herself staring into intense ebony eyes, which burned like twin braziers. His gaze locked on to hers, and a muscle jerked in his cheek.

"She's awake," he said, turning his head slightly, but his gaze never wavering from hers.

Awake? Had she fallen asleep? Surely not. She blinked several times, but before she could force her sore mouth to form a question, they passed through a doorway and entered a room she recognized as her father's bedchamber. Seconds later, Mr. Stanton gently laid her upon the maroon counterpane. She instantly missed his warmth as a chilled shudder rushed through her, but seconds later her eyes widened when he hitched one hip upon the mattress, and sat next to her on the bed, the heat of his hand pressing against her stinging shoulder. Some small corner of her mind protested that his nearness reeked of impropriety, but his presence was so comforting . . . and she felt so inexplicably in need of that comfort.

A movement caught her eye, and her gaze shifted over Mr. Stanton's shoulder, where she noted her father looking down at her with an anxious expression.

"Thank God you've come around, my dear," Father said, his voice rough. "Dr. Gibbens is on his way."

Mr. Stanton leaned closer to her. "How do you feel?"

She licked her dry lips, wincing when her tongue, which felt oddly thick, touched a sensitive spot. "Shoulder hurts. Head, too." She tried to turn her head, but immediately thought better of it when a sharp pain bounced behind her eyes, roiling a wave of nausea through her. "Wh . . . what happened?"

Something undecipherable flashed in his eyes. "You don't remember?"

Trying to ignore the aches thumping through her, she forced herself to concentrate. "Father's party. His birthday. You and I were arguing . . . and now I'm here." *Lying in bed, with you sitting so very close. Touching me.* "Feeling as if I were coshed . . . hopefully not the outcome of our disagreement."

"You were shot," Mr. Stanton said, harshness evident in his quiet voice. "In the shoulder. And it appears you hit your head quite hard when you fell. I'm sorry for the pain—I'm keeping pressure on your shoulder wound to stem the blood until the doctor arrives."

His words echoed through her pounding head. *Shot?* She wanted to scoff at his statement, but the burning ache in her shoulder and gravity of his intense regard left no doubt that he spoke the truth. And it certainly explained his nearness and touch. And obvious concern. "I . . . I do recall a loud noise."

His head jerked in a nod. "That was the shot. It came from outside, from the direction of Park Lane."

"But who?" she whispered. "Why?"

"That is precisely what we're going to find out," interjected her father, "although the why is quite obvious. These damnable criminals are everywhere. What is this city coming to? The recent rash of crimes in the area must be stopped. Why just last week Lord Denbitty came home from the opera to find his house ransacked. Tonight's debacle is clearly the doing of some bloody footpad whose weapon discharged while committing a robbery in the street."

Father's jaw clenched, and he dragged visibly shaking hands down his face. "Thank God for Mr. Stanton here. While pandemonium reigned, he kept a cool head. He ordered a footman to fetch the doctor, another to locate the magistrate, then rallied several gentlemen to conduct a search outdoors for the culprit and perhaps another victim, all while examining your injuries. Once he'd determined the ball wasn't lodged in your shoulder, he carried you here."

Catherine shifted her gaze to Mr. Stanton, who regarded her with such an intense expression, her toes curled inside her satin slippers. "Thank you," she whispered.

For several seconds he said nothing, then, with what appeared to be an effort, he offered her a half smile. "You're welcome. Thanks to my adventures with your brother, I have some experience in these matters, although you may retract your thanks when you see the mess I made of your gown. I'm afraid I had to cut off your sleeve."

She attempted a smile in return, but wasn't sure she succeeded. "No doubt the bloodstain would have proved ruinous anyway."

Father reached out and clasped her hand. "We can only be thankful you were merely grazed, and that the lead ball didn't hit anyone else before lodging itself in the wall. Egad, a mere inch or two, and you might have been killed." His lips narrowed with determination. "I vow I'll not rest until the scoundrel who did this is caught, Catherine."

The room seemed to take a sickening spin as the full ramifications of what had happened clicked into place in her mind. Before she could form a reply, a knock sounded on the door, and her father called, "Come in."

Dr. Gibbens entered the room, carrying his black leather medical bag, his long face the picture of concern as he approached her. "How is the bleeding?" he asked, setting his bag on the end of the bed.

She felt a lessening of the pressure against her shoulder. "Nearly stopped," Mr. Stanton said, with unmistakable relief. "There's a sizable lump on the back of her head, but she's coherent. She also bit her lip when she fell, but that bleeding has subsided as well."

"Excellent," said Dr. Gibbens. He stood for several seconds, then cleared his throat. "And as soon as you gentlemen leave the room, I shall examine the patient."

Mr. Stanton glowered at the doctor and appeared about to argue, but Dr. Gibbens said firmly, "I'll give you both my report as soon as I finish. In the meanwhile, you are needed downstairs. The magistrate arrived just after me."

There was no mistaking Mr. Stanton's or Father's reluctance to leave her, but they did as the doctor bid. Watching them close the door behind them, a shudder racked her, a shiver of dread that had nothing to do with the pain throbbing incessantly through her.

Father appeared convinced that she'd been shot by random accident. A robbery gone astray. But he didn't know that a growing number of people wished Charles Brightmore dead.

And that tonight someone had nearly succeeded.

Andrew paced the confines of the corridor outside Lord Ravensly's bedchamber, his insides clenched with impatience and frustration. And stark fear. How the hell long did it take to examine and dress a wound? Certainly not this long. Damn it, the party guests had departed, a witness had been found and interviewed, the magistrate had been dealt with, and still Dr. Gibbens had not emerged. He'd encountered many precarious, unsettling, and even dangerous situations in his life, but the unconditional terror and numbing horror of looking down at Lady Catherine's bleeding, unconscious form . . .

God. He paused in his pacing and leaned his back against the wall. Closing his eyes, he tunneled his hands, which still didn't feel quite steady, through his hair. All the fear and anger and desperation he'd felt since the moment that shot had rung out burst through the dam of control and restraint with which he'd surrounded himself. His knees shook, and with a low moan, he sank down to his haunches and pressed the heels of his palms to his forehead.

Damn it, he'd only ever once in his entire life felt so helpless—and that situation had ended disastrously. And under such horrifyingly similar circumstances. A shot. Someone he loved falling to the ground . . .

His every nerve ending pulsed with the need to kick down the damn door, grab the doctor by the neck, and *demand* he make Lady Catherine well. And the instant she was, he would deal with the bastard who had done this to her. But in the meantime, this waiting was eating at him. That and the fact that just prior to the shot they'd argued.

Argued, for God's sake. They'd never before exchanged a cross word. A sick sense of loss gripped him as he recalled her cool, dispassionate gaze during their conversation. Never had she looked at him like that.

"Any word on her condition?"

Andrew turned at Lady Catherine's father's voice. The Earl of Ravensly strode down the corridor, his features tight with worry.

"Not yet." Andrew rose, then jerked his head toward the bedchamber door. "I'm giving your Dr. Gibbens two more minutes. If he hasn't opened the door, propriety be damned, I'm storming the citadel."

The ghost of a smile whispered across the earl's haggard face. "How very American of you. But in this case, I must agree. In fact—"

The door opened, and Dr. Gibbens stepped into the corridor. "Well?" Andrew demanded before the earl could speak. He pushed off the paneled wall and approached the doctor, barely refraining from grabbing the smaller man by his cravat and shaking him as a dog would a rag.

"You correctly assessed the situation, Mr. Stanton. Lady Catherine's injury is, thankfully, a superficial flesh wound, which I cleansed and dressed. Thanks to your quick intervention, she did not suffer a severe loss of blood. While the bump on her head will bring some discomfort, it will not cause any long-lasting harm, nor will the cut on her lip. I expect her to make a full recovery." He removed his spectacles and polished the lenses with his handkerchief. "I've left some laudanum on the bedside table, but she refused to take any until she'd spoken with both of you. I recommend that she not be moved this evening. I'll call upon her in the morning to assess her condition and change her dressing. She is most adamant that she return to Little Longstone and her son tomorrow."

Everything inside Andrew rebelled at the thought of her being out of his sight, and he had to clamp his lips together to keep from voicing his objection.

"Headstrong gel," the earl said, his eyes suspiciously moist. "She cannot bear to be parted from Spencer. Is it wise that she travel so soon?"

"I'll give you my opinion after I examine her tomorrow," Dr. Gibbens said. "I bid you both good night." With a nod, the doctor left them.

"Come, Stanton," the earl said, opening the door. "Let us see for ourselves how my daughter is faring."

Andrew offered up a silent thank-you for Lord Ravensly's invitation, for in truth, he didn't know if he was capable of remaining in the corridor for another minute. He followed the earl into the bedchamber, then paused in the doorway.

Lady Catherine lay in the oversized bed, the maroon counterpane covering her to her chin. Bathed in the golden glow cast from the fire burning in the grate, she looked like a gilded angel. Loose tendrils of chestnut hair fanned out across the cream pillowcase, and his fingers itched to brush the shiny strands back from her soft skin. For all the times he'd dreamed of holding her in his arms, never once had he suspected that if the moment ever came, it would arrive in the guise of carrying her unconscious, bleeding form.

He approached the bed slowly, his knees threatening to wobble, his gaze minutely noting every nuance of her being. Her eyes appeared huge, and shadows of pain lurked in their golden brown depths, along with something else that looked liked fear. A small red mark marred her swollen bottom lip. Her face was devoid of color.

"Dr. Gibbens assured us you would make a full recovery," Lord Ravensly said, taking her hand between both his own. "How are you feeling?"

A grimace passed over her features. "Sore, but very grateful. My injuries could have been much worse."

The earl visibly shuddered, a sentiment with which Andrew wholeheartedly agreed. Her troubled gaze bounced between them. "Were you able to find out anything about who fired the pistol?"

Andrew cleared his throat. "One of the party guests, Mr. Sidney Carmichael, reported he was just entering his carriage when he heard the shot. He saw a man running into Hyde Park. He provided a good description to the magistrate and said he would definitely recognize the man if he saw him again. Lords Borthrasher, Kingsly, Avenbury, and Ferrymouth, as well as the Duke of Kelby were entering their carriages nearby and agree they saw a shadowy figure in the park, but none could provide a detailed description.

"The group of gentlemen who searched outside came upon an injured man near the town house. He identified himself as a Mr. Graham. Mr. Graham claims that while walking down Park Lane, he was accosted from behind. When he regained consciousness, he realized he'd been relieved of his purse and watch fob."

"I see," she said slowly. "Did the robber have a pistol?"

"Mr. Graham didn't know, but then, he never saw his attacker before he was rendered senseless."

"No doubt the scoundrel knocked him out with the butt of the pistol," Lord Ravensly fumed. "Then the weapon discharged, and here we are. Damn footpads." He shook his head, then frowned at Lady Catherine. "Now what is this nonsense Dr. Gibbens said about you wanting to return to Little Longstone tomorrow?"

"I promised Spencer I'd be home tomorrow, Father."

"We'll have the lad brought to London."

"No. You know how he hates the city. And after tonight, can you blame me for not relishing a prolonged stay in Town myself?"

"I suppose not, but I don't like the thought of you alone, isolated in the country while you're recovering. You need someone to take care of you."

"I agree," she said slowly, frowning in a way that made Andrew wonder what she was thinking. He agreed wholeheartedly with the earl, but somehow he'd expected the new "headstrong, independent" Lady Catherine to demur. To claim that her staff could adequately care for her.

" 'Tis a pity Philip cannot come to Little Longstone for an extended visit." She said the words lightly, but something in her tone caught Andrew's attention. That and the fact that she hadn't said "Philip and Meredith."

"Yes," the earl mused, "but he cannot leave Meredith now. I'd volunteer my services, but I'm afraid acting the nursemaid is not my strong suit."

Andrew forced himself not to point out that acting the nursemaid was hardly Philip's strong suit either. He looked at Lady Catherine, and their gazes met. His stomach tightened when he again saw a flash of fear, and something else he couldn't decipher in her eyes. Then her expression turned speculative, and almost . . . calculating?

Before he could decide, she said, "I believe I have thought of the perfect solution. Mr. Stanton, would you consider accompanying me to Little Longstone, then remaining as my guest? It would prevent me from having to travel alone, and I'm certain you would enjoy a visit to the country. Spencer would love to see you again and hear more of your adventures with Philip in Egypt. You had little opportunity to get acquainted at my husband's funeral.

And with Spencer there as chaperone, your visit would, of course, be above reproach and quite proper."

For reasons he couldn't explain, a warning tingled in his gut—an instinctual reaction that had served him well over the years—telling him that there was more to her invitation than met the eye. But what? And did he really want to question her motives right now? No. He'd spent the better part of the last hour trying to figure out a plausible argument for going to Little Longstone with her and staying for an extended visit, and here she'd solved the problem.

"I realize you have responsibilities in London—"

"None that cannot wait," he assured her. "It would be my honor to accompany you, then remain for a visit, Lady Catherine. You may rest assured that I will see to it no further harm befalls you." Indeed, God help anyone who attempted to hurt her again.

"An excellent solution, my dear," the earl said, with an approving nod. "You'll have company *and* protection."

"Yes. Protection . . ." Her voice trailed off. There was no mistaking her obvious relief. Clearly she didn't feel safe in London, a sentiment he could well understand. But he suspected she'd asked him to remain in Little Longstone for an extended visit for the same reason—protection. Why? Did she not feel safe in own home?

He didn't know, but he surely intended to find out.

Chapter 4

Men possess so little understanding of women because they seek out advice and information about women from other equally uninformed men. Winning his lady's favor would proceed in a much smoother manner if the gentleman simply asked her, "What do you want?" Should Today's Modern Woman ever be fortunate enough to be asked that question, it is hoped she will answer truthfully.

A Ladies' Guide to the Pursuit of Personal Happiness and Intimate Fulfillment
by Charles Brightmore

"How are you feeling, Lady Catherine?"

Catherine looked up from her embroidery to peer across the seat at her traveling companion, whom she'd managed quite successfully under the guise of needlework to ignore for the past hour—or at least as much as one can ignore a man seated barely an arm's length away. A man who seemed to take up so much *space*. She'd never realized how imposing Mr. Stanton's presence was. It was one thing to share a drawing room or dining room with him, but, as she'd discovered, quite another to share the confines of a carriage.

Her gaze met his concern-filled dark eyes. "I'm a bit achy, but all right."

"Would you like to stop for a short rest?"

In truth she would have liked nothing more than for the carriage to stop its lurching ride. Each thump and bump radiated discomfort through her aching shoulder and reminded her of the dull ache behind her eyes. But each bump brought her closer to Little Longstone and Spencer, and farther away from the nightmare of last night. Closer to the safety of her home, and farther away from whoever had fired that shot . . . that shot she was far from convinced was an accident. Closer to Genevieve, whom she needed to speak with as soon as possible. She needed to tell her dear friend about the shooting and the investigator who'd been hired to find Charles Brightmore. Warn her about the danger. Warn her she might be next.

"It is not necessary to stop," she said.

"You look pale."

"Why, thank you. Such flattery will surely swell my head—which is, thanks to last evening's fall, quite swollen enough already."

Her attempt at humor clearly sailed over his own head, for his brows bunched tighter. "You're in pain—"

"I'm *fine*. Perfectly fit. Dr. Gibbens gave his permission for me to travel—"

"After you browbeat the poor man. I believe his exact words when he departed your father's town house this morning were, 'Never in my life have I met a more obstinate woman.' "

"I'm certain you heard him incorrectly."

"I'm certain I didn't."

"Yet, I recall that last evening we'd established that most men's hearing is not all it should be."

Several seconds of silence stretched between them, and she had to stifle the sudden urge to squirm under his steady regard. "I am not most men, Lady Catherine," he finally said quietly. "You're also very preoccupied."

"I am merely anxious to get home."

"I'm sure you are. But there's something else. Something is worrying you."

"What makes you say that?" she asked, forcing a light note into her voice. Damnation, just her luck to be stuck in a carriage with the one perceptive man in all of England.

"Your uncharacteristic reticence. I've never known you to be so . . . untalkative."

"Ah. Well, that is simply because I have been engrossed in my embroidery."

"Which I find intriguing as you detest embroidery." Clearly he read the guilty flush she felt searing her cheeks for he added, "You mentioned your aversion to needlework during your visit to London two months ago."

Double damnation. The man was perceptive *and* recalled trivial details. How utterly irritating. "I'm, er, hoping to develop a fondness for the activity. And besides that, I simply have nothing to say."

"I see. In general—or to me in particular?"

She debated trying to put him off with a polite fib, but as he obviously wasn't easily dissuaded, she admitted the truth. "To you in particular."

Instead of looking offended, he nodded solemnly. "I suspected as much. About our conversation last evening . . . it was not my intention to upset you."

"You did not upset me, Mr. Stanton."

Doubt flashed across his features, raising one dark

brow. "Indeed? Then you normally resemble a teakettle on the verge of boiling over?"

"Again, I must beg you to cease your flattery. In truth, 'upset' is merely a poor choice of word. Disappointment is closer to what I felt."

"In me?"

"Yes."

"Simply because I did not agree with you? If so, that disappoints *me*."

Feeling somehow chastised, she considered his words for several seconds, then shook her head. "No, not because we didn't agree, but because you made some very strong statements without benefit of firsthand knowledge. That, to me, is unfair, which I find to be a disappointing, not to mention irksome, quality in a person."

"I see. Tell me, had I ever in any of our past meetings impressed you as being unfair?"

"Not at all, which is why I found last evening's discussion so—"

"Disappointing?"

"Yes." She cleared her throat. "Not to mention irksome."

"Indeed. We wouldn't want not to mention that."

Again silence swelled between them, uncomfortable in an inexplicable way that unsettled her. Before last evening, she'd always felt at ease in Mr. Stanton's company. Indeed, she'd found her brother's closest friend intelligent, witty, and charming, and had enjoyed the easy friendship and camaraderie that had developed between them during the half dozen or so times they'd met. His comments last evening about the *Guide*, however, had proved most disillusioning. Scandalous, appalling, trash-filled balderdash indeed. Humph. And his opinion of Charles Brightmore as a renegade who possesses little, if any, literary talent had quite set her teeth on edge. It had required all her strength not to jab her finger at his nose and inquire exactly how many books *he'd* written.

Of course, the part of her that demanded fairness had to admit that the *Guide* could be described as scandalous. While she firmly believed that the information provided in the *Guide* was necessary and valuable to women, part of her had been delighted at the brow-raising aspect of the book and had been the deciding element for her to embark on the endeavor. It gave her untold pleasure and a wickedly secret thrill to tweak the hypocritical members of Society whose ranks she'd turned her back on after their hurtful treatment of her son. That desire, that need for some bit of revenge, was clearly a flaw in her character, but there you had it. And she'd enjoyed every minute of the stir she'd created—until last night. Until she'd realized that the *Guide* had swelled into a scandal of gargantuan proportions. She shuddered to think of the horrific scandal that would ensue if Charles Brightmore's identity were to be discovered. She'd be ruined. And she wouldn't be the only one. There was Spencer to think about. And Genevieve . . . dear God, Genevieve stood to lose as much as, if not more than, Catherine if the truth came out.

Yet last evening's events suggested that more than her reputation might be at stake. Her very life could be in danger. Of course it was possible that she'd been the victim of an accident—she prayed that was the case—but the timing seemed eerily coincidental. And she was not a firm believer in coincidence . . .

He cleared his throat, yanking her from her brown study. "What would you say if I told you that I was perhaps considering the possibility of accepting your challenge to read Brightmore's book?"

Catherine stared at him for several seconds, then burst

into laughter. A combination of annoyance and confusion flickered in his eyes.

"What on earth is so amusing?"

"You. You are *perhaps considering* the *possibility* . . . if you'd given committing to read the book any wider berth, you'd find yourself afloat in the middle of the Atlantic on your way back to America." Some inner devil made her add, "Not that I'm surprised however. As Today's Modern Woman knows, most men will go to great lengths to avoid committing to anything—unless it is for their own pleasure, of course. As for you *perhaps considering* reading the book, I certainly encourage you to do so, Mr. Stanton. Not for my benefit, but for your own. Now, before another argument ensues, I suggest we discuss something else, as it is clear we are in complete disagreement on the subject of the *Guide*." She held out her gloved hand. "Truce?"

He studied her for several seconds, then reached out to clasp her hand. His hand was large and strong, and she felt the warmth of his palm even through her gloves.

"A truce," he agreed softly. His lips twitched as his fingers gently squeezed hers. "Although I suspect you're really angling for my unconditional surrender, in which case, I must warn you"—he leaned forward and flashed a smile—"I don't surrender easily."

Was it the deep, soft timbre of his voice, or the compelling yet somehow mischievous glitter in his dark eyes, or the warmth radiating up her arm from where his palm pressed against hers—or perhaps a combination of all three—that suddenly made it seem as if there was a dearth of oxygen in the carriage? She slowly extricated her hand from his. Was it just fancy that he seemed reluctant to let go?

"Your warning is duly noted." Heavens, she sounded positively . . . breathless.

"It was not my intention to argue with you—not now, or last evening, Lady Catherine."

"Indeed? What *was* your intention?"

"I'd intended to ask you to dance."

An image instantly filled her mind, of swirling across the dance floor to the lilting sounds of a waltz, her hand once again clasped in his, his strong arm around her waist.

"I haven't danced in over a year," she murmured. "I very much miss it."

"Perhaps we shall have the opportunity to enjoy a waltz in Little Longstone."

"I'm afraid not. Elaborate soirees are not usual there." Determined to erase the disturbing image of them dancing together from her mind, she asked, "Tell me more about how things are progressing at the museum."

"We've fallen a bit behind schedule with Philip's recent absence, but the building should be completed by year's end."

A frisson of guilt tickled her. "And your taking the time to accompany me to Little Longstone shall set you back even more." She swallowed the remnants of her annoyance and smiled. After all, he couldn't help but be irritating—he *was* a man. "You're a true friend—to me and my entire family—and I'm grateful." Pain throbbed in her shoulder, a physical reminder that someone might truly mean her harm. *More grateful than you know.*

"The pleasure is all mine."

He fell silent, and she once again turned her attention to the hated embroidery. With her head lowered, she peeked at him through her lashes and, noting that his attention was focused out the window, she allowed her gaze to drift over him. Thick, midnight hair, with one unruly strand falling over his forehead. Dark lashes surrounding ebony eyes that somehow managed to be compelling and composed at the same time. She liked his eyes. They were calm. Patient and steady, although often vexingly unreadable. High cheekbones, strong jaw, and a well-shaped mouth given to teasing grins and blessed with twin dimples that creased his smooth-shaven cheeks when he smiled. While he wasn't classically handsome, there was no denying Mr. Stanton was a very attractive man, and she suddenly wondered if there was a woman in his life.

"What are you thinking?"

At his softly spoken question, her head jerked upward. Their gazes met, and her heart skipped a beat at the intensity burning in those normally calm, steady dark eyes. The temperature in the carriage suddenly seemed far too warm, and she resisted the urge to snap open her fan. After a quick inner debate, she opted to tell him the unvarnished truth . . . almost.

"I was wondering if there was a special lady in London who would miss you during your stay in Little Longstone."

He appeared so nonplussed by her question, she had to laugh. "I know Meredith has attempted to introduce you to some suitable young ladies, Mr. Stanton. She *is* the Matchmaker of Mayfair, you know."

He shrugged. "She's tried on several occasions, but I've thus far managed to avoid being snared in her net."

"Ah. Studiously avoiding the altar. How very . . . manlike of you."

"On the contrary, I would very much like to have a wife. And family."

She raised her brows. "I see. You are aware that the chances of that happening would increase dramatically were you to cease avoiding being snared in Meredith's matchmaking net."

"Hmmmm. You make me sound like a fish."

"A slippery fish," she agreed with a laugh. "Well, as your friend, I feel it only fair to warn you that Meredith has told me that once she is fully recovered from childbirth, *you* are her next project."

He inclined his head. "As your friend, I appreciate the warning, however I'm not overly concerned. I know exactly the sort of woman I want—I do not require any help."

Curiosity pricked Catherine. "And what sort of woman do you want?"

"What sort of woman do you think I want?"

"Beautiful, young, amenable, nubile, soft-spoken, and demure. Worshiping the ground you tread upon would be an added plus."

He threw back his head and laughed, the rich sound filling the coach. "Do I sense a bit of cynicism, Lady Catherine?"

"Are you saying I'm wrong?"

" 'Wrong' is perhaps the incorrect term. The correct phrase would be 'utterly, completely inaccurate.' "

She didn't even attempt to hide her doubt. "Surely you don't expect me to believe you long for a hideous, buttertoothed harpy?"

"Noooo. That doesn't describe her either."

"Pray, do not keep me in suspense."

He leaned back against the squabs, his Devonshire brown coat in dark contrast to the pale gray velvet. His merriment faded, turning his expression into an unreadable mask.

"She is kind," he said quietly, his eyes serious. "Loving. Loyal. And she possesses an inexplicable something that touches me in a way no one else ever has. Here." He laid his hand across his chest. "She fills spaces that have been empty for years. With her, there is no more loneliness."

Catherine's breath seemed trapped in her lungs. She didn't know what she'd expected him to say, but it hadn't been . . . that. Empty? Lonely? And it wasn't simply what he said, but the way he said it, with that tinge of desolation resonating in his deep voice that stunned her. God knew *she'd* experienced such isolating feelings more times than she cared to remember, but Mr. Stanton?

Before she could even think of a reply, he seemed to shake off his serious mood, and a crooked smile hitched up one corner of his mouth. "And, of course, if she happened to worship the ground I tread upon, that would be an added plus."

She firmly tamped down the curiosity—and the feeling of pity—his intriguing words piqued. He'd never struck her as a man who'd suffer from loneliness, a man who would find any part of his life empty. "I do not wish to discourage you, but I feel it only fair to warn you, from my own experience, that marriage is not necessarily a cure for loneliness. However, I wish you luck in locating this paragon you've described, Mr. Stanton. I hope she exists."

"I *know* she exists, Lady Catherine."

Some imp made her ask, "Do you suppose she's read *A Ladies' Guide?"*

He shot her an odd look. "Given that it seems nearly every woman in London has read the book, it is definitely a possibility."

"If she has read it, I'm sure you'll be very pleased when you meet her."

"Pleased?" There was no missing his skepticism. "What do you mean by that?"

She smiled sweetly. "I wager if you'd read the book, you'd know."

"Ah, yes, that intriguing challenge. And if I were to take you up on it? What would I win?"

Arrogant man. Assuming he'd merit a reward for reading a book. Still, this could actually work in her favor . . .

"I hadn't had a wager in mind at all, but why not?" *Especially since I am almost guaranteed a victory.* "Whoever is victorious shall owe the other a boon—within reason—of the victor's choice." She couldn't contain her grin. "Ah, yes, I can see you now, beating the rugs and weeding the roses. Or perhaps polishing the silver. Setting the stones for the new garden pathway, fixing the stable's roof—"

"Win or lose, I'd be happy to assist with those chores. But why have they not been seen to?"

She shrugged. "It is difficult to find proper help in the country."

"I see," he murmured. "And what determines who is the winner?"

"If you read the book—the entire book, mind you—thus enabling you to engage in a well-informed discussion of the contents, you win. If you fail to do so, then I win."

When he remained silent, she murmured, "Of course, if you are afraid . . ."

"Of a simple wager? Hardly."

"Then why do you hesitate?"

"In truth, because I seriously doubt whether, in spite of my high tolerance for pain, I will actually be able to suffer through Brightmore's drivel. However, since the worst outcome is that I'd simply owe you a boon, I suppose there is no harm in accepting your wager. What period of time do you suggest?"

"Shall we say three weeks?"

He nodded. "Very well. I accept."

Catherine could barely suppress her glee. There were many chores a strong, strapping man like Mr. Stanton could do around the estate—all she needed to do was figure out which one would help her—and as an added bonus, irk him—the most. Most likely it should appall her to experience such a thrill at the thought of besting him and erasing a portion of his arrogance. It should—but it didn't.

"Of course," Mr. Stanton said, "within three weeks' time, no doubt the gossip surrounding the actual contents of the *Guide* will be supplanted by the stir that will ensue by the unmasking of Charles Brightmore."

Catherine's heart stumbled over itself. He clearly was referring to the investigator who'd been hired. Hopefully the man would not find his way to Little Longstone. But if he did, well, forewarned was forearmed. He'd certainly glean no information from *her*. Forcing a calm she was far from feeling, she laughed lightly. "Unmasking? Heavens, you make Mr. Brightmore sound like a brigand."

"There are many in London who believe he is just that."

"Including yourself."

"Yes."

"You may change your mind after you read his work—assuming you read it."

His shrug indicated he had no real intention of reading "that drivel," and even if he did, his mind would not be changed. Annoyance tickled down her spine. Aggravating man. Had she once thought him gallant? Likable? Clearly she'd been erroneously predisposed to a favorable opinion based on her brother's glowing reports of Mr. Stanton's character. The easy camaraderie they'd shared in the past must have been due to the topics they'd discussed—namely Philip and Meredith. Their wedding, and most recently the imminent birth of their child. The museum was also a common subject for discourse. A frown pulled down her brows. Casting her mind back, she realized that all of their conversations had been of a very impersonal nature. She actually knew very little about Mr. Stanton. She'd accepted him without question as a friend, as a good man, because Philip said he was. According to Philip, Mr. Stanton had saved him from several scrapes while they were abroad. He categorized his American friend as loyal, steadfast, brave, and excellent with both his fists and a rapier. Well, she had no reason to doubt he was all those things. Philip, however, had ne-glected to add, nor had she discerned on any of their previous meetings, that Mr. Stanton was also opinionated, stubborn, and irritating.

She glanced at him. He was staring out the window, a muscle pulsing in his smoothly shaven cheek, verifying the tight set of his jaw. His *stubborn* jaw. Although, she couldn't deny that it was a *strong* stubborn jaw. With an intriguing hint of a cleft in the center. Philip hadn't mentioned that. Nor had he mentioned Mr. Stanton's profile . . . the slight bump on the bridge of his nose. Most likely a souvenir from one of his pugilistic bouts. It should have detracted from his appearance. Instead, it lent him a rugged air, mixed with just a whiff of danger, reminding her that in spite of his elegant clothes, he was not of her class. Rough around the edges.

And undeniably attractive.

"You've a most intriguing expression, Lady Catherine. Would you care to share your thoughts?"

Heat flooded her cheeks. Good Lord, how long had she been staring? And why was he looking at her in that . . . speculative way? As if he'd already divined her thoughts? Humph. Just another aspect of him to term irritating.

Adopting what she hoped passed for a casual air, she said, "I was thinking that in spite of the time we've spent together over the past fourteen months, we really do not know each other very well." She lifted her brows. "What were *you* thinking?"

"Actually something quite similar—that I do not know you as well as I believed."

She wrinkled her nose and pointedly sniffed the air. "Somehow that did not smell like a compliment."

"It was not meant as an insult, I assure you." Mischief flickered in his eyes. "Would you like a compliment? I'm certain I could think of one, if it would please you."

"I beg you, do not strain yourself on my account," she said in a dust-dry voice.

He made a dismissive gesture with his hand. " 'Tis no strain, I assure you." His gaze flickered over her forest green traveling ensemble. "You look lovely."

Three simple words. Yet something about the quiet way he said "lovely," combined with the unmistakable warmth in his eyes, quivered a fluttery thrill through her. He stole any reply she might have made by focusing his attention on her mouth. "And your lips . . ." his eyes appeared to darken, and he leaned forward. Everything inside Catherine stilled—except those inexplicable flutters, which suddenly became so much more . . . fluttery. Good heavens, was he going to *kiss* her? Surely not . . .

Her own gaze riveted on his lips, and for the first time she realized what an attractive mouth he possessed. It somehow managed to appear soft and firm at the same time. The sort of mouth that would know how to kiss a woman—

"Your lips," he said softly, leaning farther still, until less than two feet separated their faces, until she had to fight the overwhelming urge to lean toward him and erase the small distance. "They look so . . . much less swollen and bruised than they did after last night's incident. Almost back to their normal loveliness."

He leaned back and shot her a grin. Whatever madness had enveloped her disintegrated like a puff of smoke, and she abruptly straightened, pressing her back against the cushion, appalled. Not so much at him, but at herself. Heat crept up her neck, and she prayed her face wasn't turning red. Good heavens, for one insane instant she'd thought he meant to . . . that she wanted him to . . .

Kiss her. But even more humiliating was the fact that she felt deflated because he hadn't. Egad, she was losing her mind.

"You see?" he said. "Contrary to your belief, I'm perfectly capable of bestowing compliments. And I'm greatly looking forward to my visit to your home, as it will give us the opportunity to discover how much more we don't know about each other."

Good Lord, the things he did not know about her, she intended to keep that way. "Wonderful. I cannot . . . wait."

Instead of taking offense at her deflating tone, his grin broadened. "Please, do not strain yourself with enthusiasm on my behalf."

Humph. How dare he have good humor when he was supposed to be abashed? Must be the American in him. Well, he might plan that they would get to know each other better during his stay, but as Today's Modern

Woman well knew, she did not have to fall in with any man's plans if she did not want to.

And based on the secrets she had to keep, Catherine most definitely did not want to.

Chapter 5

Today's Modern Woman needs to recognize that there are times when Society's restrictive rules should be roundly and soundly ignored. And the more attractive the gentleman in question, the more roundly and soundly the ignoring should be—discreetly, of course.

A Ladies' Guide to the Pursuit of
Personal Happiness and Intimate Fulfillment
by Charles Brightmore

"Bickley cottage will come into view in a moment," Lady Catherine said two hours later, pointing toward the left. "Just beyond this copse of trees."

Thank God. Andrew hoped his relief wasn't too obvious. The four-hour journey had felt more like four months. The last two hours had consisted of alternating awkward silences and stilted conversation. She'd studiously concentrated on her embroidery, but he prided himself on being able to read people, and she was clearly preoccupied about something. His instincts told him she was thinking about last night's incident, which he suspected was worrying her far more than she'd admitted.

He focused his attention out the window, taking in the verdant countryside. He couldn't wait to get out of the close quarters of the carriage, where he'd spent the last four torturous hours breathing in her delicate floral fragrance. He blew out a long, careful breath. God, did a woman exist who smelled better? No. Impossible. It had taken every ounce of his strength not to touch her, to lean closer and simply breathe her in. He had given in to the excruciating temptation and leaned closer once, and the effort he'd expended not to kiss her had cost him.

Patience. He needed to remember his campaign of subtle, gentle wooing. If he moved too quickly, he sensed she would retreat like a frightened doe. Of course, the fact that she was clearly irked with him in regards to the *Guide* didn't serve him well, although he himself found her enthusiasm for Brightmore's book and all that Today's Modern Woman rubbish irritating as well. He suspected she would not be pleased if she were to learn that he'd been hired to locate and unmask her literary idol, Charles Brightmore.

Although his quest to find the man was temporarily suspended while he remained in Little Longstone, he'd apply himself fully to the task once he returned to London. Charles Brightmore would be exposed, Andrew would collect a very handsome fee, and all this nonsense about Today's Modern Woman would fade away, which in turn would evaporate the tension that had sprung up between him and Lady Catherine. In the meanwhile, he'd take full advantage of his opportunity to spend time with her and set his wooing campaign into motion.

Less than a minute later, they rounded a corner in the path, revealing a stately white-columned, brick home nestled cozily against a backdrop of massive trees, gently rolling hills, and verdant lawns. The variant shades of green were broken by meandering trails of vivid purple-and-pink, interspersed with blankets of pastel-hued wildflowers. Shards of late-afternoon sunlight glinted off the house's gleaming, round-topped windows, drenching the mellowed brick façade in a golden glow. The entire scene reflected picturesque, country tranquillity. A calm, safe haven for her and her son, far away from the cruel pettiness of Society.

"I can see why you love it here," he said.

"It's home," she said quietly.

"It's much larger and grander than I expected. Calling it a 'cottage' is rather like referring to a ship as a rowboat."

"Perhaps. But the surroundings, the friendly atmosphere, and less formal ways here lend the house a coziness that belies it size. I fell in love with it the moment I saw it."

He turned, and his gaze drifted over her lovely profile. The soft curve of her pale cheek, the gentle line of her jaw. The slight upward tilt of her nose. The lush fullness of her mouth. *Falling in love the moment you see something . . . yes, I know exactly how that feels.*

"Buying this property, where Spencer has easy and private access to the healing warm water springs on the grounds was the one generous gesture Bickley extended to his son." She spoke softly, her voice utterly devoid of expression. She turned to face him, and he was struck by how her eyes had gone flat. Damn it all, he wanted to erase all the shadows the years of her unhappy marriage had cast upon her.

"Of course, as everyone knows, Bickley's true reason for the purchase was simply to install Spencer—and me—far away, where he wouldn't have to see, or be seen with, his imperfect son. Or the woman who had, in his words, foisted that son upon him."

Because of his close friendship with Philip, Andrew was well aware of what a selfish, unfeeling, indifferent bastard Lady Catherine's husband had turned out to be to his warm, vibrant wife, and what a poor excuse of a father for a boy who desperately needed one. He barely refrained from saying *I would have liked nothing more than five minutes alone with that bastard you married.* Instead, he said, "I'm very sorry your marriage was not a happy one."

"As am I. It began with great promise, but after Spencer's birth . . ." Her voice trailed off, and for several seconds her eyes filled with the shadows that clearly haunted her still. His fingers itched with the need to reach out and touch her. To smooth away her hurts. To soothe and comfort her as the mere thought of her comforted him.

Before he could move, however, she gathered herself and smiled. "But that's all in the past," she said. "Spencer and I love Little Longstone. I hope you'll enjoy your stay."

"I'm certain I shall."

"And you must make use of the warm springs while you're here. They are very therapeutic. I'm looking forward to taking the waters myself to ease the stiffness in my upper arm."

Andrew swallowed the apprehension that rose in his throat. He didn't relish the prospect of spending time *near* the water. *In* the water was out of the question.

He was saved from replying as the carriage jerked to a halt, signaling they'd arrived.

"Before we alight," she said, her voice low and her words coming fast, "I have a request. I would appreciate it if you did not mention last night's incident to Spencer. I don't wish to alarm him."

Andrew could not hide his surprise. "Surely he will see that you are injured."

"My sleeve hides the bandage."

"What about your lip?"

" 'Tis hardly swollen at all. I'm certain he won't notice."

"But if he does?"

"I shall tell him I bit it, which is the truth."

"Perhaps, but it is misleading nonetheless."

"I would rather gently mislead him than worry him."

The door opened, revealing a formally garbed footman who extended his hand to help Lady Catherine alight, thus ending the conversation. It was just as well since Andrew suspected any further comment on his part might have led to another argument. "Arguments are not conducive to successful courting," he muttered.

"What did you say, Mr. Stanton?" Poised in the carriage door, her hand resting upon the footman's, Lady Catherine looked at Andrew over her shoulder with a questioning gaze.

"Er, that I'm, ah, *effusive* at the prospect of, um, *cavorting*." Good God, he sounded like an ass. Also not conducive to successful courting.

"*Cavorting*?"

"Yes. In the therapeutic warm waters." He prayed his skin didn't go pale just saying the words.

"Ah." Her expression cleared, but still bore remnants that hinted she hadn't entirely abandoned the notion that he might be a bit of a dolt.

Also not conducive to successful courting.

After exiting the carriage, Andrew took a moment to look about while Lady Catherine directed the footman regarding their luggage. The drive was shaded by massive elms, sunlight spotting the gravel as it broke through the canopy of leaves. He pulled in a deep breath. The scents of late summer filled his head with a pleasing mixture redolent of grass and sun-warmed earth, and a pungent hint of hay that indicated stables nearby. Closing his eyes, he allowed an image to flicker to life, a glimmer of long ago when he'd enjoyed life in a place similar to this. Yet, as always when he permitted himself a glimpse into the past, the darkness quickly shrouded those fleeting happy memories, blanketing them with the shadow of guilt and shame. Of loss, regret, and self-condemnation. He opened his eyes and blinked away his previous life. It was dead and gone. Literally.

He turned and stilled when he noted Lady Catherine watching him with a questioning look. "Are you all right?" she asked.

As he had countless times before, he settled his painful memories and guilt deep in his heart, where they could not be seen, and showed an outward smile. "I'm fine. Just enjoying being outdoors after that long journey. And looking forward to seeing your son."

"I'm certain you won't have long to wait." As if on cue, the double oak doors leading into the house swung open, revealing a young man casually dressed in fawn breeches and a plain white shirt. He smiled and waved, calling out, "Welcome home, Mum!"

Spencer awkwardly made his way forward and Andrew's gaze was drawn to the boy's club foot. His heart pinched in sympathy for what the lad must suffer on a daily basis, not only from the physical discomfort, but the inner pain of being viewed as different. Flawed. His jaw tightened, knowing that a big part of the reason Lady Catherine and Spencer lived in Little Longstone was because of the cruelty and rejection the boy had experienced in London. Andrew well recalled the awkwardness of that age, nearly twelve years old, teetering on the brink of manhood. It had been difficult enough without the added burden of an infirmity.

Spencer was met midway down the path by his mother, who enveloped him in a hug which the boy returned with unabashed enthusiasm. A wave of something that felt like envy rippled through Andrew at the warm display of affection. He had no memory of what it was to be wrapped in a mother's embrace, as his own mother had died bringing him into the world. Spencer was nearly as tall as his mother, Andrew noted, and the lad appeared surprisingly broad-shouldered, while his gangly arms indicated he still had a lot of growing to do. He bore a striking resemblance to Lady Catherine, having inherited her chestnut hair and golden brown eyes.

Mother and son drew apart, and with a laugh Lady Catherine reached up—with her uninjured arm, Andrew noted—and ruffled Spencer's thick hair. "You're still damp," she said. "How was your visit to the springs?"

"Excellent." He frowned and leaned closer. "What happened to your lip?"

"I accidentally bit it. Nothing to worry about."

The frown cleared. "How was Grandfather's birthday party?"

"It was . . . eventful. And I've brought the most wonderful surprise." She nodded toward the rear of the carriage, where Andrew stood.

Spencer's gaze shifted, and when he caught sight of Andrew, his eyes widened. "I say, is that you, Mr. Stanton?"

"Yes." Andrew joined the duo and held out his hand to the young man. "Very nice to see you again, Spencer."

"Likewise."

"Mr. Stanton kindly consented to escort me home, and has agreed to remain on for a visit. He's promised to regale us with stories of his adventures with your uncle Philip."

Spencer's smile widened. "Excellent. I want to hear how you outsmarted the brigands who locked you in the dungeon. I couldn't pry the story from Uncle Philip."

Lady Catherine raised her brows. "Brigands? Dungeon? I've not heard of this. I thought you and Philip spent your time unearthing artifacts."

"We did," Andrew assured her. "However, as your brother possessed an uncanny penchant for landing in scrapes, I was forced to perform several rescues."

Mischief gleamed in her eyes. "I see. And you, Mr. Stanton—did *you* never find *yourself* in need of rescuing?"

Andrew did his best to look innocent and pointed to the center of his chest. "*Me?* I, who epitomizes the model of decorum—?"

"There was that time Uncle Philip helped you escape those machete-wielding cutthroats," Spencer broke in, his voice ringing with animation. "Fought them off using nothing but his cane and quick wits. They were after you because you'd kissed the one blackguard's daughter."

"A great exaggeration," Andrew said, with a dismissive wave of his hand. "Your uncle Philip is notorious for hyperbole."

Lady Catherine's lips twitched. "Indeed? Then what is the true story, Mr. Stanton? Did you not kiss the blackguard's daughter?"

Damn. How did every conversation with her of late veer down these disastrous paths? "It was more like a friendly good-bye peck. Completely innocent." No need to mention that the two hours prior to that friendly, good-bye peck were anything *but* innocent. "Her father unfortunately objected—rather strenuously, I'm afraid." He shrugged and smiled. "Just when it appeared I was about to become a human pincushion, a stranger strode into the fray, bold as you please, brandishing his cane and shouting out in some foreign language. In truth, I thought he was insane, but he quite saved the day. Turned out to be our very own Philip, and we've been friends since that day."

"What on earth did he say to them?" Lady Catherine asked.

"I don't know. He refused to tell me, claiming it was his little secret. To this day I do not know."

"Which means he must have said something absolutely heinous about you," Spencer said with a grin.

"No doubt," Andrew agreed, laughing.

"Well, Spencer and I shall look forward to hearing more about your travels during your stay, Mr. Stanton. Shall we get you settled?" She held out her uninjured arm to Spencer. They started up the walkway, and Andrew fell in behind them. He noted how firm she kept her arm, enabling her to bear a great deal of Spencer's weight as he limped down the path. Admiration for her—for both of them—hit him. He knew the emotional burdens she bore, yet she did so with humor and dignity, her love for her son shining like a warm glow of sunshine. And Spencer, in spite of the physical difficulties he faced, was obviously an amiable and intelligent young man who openly returned his mother's affection. Most certainly a lad any man would be proud to call his son. Andrew's hands clenched thinking of the boy's father rejecting him so cruelly.

They passed over the threshold, stepping into a spacious, parquet-floored foyer. A round mahogany table stood in the middle of the floor, its shiny surface bearing an enormous arrangement of fresh-cut flowers set in a porcelain vase. The bloom's fragrance filled the air, combined with the pleasant scent of beeswax. Peering beyond the foyer, he noted the wide, curved staircase leading upward, and corridors fanning out to the left and right. Several long tables decorated the corridors, all adorned with vases filled with cut flowers.

A formally attired, slightly built butler stood by the door like a sentinel, his spectacles riding low on his beaklike nose.

"Welcome home, Lady Catherine," the butler said in a voice far too deep and sonorous to come out of a man of such slight proportions. Indeed, it looked as if a stiff wind would knock the man on his posterior.

"Thank you, Milton." While handing him her bonnet and shawl, she said, "This is Mr. Stanton, my brother's business partner and a dear friend of the family. He'll be staying for several days. I've instructed that his things be taken to the blue guest chamber."

Milton bowed his head. "I shall see that the room is readied at once."

Spencer nodded toward the mahogany table. "Did you see your newest flowers, Mum?"

Andrew noted the slight flush that crept up her cheeks. "They are rather difficult to miss."

Spencer made a disgusted sound. "That one isn't nearly as large as the arrangement in the drawing room. They're turning our house into an indoor garden! Why can't they leave you alone?" He turned toward Andrew, clearly seeking an ally. "Don't you think they should leave her alone?"

"They?"

"The *suitors*. Lords Avenbury and Ferrymouth. The Duke of Kelby. Lord Kingsly. Then there's Lord Bedingfield, who recently purchased the estate bordering ours to the west. Between them, they send enough flowers to make one feel as if one is living in a botanical prison."

Spencer made a disgusted sound. "I feel as if I'm choking on flowers. Don't you think they should stop?"

Hell, yes. Andrew forced himself not to shoot the floral tribute a sizzling glare. Before he could answer, Lady Catherine, whose blush had deepened to rose, said, "Spencer, that is very discourteous. Lords Avenbury and Ferrymouth and the others are merely being polite."

Andrew swallowed the irritated *humph* that rose in his throat. Polite? Hardly. He had to bite his tongue to refrain from announcing that a man didn't send a woman enough flowers to sink a frigate just to be polite.

"Shall I arrange for tea?" Milton asked, wading into the awkward silence.

"Yes, thank you, but just for two. In the drawing room." She turned to Andrew. "I'll see you settled in, but then I'm afraid I have a previous appointment." She touched Spencer's sleeve. "Will you entertain Mr. Stanton while I'm gone?"

"Yes. Is your appointment with Mrs. Ralston, or with Dr. Oliver?"

"Doctor?" Andrew asked, his gaze jumping to Lady Catherine. "Are you ill?"

"No," Lady Catherine said quickly. "My appointment is with Mrs. Ralston."

Spencer turned to Andrew. "Mrs. Ralston is my mother's greatest friend. Unless the weather is foul, Mum walks to her house every day to visit and help her."

"Help her?" asked Andrew.

Spencer nodded. "Mrs. Ralston has arthritis in her hands. Mum writes letters for her and tends her flower beds."

Andrew smiled at Lady Catherine. "Very kind of you."

She appeared to blush. "Genevieve is a very dear lady."

"And fortunate to have such a staunch friend." Andrew returned his attention to Spencer. "And who is Dr. Oliver?" he asked casually.

"*Another* suitor, although he's quite nice, and isn't wealthy enough to send these gargantuan bouquets. No, the doctor merely gazes upon Mum with mooning eyes." Spencer proceeded to demonstrate "mooning eyes" by adopting a simpering expression and fluttering his lashes.

If any other woman besides Lady Catherine were involved, Andrew would have found the boy's antics highly entertaining. Instead, he grimly noted that Lady Catherine's cheeks flamed to crimson. He clearly recalled Philip mentioning that one of Lady Catherine's admirers was a village doctor. Based on her reaction, he strongly suspected this was the man.

"What nonsense, Spencer," she said. "Dr. Oliver makes no such faces and is merely a friend."

"Who stops by every day."

"Not *every* day. And besides, he is only being polite."

"It would appear that there is an abundance of polite gentlemen in Little Longstone," Andrew said dryly.

Spencer looked toward the ceiling. "Yes. And they're all intent upon courting my mother."

"It cannot be considered courting if I do not respond," Lady Catherine said in a firm voice. "Their interest will cease once they realize I am not interested."

Andrew cleared his throat. "Based on these"—he waved his hand, encompassing the trio of floral arrangements visible—"they have not yet realized that."

"Lord Bedingfield now knows," Spencer said. "I told him myself when he called upon you yesterday afternoon."

"What on earth did you say to him?" Lady Catherine asked.

"I said, 'My mother is not interested in you.' "

A noise that sounded distinctly like a poorly smothered laugh emitted from Lady Catherine, followed by a cough. Andrew bit back a smile of his own. Spencer was indeed a good lad.

"And what did Lord Bedingfield say?" Catherine asked.

Spencer hesitated, then shrugged. "Just something about children being seen and not heard."

Milton cleared his throat. "Actually, his lordship said something extremely unpleasant which does not bear repeating, at which time I instructed him to leave before I set the dogs upon him."

Andrew's jaw clenched at the realization that Lord Bedingfield had clearly said something unkind to Spencer.

"We don't have any dogs," Lady Catherine said.

"I did not feel it was necessary to point that out to his lordship, my lady."

Although there was hurt in his eyes, a smile flirted around the edges of Spencer's mouth. "Where upon Lord Bedingfield departed, only to trip as he crossed the threshold—"

"—My foot somehow got in his way," Milton said with a stoic expression. "Most unfortunate."

"I'd never before seen the shade of red he turned," Spencer said, his grin now full. "Can't imagine how angry he would have been if he'd known we don't actually have any dogs."

"Yes, I fear his lordship won't be coming back," Milton said with a perfectly straight face. "A thousand apologies for my clumsiness, Lady Catherine."

"I shall endeavor, somehow, to find forgiveness in my heart," she replied in an equally serious voice. She then turned and shot her son a huge wink.

Well, that was one suitor gone, Andrew thought with an

inward grim smile. Unfortunately, there were still quite a few more who needed to go.

While her coachman remained with the carriage, Catherine entered Ralston cottage's modest foyer.

"Good afternoon, Baxter," she greeted Genevieve's imposing butler, tilting back her head to meet his obsidian gaze. "Is Mrs. Ralston at home?"

"The mistress is always at home for you, Lady Catherine," Baxter announced in his deep, gravelly voice. Relieved, Catherine surrendered her velvet bonnet and cashmere shawl to Baxter's ham-sized hands.

No matter how many times she saw him, Baxter's sheer height and breadth never ceased to amaze Catherine. He stood at least six inches over six feet, and his impressive muscles strained the confines of his formal black attire. His proportions, combined with his bald head, not to mention the tiny gold hoops adorning his earlobes, or the fact that he tended to answer questions with a monosyllabic growl, lent him a most intimidating air. Certainly no one encountering Baxter would ever suspect that he loved flowers, clucked over Genevieve's brood of cats like a mother hen, and baked the most delicious scones Catherine had ever tasted. He guarded Genevieve and her menagerie as if they were the crown jewels, and referred to Genevieve as "the one wot saved me."

Catherine knew they'd known each other in Genevieve's "former" life—the one she'd lived before settling in Little Longstone, and she was thankful Genevieve had a strong friend to help her. And protect her. Baxter's hands alone looked as if they could pulverize rock, and, according to Genevieve, they had on more than one occasion. Catherine prayed they would not need to know such violence again.

Baxter escorted her to the drawing room, then retreated. Five minutes later, Genevieve entered the room, her beautiful face alight with pleasure. A pastel green muslin gown adorned her lush figure, and her pale blond hair was arranged in the simple chignon she favored, a style that highlighted her pansy blue eyes and full lips. At two-and-thirty, Genevieve's complexion remained creamy, and even the faint lines etched around her eyes and on her forehead could not detract from her beauty.

"What a lovely surprise," she said, crossing the blue-and-cream Axminster rug with her slow, measured steps. "I thought you'd be too weary after your journey to visit today."

As was her custom, Genevieve blew her a kiss in greeting, touching her lips to her gloved fingertips. Catherine returned the gesture, her heart pinching with sympathy for her friend at her misshapen hands that even the heavy gloves could not hide. In all the years they'd been friends, Catherine had never seen her friend's hands bare.

"I had to come," Catherine said. "There is something we must discuss."

Genevieve gave her a sharp-eyed look. "What happened to your lip?"

"That is part of what we need to discuss. Come, let us sit."

Once they were seated on an overstuffed brocade settee, Catherine told her friend about the shooting.

"Dear God, Catherine," Genevieve said, her eyes filled with concern. "What a horrifying ordeal. How do you feel now?"

"A little achy and sore, but much improved. The wound was superficial"

"How fortunate. For all of us." Her expression grew fierce. "Hopefully the scoundrel who did this will be apprehended. When I think about what might have happened with a stray shot . . . you, or anyone else at the party, could have been seriously injured. Or killed." A delicate shudder shook her frame. "An absolutely horrifying accident. I'm so relieved you weren't seriously hurt."

"As am I. But . . ." Catherine drew a deep breath. "Actually, I'm not convinced that it was an accident." She quickly told Genevieve about the conversation she'd overheard just prior to the shooting, concluding with, "I'm praying it was indeed just a random incident, but I'm frightened. Afraid that it might have been specifically directed at me. That someone, perhaps this investigator, has discovered my connection to Charles Brightmore. And if that is so . . ."

"Then I would be in danger as well," Genevieve said slowly, her expression turning to one of deep sorrow and regret. "Oh, Catherine. I am so sorry that your involvement with me, with my book, has placed you in this untenable situation. This must be stopped. Immediately. I shall travel to London tomorrow to speak with our publisher and instruct Mr. Bayer to reveal that *I* am Charles Brightmore."

"You shall do nothing of the kind," Catherine said firmly. "That would only serve to place you in more imminent danger and destroy your reputation."

"My dear, do you think that matters when compared to your *life?* I can always leave and resettle elsewhere. You have Spencer to think about."

"You will not leave here," Catherine insisted. "You need the warm waters for your hands and joints as much as Spencer does."

"There are other warm springs in England. In Italy." She looked down at her hands and her lips tightened.

"I've cursed these crippled hands so many times. They cost me my livelihood. The man I love . . ." A humorless laugh pushed past her lips. "After all, who wants a mistress with hands like these? No man wants to be touched with such ugliness. But never have I cursed them more than I do now. If I were physically capable to write, to hold a pen, I never would have enlisted your aid to author that cursed book."

"Please do not say that. I wanted to help you. Writing the book, listening to your dictation, being involved, gave my life a sense of purpose that had been lacking for years. You think you took something from me, but just the opposite is true. You've given me more than I can ever repay."

"As you've always given me, yet you cannot deny I've taken away your sense of safety, that this enterprise I involved you in has placed you in danger."

"We can't be certain that is true. Crime is rampant in London, and this very well could have been an accident."

"Yet how will we determine that?" Genevieve asked. "We cannot simply wait until one or both of us is harmed. Or worse. This must be stopped. Immediately. I must speak with Mr. Bayer."

"I beg you not to, at least for a day or two. There was a witness who can identify the culprit. My father promised to write to let me know if the perpetrator is caught. If he is, then our worries are for naught. Let us wait to hear from Father."

Genevieve worried her lowered lip, then finally jerked her head in agreement. "Very well. However, if you haven't heard from him by tomorrow evening, I am going to London the following day. In the meanwhile, we must do something to guarantee your safety. Baxter will see to it that no harm comes to me, but I fear that although Milton and Spencer are brave, they cannot offer you adequate protection should the need arise."

"I have already taken care of that. My brother's American friend, Mr. Stanton, accompanied me to Little Longstone and is remaining for a visit."

"But is he capable of protecting you?" Genevieve asked in a dubious voice.

An image of Mr. Stanton carrying her in his strong arms flashed through her mind, and to her mortification, heat crept up her neck. "Er, yes. He is definitely capable."

Genevieve's gaze turned speculative, then she hiked up one perfectly arched blond brow. "Indeed? Well, I am vastly relieved. I recall you mentioning this Mr. Stanton, but only in the vaguest terms. What is he like?"

"Annoying and opinionated," she answered without hesitation.

Genevieve laughed. "Darling, all men are *that*. Does he possess any good traits?"

Catherine shrugged. "I suppose if pressed to do so, I could think up one or two." When Genevieve continued to wait with an expectant expression, Catherine looked toward the ceiling and blew out a resigned sigh. "He was apparently quite helpful after I was injured last evening. And, um, he does not have an unpleasant body odor."

Something that looked suspiciously like amusement flashed in Genevieve's eyes. "I see. Quick-wittedness and a commitment to personal cleanliness are indeed good traits in a man. Tell me, how precisely did he prove helpful after the shooting?"

Another wave of heat engulfed Catherine. "He applied pressure to the wound until the doctor arrived."

"Excellent. Clearly he knows something about treating injuries." Her eyes widened. "Oh, but please tell me the doctor didn't examine you right there in the drawing room!"

"No." *Damnation, but it was warm in here.* Knowing Genevieve would eventually worm the information from her, Catherine met her gaze squarely and said in her best noncommittal voice, "Mr. Stanton was kind enough to carry me to my father's chamber so as to remove me from the prying eyes of the other guests."

"Ah, a man of discretion as well," Genevieve said with an approving nod. "And I take it you ascertained the fact that he does not possess an offensive body odor while he carried you."

"Yes."

"And obviously he possesses superior strength."

Catherine shot her friend an arch look. "Are you implying that I weigh more than I should?"

Genevieve's musical laugh rang out. "Of course not. I merely meant that only a strong man could carry a woman from the drawing room to the bedchamber—a journey that naturally requires navigating stairs—all while applying pressure to her wound. Very impressive. Does he possess any fortune?"

"I've never asked."

Genevieve shook her head. "My dear, you must have some idea. How are his clothes?"

"Very fine. Expensive."

"His residence?"

"Rooms on Chesterfield. I do not know their condition as, naturally, I've never visited."

"A fashionable part of town," Genevieve said with approval. "So far he sounds quite promising."

"Promising? For what?"

Genevieve's innocent expression resembled that of an angel. "Why as adequate protection for you, of course."

"A fortune and tailored clothing are not prerequisites. He is an expert fencer and accomplished pugilist, and brawny enough to present a threatening presence. That is all I require."

"You are right, of course. And a pugilist, you say. I suppose he bears many scars and healed broken bones. Pity." Genevieve blew out a sigh. "I gather he is remarkably unattractive?"

Catherine's fingers fidgeted with the velvet cord of her reticule. "Well, in all fairness I wouldn't say *that*."

"Oh? What *would* you say?"

That this conversation has taken a most unsettling turn. An image of Mr. Stanton, sitting across from her in the carriage flashed in her mind, his dark eyes steady on hers, a teasing smile playing about his lips. She cleared her throat. "While Mr. Stanton is not classically handsome in any sense, I can see where a certain sort of woman might find him . . . not unappealing."

"What sort of woman?"

The living, breathing sort. The words popped unbidden into her mind, appalling her. Heavens, she was losing her senses. "I really wouldn't know," she said, much more stiffly than she'd meant to. "Perhaps the nearsighted sort?"

Unfortunately, Genevieve ignored her stiff tone. "Oh, dear. Poor man. What exactly does Mr. Stanton look like?"

"Look like?"

Concern clouded Genevieve's eyes. "Darling, are you certain that bump on your head is not more serious than you thought? Your manner is most odd."

"I'm fine." She drew a deep breath. "Mr. Stanton looks like . . . he has . . ." *Dark, compelling eyes that you must actually force yourself to look away from. A slow, engag-*

ing smile that for some insane reason makes my heart beat faster just thinking about. A strong jaw, and that lovely mouth that looks both firm and delightfully soft at the same time. Silky, dark hair, strands of which fall over his forehead in a manner that makes one's fingers itch to brush the locks back into place—

"He has what, darling?"

Genevieve's voice jerked Catherine from her reverie with a start. Good Lord, her thoughts had positively run amuck. Perhaps she *had* bumped her head harder than she'd thought. "He has dark hair, dark eyes, and a, um, rather nice smile." Her conscience balked at the lukewarm description of Mr. Stanton's smile as "nice," but she firmly swatted her inner voice aside.

"So he's just very ordinary."

Ordinary? Catherine tried to attach that word to Mr. Stanton, and was spectacularly unsuccessful. Before she could think up a reply, Genevieve continued, "Well, that is just as well. He is here to protect you. If you were attracted to him, you might consider entering into a liaison with him, and that could lead to all sorts of complications that could distract him from his duties."

"I can assure you that a liaison with Mr. Stanton—or anyone else for that matter—is the furthest thing from my mind."

Genevieve smiled. "Then thank heavens you do not find him the least bit attractive."

"Yes, thank heavens."

Yet even as those three words passed her lips, her inner voice whispered three words of its own.

Liar, liar, liar.

Chapter 6

Many men feel disinclined to give a woman what she wants if she is bold enough simply to ask for it. In addition, many men disregard superb ideas simply because they were suggested by a woman. Therefore, the most expeditious way for Today's Modern Woman to get what she wants and to implement her ideas is to lead the gentleman in question to believe that it was his *idea all along.*

A Ladies' Guide to the Pursuit of
Personal Happiness and Intimate Fulfillment
by Charles Brightmore

Andrew leaned his shoulders against the white marble mantel in the drawing room and tried his best not to glare at the monstrous floral tribute that dominated the room. Clearly he was not entirely successful—either that or Spencer was clairvoyant—because the lad said, "Dreadful, isn't it?"

He turned his attention to Spencer, who sat on an overstuffed brocade settee next to the fireplace. The boy's attention was fixed upon the trio of fruit tarts remaining on the silver platter Milton had served with their tea.

"Dreadful," Andrew agreed. "Whoever sent that bouquet must have emptied every flower shop in the district."

"The Duke of Kelby," Spencer said, plucking a strawberry-topped tart from the tray. "Horrendously wealthy, although I'm certain the flowers came from his private conservatory, not a local shop."

Bloody hell. The quizzing glass sporting, carplike duke was horrendously wealthy. With his own damn private conservatory.

Before Andrew could comment, Spencer looked up at him with a worried frown. "Is my mother all right?"

Wariness skittered through Andrew. "What do you mean?"

"She seemed worried. Did something happen in London to upset her?"

Damn it, he didn't want to lie to the boy, yet he couldn't ignore Lady Catherine's request not to mention the shooting. "I think the journey back to Little Longstone exhausted her," he said carefully.

There was no mistaking Spencer's relief, and Andrew felt like a cad of the first order for not being honest with the lad. God knows he'd uttered an uncountable number of lies over the years without so much as batting an eye, but being less than truthful with this young man did not sit well at all.

Anxious to change the subject lest he be forced to say something else less than truthful, he asked, "Tell me, what sort of man is this duke?"

"Don't really know. But he looks like a carp. I'd say he belongs in your museum with the rest of the relics." Spencer stuffed half the tart in his mouth with a huge, enthusiastic bite that had Andrew holding back a grin. He swallowed, then added, "But it's not just that he's carplike. He doesn't *care* about my mother."

"And how do you know that?"

Spencer jerked his head toward the flower monstrosity. "Because he sent her those. She hates large, ostentatious displays like that. If he knew anything about my mother, he'd know that she'd prefer a single bloom."

Andrew made a mental note of that useful information, and, burying the guilt that pricked him at questioning Spencer, he asked, "What else does your mother like?"

Spencer screwed up his face, clearly giving the matter serious thought. "Girl things," he finally said.

"*Girl* things?"

"Yes. You know, gowns and ribbons and flowers and such. But simple. Not like that." He pointed toward the huge bouquet.

Hmmm. Not much help there. "What else? Jewelry, I suppose?"

Spencer shook his head. "No. Or at least not very much I don't think, as she rarely wears any. Mum likes animals. Walking in the gardens. Tending her flowers. Taking the waters. And strawberries. She's very fond of strawberries." He popped the other half of the tart into his mouth and grinned. "Me too."

Andrew smiled in return. "Me three." He leaned down, to help himself to a strawberry tart, which he ate with only marginally less gusto than Spencer, eliciting a laugh from the boy.

"Well, I'm glad that the duke doesn't know what Mum likes," Spencer said, his expression sobering, "or any of those other gentlemen who are trying to win her favor. She doesn't need them. *We* don't need them." His gaze wandered down to his misshapen foot, and his jaw tightened. When he raised his gaze, Andrew's heart lurched at the thousand hurts he read shimmering in Spencer's eyes.

"I wish I could make them all just take away their flowers and invitations and gifts and leave her alone," Spencer said, a quiver evident in his fervent voice. "I wish I was strong and could fight. Like you. Then they'd leave her alone."

"I fight gentlemen in the pugilist's ring," Andrew said gently. "I don't make a habit of going about popping dukes in the nose—even if they do send horrible flower arrangements." *Of course, I could change my policy on that . . .*

Spencer didn't respond with the smile Andrew had hoped for. "Uncle Philip said you are also an expert fencer."

"I'm passable."

"Uncle Philip said you've defeated him, and he *is* an expert." Before Andrew could reply, Spencer rushed on, "Who taught you to fight with your fists?"

"My father gave me some instructions—after I arrived home one afternoon with a bleeding nose, swollen lip, and two blackened eyes. The rest I learned the hard way, I'm afraid."

Spencer's jaw dropped. "Someone hit you?"

"*Hit* is an understatement for the thorough thrashing I received."

"Who would do such a thing? And why? Weren't they afraid of you?"

Andrew laughed. "Hardly. I was only nine years old at the time, and as scrawny as they come. I was walking home after a successful afternoon of lake fishing when two local boys set upon me. They were both about my age, but far less scrawny than I. After they blackened my eyes, they relieved me of my fish."

"I wager they wouldn't attempt such a thing now," Spencer predicted.

"I'd certainly give them a better showing than I did back then," Andrew agreed.

"Did they ever do it again?"

"Oh, yes. They waited for me every week, the same spot, on my way home from the lake. I changed my return route, but they quickly caught on to that ploy. They made my life excessively miserable for several months." Memories swept over him, of his shame at returning to his father without the fish he'd been sent to catch. The humiliation of shedding tears of pain and frustration, in spite of his best efforts not to, in front of his tormentors. His father looking at him through shrewd, yet calm eyes. *How many more times you gonna let those whelps beat the tar out of you and steal our dinner, son?* Wiping his bloody nose with the back of his hand, fighting back tears. *None, Pa. They ain't gonna beat me next time. Show me again how to fight them . . .*

"And then what happened?"

Andrew blinked and the memory dissipated as if blown away on a gentle breeze. "I learned how to fight. How to protect myself. Then I bloodied *their* noses. Only had to do it once."

Spencer's lips pressed together into a thin line. "I'd wager your father was proud of you when you succeeded in subduing those ruffians."

There was no missing the pain in those words, and Andrew's heart squeezed for this young man whose hurts obviously ran so deep, and who, in spite of having all his mother's love, still longed for a father's love and acceptance as well. "My father was proud," Andrew agreed softly, refusing to acknowledge the lump of emotion threatening to clog his throat. "And very relieved that we wouldn't be losing our fish any longer."

"Why didn't your father go with you to the lake so the boys wouldn't set upon you?"

"You know, at the time, I asked myself, and him, that

very question. And I've never forgotten what he said. He told me, 'Son, a man doesn't let anyone else fight his battles for him. If someone else has to fight for your pride, then it isn't yours at all.' " He smiled. "My father was a very wise man."

"Was?"

Andrew nodded. "He died the year I turned sixteen."

Spencer's solemn expression indicated he understood losing a father. "Do you . . . think of him often?"

It was clear by his tone that the question was serious to Spencer, so Andrew thought carefully before answering. "After he died, I thought of him all the time. I tried not to, I pushed myself, worked harder, trying to exhaust my body and mind so I wouldn't think of him because every time I did, it . . . hurt. He'd been my best friend, and for my entire life, we were all we had."

"Where was your mum?"

"Died birthing me."

"So you and your father were alone," Spencer murmured. "Like me and my mum."

"Yes, I suppose we were. As the years passed, the pain of his death became less sharp. Rather like a knife whose blade loses it edge—it can still cut, but not as keenly. I still think of him every day—it just doesn't hurt as much now."

"How did he die?"

Another image flashed in Andrew's mind, filling him with acute pain, and he realized that he hadn't been entirely honest with Spencer about the grief dulling over time. "He drowned. A heavy fog rolled in one night while he was at the wharf, and he lost his bearings. Stepped off the dock." Emotion tightened his throat. "He was a strong, hearty man who could do a thousand things, but he couldn't swim."

"I'm sorry."

"As am I."

Spencer's gaze again drifted down to his damaged foot and for nearly a minute, the only sound in the room was the ticking of the mantel clock. Finally, he looked up. "Isn't it odd that the one thing your robust father couldn't do is the only thing I *can* do."

"You can do more than swim, Spencer."

He shook his head. "No. I cannot fence. Or fight. Or ride." His voice took on a bitter, resigned edge that broke Andrew's heart. "I can't do any of those things. It's why my father hated me, you know."

Andrew pushed off from the mantel and sat beside Spencer. Leaning forward, Andrew rested his elbows on his spread knees and clasped his hands, searching for the right words. He wanted to refute the boy's statement, assure him his father had cared for him, but Spencer was no longer a child, and far too intelligent to accept such empty platitudes.

Turning to look at him, Andrew said, "I'm sorry that your relationship with your father was estranged and that he didn't know what a fine young man you are. That was truly his loss, and *his* decision—one that in no way reflects poorly on you."

Surprise, and gratitude, flashed in Spencer's eyes before his expression went flat. "But he wouldn't have hated me if I were like other boys."

"Then learn from his mistake, Spencer. Outward appearances are a poor way to judge a person. Just because someone is beautiful or without physical imperfection does not mean he possesses integrity or a good character. *Those* are the things upon which a person should be judged."

Spencer looked away and plucked at his jacket sleeve. "I wish everyone felt that way, Mr. Stanton."

Andrew debated for several seconds, then gave in to his inclination and patted Spencer's shoulder in what he hoped was a comforting gesture. "So do I. But unfortunately we can't control other people's actions. Or words. Only our own. And you're wrong, Spencer. You *could* do those things. If you really wanted to."

Spencer gazed back at him with eyes too young to hold all the hurt and cynicism shimmering in their depths. "I can't."

"Have you ever tried?"

A humorless laugh escaped the boy's lips. "No."

"My father, who we've already established was a very wise man, was fond of telling me, 'Son, if you always do what you've always done, you'll always be where you've always been.' " He kept his gaze steady on Spencer's. "Is that what you want? To always say that you cannot do something that you want to do?"

"But how can I do them? Have you not noticed this?" He jabbed his finger toward his foot.

"Of course I noticed. But it hasn't stopped you from walking. Or swimming. Your foot is damaged, but your mind is not. I'm not suggesting that you aspire to become the best fencer or pugilist or rider in England—only that you aspire to be the best *you* can be. Tell me, what is your favorite food—the thing you love above all else?"

The boy looked confused at the abrupt change of subject, but he answered. "Cook's fresh-baked scones with strawberry jam."

"How do you know they're your favorite?"

"Because I tried them . . ." His voice trailed off as understanding dawned in his eyes.

"Exactly. You wouldn't have discovered your very favorite food if you hadn't tried it the first time. I wouldn't have known that I could pound the piss out of those ruffians if I hadn't tried. If I hadn't wanted to. If I hadn't been determined. The only thing stopping you from doing the things you want to do is *you*, Spencer. By thinking that you can't."

A heartbreaking combination of doubt, confusion, and hope ignited in his eyes. "You think I can?"

"I know you can."

"You'd teach me?"

"You've only to ask."

"But . . . what if I fail?"

"You can only fail if you don't try. If you don't take that first step, you'll never know how far you might go. If you at least make an attempt, you've already succeeded."

"Are those more words of wisdom from your father?"

"No. Those are hard-won lessons I had to learn for myself. Lessons no one offered to teach me."

"The way you're offering to teach me."

"Yes."

He frowned and plucked at his sleeve again, clearly debating. Finally, he said, "Mother won't like it, you know. She'll be afraid I'll hurt myself." A red flush stained his cheeks. "In truth, I might be a bit afraid of that myself."

"We'll go very slowly. A great deal of it involves balance, and I've a number of ideas how to help you with that. And if, at any time, you want to cease our lessons, we shall."

The boy drew a deep breath, then straightened his spine. Andrew's heart warmed at the combination of determination and tentative eagerness shining in his eyes. "When can we begin?" he asked. "Tomorrow?"

"Tomorrow it is."

"Best to do it when Mother won't be about," Spencer said, his voice dropping to a conspiratorial level. "I'd suggest after breakfast. That's when she spends an hour in her rooms seeing to her correspondence."

"Agreed."

"After our lesson, I'll take you to the warm springs. It will be especially fine to soak after our exertions."

Andrew managed a weak smile. "The warm springs. Yes, that sounds delightful."

He made another quick mental note—to fabricate something that required his immediate attention after his lesson with Spencer so as to avoid the trip to the warm springs. He had no intention of getting anywhere near the water. *Like father, like son . . .*

Chapter 7

Today's Modern Woman should not be afraid to take the upper hand during lovemaking. Touch your lover in the manner you'd like to be touched. Although he may at first express surprise at such bold behavior, be confident that your forthrightness will ultimately lead to very satisfactory results.

A Ladies' Guide to the Pursuit of Personal Happiness and Intimate Fulfillment
by Charles Brightmore

Catherine arrived home from her visit with Genevieve feeling unsettled. Between their conversation about Mr. Stanton and the shooting, she was more than a little perturbed.

Surrendering her bonnet and shawl to Milton, she asked, "Have any messages arrived from my father?"

"No, my lady."

Fustian. Swallowing her disappointment, she asked, "Where is Spencer?"

"Taking his afternoon rest."

"And Mr. Stanton?" She pressed her lips together, thoroughly annoyed that her heart seemed to skip a beat just saying his name.

"When last I saw him, he was on his way to his bedchamber, presumably to rest before dinner. Shall I arrange for tea for you, my lady?"

"No, thank you." Certainly she was relieved, not disappointed, that Mr. Stanton wasn't about. "The weather is so delightful, and as I took the carriage to visit Mrs. Ralston, I believe I'll walk to the stables and see how Fritzborne is faring." Her head groom had injured his hand while repairing the stable roof just before she'd left for London. "How is he?"

"His usual self again, although I believe the air surrounding the stable still bears an odd hue from the colorful language he spewed after he smashed the hammer down on his thumb."

Catherine smiled, well imagining Fritzborne's tirade. She exited the house and struck out across the lawns, heading toward the stables. Late-afternoon sunlight kissed the sky, gilding the fluffy white clouds in a blanket of vivid golds and oranges. She breathed deeply of the warm, flower-scented air, allowing peace to infuse her, the sense of tranquillity that the yellow haze and crowds and odors of London always stole from her.

Yet the calm she sought and had never failed to find somehow eluded her. Obviously the shooting still badly disrupted her peace. A little more time at home, surrounded by Spencer and the familiar atmosphere and things she loved would help her recapture her equilibrium.

The stable's huge weathered wood doors were flung wide open. After crossing the threshold, she stood just inside the doorway for several seconds, blinking to adjust her vision to the dim interior. The murmur of a deep voice reached her ears from the far corner, where Venus was stalled, followed by a soft nicker. A smile pulled at Catherine's lips at the familiar sound her favorite mare made when being brushed. She started forward, anticipating her chat with Fritzborne and a friendly nuzzle from Venus. The rich scents of fresh hay, leather, and sun-warmed horseflesh filled her head, easing away her tensions.

When she stopped in front of the stall, however, she froze. And stared.

It was not Fritzborne, but Mr. Stanton who stood in the stall, brushing Venus with long, sure strokes. Mr. Stanton, who'd discarded his jacket and cravat. Mr. Stanton, who'd rolled back his shirtsleeves, revealing muscular forearms that flexed in the most fascinating manner with each passage of the brush over Venus's back. Mr. Stanton, dressed in fawn-colored riding breeches that hugged his long legs in a way that made her mouth go dry.

Sweat had dampened a T across the white linen shirt stretched across his broad shoulders and down the center of his back. His hair was disheveled, dark strands falling over his forehead with his exertions. He looked completely undone, yet for some unfathomable reason, the word that burrowed into her mind was *delicious.*

Any modicum of serenity she'd managed to regain evaporated like steam. She stood, transfixed, her gaze roaming over his masculine form in a manner that should have appalled her—that *did* appall her—but not enough for her to cease.

The sight of his strong, long-fingered hands easing over Venus, while his low-pitched voice murmured soothing words, filled Catherine with a longing that frightened her in its intensity. She needed to leave—

He looked up, and their eyes met. His hand stilled, and she fancied his eyes darkened. Heat rushed through her at his intense regard, and she barely refrained from dabbing at her forehead with the back of her hand. And what on earth was wrong with her stomach? It felt so very odd . . . clearly she'd eaten something that hadn't quite agreed with her.

"Lady Catherine. I did not know you were here."

"I . . . I just arrived."

He set down the brush, then walked slowly toward her. Her toes curled inside her shoes, and she had to force herself not to back up, to flee his presence, a sensation that irked her. Well, at least now she was irked. That was certainly better, and far safer than . . . not being irked.

"Where is Fritzborne?" Good heavens, had that husky voice come from her?

"Out exercising Aphrodite. Very romantic names for your horses."

"I enjoy mythology. Milton said you were in your bedchamber."

"I was, but only long enough to change into riding clothes. I felt the need for some fresh air."

A feeling she could well understand, especially as it seemed someone had sucked all the air from the stables.

He opened the stall door and smiled. "Would you care to join us?"

Even as her mind told her to decline, her feet moved forward. She entered the stall and ran her hand over Venus's satiny nose. The horse nickered and pushed affectionately against her palm.

"She's a beautiful animal," Mr. Stanton said, picking up the brush once again.

"Thank you. Did you ride her?"

"Yes. I hope you don't mind."

"Not at all. She loves to run."

Silence swelled between them as Catherine watched him glide the brush over Venus's glossy chestnut back.

Her attention was riveted on the tensile strength of his arms and the way the linen of his shirt pulled across his chest with each long stroke.

"How was your visit with your friend?"

Her gaze snapped back to his, and she experienced the unsettling sensation that he was aware she'd been watching him. "Fine. And your visit with Spencer?"

"Very nice indeed. He's an exceptional young man."

There was no mistaking the sincerity in his voice or his eyes, and some of the tension left her shoulders. Running her fingers through Venus's brown mane, she smiled at him across the horse's back. "Thank you. I'm very proud of him."

"As well you should be. He's very intelligent and remarkably mature."

"He excels at his studies. His tutor, Mr. Winthrop, is in Brighton, visiting his family as he does for a month every summer. Yet even during his absence, Spencer reads avidly. As for his maturity, I suppose some of it stems from the fact that he spends all his time with adults."

She watched him as she spoke, noting how he did not waste a single stroke, and except for the sheen of exertion dampening his skin, appeared tireless. "Venus tends to be skittish around strangers," she remarked. "You obviously have a way with horses."

"No doubt because I spent my youth working in stables."

Catherine blinked at this bit of news. "I did not know that."

He glanced at her, and she had to clench her hands to keep from reaching out to brush back the silky ebony hair spilling across his forehead. Damnation, he should *not* look so appealing. If *she* were sweaty, rumpled, with her hair in disarray and scented with horse, she wouldn't look in the least appealing.

"There is a great deal we don't know about each other, Lady Catherine," he said softly.

His voice, his words, flowed over her like warmed honey, filling her with the unsettling realization that he was right. And the even-more-unsettling realization that she wanted to know more about him. Everything about him. She hadn't ever thought of what his life in America had been like. Clearly he came from humble beginnings if he'd worked in a stable. Surely that wasn't a fact she should find so interesting. And obviously he'd had a family there. Friends. Women . . .

Which certainly wasn't a fact she should find so disturbing.

"I am hopeful we can remedy that and become better acquainted during my stay," he added.

The distressing and alarming realization suddenly dawned that she harbored that very same hope. Adopting her briskest tone, she said, "But we already have become better acquainted, Mr. Stanton. Thus far we have learned that we have very little in common and hold diametrically opposed opinions on a number of subjects."

Instead of looking offended, one corner of his mouth curved upward in clear amusement. "Such a pessimistic view, Lady Catherine. But whereas you choose to view the glass as half-empty, I prefer to see it as half-full. While our literary tastes may differ—"

"—*Drastically* differ."

He inclined his head in agreement. "We do both enjoy reading. And we agree that your son is a fine young man. And that Venus is an exceptional horse."

"Yes, well, I'm certain we could also agree that the sky is blue, the grass green, and my hair brown."

"Actually, right now the sky is streaked with crimson

and gold, the grass is better described as emerald, and your hair . . ."

His voice trailed off, and his gaze shifted to her hair, making her suddenly conscious of the fact that she'd left the house without her bonnet.

"The lovely chestnut color of your hair, the richness of the deep golds and subtle reds layered through the strands, is not well served when described as merely 'brown.' " He slowly reached out, and a heated tingle of anticipation raced through her. His fingers brushed just above her ear, halting her breath.

"Except for this," he said, holding out a piece of hay pinched between his thumb and index finger. "*This* can be described as brown, although I must tell you, I believe most ladies prefer to decorate their hair with ribbons."

Catherine sucked in a breath and clenched her teeth in annoyance, although she could not decide if she were more annoyed at him for throwing her so off-balance, at herself for allowing him to do so, or at him for not appearing the least bit off-balance. Well, clearly she was more annoyed at him as she had *two* reasons.

"And," he added, "we clearly share a love of horses . . . do we not?"

"I can't deny I love them." She threw him an arch look. "Horses never argue with you."

He threw an equally arch look right back at her. "No, they never do." He walked around Venus to stand beside her. She inhaled sharply and caught a pleasing whiff of sandalwood.

"Our last conversations seem to have ended . . . awkwardly," he said, "and I feel bad about it. Can we call a truce?"

Dear Lord, she didn't want to call a truce at all. She

wanted to summon up the irritation she'd felt toward him, which was far preferable to this heated, almost painful awareness of him. Of his strength. And height. And compelling eyes. And the sight of him, rumpled, the strong, tanned column of his neck visible where he'd removed his cravat.

When had their relationship taken this unsettling turn? She didn't know, but she dearly wished she could retravel that road and avoid the disastrous detour she'd somehow taken. "I seem to recall asking you something similar," she said.

"Yes. Although I suspected you really wanted my complete surrender."

"And is that what you want, Mr. Stanton? My complete surrender?"

Something flickered in his eyes. "Are you offering it, Lady Catherine?"

He hadn't moved, yet somehow it seemed as if he'd drawn closer to her, and she took an involuntary step backward. Then another. Her back bumped into the rough, wooden wall.

"Today's Modern Woman does not surrender, Mr. Stanton. If the occasion calls for it, she may consider a graceful capitulation."

"I see. But only if the occasion calls for it."

"Precisely."

"Well then." He stepped forward, stopping less than an arm's length away. He looked down at her, his eyes filled with something she couldn't read, along with a hint of unmistakable amusement.

Amusement? Aggravating man. How dared he be amused when she was so . . . unamused. Out of sorts. And damnation, breathless by his nearness. She pressed herself harder against the wall, but compensated for her cowardice by raising her chin a notch.

He reached out and captured her hand in his, and her breath backed up in her throat at the sensation of his skin touching hers. She detected the roughness of calluses and realized she'd never been touched by hands like his—hands that did not bear the softness of a gentleman's. Her hand looked pale and small and fragile against the tanned strength of his, yet his touch, while strong, was infinitely gentle. She watched, transfixed, as he slowly raised her hand to his mouth.

"I don't believe I've ever witnessed a graceful capitulation, Lady Catherine. I shall look forward to it—should the occasion arise." The words whispered over her skin, stunning her with a flash of heat. Then, with his gaze on hers, he pressed a warm kiss to her fingertips.

Oh, my. The sensation of his mouth touching her fingers sizzled pure pleasure up her arm. Before she could recover her breath, he lowered her hand and released it, and she pressed her lips together to contain her disappointment.

His touch was . . . lovely. Gentle, yet with an underlying intensity that made her feel as if her skirts had caught fire. It had been so very long since a man had touched her. Yet she hadn't realized that she'd missed it so very much until just now. And never had a touch inspired such a blaze of heat . . .

Catherine gave herself a mental shake. Good heavens, this wouldn't do at all. She surreptitiously wiped her fingers on her gown in a vain attempt to remove the provocative feel of his lips from her skin. "I cannot imagine such an occasion arising, Mr. Stanton."

He had the nerve to smile. "Hope springs eternal, Lady Catherine."

Humph. The best thing clearly was for her to retreat

and remove herself from his disturbing presence. "If you'll excuse me, Mr. Stanton . . ." She turned and walked toward the stall door. "I'll see you at dinner."

Instead of merely letting her leave, he reached out and opened the stall door for her. Not about to let him ruin her perfect exit, she swept through the opening like a ship under full sail.

He immediately fell into step beside her. "I've finished grooming Venus, and as there is something I need to discuss with you, I'd be happy to escort you back to the house."

She bit the inside of her cheeks. She had no desire to discuss anything with this vexing man.

Vexing. She instantly brightened. Yes, he was vexing. Irritating. She could not, would not, find such a man attractive. Perhaps she should engage him in conversation regarding the *Guide* so as not to forget exactly how irritating and vexing he was. To remind herself how little they had in common. Because she somehow seemed constantly to forget.

Marching from the stables, she struck out for the house at a brisk pace, intent upon her plan of retreat. He not only kept up with her easily, but looked as if he were just strolling along while doing so.

"Are we late?" he asked.

"Late?"

"Based on the speed of your gait, which quite resembles a gallop, by the way, I was wondering if we were perhaps late for dinner."

"I enjoy a brisk walk. It is, um, very good for the constitution."

"You are clearly feeling better. Is your arm hurting?"

"Only faintly. What did you wish to discuss with me?"

"When do you plan to tell Spencer what happened?"

"Why do you ask?"

"He asked me this afternoon if something had upset you in London. Clearly he sensed something in your manner."

"What did you tell him?"

"That our journey to Little Longstone had exhausted you."

"Which is true."

"Yes, but it wasn't the *truth*, and I did not like being less than honest with him. I'd like to know when you plan to tell him, as I wouldn't want to mention the incident to him before you've done so."

"I would prefer that you not mention it at all."

She felt, and ignored, the weight of his stare. "Surely you intend to tell him what happened."

"What would be the point? He'd only worry needlessly."

"But what if he finds out from someone else? Your father. Or Philip, whom your father has most likely notified. Or Meredith."

Damnation, the man had a point, and about something that was none of his business, which only served to vex her further. "I agree that the news should come from me—*if* I decide to tell him. Therefore, I shall write to Father and Philip and ask them not to mention the incident."

"I fully understand your concern for your son, indeed it is admirable. Still, don't you think Spencer would prefer the truth—especially since you can assure him you're going to make a full recovery? I believe he deserves as much. A lad on the brink of manhood does not appreciate being treated like a child."

"When did you become an expert on children, Mr. Stanton—and my child in particular?"

"Actually, I know nothing about children, except that I once was one."

"So you consider this the voice of experience speaking?"

"Yes, as a matter of fact. No one likes being lied to."

She halted, swung around to face him, and treated him to her most glacial stare. "As much as I'm *excruciatingly* grateful for your *unsolicited* advice, I really think *I* know how best to handle this situation. Spencer is *my* child, Mr. Stanton. You barely know him. I've raised him alone—and without interference—from the moment he was born. If I decide to tell Spencer, I will do so in my own way, when we have a quiet moment together, so as to minimize his worry."

He said nothing for several seconds, just stood, the breeze blowing his hair, his gaze steady on hers in a way that made her want to squirm and perhaps examine her behavior, but she feared it would not hold up well to intense scrutiny. After all, hadn't she been living a lie these last months regarding her connection to the *Ladies' Guide*? And she was increasingly, uncomfortably aware that something about this man affected her behavior in ways she didn't understand. And wasn't certain she liked.

Finally, he inclined his head. "Spencer was already worried about you. And it bothered me to step around the issue with him. I well recall how difficult it was to be a boy that age. No longer a child, not yet an adult. I knew I was capable of much more than anyone gave me credit for, and I think perhaps Spencer is as well. However, I offer my apologies. I meant no offense."

"Indeed? I suppose then that you thought I'd consider it a compliment to be called a liar?" She shoved aside her inner voice that whispered *you* are *a liar.*

"I did not intend to call you such."

"What *was* your intention?"

"Merely to encourage you to tell him what happened. As soon as possible."

"Very well, Mr. Stanton. Consider me encouraged." She raised her brows. "Now, is there anything else you feel we need to discuss?"

He blew out a breath and raked a hand through his hair in a gesture of clear frustration. Good. Why on earth should *she* be the only one out of sorts? "Only that I'm not certain how *another* conversation has deteriorated into an argument."

" 'Tis no mystery, Mr. Stanton. It is because you are opinionated, irritating, and altogether aggravating."

"A statement that is very much like the lake calling the ocean 'wet,' Lady Catherine."

She opened her mouth to respond, but he touched his index finger to her lips, effectively cutting off her words.

"However," he said softly, the warmth from this finger heating her lips, "in addition to finding you opinionated, irritating, and altogether aggravating, you are also intelligent, beautiful, a wonderful mother, not to mention delightful company—at least most of the time."

His finger slipped slowly away from her mouth, and she pressed her lips together to keep from involuntarily licking them.

" 'Til dinner, Lady Catherine." Offering her a formal bow, he turned and walked toward the house, leaving her to stare after him, robbed of speech.

Her lips still tingled from the gentle pressure of his finger, and now that he couldn't see her, she flicked out the tip of her tongue to taste the warm spot.

She was outraged. Completely. Who was he to tell her how to handle her son? Or to suggest that he found her as opinionated, irritating, and altogether aggravating as she found him? And then to turn around and dare call her intelligent, beautiful, a wonderful mother, and delightful company—at least most of the time. Clearly he was a scoundrel of the first order. A scoundrel who—

Thinks I'm beautiful.

A completely unacceptable delighted shiver quivered down her spine, and she heaved out the sort of prolonged, feminine sigh she'd believed herself long past heaving. Lifting her hand to shade her eyes against the last remnants of the setting sun, she stared at his retreating backside.

And damnation, what a fine-looking backside it was.

She watched him climb the stone steps to the terrace, and after he'd disappeared through the French windows leading into the house, she roused herself from her slack-jawed stupor and strode toward the house. She felt in great need of a restorative cup of tea. Two cups of tea might well be needed to settle her ruffled feathers. Three would not be beyond the realm of possibility.

Chapter 8

Today's Modern Woman must not fear acting upon the attraction she feels for a man, yet she should recognize that it is possible to be bold and discrete at the same time. An "accidental" brushing against his body, a whisper only he is meant to hear, will thoroughly capture his attention.

A Ladies' Guide to the Pursuit of
Personal Happiness and Intimate Fulfillment
by Charles Brightmore

"It's your turn, Mum."

Catherine's chin jerked up, and she met her son's smile across the dining room table. Heavens, how long had she been lost in her own thoughts, staring at her dinner of peas and poached turbot?

She blinked away her preoccupation and forced a smile. "My turn?"

"To share an 'I wish I had not done that' story." His grin widened. "Tell Mr. Stanton about the time you were stuck in the tree."

In spite of her best effort to remain focused on Spencer, her errant gaze shifted to Mr. Stanton. *Why* could she not keep from looking at the man? All through dinner she'd surreptitiously peeked at him from beneath her lashes, unable to forget her conversation about him with Genevieve. All evening she'd hoped in vain that a note would arrive from her father relating the news that the culprit was caught, thus relieving her mind that she faced any danger. Then there would be no further need for Mr. Stanton to remain in Little Longstone. His increasingly disturbing presence could return to London, thus ending this unwanted . . . whatever it was. Yes, the moment he was gone from her home, she would forget him.

In the meanwhile, it was damned difficult to contemplate forgetting him when he sat not ten feet away from her, looking large and masculine and incredibly attractive in a Devonshire brown jacket and snowy linen shirt. His dark eyes studied her with an arresting combination of warmth, interest, amusement, and something else that she couldn't define. But whatever that something else was, it tingled heat down to her toes.

One dark eyebrow quirked upward. "Stuck in a tree?" Mr. Stanton repeated. "My curiosity is aroused, Lady Catherine. Please, you must share this tale. How did such an unfortunate predicament occur?"

"I was rescuing a kitten."

"Don't tell me you climbed a tree to do so."

"Very well. I won't tell you that. However, by not doing so, it shall be very difficult to continue my story."

There was no mistaking his surprise, but rather than feeling abashed at his stunned expression, she barely suppressed a laugh of delight at shocking him.

"In that case, tell me what you must to continue."

She inclined her head in acquiescence. "Several years ago, Fritzborne brought home a cat he'd found wandering in the woods. In a remarkably short time, we found ourselves the proud owners of a litter of kittens. They were adorable, but the most mischievous little beasts ever born. The one we named Angelica was, ironically, the most devilish of the group. One day, while Spencer and I were returning from the springs, we heard a pitiful sound. We looked up and saw Angelica perched on a high limb of an elm. She required rescuing, so I did the job." She cleared her throat and stabbed a pea onto her fork. "The end."

"But Mum, you left out the best part," Spencer protested. "The part where *you* became stuck." His eyes alight with animation, he turned toward Mr. Stanton. "Mum's gown became tangled in the branches. When she couldn't free herself, I went to the stables to fetch Fritzborne. We returned to the tree with a sturdy rope and a basket. Fritzborne tossed the rope to Mum, affixed the basket, then with a bit of ingenuity, Angelica was lowered to the ground in the basket."

"Leaving your mother still stuck in the tree," Mr. Stanton said.

"Yes," Catherine interjected with an exaggerated sniff. "While that dastardly kitten ambled off as if nothing had occurred."

"How did you get down?"

"Fritzborne returned to the house to fetch scissors, which he sent up in the basket," Catherine said. "Of course, Milton, Cook, and Timothy the footman, had returned with him. While I sat upon the branch, hacking away with the scissors to free my gown, the group of them stood below, arguing how best to get me down. Spencer, bless him, came up with the winning suggestion. I tied the rope around the branch I sat upon, then simply slid down. The end."

Spencer sent her a long-suffering look. "Mum . . . ?"

She wrinkled her nose at him. "Oh, very well. I was so proud of myself for successfully sliding down the rope, I decided to let go a few feet from the ground and give my audience a graceful curtsy. Unfortunately I landed in a slippery patch of mud. My feet went up, and my bottom went down." She gave them both a rueful smile. "Luckily the mud was quite soft, as were my petticoats, and nothing save my pride was hurt. However, no stretch of the imagination could call the outing dignified. And my dress was beyond ruined. Most assuredly an episode I call 'I should not have done that.' "

She sipped her wine, then said, "Once I'd assured everyone I was unharmed, they all burst out laughing over my horribly disheveled appearance."

"You should have seen her, Mr. Stanton," Spencer said, his eyes filled with humor. "Leaves in her hair, dirt on her nose, gown muddy and chopped off."

"Yet I'm certain you still managed to look enchanting," said Mr. Stanton.

An unladylike snort escaped her even while warmth at his compliment flowed through her. "I'm afraid I looked the exact opposite of 'enchanting.' However, some good did come out of the debacle as the 'I should not have done that' tradition was born that day. Since then, Spencer and I often relate such tales to each other in an attempt to spare each other embarrassment." She shot Spencer a mock fierce frown and shook her finger at him. "Learn from my folly, son."

Spencer adopted an equally serious expression. "Rest assured, should I ever slide down a rope from a tree, I will make certain not to land in a slippery mud hole."

She gave Mr. Stanton a conspiratorial smile. "You see how marvelously it works?"

"I'm duly impressed," Mr. Stanton said, his returning smile filled with a warmth that suddenly made her feel a bit breathless. "Except for your gown, a happy ending all around. What ever became of Angelica?"

"Oh, she's still here, prowling the grounds and the stables, along with several of her siblings and some children of her own."

"An impressive tale of courage, Lady Catherine," Mr. Stanton said, "but I'm amazed that you even thought to climb the tree in the first place."

"Oh, Mum used to climb trees all the time when she was my age," Spencer said, a note of pride in his voice.

Mr. Stanton's gaze never left hers. "Indeed? Your brother never told me that, Lady Catherine."

"Most likely because my brother doesn't know about my youthful predilection for scrambling up trees." A chuckle she couldn't contain escaped her. "Although he should, seeing as he was the victim of it—but he never solved that particular mystery."

Unmistakable interest flared in his eyes. "What's this? Something Philip doesn't know? You must tell me."

She adopted her most prim expression. "My lips are sealed."

"That's wretched, Mum," Spencer declared. "You mentioned it, so now you *must* tell."

Mr. Stanton's brows rose, and he looked at Spencer. "You don't know what she's talking about?"

"I've no idea. But unless she wants us to expire from curiosity, she'll tell us."

She tapped her pursed lips with her fingertips. "I suppose I can't have *that* weighing upon my conscience. But you must promise never to tell."

"Promise," both Spencer and Mr. Stanton said dutifully.

"Very well. When I was about Spencer's age, I would

climb the tree outside Philip's bedchamber at night and toss pebbles at his window."

"Why did you do that?" Spencer asked, his eyes wide.

"He was my older brother, darling. It was my *responsibility* to annoy him. He was convinced the noise was some horrid bird pecking at his window. He'd open the French windows and charge onto his balcony, flapping his arms and saying the *naughtiest* words, promising all manner of retribution when he caught the guilty bird."

"That's horrible, Mum," Spencer said, but ruined the scolding by laughing.

"He never discovered it was you and not a bird?" Mr. Stanton asked, his amusement evident.

"Never. In fact, I've never told anyone, until now."

"I am honored to be taken into your confidence." He chuckled. "Although I would dearly love to tell Philip that I know something he does not." At her frown, he raised his hands in mock surrender. "But I'll keep my promise not to tell. I'm a man of my word."

"When did you finally stop tossing the pebbles, Mum? Did Grandfather discover you?"

"Heavens, no. Your grandfather would be properly shocked if he knew I'd even *thought* about climbing a tree. I'd tied a small basket to one of the tree's branches, and in it I kept my supply of pebbles. One night I reached my hand into the basket and was horrified to discover that it had become infested with *worms*." A shudder ran through her at the memory. "I do *not* like worms. That episode quite cured me of my tree-climbing tendencies."

"And rather served you right," Mr. Stanton said, his grin teasing.

"Yes," Catherine agreed with a laugh. "I fear I well deserved the sobriquet of 'Imp' that Philip bestowed upon me. Surely he's told you what a devil I was."

"Oh, he did." The amusement slowly drained from Mr. Stanton's expression. "But he also said that he was an awkward, clumsy, serious, pudgy youth who you coaxed from shyness by teaching him how to laugh and smile. How to take time for fun. That your exuberance, loyalty, and love saved him from what would otherwise have been a very lonely childhood."

A swift jolt of emotion caught Catherine by surprise, swelling her throat, while images of her and Philip as children blinked through her mind. She swallowed hard to find her voice. "His peers often treated him unkindly, which never failed to infuriate me. I only wanted to make him as happy as they'd made him sad. Philip was, and still is, the very finest of brothers. And of men."

"I agree," Mr. Stanton said. "Actually, Lady Catherine, I would not be surprised if Philip suspected it was you outside his window and climbed that tree, whereupon he'd have discovered your little basket of pebbles. I assume he was aware of your aversion to worms?"

Catherine blinked, nonplussed, then shook her head and chuckled at her own folly. "Yes, he was. I'll make a point of asking him about the incident when I see him next. That devil. As neither of you gentlemen has any siblings, I would not expect you fully to appreciate the need for brothers and sisters to irritate each other. Although it was all done in fun."

"Mum still does impish things, you know," Spencer announced.

Mr. Stanton looked immediately interested. "Oh? Like what?"

"She slides down the banister."

Amusement-filled dark eyes assessed her. "Why, Lady Catherine, is this shocking statement true?"

"Sometimes I'm simply in a bit of a hurry to get downstairs," she said as primly as she could.

"And sometimes she wakes me after Cook's gone to bed so we can steal to the kitchens and find ourselves a grand snack."

"Spencer is a growing boy who requires a great deal of nutrition," she said even more primly, although the effect was ruined when she felt her lips twitching.

"She sings songs with naughty lyrics while she works in the garden."

"Spencer!" Catherine's face heated. Good heavens, she hadn't realized he had heard. "I'm certain you, ah, misunderstood."

"Not a bit. You tend to sing rather loudly. And off-key." Spencer grinned at Mr. Stanton. "Mum couldn't carry a tune in basket."

"Will you regale us with a selection, Lady Catherine?" Mr. Stanton teased.

A bubble of horrified laughter escaped her, and she coughed to cover the sound. "Perhaps some other time. And now that everyone knows far more about me than they should, it is your turn, Mr. Stanton, to share an 'I should not have done that' tale."

He leaned back in his chair and tapped his fingers against his chin. After several seconds of consideration, he said, "The day I arrived in Egypt, after being on board a ship for weeks, I wanted two things: a hot, decent meal, and a hot, decent bath. After I'd eaten, I found a bathhouse on the outskirts of Cairo. Feeling well fed and clean, I departed, only to discover that I'd inadvertently ventured into an area known for cutthroats and thieves. Fortunately, I managed to get out alive. Unfortunately, I was robbed before I managed to escape."

"Why did you not defeat the brigand with your fists?" Spencer asked, his eyes wide.

"Brigand*s*. There were four of them. And as they all had knives *and* pistols, I'm afraid I would not have fared very well."

"What did they steal from you?"

"My money. And my . . . clothes."

Spencer's jaw dropped. "Never say so! *All* your clothes?"

"All my clothes. Right down to my boots, which quite irked me as they were my favorites."

"So you were . . . ?" Spencer's voice trailed off in disbelief.

"Naked as the day I was born," Mr. Stanton confirmed.

"What did you do?"

"I briefly debated fighting them to get my clothes back, but decided my life was not worth the risk. Fortunately, they seemed disinclined to do away with me. Indeed, I think they were highly amused at leaving me to find my way home in broad daylight, naked as a babe."

Heat whooshed through Catherine, and her throat went dry at the thought of Mr. Stanton, freshly bathed, standing in a column of golden sunlight. Naked.

She instantly recalled the chapter in the *Guide* dedicated to instructing Today's Modern Woman on some of the many things she could do to, and with, a naked man. Her recollection did nothing toward cooling the inferno that seemed to have engulfed her.

"Did anyone see you?" Spencer asked, his eyes agog. Catherine prayed she did not wear a similarly rapt expression and barely resisted the urge to fan herself with her linen napkin.

"Oh, yes, but I just kept running as fast as I could. I finally filched a sheet from someone's laundry, which afforded me a small measure of my lost dignity. Not one of my more stellar episodes, and while I can laugh about it now, it was not at all humorous at the time. Yes, wandering about Cairo on my own was just one of many 'I should not have done that' moments." He grinned. "Would you like another?"

"Yes!" said Spencer.

"No!" said Catherine at the same time. Mr. Stanton naked, wandering about in a sheet, robbed by armed ruffians, *naked* . . . Lord only knew what else he'd done, and she was quite certain she did not want to know. Yes, quite certain.

A nervous laugh escaped her, and she rose, signaling the end to their meal. "Perhaps another time. For now, I suggest we retire to the drawing room. Do you play cards, Mr. Stanton? Chess? Backgammon?"

"I enjoy all three, Lady Catherine. What would be your pleasure?"

To see you naked. Catherine barely suppressed the horrified squeak that rose in her throat. Good God, where had *that* ridiculous thought come from? Of course she did not want to see him naked. The absurd, inappropriate notion was clearly just a consequence of his absurd, inappropriate story. *Yes, that's all it was.*

Straightening her shoulders, she said, "Why don't you and Spencer play while I enjoy my needlework by the fire?"

"Very well." He turned to Spencer. "Backgammon?"

"My favorite," Spencer said.

She led the way toward the drawing room and mentally congratulated herself on her excellent plan. She'd now have her needlework to concentrate on rather than her unsettlingly attractive guest.

An hour later, however, she realized that her plan was not so excellent after all. It was nearly impossible to focus her attention on the intricate flower pattern of her hated embroidery when her gaze continually strayed in the most annoying manner across the room to the French windows, where Mr. Stanton and Spencer sat, the backgammon board resting on a cherrywood table between them. Damnation, when had she lost control over her own eyeballs? Even when she managed to stare at her work, she accomplished little, for her entire being was focused upon trying to hear snippets of their conversation—a conversation Spencer was clearly enjoying.

The deep rumble of Mr. Stanton's laugh mingled with Spencer's chuckle, and for the hundredth time, Catherine's hands stilled, and she peeked at the pair from beneath her lashes. Spencer's mouth was stretched in a boyish, ear-to-ear grin. Pure delight emanated from him, and the fact that no shadows lurked in his eyes squeezed her heart with maternal love.

Spencer laughed again, and she gave up all pretense of needlework. Setting her project aside, she leaned back against the soft brocade of her wing chair, and just indulged in watching her son enjoy himself. She loved to see him smile and laugh, and he did so far too seldom in her opinion. During the last year he'd taken to solitary walks, wandering the estate's gardens and trails that led to the warm springs. While he basked in the freedom afforded by the vast grounds, she worried that he spent too much time alone in sad reflection. She gave him the privacy he needed, but made certain that they still spent time together every day—talking, reading, sharing stories, eating their favorite foods, enjoying the gardens and each other's company.

Now, sitting across from Mr. Stanton, Spencer looked happy, carefree, and relaxed in a way she rarely witnessed when he was in the company of anyone besides his familiar, immediate circle. Normally he was wary and withdrawn with strangers, fearing they would jeer at him or pity his condition. But clearly he harbored no such fear with Mr. Stanton.

Catherine's gaze shifted to the man who'd invaded her thoughts far too often since last evening. His chin was propped upon his palm as he studied the backgammon board, while Spencer hooted with mock-diabolical laughter, predicting his defeat. It suddenly struck her how cozy and domestic this scene—indeed this entire evening—was, and acute yearning washed over her.

How many times during her marriage had she hopelessly wished to experience a pleasurable home-and-hearth scenario such as this? How many hours had she foolishly wasted inventing scenes in her mind, of her, Bertrand, and Spencer enjoying a meal, then father and son laughing over a game board, while she looked fondly on? More than she could count.

The fact that that vivid, longed-for image she'd held so dear to her heart had come to life before her eyes, prominently featuring Mr. Stanton, filled her with an aching sensation she could not name. He had not figured in the tableau she'd imagined. Yet even though his presence should have been all wrong, it somehow felt most disturbingly right.

She gave herself a mental shake. Good Lord, she was long past hoping for and wanting such a domestic scene. She and Spencer did not need anyone else in their lives. Still, looking at Spencer's joyful expression, the animation with which he spoke to Mr. Stanton, filled her with a rush of gratitude toward her guest for the kindness he was extending toward her son. While Mr. Stanton possessed many qualities *she* found irksome, clearly Spencer enjoyed his company.

At that instant, Mr. Stanton turned, and their eyes met.

Heat sizzled through her, skittering jitters to her stomach, and her toes involuntarily curled inside her satin slippers. How did he manage to throw her so off-balance with a mere look? How was it that his presence in her home simultaneously comforted yet agitated her? And why, oh why, was she so intensely *aware* of him?

His lips curved upward in a slow smile, then he returned his attention to the backgammon board. She snapped her lips together, horrified to discover that they'd been slightly parted as she'd gawked at him. With grim determination she snatched up her embroidery and jabbed the needle into the material.

"He is annoying and presumptuous and really, not even all *that* attractive," she muttered under her breath. "Why, I've known dozens of men far more handsome."

Perhaps. But none of them weakened your limbs the way this man does, her inner voice taunted.

She pressed her lips more firmly together. Fustian. If her limbs were weak, it was merely due to fatigue. She'd suffered an exhausting ordeal. 'Twas merely weariness playing with her body and emotions. After a good night's sleep, everything would fall back into its proper place.

Stiffening her spine, she jabbed the needle through the linen once again. Very well, she found the man attractive. But only slightly, and in a strictly *physical* way. She certainly had no intention of acting upon these unsettling feelings. Therefore, her best recourse was to avoid him as much as possible—a challenge, as the entire purpose for him being there was to protect her should the need arise—but nothing said they had to be in the same *room*. And even if she found herself in the same room with him, nothing said she had to *converse* with him. Or *stand* near him. She could simply ignore him.

Relief swept through her. Avoid and ignore would be her strategy—surely easy enough tasks to accomplish.

Her inner voice chimed out something that sounded suspiciously like *in a pig's eye*, but she managed, with a great deal of effort, to ignore it.

Chapter 9

If Today's Modern Woman wishes for her gentleman to express more passion, she should boldly explain to him that while a kiss upon the hand can *be employed to demonstrate fervent regard, it is not the most effective method as it can also symbolize nothing more than a sign of brotherly or sisterly fondness. It is nearly impossible, however, to misinterpret the meaning behind a kiss on the lips. Or the nape. Or the spine . . .*

A Ladies' Guide to the Pursuit of
Personal Happiness and Intimate Fulfillment
by Charles Brightmore

After a fitful night, which she firmly attributed to her worries about the shooting, Catherine put her avoid-and-ignore strategy into immediate effect by taking an early, solitary breakfast in her bedchamber. She knew Spencer would not be about so early, and she had no intention of risking a cozy breakfast with only Mr. Stanton for company. After her meal, Catherine spent the remainder of the morning sitting at her desk, catching up on her correspondence. When she finished, she dressed carefully, relieved that the ache in her arm had faded so as to be barely noticeable. She spent extra time on her appearance, and told herself it was because she wished to appear presentable when she visited Genevieve this afternoon.

Deciding it was well past the time to check on Spencer, who surely would have arisen by now, and perform polite hostess duties toward Mr. Stanton, she headed downstairs, looking forward to a cup of tea.

When she entered the foyer, she was immediately greeted by Milton, who held out a silver salver bearing a sealed note.

"This just arrived from London, my lady."

Catherine's heart quickened as she recognized her father's distinctive bold, cursive scrawl. Deciding the tea could wait, she took the note, nodded her thanks, then headed directly back to her bedchamber. The instant she closed the door behind her, she broke the seal and scanned the contents.

Dear Catherine,

I am happy to report that the scoundrel who fired the shot last night has been apprehended. The man, a ruffian by the name of Billy Robbins, is well-known to the magistrate for perpetrating robberies in Mayfair and elsewhere. Thanks to the information provided by Mr. Carmichael, Robbins was identified and captured near the docks. As we suspected, you were the victim of a robbery gone awry. Robbins, of course, insists he is innocent, but as we all know, Newgate is filled with "innocent" men.

While this news cannot erase the harrowing ordeal you suffered, you at least now have the satisfaction of knowing that the culprit responsible can no longer hurt anyone. Please extend my regards to Spencer and Mr. Stanton, and I look forward to seeing you all again soon.

With love,
Your father

Catherine closed her eyes and blew out a sigh of heartfelt relief. It had been an accident. Thank God. She was not in danger. Nor was Spencer. Nor Genevieve. Charles Brightmore's identity was safe. Yes, there was still that investigator Lord Markingworth and his friends had hired, but since the publisher of *A Ladies' Guide* would never reveal her and Genevieve's secret, the man would eventually have to admit defeat. The chances of his investigation leading him to Little Longstone were so minute as to be nonexistent.

She opened her eyes, smiled, and drew in what felt like her first easy breath since she'd secreted herself behind her father's Oriental screen. Now her life could resume its tranquil course, without threat of danger. Without need of protection—

Without need of Mr. Stanton.

Her smile froze. She no longer required the protection and security his presence afforded. He could leave Little Longstone. Right away—although she supposed it would be insupportably rude to suggest he depart sooner than tomorrow morning. And since she rarely traveled to London, she need not worry about seeing him again in the near future.

Mr. Stanton's imminent departure was good. *Very* good. No more necessity for avoid-and-ignore tactics. The man was a blight on her peaceful existence, and the sooner he departed for London, the better. She was happy. Ecstatically so.

Her inner voice coughed to life to inform her she'd somehow managed to confuse "ecstatically happy" with "utterly miserable."

Botheration, she needed to find a way to somehow muzzle that damnable voice.

"May I have a moment of your time, Mr. Stanton?"

Andrew paused at the top of the staircase. He gripped the mahogany banister and suppressed a sigh at the way his heart skipped a beat at the mere sound of her voice.

He'd spent the entire morning—not to mention a number of the predawn hours when sleep had eluded him—replaying the wonder of last evening in his mind. Sharing a meal and silly stories with her and Spencer, laughing together, enjoying after-dinner games—it was a cozy, domestic scenario he'd played out in his dreams more times than he could count. And the reality had exceeded all his imaginary expectations. By God, he couldn't wait to repeat the experience tonight.

And every night, for the rest of their lives.

Had she noticed how well the three of them fit together? How very *right* last night had been? Well, if it had somehow escaped her notice, he certainly intended to remedy that tonight.

Turning, he watched her approach. An artful array of chestnut curls framed her face in a becoming style that made her golden brown eyes appear luminous. Her pale peach muslin gown highlighted her creamy skin. The gown and its neckline were properly modest, yet rather than inspiring propriety, Andrew's imagination ran wild with what delights her demure clothing covered.

As she neared him, the subtle scent of flowers invaded his senses, and he tightened his grip on the banister to keep from reaching out to touch her.

"You may have as many moments as you wish, Lady Catherine."

"Thank you. In the library?"

"Wherever you wish." *Whenever you wish. However you wish. Whatever you wish.* He clenched his jaw to contain the words that threatened to break free of his heart. This was hardly the time or place to blurt out that he was madly in love with her, desired her to the point of pain, and wanted nothing more than to grant her every wish.

He followed her down the stairs and through the corridor, admiring the subtle hints of feminine curves revealed when she walked. His gaze wandered upward and fastened on her vulnerable, smooth nape, left bare by her upswept coiffure—bare except for a single curl that bisected her pale skin with a shiny chestnut spiral.

His fingers flexed, and he locked his elbows to keep from reaching out to glide his fingertip over that beguiling solitary curl. So intent was he on looking at the tendril, he didn't notice that she'd paused in front of a closed door. Didn't notice until he walked right into her.

She gasped and reached out, pressing her palms against the oak panel to maintain her balance and keep from plunging headlong into the door. His hands came forward and slipped around her waist.

For several stunning seconds neither moved. Andrew's mind shouted at him to release her, to step back, but his hands and feet refused to obey the command. Instead, his eyes slid closed, and he absorbed the intense pleasure of her body pressing against his from chest to thigh. Her scent, that alluring essence of flowers, surrounded him like a seductive cloud. He had only to turn his head slightly to press his lips to her fragrant skin that was so close . . . so tantalizingly close.

Before he could think, before any reason why he shouldn't invaded his mind, he gave in to the overwhelming longing. His lips touched the ivory skin just behind her ear, gentle as a breathless whisper, so softly he wondered if she even realized what he'd done—and that it was done deliberately.

But he knew, and the effect upon him, the assault on his senses, was anything but soft. Desire—fierce, hot, and so long denied—slammed into him, and he squeezed his eyes shut tighter in a vain attempt to curb the needs clawing at him.

Her utter stillness, the rigid set of her spine, roused his common sense. Summoning all his strength, he forced himself to slip his hands from her waist and step back. "I beg your pardon," he said in an unsteady voice that sounded as if he'd swallowed gravel. "I was not watching where I was going."

She said nothing for several seconds, then cleared her throat and lowered her hands from the door. "Apology accepted."

He stilled at the slight quaver in her voice. Was the unsteadiness of her words the result of embarrassment or anger? Or was it possible that she'd been as affected by those few seconds as he? He silently willed her to turn around, so he could look at her face, read her eyes, to see if any hint of desire existed, but she did not oblige him. Instead, she opened the door and quickly headed toward the marble fireplace lining the far wall.

Andrew crossed the threshold, then closed the door behind him. The click reverberated in the heavy silence, a silence he was sorely tempted to break by pointing out that his begging her pardon had not been an *apology*. He certainly wasn't sorry he'd had the unexpected opportunity to touch her—although perhaps he should be. The exquisite feel of her was now embedded in his mind, and his body, his lips, still tingled from the impact.

He grimaced and shifted. Although it irked him that she continued to stare into the low-burning flames and ignore him, it was for the best. If she turned around right now, she would surely notice just how much their brief encounter had affected him.

"Would you mind if I have a drink?" he asked, hoping one of the group of crystal decanters set on the round, mahogany table next to the settee contained brandy.

She did not turn. "Please, help yourself."

"Would you care to join me?"

She surprised him by saying, "Yes. A sherry, please."

Andrew crossed to the decanters. He took his time pouring the two drinks, pulling in slow, deep breaths until he'd gained control of his emotions and body. He then walked to the fireplace, stopping a safe distance away from her.

"Your sherry, Lady Catherine."

She finally turned to face him. Hectic color stained her cheeks, but whether the beguiling hue was due to embarrassment, the warmth of the fire, or desire, he couldn't tell. She regarded him with a perfectly calm, cool expression that snaked irritation down his spine. Well, obviously it hadn't been *desire.* Trying his best to match her unconcerned look, he handed her the crystal cordial glass.

"Thank you." She took the glass, and he noted that she was very careful to not allow their fingers to touch. She shifted her gaze from him and sipped her drink. He followed suit, resisting the urge to toss back his potent brandy in one gulp.

After taking a second sip, she slipped a piece of ivory

vellum from the pocket in her skirts and held it out for him. "This arrived a short time ago from my father. The man responsible for the shooting has been apprehended."

Andrew set down his drink, took the note, then quickly scanned the contents. Billy Robbins. His jaw tightened when he read the name of the man who'd injured Catherine. The man who could have so easily ended her life. *Be happy Newgate has you and not me, you bastard.*

When he finished reading, he handed her back the note. "I'm relieved the scoundrel was caught. Thank goodness Mr. Carmichael was so observant."

"Yes. We all owe him our thanks." She tucked the note back in her pocket. "As this man's capture means that there is no longer a threat of danger to me—"

"*No longer?*" Andrew's eyes narrowed. "I was not aware there *was* a threat of danger to you. What are you talking about?"

A flicker of what looked like fear flashed in her eyes, but disappeared so quickly he couldn't decide if it was real or imagined. She pressed her lips together for several seconds, then said, "I meant there is no longer a threat of danger to my *health*. I'm feeling very well, and Milton and my staff can fully see to my needs. Without any assistance."

Understanding dawned, along with a healthy dose of annoyance, and, damn it, hurt. She wanted him to leave Little Longstone.

"I can arrange to have my carriage at your disposal tomorrow morning," she continued. "While I appreciate your kindness and thank you for escorting me home, I wouldn't want you to sacrifice any more of your valuable time away from your work in London."

Before Andrew could think of a suitable reply—having wisely decided that *Hell no, I'm not leaving was* not *suitable*—a knock sounded on the door.

"Come in," Lady Catherine said.

The door opened, and Spencer shuffled into the room. His smile faded as his gaze bounced between his mother and Andrew. "Is something amiss, Mum?"

She appeared to square her shoulders, then offered Spencer a smile. "No, darling. Did you need to speak to me?"

Spencer looked clearly unconvinced. Instead of answering his mother's question, he asked, "What were you just talking about?"

Lady Catherine set down her drink, then crossed the pale green Axminster rug to bestow a kiss upon Spencer's cheek. "Transportation arrangements. Mr. Stanton will be leaving us tomorrow to return to London."

"Leaving? *Tomorrow?*" There was no mistaking the boy's dismay. He turned toward Andrew and gazed at him with eyes brimming with confusion and hurt. "But why? He only arrived yesterday."

Lady Catherine said, "Mr. Stanton has many responsibilities in London, Spencer, even more with your uncle Philip unavailable. While he was kind enough to leave his work at the museum to escort me home, he must return to his duties."

"But why must he leave so soon? We've only just started—" He clamped his lips together and shot Andrew an imploring look.

"Started what?" Lady Catherine asked.

"A surprise for you," Andrew cut in. "Something Spencer and I discussed yesterday afternoon. I promised to lend my assistance."

She raised her brows. "What sort of surprise?"

Pure chagrin washed over Spencer's face. Before the boy could reply, Andrew again spoke up. "If we told you, it wouldn't be any sort of surprise." He shot Spencer a conspiratorial wink. "I believe we need to fetch the dictionary for your mother, Spencer, so she can look up '*surprise.*' "

"I know you're not normally fond of surprises, Mum," Spencer said in a rush, "but you'll like this one. You'll be proud of me, I know, when we're finished."

"I'm already proud of you."

"Then you'll be more proud."

She studied her son's face for several seconds, then she turned toward Andrew. "You *promised* him this . . . whatever it is?"

"I did."

"You did not mention this to me earlier."

"It had not occurred to me to do so as that is the nature of a surprise. Also, I hadn't anticipated my visit here being quite so short in duration."

Silence filled the room, and Andrew could almost hear the wheels turning in her mind. Why was she suddenly so anxious to get rid of him? Was there some aspect of her life that she worried he'd discover? Her earlier words, *this man's capture means that there is no longer a threat of danger to me* bothered him greatly. The fact that he'd detected fear in her eyes more than once since the shooting made her explanation of "danger to my health" ring untrue. Had she lied? If so, why?

There were only two other reasons he could think of that would make her anxious for him leave. If she were interested in forming a relationship with a man—like perhaps one of her many bouquet-sending suitors—Andrew's presence in her home could put a damper on her plans. But that made little sense since she'd made it plain that she did not wish to form an attachment.

The other reason made his heart pound with hope. *If she vehemently did not want to form an attachment, yet found herself attracted to me . . .*

She'd want him to leave. As soon as possible. Could that be why she'd acted so prickly around him lately—because she was fighting desire?

He shook himself from his reverie and looked at her. She looked very disgruntled—rather the way Andrew imagined a general would if his brilliant military campaign was just outmaneuvered. Hmmm. This was *very* promising.

"How long will this surprise take to complete?" she asked him.

"At least a week," Andrew said, certain that a halo magically appeared above his head to accompany the angelic expression into which he arranged his features.

"A week!" There was no mistaking her dismay—or the suspicion ripe in her voice.

Spencer instantly brightened. "You can stay that long, Mr. Stanton?"

"Yes," Andrew said.

She shot him an undecipherable look, then turned toward Spencer, whose eyes were filled with a heartbreaking combination of excitement and hope. There was no mistaking she was torn. Finally, she reached out and ruffled the boy's dark hair.

"A week," she agreed.

Spencer's smile could have lit a darkened room.

"Well, now that that's been settled," said Lady Catherine, "I shall depart for my visit with Mrs. Ralston."

"Is your friend's home on the way to the village?" Andrew asked.

"As a matter of fact it is. Why?"

"Would you mind if I came along? There are some items I need to purchase and would like to visit the local shops."

"What do you wish to purchase?"

He made a *tsk*ing sound and waggled his finger at her. "Cannot tell. All part of the surprise."

"Perhaps we have on hand whatever these supplies are."

"I've already ascertained that you don't." He turned to Spencer. "Would you care to join me, Spencer?" he asked casually.

Andrew instantly sensed the tension that filled the silence. He knew Spencer rarely left the security of the grounds, and perhaps it was too soon to encourage this outing to the village, but they'd made such great strides this morning during their first horseback-riding lesson, Andrew hoped to keep their momentum going.

Several more seconds of silence passed, and Andrew could see Spencer was conflicted.

Lady Catherine cleared her throat. "That is very thoughtful Mr. Stanton, however, Spencer doesn't like to venture—"

"I want to go," Spencer cut in.

"You do?" There was no mistaking his mother's amazement.

Spencer nodded vigorously, and Andrew wondered if the lad was trying more to convince his mother or himself of his decision. "I want to help with the surprise." He lifted his chin. "I'll be fine, Mum. Mr. Stanton will keep me safe. I want to go. Truly."

She hesitated for several heartbeats, and Andrew could plainly see her surprised pleasure at Spencer's words. Indeed, he fancied she blinked back tears. Finally, she smiled at her son. "I'd be delighted to have the company. I'll have the carriage brought around. You can drop me at Mrs. Ralston's cottage, then continue on to the village. No need to return for me—I'd enjoy a brisk walk home."

"Can we use the curricle instead?" Spencer asked.

"That way Mr. Stanton can show me how to handle it." He turned to Mr. Stanton with a hopeful expression. "You do know how, don't you?"

Andrew nodded. "Yes, but a curricle only seats two people."

"We can all squeeze onto the seat," Spencer insisted. "I do not require much room at all. Besides, it's only a short ride to Mrs. Ralston's, and then there'd only be two of us since Mum wishes to walk home."

Andrew turned to Lady Catherine, who was clearly stunned by this turn of events. Keeping his voice and expression perfectly bland, he said, "I'm amenable to trying Spencer's plan, if you are, Lady Catherine. If we discover the seat is too crowded, I would be happy to walk beside the vehicle to Mrs. Ralston's house."

She looked at him with a combination of worry and hope. "Do you promise not to travel swiftly during this lesson?"

He laid his hand over his heart. "I swear I would never do anything to place Spencer, or you, in any danger."

Her gaze drifted back to Spencer and she smiled. "Very well. The curricle it is."

Forty-five minutes later, Spencer, under Mr. Stanton's patient tutelage, successfully brought the pair of matching bays to a halt in front of Genevieve's cottage. Catherine's heart contracted at the utter delight and triumph etched on her son's face.

"I did it," he said, his cheeks flushed with victory.

"Yes, you did," she agreed. "And marvelously well. I'm so proud of you—" Her throat swelled, cutting off her voice, and to mask her emotion, she pulled him to her for a hug. Spencer's arms wrapped around her, and with her cheek pressed to his, she looked over his shoulder and met Mr. Stanton's steady, dark-eyed gaze.

Her heart thumped against her ribs, and the myriad of confusing, conflicting emotions this man inspired assailed her once again. But one rose swiftly to the surface—gratitude. She was deeply grateful to him for giving this joy to Spencer. Blinking back the moisture that ridiculously threatened behind her eyes, she smiled at him. *Thank you,* she mouthed silently.

His lips curved upward in a warm smile that stalled her breath. *You're welcome*, he mouthed back.

"My goodness, is that Master Spencer at the reins of this fine equipage?"

At the sound of Genevieve's rich, sultry voice, Catherine yanked her gaze from Mr. Stanton and released her son.

"Good afternoon, Mrs. Ralston," Spencer said, grinning hugely. "Yes, 'tis I. I've just learned to drive it."

Genevieve approached the curricle from the flower-lined path leading to her cottage, her avid gaze taking in the three passengers squashed into the seat. Dressed in a cheery yellow muslin gown decorated with sprigs of embroidered lilacs, she looked like a breath of late-summer sunshine. "Why, I nearly did not recognize you, Master Spencer," she said, her smile directed at the lad. "You've grown into quite the strapping young man since I saw you last."

There was no missing Spencer's flush of pleasure at her words. "Thank you, Mrs. Ralston."

"And whom have you brought to see me today?" she asked with a teasing grin.

"Well, my mum, but you already know her."

"Yes, Lady Catherine and I are well acquainted."

"And this is our friend, Mr. Stanton. He traveled all

about Egypt with my uncle Philip. You should ask him about the time his clothes were stolen by knife-wielding brigands."

Heat rose in Catherine's cheeks as the thought of a naked Mr. Stanton slammed into her mind. Genevieve's smiling gaze swept over Mr. Stanton with unabashed interest. "I am curiosity itself."

Catherine cleared her throat. "Genevieve, allow me to *properly* introduce Mr. Andrew Stanton, my brother's business partner in his museum venture. Mr. Stanton, my dearest friend, Mrs. Ralston."

Mr. Stanton unwedged himself from the seat and jumped nimbly down. He offered Genevieve a formal bow and a friendly smile. "A pleasure, Mrs. Ralston."

"Likewise, Mr. Stanton. Welcome to Little Longstone. Are you enjoying your visit?"

"Very much. It's been a long time since I've had the opportunity to take pleasure in such fresh air and tranquil, colorful surroundings." He indicated the profusion of well-tended blooms surrounding them. "Your garden is exceptional."

Genevieve beamed. "Thank you. It is entirely Catherine's doing. She resurrected the entire area from the weed-infested, overgrown disaster it was when I purchased the cottage. She won't hear of me hiring a gardener."

"A stranger?" Catherine interjected, her voice filled with mock horror. "Tending my darlings? Never!"

"You see?" Genevieve said to Mr. Stanton with an arch grin. "A very headstrong woman."

"Indeed?" Mr. Stanton said, his face the picture of exaggerated shock. "I hadn't noticed."

A delighted laugh trilled from Genevieve. "Will you join us for tea?"

"Thank you, but Spencer and I are on our way to the village."

"Another day then?"

"I wouldn't want to intrude on your visit with Lady Catherine."

"Nonsense. I simply must hear about these knife-wielding ruffians."

He laughed. "In that case, I'd be honored to join you another day." After a brief nod of thanks, he walked to Catherine's side of the curricle and raised his hand. "May I assist you, Lady Catherine?"

Catherine stared at his hand and swallowed. She did not want to touch him. Her brutally honest inner voice immediately branded her a liar, and she clenched her jaw. Botheration. All right, she *wanted* to touch him. But she greatly feared doing so. Feared her reaction, especially if it was anything like what she'd experienced when he'd walked into her in the corridor . . .

Oh, stop being ridiculous, she chided herself. It was merely his hand. Helping her so she didn't ignominiously tumble to the ground from her perch. Besides, it wasn't as if she'd actually have to *touch* him, as they both wore gloves. Giving what she hoped passed for a cool, unconcerned smile, she placed her hand in his.

His fingers wrapped around hers in a sure, strong grip, and warmth permeated through her gloves to sizzle up her arm. An accompanying heat blossomed on her cheeks, and she prayed no one would notice. The instant her feet touched the ground she snatched her hand away as if he'd burned her.

"Thank you." Shielding her eyes against the sunlight dappling through the trees, she smiled up at Spencer. "Enjoy your outing."

"I will, Mum."

Mr. Stanton turned, as if to climb back onto the curricle, but instead he leaned toward her. "Don't worry," in said in a low voice only she could hear. "I'll take good care of him."

He swung himself into the seat, then with a smile and a nod at her and Genevieve, he instructed Spencer to go. Seconds later the curricle was heading off toward the village.

Catherine watched the vehicle until it rounded the corner at the end of the lane and disappeared from view. She then turned toward Genevieve, and said, "I have news." Pulling her father's letter from her reticule, she passed the missive to Genevieve.

After reading the letter, Genevieve handed it back and offered a relieved smile. "So there is no need to worry."

"None. Well, except for the investigator Lord Markingworth and his friends hired, but I cannot see how he could discover our identity."

"Excellent." She looked down the lane where the curricle had traveled. "So that was Mr. Stanton," her friend said, her voice ripe with . . . something. "He is much different than I'd envisioned based on your description."

"Indeed? And what had you envisioned?"

Genevieve laughed. "Certainly not that alarmingly attractive man with the devastating smile and soulful eyes. Darling, your description of him in no way did him justice. *I* could sum up that glorious man in two words: *absolutely divine*."

Something that felt suspiciously like jealousy fluttered through Catherine. "I never said he was *ugly*."

"No, but neither did you give any hint that he was so"—she blew out a dreamy-sounding sigh—"so *absolutely divine*. Masculine and strong. Did you *see* those lovely dimples when he smiled?"

God, yes. She'd had a great deal of trouble prying her avid gaze away from them. "I hadn't particularly noticed, but now that you mention it, yes, I suppose he does have dimples."

"He seems to have formed a bond with Spencer."

"Yes. They are working together on some sort of surprise for me."

"Indeed? What sort of surprise?"

"If I knew, it wouldn't be a surprise," Catherine said with a smile, mimicking Mr. Stanton's earlier words to her. "When Mr. Stanton asked Spencer to accompany him to the village, I thought for certain it would turn into an awkward moment. I was stunned when Spencer accepted. I'd ceased asking him to join me several years ago, as I knew he would only refuse to leave the estate grounds." A sheepish smile pulled at her lips. "If I weren't so pleased with Spencer's change of heart, I'd be irked that Mr. Stanton achieved in a mere twenty-four hours something I've been unable to accomplish."

"Obviously the reason behind your son's unusual decision rests with Mr. Stanton. Your guest's presence is clearly having a positive effect on Spencer."

"Yes." Unfortunately he wasn't having an effect only on Spencer.

Genevieve's gaze searched hers, and all traces of amusement vanished. "He cares for you."

It felt as if the bottom of her stomach landed on her toes. Adopting a light tone, she said, "Of course he does. He's my son."

Genevieve regarded her with a sharp-eyed gaze that made Catherine want to squirm. "I was not talking about your son."

Catherine arranged her features into what she prayed passed for surprise. "Oh. Well, any 'caring' Mr. Stanton might feel toward me is merely a politeness toward his best friend's sister."

"You are wrong, Catherine. I cannot fathom how you don't see it. Are you not aware of the way he looks at you? Believe me when I tell you, there is nothing merely polite about it."

Heat singed Catherine's cheeks. "I fear you are in need of spectacles, my dear."

"I most certainly am not. Has he not told you how he feels about you?"

"As a matter of fact, he has. He thinks I am opinionated and annoying." *And beautiful.*

Genevieve laughed. "Oh, yes, he is well and truly caught. Darling, he may think you're opinionated—which you are, and annoying—which everyone is on occasion, but he still desires you."

"Pshaw," she scoffed, attempting her best to ignore the sudden thumping of her heart. Heavens, could Genevieve be right? And if so, why did the notion of Mr. Stanton desiring her speed up her heart rate rather than appall her?

"You may 'pshaw' all you wish, but, as you know, I am most experienced in these matters, Catherine. The man is deeply attracted to you. And the fact that you refuse to see what is staring you in the face suggests to me that you care for him as well."

"I most certainly do not! As I've already told you, the man is utterly irritating."

"But very attractive."

"Stubborn and opinionated."

"Something you have in common," Genevieve said, with a teasing grin.

"Argumentative."

"But kind to your son."

That stopped Catherine cold. "Yes," she agreed softly, feeling decidedly off-balance.

"And I do not believe I have ever seen a more lovely mouth on a man."

A statement that threw her even further off-balance. An image of Mr. Stanton's lovely mouth flashed in her mind. His lovely mouth that had brushed so softly against her skin . . . hadn't it? It had happened too quickly, occurred so softly. The feel of him pressed behind her had stalled her heart. Rendered her breathless. Shot spears of hot yearning through her that weakened her knees.

And it had all happened in the space of two heartbeats.

Good Lord, what would have happened if they'd had three heartbeats? Or half a dozen?

"Catherine? Are you all right? You look flushed."

No doubt because she felt as if someone had lit fire to her skirts. Blinking away her errant thoughts, she said, "I'm fine. It's merely warm standing here in the sun."

"Then let us go inside and enjoy some tea. Baxter has just baked a fresh batch of scones."

Hot tea was not at all what she was craving, but seeing that it was much safer than what she feared she *was* craving, she decided tea was a wise choice.

But while she had a reprieve from Mr. Stanton right now, she faced another cozy evening at home tonight. Sharing a meal and stories and games. Avoid and ignore. Yes, she needed to recall her watchwords. She simply had to avoid and ignore these insane yearnings Mr. Stanton's presence caused.

But how?

"Tell me," Genevieve said, as they entered the cottage, "do you and Mr. Stanton plan to attend the Duke of Kelby's soiree this evening? According to the village gossip, a group of guests arrived this morning from London, so it promises to be an interesting diversion."

Catherine recalled the invitation among the morning's correspondence. She had not considered attending, as she did not wish to offer the duke even the slightest encouragement. "I don't think . . ." Her voice trailed off as she realized that the soiree provided the perfect opportunity to avoid another cozy evening at home.

She smiled. "I don't think I'd miss it for the world."

A gloved hand fisted in the heavy, forest green velvet drapery and pushed the material aside. The village of Little Longstone beyond the window bustled with activity, but the only sound in the room was the ticking of the mantel clock and a slowly exhaled breath of frustration.

Look at those fools, walking about, talking, laughing, shopping, as if they hadn't a care in the world. As if lives hadn't been ruined.

But no more would be ruined. *I'll see to it.*

The curtain fell back into place.

You managed to survive last time. You won't survive next time.

Chapter 10

Today's Modern Woman may well find herself the object of affection of more than one gentleman. This is an enviable position as it is always good to have a choice. If, however, she eventually decides that one must be chosen over the others, the best way to discourage the excess gentlemen is to make it plain her affections are claimed elsewhere.

A Ladies' Guide to the Pursuit of
Personal Happiness and Intimate Fulfillment
by Charles Brightmore

That evening, Andrew sat across from Lady Catherine in her carriage en route to the Duke of Kelby's soiree. While he would have preferred another cozy, laughter-filled evening like last night rather than a gathering where God only knew how many men would be vying for Lady Catherine's attention, he intended to make the most of whatever courting opportunities the night might bring. And if one of those opportunities was the chance to discourage the competition, so much the better. With his impending departure from Little Longstone hanging over his head like a dark cloud of doom, he refused to squander any time.

Just then Lady Catherine smiled at him and *bloop* went his heart. Dressed in a pale turquoise muslin gown, with matching ribbons woven through her shiny chestnut curls, she stole his breath. By God, he could not wait for the day when he could freely draw her into his arms and kiss her rather than gawk at her from a distance.

Returning her smile, he said, "The color of your gown reminds me of the beautiful, sparkling clear waters of the Mediterranean. You look"—his gaze drifted over her, resting for several seconds on her lips before meeting her eyes once more—"stunning."

Catherine felt the heat of color bloom on her cheeks. "Thank you." Her gaze flicked over his dark blue jacket, neatly tied cravat, and cream breeches, and she had to press her lips together to contain a sigh of feminine appreciation. Was it possible for a *man* to look stunning? One look at her companion told her that clearly it was. "One could say the same about you."

"One *could*?" he teased. "Or one does?"

His smile nearly stole her breath. "Are you attempting to extract a compliment from me, Mr. Stanton?"

"Heaven forbid. I am merely trying to ascertain whether you inadvertently gave me one."

She pursed her lips and pretended to give the matter grave thought. "My goodness. It appears I did."

"Then I thank you, my lady. Indeed, I don't believe I've ever been called 'stunning' before. Tell me, did Spencer tell you about our adventures in the village?"

"Yes, although apparently not *everything*, as he didn't wish to ruin your surprise. It sounds as if you two had a jolly time."

"We did."

"He said that quite a few people looked at him rather oddly, but that 'Mr. Stanton fixed everything.' He said you introduced yourself and Spencer to everyone you met, and to all the shopkeepers whose stores you visited."

Mr. Stanton nodded. "When people realized he was your son, they were very kind. Everyone we spoke to sent you their best regards. Some people did stare, but I assured Spencer they were most likely only curious, not unkind."

"He told me that you said if anyone was unkind to him, you'd pound the, um, piss out of them."

"My exact words," Mr. Stanton agreed without hesitation.

She couldn't contain the grin pulling at her lips. "Well, while the method might perhaps be a bit uncivilized, I'm grateful for the thought. I trust the good people of Little Longstone did not see fit to make you put your pugilistic talents to use?"

"They were all the personification of kindness. In fact, we even saw someone I know. One of the museum investors."

"Oh? Who was that?"

"Mrs. Warrenfield. She suffers from numerous maladies and is visiting Little Longstone to take the waters. She mentioned the duke's party this evening—I assume she'll be attending." He hesitated, then said, "You were surprised that Spencer wished to venture into the village."

"In truth, I was stunned. Spencer loves to wander about the estate, walking to the springs and strolling in the gardens. The property is private, and I'm grateful he has such a place, where he can strike out on his own a bit as it builds his strength and allows me to not worry—which, I'm afraid, I tend to do. But he's always been adamant about not wanting to venture off the grounds; some years ago I simply stopped asking if he wanted to join me."

"I realize you were worried about him, worried for him, and I appreciate that you trusted me enough to allow him to accompany me. Spencer appreciated it as well."

"I didn't doubt he was in good hands. While I freely admit I was concerned that someone might hurt Spencer's feelings, I was confident that you wouldn't hesitate to—"

"Pound the piss out of them? It would have been my very great pleasure."

She lowered her gaze, and she plucked at the satin strings on her reticule. "After Spencer told me about your afternoon in the village, I told him about the shooting." Looking up, she met his gaze squarely. "I give you leave to say 'I told you so.' "

"He was upset."

"That is putting it mildly. He insisted I tell him every detail, questioning me in a manner I suspect a Bow Street Runner might use to interrogate a crime suspect. It required a great deal of reassuring on my part to convince him I was fine."

"Are you?"

"Yes, I'm perfectly fit."

"Did that argument convince Spencer?"

"Not exactly. He demanded to see my injury. After he saw for himself that it was barely more than a scratch, our conversation took a turn for the better."

"He was hurt that you hadn't confided in him."

"Hurt, angry, worried. His expression was one I hope to never see again."

"Spencer worries about you just as you worry about him. We cannot always protect the people we love from worry, as much as we might want to. Sometimes we just have to let them worry."

"Spencer said something very similar—right after he reminded me that he is no longer a child. He then made me promise never to hide something important from him." One corner of her mouth lifted. "I, of course, extracted a similar promise from him."

"So everything was well in the end."

She nodded. "I believe in the back of my mind I had every intention of telling him, but I took umbrage at your telling me I should. I haven't had a man underfoot telling me what to do in many years."

"I'm certain you meant underfoot in the nicest way," he said with a flash of his dimples. "And I wasn't trying to tell you what to do. I was merely suggesting."

"I realize that—now. However, at the time I reacted badly, and I'm sorry." She shot him a sheepish grin. "I'm afraid that Today's Modern Woman does not like being ordered about."

He drew back in exaggerated surprise. "Indeed? I hadn't noticed that at all."

She laughed. "As for Spencer, he became very manly about wanting to take care of me."

"Yes, well, I'm afraid that that is what men like to do with women they love—take care of them."

His softly spoken words set up a fluttering in her stomach. "Yet Today's Modern Woman can take care of herself."

"Still, it is nice to have someone to share both the good and bad things life offers."

She considered his words for several seconds, then nodded. "Yes, I suppose that is true."

He leaned forward and rested his forearms on his knees and regarded her solemnly. Her breath caught with awareness at his sudden proximity, filling her head with his clean, masculine scent. Her heart thumped hard at the serious expression in his dark eyes.

Silence swelled for several seconds, then he said, "Do

you realize that we've been in this coach for nearly a *quarter hour*, and we've yet to argue? In fact, unless I am mistaken, we actually just *agreed* on something."

She blinked. "By God, you're right."

"Again we agree!"

"And this in spite of the fact that the words 'Today's Modern Woman' were spoken."

"Three times," he said.

"Twice."

"Ah. I knew it was too good to last."

She couldn't help but smile at him, and she absorbed the warmth that suffused her when he smiled in return. The carriage jerked to a stop, and she forced her gaze away from him to look out the window. They'd arrived at Kelby Manor.

A house filled with people where she would not have to spend a cozy evening alone with Mr. Stanton. Which was precisely what she needed.

For, as their enjoyable carriage ride had just illustrated, Mr. Stanton was proving increasingly difficult to avoid and ignore.

Swirling a brandy in one of the duke's fine crystal snifters, Andrew stood in a group of gentlemen who were discussing some nature of farming techniques. Or perhaps they were discussing sheep. Or was it finances? As his attention was firmly fixed across the room, he wasn't quite certain.

Lady Catherine stood near the fireplace chatting with her friend Mrs. Ralston, and while he could have happily stared at Lady Catherine's lovely profile all evening, he was currently more intent upon the men casting their gazes in her direction.

Based on the number of gentlemen attending whom

Andrew had met at Lord Ravensly's birthday party in London, the duke had obviously made good on his promise to invite his friends to take the waters. Standing near the punch bowl, Lords Avenbury and Ferrymouth were staring at Lady Catherine as if she were a sweet in the confectioner's shop. Then there was Lord Kingsly, that married reprobate, eyeing her in a way that had Andrew tightening his grip on his snifter. And near the French windows stood Dr. Oliver, to whom Andrew had been introduced shortly after arriving, making what he assumed were his "mooning eyes" at Lady Catherine. It wouldn't take much convincing for Andrew to blacken both of his damned mooning eyes—

"—Don't you agree, Mr. Stanton?"

Andrew jerked his attention back. The duke, Lord Borthrasher, Mr. Sidney Carmichael, and Lord Nordnick all looked at him with expectant expressions. "Agree?"

"That women today are becoming far too bold in expressing their opinions," said the duke.

"I have noticed, yes," he said dryly. "Yet I prefer a lady to say what she thinks."

"But often what they're thinking is utter nonsense," protested Lord Borthrasher.

"I suppose that depends on the lady," Andrew said.

"Well, they're just far too opinionated if you ask me," the duke said. "My nieces, for instance." He jerked his head toward the trio of pastel-clad young ladies twittering near the open doors leading to the terrace. "Haven't an intelligent thought amongst the silly lot. Earlier today the youngest informed me that she had no intention of marrying for fortune—she would only marry for *love*. Ridiculous gel. 'Tis a father's responsibility to arrange marriages based on the advantageous joining of fortunes and properties."

"Extremely unfashionable to be in love with one's wife," Lord Borthrasher remarked. He turned to Lord Nordnick. "Hope you're planning to choose wisely, Nordnick."

A deep flush crept up the young man's neck. "Surely it is possible to make an advantageous match with a woman one also loves."

"Nonsense," said the duke, with a wave of his hand. "Choose a wife based on her family and fortune, then count your blessings if she is someone you can live with without undue stress. Save your love for your mistress."

Lord Nordnick looked at Andrew. "You're an American, Mr. Stanton. As such, do you have a different opinion?"

"Yes. Rather than marrying a woman I could live with, I'd marry the woman I couldn't live without."

Lord Borthrasher harrumphed. "And you, Carmichael? What is your opinion?"

"It is a father's right and duty to have his daughter marry as he sees fit," said Mr. Carmichael.

Andrew tensed. Before he could stop himself, he asked softly, "And if the daughter disagrees with her father's choice of groom?"

Mr. Carmichael turned toward him with a measuring look. He raised his hand to stroke his chin, and the diamond on his ring flashed. "She would be wise not to. Interfering with such arrangements is begging for disaster."

"Well, I'm hopeful my brother-in-law will be able to marry off those three silly chits of his," the duke said. "The sooner the better, I say."

A movement across the room caught Andrew's attention, and he turned. Dr. Oliver was heading toward Lady Catherine. "If you gentlemen will excuse me?" With a nod, he stepped out of their circle. Before he crossed the room, however, he leaned behind Lord Nordnick and said quietly, "I have it on the best authority that Lady Ophelia holds a fondness for tulips."

Satisfied that he'd done what he could for Nordnick's courting attempts, it was time to see to his own. As he made his way across the room, his gaze raked over Dr. Oliver in critical assessment. He'd hoped the doctor would prove old, decrepit, and frail. Bald. With a hideous paunch. And brown teeth. Or better yet, no teeth. With a countenance that resembled that of a hound. An ugly, no-tooth, paunchy, bald hound.

Unfortunately the doctor was tall, robust, and certainly not much over thirty, if he were that old. Andrew watched grimly as Dr. Oliver's face—his damned good-looking face—lit up like a bloody candle as he approached Lady Catherine. His grin displayed a set of perfectly even white teeth. Andrew felt a strong urge to uneven those teeth.

"A word with you Oliver?" he asked, strategically waylaying the man before he reached the fireplace.

Dr. Oliver halted and nodded at Andrew. "Of course. Didn't have much of a chance to speak with you when we were introduced earlier. Pleasure to meet the explorer fellow who's starting the museum with Lady Catherine's brother. Tales of your exploits with Lord Greybourne have provided many hours of entertaining conversation between Lady Catherine and myself."

"Have they indeed?" Andrew said silkily. "Did she tell you the legend of the unfortunate suitor?"

Dr. Oliver frowned, then shook his head. "I don't believe so."

"Very sad tale. A misguided young man—who oddly enough was a physician—set his sights on the object of another man's affections. As the lady was extremely lovely, the man—who was a very reasonable gentleman—

understood the physician's fascination with her and decided he would give the physician fair warning. He looked the physician straight in the eye, and said, 'The lady regards you as nothing more than a friend, and you'd be wise to remember that. If you make any further advances toward my woman, I'll be forced to hurt you.' " Andrew shook his head sadly. "Frightfully barbaric lot, those ancient Egyptians."

Understanding slowly dawned in the doctor's gaze, and his jaw tightened. "You don't say. So what did the doctor do?"

"According to the legend, he backed away. A most intelligent decision."

They stared at each other for several seconds, then Dr. Oliver said, "I'm certain that if the physician backed away, it was because he realized that the lady did indeed regard him only as a friend. Not because he was a coward." He leaned forward and lowered his voice. "Because if the lady had given the physician any indication that her regard was deeper than friendship, well, then, I think the other gentleman would have had a fight on his hands."

Andrew kept his expression impassive, but he mentally applauded the doctor. If not for Lady Catherine, he might actually like this man. "I think we understand each other."

"Yes, I believe we do. If you'll excuse me, Mr. Stanton . . ." With a curt nod, the doctor left him and headed toward the punch bowl.

Excellent. Another suitor taken care of. Andrew glanced around and when his gaze settled on Lord Kingsly, his eyes narrowed. Clearly Kingsly, as well as several other gentlemen, would do well to hear the tale of the unfortunate suitor.

Catherine stood alone at the fireplace, sipping her sherry, awaiting Genevieve's return. When Genevieve had excused herself for a moment, Catherine had actually been relieved. For the first time in their long acquaintance, she'd had difficulty following her friend's conversation. She'd been forced to say "pardon?" three times, and it was all *his* fault.

This evening was not going at all as she'd intended. Oh, the avoid portion of her plan was working splendidly—shortly after arriving she'd left Mr. Stanton in the company of the duke and several other gentlemen, then had joined Genevieve. It was the ignore portion of her plan that was failing miserably. She knew every time Mr. Stanton moved about the room. Every time he spoke to someone new. Every trip he made to the punch bowl. In desperation she'd finally maneuvered herself so that her back was to the room, but then she found herself straining her ears for the sound of his voice and stealing quick peeks over her shoulder to ascertain his whereabouts.

Never in her life had she been so excruciatingly aware of someone. Never in her life had she found it so completely impossible to ignore someone. It was an unsettling, confusing sensation, and she was quite sure she did not like it one bit.

Genevieve rejoined her, and said in an undertone, "Darling, I just overheard the most *fascinating* conversation."

"Oh? Between whom?"

"Your Mr. Stanton and Dr. Oliver."

Warmth rushed into Catherine's cheeks. "He is not *my* Mr. Stanton, Genevieve."

"Based on what I just heard, I rather think he is whether you want him or not. He's just staked his claim to Dr. Oliver, very cleverly I must say, under the guise of a tale called 'the legend of the unfortunate suitor.' "

"Staked his claim? What do you mean?"

Catherine listened intently as Genevieve related the conversation she'd overheard. When she finished, Genevieve heaved a delighted sigh. "That man is simply *divine*, Catherine."

Heat scorched Catherine, and she tried to convince herself it was the heat of embarrassment. Of outrage at Mr. Stanton's temerity. Yet as much as she wanted to, she couldn't deny the almost primitive feminine thrill racing through her.

"Oh, to be desired like that again . . ." A slow, devilish smile curved Genevieve's lips. "If not for my hands, I believe I would offer you some competition for Mr. Stanton."

A swift, strong, and undeniable shot of jealousy pulsed through Catherine. "You are welcome to him," she said stiffly.

Genevieve laughed. "Darling, if only you meant that, and my hands were not crippled, and the gentleman not so thoroughly enamored of you—" She cut off her words and leaned closer to Catherine to whisper, "Here he comes."

Before Catherine had a chance to draw a deep breath, Mr. Stanton stood before her. "May I join you ladies?"

"Certainly, Mr. Stanton," said Genevieve, with a beaming smile. "This is a delightful party, is it not?"

"Indeed it is. I'm enjoying myself immensely."

"You've been very social, Mr. Stanton," Catherine said, pleased her voice sounded so cool in contrast to the heat singeing her. "I believe you've spoken to everyone in the room."

"Just trying to spread a little cheer."

"We were just speaking about competition," Genevieve said, her blue eyes filled with innocent warmth.

Catherine's belief that her cheeks couldn't grow any hotter was proven incorrect, and she shot her friend a repressive look—a look Genevieve blithely ignored.

"Competition?" Mr. Stanton repeated. "In regard to sporting events?"

Genevieve shook her head. "In regard to matters of the heart. Would you care to share your opinion?"

Mr. Stanton's gaze shifted to Catherine, and the compelling look in his dark eyes stilled her. Then he turned his attention to include Genevieve in his answer. "Identify the competition," he said, "then outmaneuver it."

"Excellent advice," Genevieve said, nodding in an approving manner. "Don't you agree, Catherine?"

Catherine had to swallow twice to locate her voice. "Er, yes."

"The music is about to begin," said Genevieve. "Do you know how to do our country dances, Mr. Stanton?"

"Passably well."

"Waltz?"

Mr. Stanton smiled. "Extremely well."

"Excellent. I'm certain you won't lack for partners." Genevieve leaned forward and lowered her voice in a conspiratorially manner. "The duke's nieces have taken a keen interest in you."

"What?" Mr. Stanton and Catherine said at the same time.

"The duke's nieces. They're quite smitten."

Catherine's gaze shot over to the trio of young ladies. Three fascinated gazes were fastened on Mr. Stanton as if he were a new species of exotic animal. An unpleasant, unwelcome cramp Catherine was beginning to recognize all too well squeezed her.

The string quartet played a series of arpeggios, then launched into their first selection, a waltz.

Mr. Stanton turned toward Catherine and offered a formal bow. "As we were unable to share a dance at your father's birthday party, may I request the honor now?"

Common sense indicated that dancing with him, being held in his arms, did not fit in at all with her avoid-and-ignore plan. But everything female in her longed to accept his offer. It had been so long since she'd danced. And she wanted so very much to dance with *him* . . .

"I'd be delighted," she said.

Lightly resting her fingers on his proffered forearm, they made their way to the dance floor. He turned her to face him, and her breath caught at the expression in his eyes. Before she could decipher that look, however, her hand was engulfed in his, his palm settled firmly at the base of her spine, her hand rested on his broad shoulder, then . . . pure magic.

The room swirled by in a rainbow blur as he led her expertly around the gleaming floor. Warmth spread through her from where his hand touched her back, encompassing her in a heated glow as if she stood in a ray of summer sunshine. She could feel the supple strength of his shoulder beneath her fingertips, and pleasurable tingles radiated up her arm from between their clasped palms. His scent, that pleasing mixture of clean linen, sandalwood, and something else that belonged to him alone, filled her head, rendering her almost giddy.

She felt as if she were soaring, flying in his strong arms as everything, everyone, faded into the background except this man whose gaze never left hers, whose rapt expression somehow made her feel womanly and beautiful. Feminine and exciting. Young and carefree. Invigorated, her heart pounded with exhilaration, infusing her with a sense of freedom such as she'd never known, forcing her to call on all her breeding so as not to throw her head back in a most unladylike manner and simply laugh with pure and utter delight.

When Mr. Stanton led them to a stop, she hadn't even

noticed that the song had ended. For the space of several heartbeats, neither moved, standing as if locked in a motionless dance. Erratic breaths puffed from between her parted lips, although whether her labored breathing was due to the exertions of the dance or the man still touching her, she couldn't tell. Gazing at him, it seemed as if his dark eyes held hundreds of secrets, thousands of thoughts, and she suddenly found herself desperate to know each and every one of them.

Applause for the musicians roused her from her stupor. He slowly released her, and she instantly mourned the loss of his warmth and strength. After forcibly gathering her wits, she clapped politely and smiled at him. "You do indeed waltz extremely well, Mr. Stanton."

"My lovely partner inspired me."

"I fear I am frightfully out of practice."

"You gave no indication of it, but please consider me at your disposal should you wish to hone your skills."

The temptation to spend hours indulging in the delicious sensation of whirling around the dance floor with him nearly overwhelmed her.

No, to dance with him again would be most unwise. And prove yet another failure to her avoid-and-ignore plan. Yet she had no desire to dance with anyone else present.

The sound of feminine laughter caught her attention, and she turned. The duke's three nieces were descending upon them, their gazes riveted on Mr. Stanton, each girl clearly hoping for an invitation to dance.

And Catherine realized, quite unsettlingly, that not only did she have no desire to dance with anyone else save Mr. Stanton, but she did not desire Mr. Stanton to dance with anyone other than she. His earlier words echoed through her mind: *Identify the competition, then outmaneuver them.*

Looking up at him she said softly, "I fear I'm feeling a bit . . . overheated. Would you mind terribly if we went home?"

Instant concern flashed in his eyes, pricking her conscience, although she felt, in truth, quite overheated. "Of course not. We'll leave immediately."

She tried, very hard, to ignore the glow of pleasure suffusing her at his agreement as it boded very poorly indeed for her avoid-and-ignore plan.

She tried, but she failed.

Chapter 11

Every so often fate smiles, presenting Today's Modern Woman with the rare and precious opportunity to obtain her heart's most secret desire. If she should find herself in such a fortunate, glorious circumstance, she should heed those wise words, Carpe Diem, *and not hesitate to seize the day, as it may be her only chance. Be a woman of action, not a woman of regret, for it is those things we do not do that bring us sorrow.*

A Ladies' Guide to the Pursuit of
Personal Happiness and Intimate Fulfillment
by Charles Brightmore

Andrew paced the confines of his bedchamber, alternating between staring into the low-glowing embers in the grate, and looking out the window into the moonlit garden below. He stalked past the bed, shooting the navy blue counterpane a dark scowl. Comfortable as the bed looked, there was no point in lying down, for he knew all too well sleep wouldn't come. His mind, his thoughts, were too full. Of her.

Catherine. With a groan, he paused in front of the

glowing embers in the grate and dragged his hands down his face, vividly recalling her exhilarated expression as they'd waltzed this evening. The exquisite feel of her in his arms, her beautiful eyes glowing with delight, her delicate floral scent filling his head. It had required every ounce of his self-control not to simply yank her against him and profess his love in front of the entire assemblage of guests.

While tonight's pleasant carriage ride and waltz had afforded him a flicker of hope regarding his wooing campaign, that light had been all but extinguished when they'd arrived back at Bickley cottage and she'd immediately excused herself and retired.

One week. He had one bloody week to court her. Make her fall in love with him. Change her mind about wanting to marry again. Convince her that they belonged together. That in spite of his nonnoble birth, he would be a worthy husband to her and a good father to Spencer. That he loved her so much he ached.

He squeezed his eyes shut as dread suffused him. One week—for unless something drastic happened, he strongly sensed she wouldn't invite him to remain longer, and in any event, he needed to return to London to oversee the museum. No, in one week's time, he'd return to his life in Town, and she'd remain here.

One week. Even if he were, by some miracle, able to accomplish all those seemingly impossible tasks, managed to convince her to share their futures, he couldn't ignore what might happen when he revealed his past. Would she reject him when he confessed to her the secrets he'd never told anyone? The circumstances that had forced him to leave America?

Opening his eyes, he stared into the fire, futilely seeking answers in the dancing orange flames. His conscience fought the same battle it waged every time he mulled the daunting question of whether or not to reveal his past. He hated the thought of lying to her, of there being any secrets between them. Liked to think if the time should ever arise that he'd tell her.

But would he? God help him, he didn't know. If he were lucky enough finally to win her favor, would he, could he risk losing her by telling her the truth? His conscience prodded him to tell her. She deserved the truth. But then came the rationalization that always twisted his guts into a knot—no one knew except him. If he didn't tell her, she'd never find out.

Blowing out a long breath, he tunneled his hands through his hair and shoved the matter from his mind, leaving it once again unresolved. What he needed to concentrate on now was revising his courting strategy, because thus far his carefully thought-out plan was not the smashing success he'd hoped for. He needed a new plan, and given his time constraints and the fact that other suitors hovered on the horizon, it needed to be a brilliant, not to mention drastic, plan. But what? *Damn it, I need help. I need—*

An idea popped into his mind, and he stilled for several seconds. Yes . . . that might be the very thing to help him. With a purposeful stride, he crossed the blue-and-gold Persian rug to the wardrobe and pulled his brown leather portmanteau from the back corner. Reaching inside, he carefully unfastened the hidden pocket in the lining and withdrew the item he'd secreted there after purchasing it in London the morning they'd departed for Bickley cottage.

A Ladies' Guide to the Pursuit of Personal Happiness and Intimate Fulfillment by Charles Brightmore. He turned the slim, leather-bound volume over in his hands.

She'd wagered that he wouldn't read it, but he'd prove her wrong. Not only would he read it, hopefully he'd learn something from this Charles Brightmore that might inspire a new wooing campaign. At the very least, he'd win his wager with Lady Catherine and be entitled to a boon . . . a prospect ripe with possibilities.

He pulled the wing chair closer to the fire and settled into the comfortable upholstery. Shouldn't take more than an hour or so to read the book. Then he'd map out his new campaign.

This time he'd go into battle armed to the teeth.

Ensconced in her bedchamber in the comfort of her favorite wing chair next to the fireplace, Catherine leaned her head back against the soft upholstery and closed the slim leather volume. Pressing the book against her chest, she squeezed her eyes shut and cursed her folly at once again reading the words that filled her with dark yearnings. Stark needs. And insatiable curiosity.

Snippets of passages from *A Ladies' Guide* invaded her brain, igniting desires she'd tried so hard to suppress.

The leisurely caress of a man's hand up the length of a woman's thigh . . . the incredible sensations experienced by both partners when the woman takes his hardness slowly into her body . . . making love in the light so as to see every nuance of passion your lover is feeling . . . learning each other's intimate secrets with hands and lips and tongues . . . a naked man will provide a feast of delights for the woman willing to explore . . .

A soft moan escaped her lips. Heat that had nothing to do with the low-burning fire in the grate swamped her. She could feel her pulse throbbing at the base of her throat. Between her thighs. Her breasts felt heavy and swollen and almost painfully aroused.

Lifting one hand, she slowly cupped the sensitive flesh through the material of her gown. Her nipple, hard and aching, pressed against her palm. She gently squeezed, shooting ribbons of fire to her womb, increasing rather than relieving her discomfort. Setting the *Guide* aside, she rose and paced the length of the room.

Dear God, the things Genevieve had described in the *Guide* . . . incredible, unthinkable, unbelievably tantalizing things. While she'd taken dictation from Genevieve, writing in a shaky hand such intimate wonders, she'd questioned whether Genevieve was creating fiction. But her friend had assured her she was not. Genevieve had spent ten years as the mistress of an earl, captivating him with her sensual prowess. Prowess she'd learned as a result of tutelage from her mother, who'd spent her entire adult life as a mistress, and Genevieve's own imagination, which was inspired out of deep love for her earl. *It was very unwise for me fall in love with him, Catherine,* Genevieve had said. *It broke my heart when he ended our liaison. He found someone younger. Prettier. He no longer wanted my ugly hands to touch him . . .*

Catherine paused near the window. Leaning her forehead against the cool glass, she stared out into the darkness, seeing nothing save the images bombarding her. Herself and Mr. Stanton . . . hands exploring. Mouths touching. Limbs entwined.

What would his large, strong, callused hands feel like caressing her? His lovely mouth kissing her? His long, muscular legs pressing against hers?

She actually felt feverish. She should *not* have reread that book. Should have allowed her wants and needs to remain dormant. And surely they would have. If Mr. Stanton had not brought them roaring to life.

After she'd helped Genevieve write the book and had

learned of the wonders that could physically exist between a man and a woman, she'd been stunned. *Never* had she experienced anything like that with Bertrand.

After being exposed to the tantalizing information in the *Guide*, however, her thoughts had much more frequently strayed to sensual matters, piquing her long-suppressed desires and her curiosity. Since embarking on writing the *Guide* eleven months ago, shortly after Bertrand's death, how many nights had she lain in her lonely bed, her body throbbing with newly awakened, unfulfilled needs? More than she cared to recall. Her attempts to ease the aching had left her only more frustrated.

In the past, whenever she'd imagined a lover touching her, the man's image had been shadowy and unformed.

Not anymore.

Mr. Stanton's face filled her mind's eye, igniting her imagination and fantasies in a way they'd never been lit before. He was no figment of her imagination, but a flesh-and-blood man. Who had called her beautiful. Who'd made her feel as if she were soaring above the clouds when he waltzed with her. Who could inspire pleasurable tingles with a mere glance. Who, Genevieve believed, cared for her—or at the very least, desired her.

Desired her. She closed her eyes and blew out a long breath at the myriad sensual images that inspired. Images that did nothing to cool her arousal or relax her tension. She longed for the oblivion of sleep, but knew from experience that sleep would not come.

As they always did when her body and mind would not relax, the springs beckoned with their soothing warmth. She loved the privacy of taking the waters in the dark, alone, only her and the gentle night sounds surrounding her. Turning from the window, she crossed to her wardrobe and pulled out the thick, quilted robe that accompanied her on all her nighttime excursions.

She needed the soothing waters on her like she never had before.

Andrew paused on the dark path and strained his ears. A splash of water. Must be nearing the warm springs, or perhaps the small lake Spencer had mentioned. A shudder ran through him. He'd best take care lest he inadvertently locate the springs or the lake with his body, in which case this would be the last nighttime stroll he'd ever take.

Another soft splash sounded, seeming to come from behind an outcropping of rocks outlined in the moonlight about a dozen yards ahead. Might as well look at the damnable springs, so as to be prepared in case he could not find an excuse to avoid going there with Spencer. If forced, he'd look, but wild horses would not drag him into the water.

He took several steps forward, but then froze when another sound reached his ears. Something that sounded distinctly like . . . humming? Followed by a long purring *hmmmmm* of unmistakable pleasure. Unmistakable pleasure that sounded distinctly feminine. Surely it couldn't be—

Cutting off the thought before it could take root and fill his head with a hundred fantasies, he moved forward. Quickly, silently, he approached the outcropping. Keeping to the shadows, he moved around the rocks until his view was unobstructed. And his heart nearly stalled.

A circular pool of water, approximately twelve feet in diameter, surrounded by the rocks on three sides, met his stupefied gaze. Sinuous curls of steam, glowing in the moonlight, wafted upward from the water . . . and surrounded Lady Catherine in an ethereal fog.

He blinked, certain that his desperate imagination had conjured her up, but when he opened his eyes, she remained.

Submerged in the steamy water up to her neck, eyes closed, a half smile playing about her lips, she breathed out another long purr of pleasure.

As if in a daze, he stood perfectly still, utterly transfixed by the sight of her.

He meant to do . . . something. Make his presence known, or slip away, but she reached up and slowly pulled pins from her upswept hair, and he lost the ability to move. Dark curls tumbled down, over her shoulders, and he instantly imagined combing his fingers through the strands, burying his face in those soft, fragrant tresses.

She opened her mouth, took what appeared to be a deep breath, then sunk below the surface. Andrew's brows snapped together. Damn it. He hated to see anyone disappear beneath the water like that. And where the hell was she? Why was she under for so long?

His eyes scanned the surface. Why hadn't she yet reappeared? She shouldn't be under this long. How much time had passed? Surely only a few seconds, but still, tiny talons of panic clawed at him.

He started forward. What if she'd become entangled in something beneath the water? How could he hope to save her? He couldn't swim. They'd both die. He'd jump in to save her, but would he be able to do so before he sank like a stone?

Still she didn't reappear. Sweat broke out on his forehead, and the talons of panic gave way to stark terror that clamped around his heart.

"Catherine," he yelled, breaking into a run. "Cath—"

Her head broke the surface, and he skidded to a halt about three feet from the edge of the spring.

She opened her eyes, caught sight of him, and gasped. "Mr. Stanton!" Her eyes widened to saucers. "What are you doing here?"

His breath still came in ragged pants, his lungs working like a bellows. He squeezed his eyes shut and tried to regain control of his emotions. He actually felt weak-kneed. Weak-kneed and angry as hell.

He moved to the edge of the spring in one furious stride and glowered down at her. "A more apt question is *what the hell are you doing here*?"

Her mouth dropped open, and she simply stared. He didn't know if she were more shocked by the clear menace in his stance and voice or by his use of an obscenity. But at the moment he simply didn't care.

"Have you taken leave of your senses to come out here alone?" he fumed. "At night? To *swim* alone? Does anyone even know that you are here? What if something had happened to you? What in God's name were you thinking?"

She blinked several times, then pressed her lips together. Muttering something that sounded suspiciously like *irritating, overbearing man,* she reached for the side of the pool. Before he realized what she was about, she'd gracefully hoisted herself out of the spring onto the rocky ledge. Then, water sluicing down her body, she stomped over to him.

Every thought he'd ever had, and a few he hadn't yet managed to think, drained from his head and flopped onto the ground at his feet—to join his jaw.

She looked like a pale sea nymph, her dark hair slicked back, the dark curls flattened straight by the water, falling to her waist. Her body was covered, or more aptly not covered, in a wet chemise that clung to her form as if painted on—with transparent paint. His stupefied gaze traveled downward, over her delicate clavicle, to the generous swell of her breasts, topped with dusky, hardened nipples. The indent of her waist. The flare of her hips. The shadow of the dark triangle nestled between her shapely thighs. Over her calves, right down to her slender ankles and dainty feet.

She halted less than two feet in front of him, and he snapped his gaze back up to her face. The ice emanating from her glare was surely meant to freeze him where he stood.

"No, Mr. Stanton," she said in a voice throbbing with anger, "I have not taken leave of my senses. I often visit this warm spring alone at night, as I enjoy the solitude. I was not *swimming*, I was soaking. There was no risk as not only am I an excellent swimmer, but the water in the spring is no deeper than my shoulders. No one knows I am here, but I assure you I am perfectly safe. Little Longstone is not London, and dangerous persons, with the obvious exception of *you,* do not skulk about in the bushes. And now that I've answered all your questions, perhaps you'd enlighten me as to what the hell *you* are doing here?"

He wanted to answer her, but God help him, he couldn't find his voice. The sight of her, wet, beautiful, angry, stole his ability to speak. Damn near stole his ability to breathe.

She planted her fists on her hips. "Were you spying on me? Trying to frighten me?"

He frowned, shook his head, and swallowed. "No." His voice sounded rusty, as if he hadn't used it in a decade or two. "I couldn't sleep. Wanted some air. I heard splashing . . . and there you were. I hadn't recovered from my surprise when you went under the water. It seemed you were under far too long. I thought you were drowning." He could barely push the last word past his lips.

Unable to stop himself, he reached out and trailed unsteady fingers over her cheek. Her skin was smooth, warm and wet beneath his fingers. Her eyes widened at the gesture, but she did not pull away.

"I'm sorry for shouting at you. I thought you were drowning . . ." His fingers slipped from her cheek, and he fancied he saw disappointment flash in her eyes. Reaching down, he clasped her hands, then pressed them against his chest over the spot where his heart still raced. "Can you feel how scared I was?" he asked, drinking in the sensation of her hands on him, wishing his shirt would magically disappear.

Her head jerked in a tiny nod. "I . . . I'm sorry as well. I was only wetting my hair."

He inhaled, and the delicious scent of her warm, wet, nearly naked body filled his head, intoxicating him. His sudden spate of anger died as quickly as it had flared, replaced by a roar of desire that threatened to bring him to his knees. All the feelings he'd held in check for so long rushed to the surface, sweeping away his restraint like a feather cast upon rough seas. He wanted her so badly . . .

He released her hands, cupped her face in his palms, then slowly lowered his head.

At the first gentle brush of his lips against hers, he stilled, absorbing the incredible realization that he was actually kissing her, memorizing the sensation. He brushed his lips over hers again, and a tiny gasp escaped her. Her fingers curled against his chest, her lips parted slightly, and the longing that he'd held back for so long burst.

With a groan, he erased the space between them in one step. Wrapping one arm around her waist, he clasped her tightly against him. He sifted a hand through her damp hair, then deepened their kiss.

Catherine stood in the strong circle of his arms and simply allowed the onslaught of sensations battering her to take over. Warm. He was so warm. She felt as if he'd wrapped her in a velvet blanket.

Solid. The sensation of her body pressed against his from chest to knee stole her breath. Her fingers curled, then splayed against his chest, and she could feel the hard muscles beneath the fine linen. His heartbeat thundered against her palms, and she absorbed every slap, knowing her heart was beating at the same frantic speed.

She parted her lips and was rewarded with the erotic, delicious sweep of his tongue against hers. He tasted dark and exotic, with a faint trace of brandy.

More. How she wanted more of this heady wonder, more of these sensuous delights. She pressed herself closer to him, reveling in his arousal pressing against her belly. A low groan vibrated in his throat, and she glided one hand up to touch the sound. He wore no cravat, and her fingers brushed over the shallow indentation at the base of his throat, then slipped beneath the material to touch his warm, firm skin before sliding upward to ruffle through his thick hair.

His hold on her tightened, and she strained closer, squirming against him. *More. Please, more . . .*

He answered her silent plea, slanting his mouth over hers in a long, slow, deep, tongue-mating kiss that dissolved her bones. His large hands tunneled through her hair, then moved slowly down her back, as if trying to memorize every inch.

When his palms reached the small of her back, he left her lips and trailed his mouth along her jaw, then down her neck with a series of heated, nipping kisses. Shivers of delight shook her and she leaned her head back to give him better access.

He blazed a trail back up her neck, then found her lips once more, destroying her with another hot, open-mouthed, lush kiss that made her feel as if she were a mound of gunpowder on the verge of exploding. A long, need-filled groan rumbled upward from the vicinity of her toes. He gentled the kiss, then raised his head, and her groan turned to one of protest.

She forced her eyes open and stilled. A feminine thrill unlike any she'd ever felt before suffused her at the fire burning in his gaze. Never had a man looked at her like that. With such heat. Such passion. Such reverence. Such raw hunger. She felt a tremor run through him and clearly saw his fight for self-control . . . a fight that part of her badly wanted him to lose. The feminine part that longed to feel his kiss again. His hands on her body. Skin to skin.

One strong arm released her, and he brought his hand to her face. Slowly his fingertips brushed over her brow. Her cheeks, her lips, all while his other arm held her tightly against him—which was good, as she suspected she'd slither to the ground in a boneless, heated heap. He swallowed, then whispered one word.

"Catherine."

It sounded like a sensual caress. Deep and raspy, with a hint of wonder. The sound tickled over her skin, making her feel wicked and decadent. More womanly and alive than she'd felt in years. There was only one word she could answer in reply.

"Andrew."

A slow smile tilted up his lips. "I like the way my name sounds when you say it."

"It was all I could think of to say, except Oh, my."

"I am in complete agreement."

"Is this possible? That we agree *again* this evening?"

"Shocking, but true. However, you sound surprised that you would think to say *Oh, my* about our kiss."

"I confess I somewhat am. Are you not?"

He shook his head. "I didn't doubt for a moment it would be like that. The only thing that surprises me is that I managed to summon the fortitude to stop."

"You'd thought about kissing me?" She blessed the cover of darkness that kept him from seeing the flush that heated her cheeks at her forward question, but she wanted to know. Needed to know.

"Yes. Does that . . . upset you?"

No. It excites me. Almost unbearably. "No." Her eyes searched his, and after a quick debate, she uttered the unvarnished truth. "I've never been kissed like that."

He cupped her cheek in his callused palm and brushed his thumb lightly over her lips. "Good. I like to be first."

A dozen sensual images collided in Catherine's mind, and she realized this man could represent a great many "firsts" for her—firsts her body was aching to experience. The arousal still pressing against her belly and the hard, fast thumping of his heart beneath her palms indicated he wouldn't be averse to the idea.

But she could not make such an important decision, like whether or not to take him as a lover, while wrapped in his arms. She needed to think. And in order to do so, she had to put some space between them.

She slowly stepped back, until three feet separated them. His gaze wandered down her body. Her wet chemise clung to her skin, revealing everything to his avid gaze, but instead of feeling shy, she reveled in the intense need and desire etched on his face.

"You're beautiful, Catherine. The most beautiful woman in the world."

The desire his words fueled in her left her shaking and

frightened. Hoping to cool the fire racing through her, dispel the sensual tension bouncing between them, she attempted a laugh. "How can you possibly say that? You haven't met every woman in the world."

"I don't need to touch fire to know it would burn me. I don't need to smash a hammer on my finger to know it would hurt. Or eat a sweet from the confectionary to know I'd want another one. Some things, Catherine, you just *know*." He reached out and lightly grasped her hand, entwining their fingers. "I also know that our next kiss will be even more *Oh, my* than the one we just shared. And the one after that . . ." He raised their joined hands to his lips and pressed a warm kiss against the sensitive skin on the inside of her wrist. "Indescribable."

"Our *next* kiss, Mr. Stanton? What makes you think there will be a next kiss?"

"As I said, some things you just *know*."

Another bout of heat whooshed through her. Good heavens. It was time to end this interlude before their next kiss happened right now. Turning, she strode to the flat rock where she'd placed her robe. After slipping her arms into the sleeves, she tightened the sash around her waist. When she turned around, he stood not two feet away. She drew in a sharp breath, and her head filled with his delightful, musky the scent.

"Andrew," he said softly.

"I beg your pardon?"

"Just now you called me Mr. Stanton. I'd prefer you call me Andrew. Just as I'd prefer to call you Catherine."

She'd called him that to put a bit of emotional distance between them, but she doubted her ability ever to think of him in such formal terms again. Not now that she knew the texture of his skin. The silkiness of his hair. The sensation of his tongue stroking hers. And she could not deny that she liked the sound of her name coming from his lips. Amazing how simply dropping the word "Lady" changed . . . everything.

"I suppose we're on a first-name basis now. Very well . . . Andrew." His name tasted decadent, luscious upon her tongue.

He reached out and clasped her hands in a warm grip. "Are you sorry about what happened between us, Catherine?"

She shook her head. "Not sorry. But . . ." Her voice trailed off, unable to find the right word to describe the jumble of emotions careening through her.

"Scared?" he guessed. "Confused?"

Botheration, when had she become so transparent? "Do you have clairvoyant capabilities, Andrew?"

"Not at all." He lifted her hands, one at a time to his mouth, his gaze never leaving hers. "I only suggest those because they are some of the things I'm feeling."

"Scared? You?" She meant to laugh, but the sound came out as a breathless sigh when his tongue brushed the center of her palm.

"Terrified is actually closer to the truth."

The fact that this strong, virile man would admit such a thing touched her in a way she couldn't describe. "Why?"

"I'd say for the exact same reasons you are."

"Because as pleasant as our kiss was, you're not sure it was a good idea?"

"No. I think it was a good idea. And Catherine, our kiss was much more than 'pleasant.' "

"Must you disagree with *everything* I say?"

"Only when you're wrong. And you're wrong to describe what happened between us with a bland word such as pleasant."

Well, she certainly couldn't argue with that. "Why are you scared?"

He said nothing for several long seconds, clearly considering how to answer her. Finally, he said, "I'm afraid of tomorrow. I'm afraid that once we leave here, once we go our separate ways for the rest of the night, that when I see you again tomorrow you'll have forgotten what we shared here. Or if not forgotten, then you'll have decided to ignore it. I'm afraid you'll look at me with coolness rather than heat in your eyes. I'm afraid that you'll stop what we could share together before it's even had a chance to start."

She cleared her throat. "I don't think there is anything I can say right now to allay your fears. But I can assure you that I will not forget what we shared this evening."

A ghost of a smile touched his lips. "Something else for us to agree upon, for I will not forget it. Not if I live to be one hundred. Now you tell me—what are you confused about?"

She toyed with the idea of lying. Or simply leaving. But it was most likely best that she should speak her mind. "My mind and my common sense are telling me to walk away and not look back. Everything else in me, however, does not want to do that. I am not a naive, virginal miss, and I know where this . . . flirtation could lead. However, I've more than just myself and my desires to consider. Therefore, I have a great deal of thinking to do. And decisions to make."

"As do I."

"Indeed? What sort of decisions do you have to make?"

A hint of deviltry sparkled in his eyes. "I must decide how best to entice you to make the decision *I* want you to make."

Matching his mischievous tone, she said, "You realize, of course, that arrogance is a most irritating character trait that will certainly not tip the scales in your favor during my decision-making."

"I spoke not out of arrogance, but out of honesty—a trait most people appreciate and find admirable."

"Are you saying you intend to *seduce* me?"

"I'm saying I intend to court you."

Catherine's heart skipped. A ridiculous reaction to a ridiculous statement. "Don't be ridiculous."

He raised his brows. "You'd prefer not to be courted?"

"There is no point in your doing so."

"So you'd prefer simply to be seduced."

"Yes. I mean no! I mean, oh!" She stepped away from him and pulled her robe tighter around her. "You are so—"

"Irrepressible? Irresistible?"

Amusement she couldn't deny rippled though her, and her lips twitched. "I was going to say irritating."

"I must confess, I like my choices much better."

"Yes, I'm certain you do."

"Why is there no point in me courting you?"

"Courting is a precursor to marriage, and as I've no intention of marrying again, your efforts would be wasted."

"A man cannot court a woman simply because he enjoys her company?"

"Do you enjoy my company, Mr. Stanton?"

"Andrew. And yes, I do. When you're not being so prickly. Although, I must admit that I enjoy your company even when you are prickly. I just enjoy it more when you're not."

"I am not prickly."

"If you don't think so, clearly you do not know the definition of the word. Between that and not knowing what a surprise is, I think it might behoove me always to keep a dictionary in easy reach."

"Is this your idea of courting me? Irritating me until my head hurts?"

"No. However, I don't see that it makes much difference as you've said you don't wish to be courted."

Catherine bit her lips, not certain if she were more amused or vexed. Shooting him an exaggerated frown, she asked, "Do you know who is more annoying than you?"

His eyes twinkled with clear amusement. "No, but I'm certain you're about to tell me."

"No one, Mr. Stanton. I've never met anyone more annoying than you."

"Andrew. And how fortunate that I so enjoy being in first place."

He smiled, a beautiful, full smile, complete with the enticing dimples that had her pressing her lips together to keep from responding in kind. Botheration, where had her irritation disappeared to? She shouldn't feel like smiling. She was supposed to be irked. Annoyed. Why then did she feel so utterly . . . charmed?

Clearly it was time that she took her leave of him.

She stepped forward, but he stopped her by lightly grasping her upper arm. All vestiges of humor left his eyes, and he reached out to trail a single fingertip down her cheek. "I think we shared something good here tonight, Catherine."

A tingle tripped down her spine. How did he elicit such a strong physical reaction from her with just the whisper of a touch? Although she desperately wished it otherwise, she could no longer lie to herself and deny that she found this man irresistibly attractive.

Now the only question was, what did she intend to do about it?

Chapter 12

Today's Modern Woman must realize that it is not a crime to be selfish upon occasion. In many aspects of life, women are expected to, indeed ofttimes forced to, put the wants and needs of others above her own. In many instances these sacrifices are admirable. In other instances, however, they are foolhardy. Today's Modern Woman should take the time to look in a mirror, and say to herself, "I want *this, I deserve this, I am going to have it."*

A Ladies' Guide to the Pursuit of
Personal Happiness and Intimate Fulfillment
by Charles Brightmore

"Are we almost finished, Mr. Stanton?" Spencer asked for the third time in the last quarter hour.

Crouched on the rough wooden floor of a little-used part of the stables, Andrew smiled over his shoulder. Spencer stood next to a bale of hay, holding a broom—for the first time in his life. When Andrew had handed him the tool half an hour ago, Spencer had stared at the wooden handle for several seconds as if it were a snake, but then he got into the spirit of the task. The sheen of hard work glistened on the young man's face, as did clear satisfaction in the fruits of his labors.

"The floor looks good," Andrew said. "I just need to hammer a few more nails. Then we can begin."

While Andrew set another nail in place, Spencer cleared his throat. "I want to thank you for taking such good care of my mother after the shooting."

Andrew turned around, giving the boy his full attention. "It was my pleasure to do so, Spencer."

"I would have thanked you sooner, but she did not tell me about it until yesterday." He looked down and plucked a piece of hay from the bale. "When she first told me, I was not only angry at her, but at you as well for not telling me."

"It wasn't my place to tell you, Spencer. And your mother's intentions were good. We all try to protect the people we love."

"I know. Mum and I talked about it. I'm not angry anymore. She promised not to keep any more secrets from me."

"Good." Andrew crossed to the bale of hay and extended his hand. "I hope we are still friends?"

Spencer's head jerked up, and his serious gaze met Andrew's. Reaching out, he clasped Andrew's hand in a strong grip and nodded. "Friends. But . . . no more secrets."

Guilt hit Andrew like an open-handed slap, and he merely nodded in response, not willing to give voice to such a blatant falsehood. His entire life was based on secrets. And lies.

He released Spencer's hand, then stepped back to retrieve his hammer. "I'll finish this so we can begin," he said. Burying his regret at being less than honest in the face of Spencer's trust, he set a nail in the wood and pounded out his frustrations.

Ten minutes later, Andrew completed the task, and he stood to survey his handiwork. While Spencer had cleared away the dust and cobwebs from the area, he'd affixed three dozen wood rectangles, each approximately the size of a brick, to the floor to form a wide circle. Yes, this would do very nicely.

"Ready?" Andrew asked.

"Yes. And eager." He indicated the wood blocks with his chin. "*Now* will you tell me what those are?"

"They're to aid your balance during our pugilism lessons. Once you are steady on your feet, there is no reason why you cannot do well. Allow me to demonstrate. Brace the side of your weak foot along the wood, then step forward with your strong foot, keeping most of your weight on the forward leg."

After Spencer had done so, Andrew said, "As long as you keep your weight forward, the wood will keep your weak foot from sliding, thus preventing you from falling backward."

Spencer slowly flexed his knees several times, then a broad smile lit his face. "I say, that's quite ingenious, Mr. Stanton."

Andrew took a bow. "Thank you. I'm certain you did not mean to sound so shocked."

The boy's smile faded, and he looked distressed. "Oh, no. I—"

" 'Twas a jest, Spencer. Now, let's start with the basics. There are two basic principles to pugilism. Any idea what they are?"

"To punch the other fellow and not let yourself get punched."

"Exactly." Andrew cocked his head. "You seem to know a great deal about this. Are you certain you've never done this before?"

"Most certain," Spencer said, his face perfectly serious.

Andrew suppressed his smile. "In order to do those two

things, you must know how to deliver a punch and how to block or avoid a punch."

"I imagine speed is very important in this sport," Spencer said, his voice wistful.

"It is. But it is not the only thing. Timing and the ability to outthink your opponent are just as important. What you may lack in speed, you will make up for in intelligence. And you'll recall that the goal here is not to become the most feared pugilist in the kingdom—only the best that you can be."

"But what if I can't do it at all?"

"If you try, then discover that you can't do it, that's fine. Not everyone can excel at everything he attempts, Spencer. The important thing is to try. I truly believe you can do this. If I didn't, I wouldn't have hammered this makeshift ring into place. If it turns out I'm wrong, then so be it. If nothing else, you'll have learned you don't like it."

"You won't think I'm . . . foolish? Or stupid?" He looked at the ground. "Or a failure?"

The worry and resignation in the boy's voice tore at Andrew. Reaching out, he placed his hands on Spencer's shoulders and waited until Spencer looked up to meet his gaze. "Whether you excel at this or not, I would never think you to be anything less than a courageous, intelligent, successful young man."

The hope that flared in the lad's eyes made the space around Andrew's heart go hollow. Spencer blinked, then swallowed. "Do you truly mean that?"

"You have my word." He released his shoulders, then ruffled his hair. "Indeed, I envy your courage."

"*You?*" The word was a snort of disbelief. "You and Uncle Philip are the bravest men I know."

"Thank you, although I believe we are the *only* men you know," he teased.

Spencer's face flushed bright red. "That's not true. I know—"

"I was jesting, Spencer."

"Oh. I . . . knew that." He frowned. "What sort of courage do I have that you envy?"

Andrew paced before the boy several times, debating, then halted. "If I tell you, do you promise not to think *me* foolish or a failure?"

Spencer's eyes widened. "I'd never think such a thing, Mr. Stanton. I promise."

"Very well." Andrew raked his hand through his hair, then drew a deep breath. "Icannotswim," he said in rush. There. He'd said it. Out loud.

"I beg your pardon?"

Damn. It appeared he'd have to say it again. "I. Cannot. Swim."

Spencer's eyes widened further. "Never say so. Are you certain?"

"Very. I never learned. As you know, my father did not know how to swim, and who else would have taught me? After he drowned, any enthusiasm I might have had for the water abruptly left me. The last time I was in the water, except for a bathtub of course, was during some ridiculous reenactment of an ancient Nile canoe crossing your uncle insisted I participate in. I was too embarrassed to admit I couldn't swim, so against my better judgment I did it. The canoe overturned, and I nearly drowned." A shudder ran through him as he relieved the stark terror of the water closing over his head. Filling his lungs. Shaking off the memory, he gazed steadily at Spencer. "Believe me, I understand your trepidation about trying something over which you feel you have no control. But I'll help you. You can do it. If you really want to."

"So could you, you know."

He smiled. "I already know how to fight."

"I meant swim. Have you ever tried to learn?"

"No. As much as I hate to admit it, I'm afraid of the water."

"But you crossed an entire ocean!"

"And don't think I wasn't scared. Believe me, I stayed far away from the rails."

"I could teach you to swim, you know. We could start today! Right after our pugilism lesson."

Andrew actually felt the blood drain from his face. "*Today?* No, I don't think—"

"I could teach you to swim, Mr. Stanton," Spencer went on, his eyes alight with eagerness. "Won't you allow me to try? I'd be honored to teach you something in return for everything you're teaching me. And once you learn, you can take the waters with me and Mum—not that you need to know how to swim to take the waters. The springwater would only reach your chest."

The "no" that had hovered on Andrew's lips fell away as he considered this opportunity. If he learned to swim . . . he instantly imaged him and Catherine together at night in the spring, kissing, touching in the warm, soothing water. Then a relaxing, fun-filled family afternoon, splashing and swimming with Spencer and Catherine.

"Mr. Stanton?"

Andrew roused himself from his brown study. "Yes?"

"If you try, then discover that you can't do it, that's fine. Not everyone can excel at everything he attempts. The important thing is to try."

One corner of Andrew's mouth pulled up. "Surely it is written somewhere that 'thou shalt not use a man's own words against him.' "

"Unfortunately for you, that is not written anywhere,"

Spencer said positively. "And surely you cannot expect me to take your advice if you're unwilling to take it yourself."

Andrew blinked. The lad had him there. "Have you ever considered becoming a barrister?"

"No. But if I stand a chance of winning this—my first case—I may consider it." He reached out and laid a comforting hand on Andrew's shoulder. "I know it will be difficult, especially after what happened to your father. But a very wise man recently told me that if you always do what you've always done, you'll always be where you've always been."

Andrew shook his head. "Hoist upon my own petard," he muttered.

"I appreciate your trust in sharing your secret with me, sir," Spencer said in a very serious voice. "I give you my word it is not misplaced."

There was no missing Spencer's strong desire to be needed, to be important, to be good enough at something to teach someone else. It was all right there in the young man's eyes, calling out to Andrew. It was a call he couldn't ignore.

"All right," he agreed. "I'll try it. *One* time," he added hastily when Spencer's face lit up with an eager smile. "But if I don't like it, we stop. Immediately."

"Agreed. But first our pugilism lesson."

Andrew nodded. "Ready?"

Spencer made two fists and struck a fighting pose. "Ready."

"Have you taken to studying tea leaves, Catherine?"

At Genevieve's question Catherine jerked her gaze up from her teacup and blinked. "I beg your pardon?"

"I wondered if you'd developed an interest in tea leaves

since clearly there is something fascinating in the bottom of your cup."

Heat rose in Catherine's cheeks. "Forgive me, Genevieve. I'm a bit preoccupied."

"Yes, I can see that. Is something amiss?"

Catherine looked at the warm concern in Genevieve's blue eyes, and to her consternation felt hot moisture press behind her own eyes. "Not amiss, precisely, but there is something troubling me."

"I'd be happy to listen if you'd like to tell me."

"I don't really know how or where to begin."

Genevieve nodded slowly. "I see. This concerns Mr. Stanton."

Catherine stared. "Good Lord, either I've become completely transparent, or everyone around me has developed clairvoyant tendencies."

"There is nothing of a transparent or clairvoyant nature at work here, darling. 'Tis just that I know you so well, and the fact that since I have a great deal of experience in these matters, I can easily recognize the signs."

"These matters? Signs? What do you mean?"

"Why, I'm talking about you and Mr. Stanton. Last evening. The way he looked at you. The way you tried so hard not to look at him. The way you waltzed together."

"I . . . I don't know what to say. My thoughts are so confused, I'm not certain how to describe them."

"Catherine, there's nothing to be confused about. I understand completely."

A humorless laugh escaped Catherine. "Then perhaps you could explain it to me."

"Gladly. You find Mr. Stanton very attractive—in spite of the fact that you do not wish to."

"I don't wish to," Catherine agreed emphatically. "And what makes it worse, I cannot fathom *why* I find him so fascinating. He is the most irritating man I've ever encountered."

"Which is why you find him so fascinating," Genevieve said with a soft laugh. "He is challenging in that he does not fall at your feet and agree with everything you say like the rest of the men seeking your favor. Yet he is kind and holds you in the highest regard. To say nothing of the fact that he is a delight to look at." Genevieve's sharp-eyed gaze studied her for several seconds. "I'm guessing he kissed you."

Fire erupted in Catherine's cheeks. "Yes."

"He is a man who knows how to kiss a woman."

"Truer words have probably never been spoken."

"Did you make love with him?"

A heated tremor sizzled through Catherine at the mere thought. "No."

"But you want to." Clearly, Genevieve needed no confirmation of that because before Catherine could speak, she continued, "Obviously he wishes to. Did he give you any indication what his intentions are?"

"He said he intends to court me."

"Ah!" Genevieve's eyes sparkled. "Not only is he charming, handsome, intelligent, and—"

"Irritating. You seem to keep forgetting that—"

"—Well traveled, he is honorable as well."

Feeling decidedly like a hen whose feathers were badly ruffled out of place, Catherine said tartly, "As I told him last evening, there is no point in courting me, as I've no intention of marrying again."

"So you wish for him merely to seduce you," Genevieve said with a matter-of-fact nod. "You could easily convince most men to agree to your terms, but one can tell at first glance that your Mr. Stanton is not most men."

"He is not *my* Mr. Stanton."

Genevieve brushed the comment away with her gloved hand. "I do not see him turning down the opportunity to become your lover, but his intention to court you leads me to think he will not be satisfied with that arrangement in the long run."

"Yes, I'm certain he'd tire of me after a time." The words felt like sawdust in Catherine's mouth, and she sipped her tea to relieve the discomfort.

"You misunderstand, my dear. Mr. Stanton stated he wishes to *court* you. He wants a *wife*. He will grow tired not of you, but of the nonpermanent nature of your relationship. When he does, he will push for you to marry him."

"He will not succeed."

"Then it is my guess that he will end your relationship at that time."

Catherine ignored the odd feeling that pervaded her at the bald statement, and laughed. "I was not aware that gentlemen ended relationships because the *woman* refused to get married. What sort of man would want the responsibility of a wife, especially a wife who comes with another man's child, when he could have the carefree enjoyment of a mistress?"

"The sort of man who wants a family. Permanence. A woman and child to share his life with. A man who is capable of giving a woman all the things a man like your husband was not. The sort of man who is in love." Genevieve shrugged. "Mr. Stanton could be any one of those—or perhaps all of them."

"He cannot possibly be in love with me, Genevieve. We barely know each other."

"It does not take long to fall in love." A wistful, faraway look entered Genevieve's eyes, and Catherine knew her friend was thinking of her former lover. Genevieve appeared to give herself a mental shake, then offered Catherine a sad smile. "Indeed, it can happen distressingly fast. And unfortunately, Cupid's arrow often strikes our hearts at inconvenient times and makes us fall in love with very inconvenient people. Lord knows I am a perfect example of that."

"I am *not* in love with Mr. Stanton. Heavens, I don't even particularly *like* him!"

"Actually, I meant Mr. Stanton, my dear. It certainly is inconvenient for him to have feelings for a woman who is dead set against marriage. To say nothing of a woman who is his social superior. And I believe you like him more than you think. Certainly more than you are willing to admit."

An instant denial rose to Catherine's lips, but she found she could not utter the words. Instead, she set her teacup aside and rose to pace in front of the floral chintz settee. "I cannot deny I am faced with deciding what to do with this . . . inconvenient attraction to Mr. Stanton."

"It isn't difficult, Catherine, as you only have two options: ignore your feelings, or enjoy them and indulge in an affair."

Catherine shook her head. "It is not that simple. There are things I must consider before making such an important decision."

"It is precisely that simple. You want him, he wants you, neither of you are attached, neither are innocents—what else is there to consider?"

"My son, for one thing. What if he were to find out I'd taken a lover?"

"Well, naturally you would be extremely discreet,

Catherine. Not only to protect Spencer, but yourself as well."

"Someone could still find out."

"Yes, but no one said that taking a lover was free of risk. Oftentimes the risk itself lends an air of excitement to the affair."

"What about the fact that Andrew lives in London?"

"He may live in Town, but he's in Little Longstone *now*."

"But he will return to London in a week's time."

Genevieve raised her brows. "I would think that would be perfect. You do not want a permanent relationship, and he is leaving Little Longstone in one week. What could be more ideal?"

Catherine halted in her pacing in front of the fireplace. "I had not considered it quite that way."

"Perhaps you should."

Gripping the edge of the mantel, she tipped her head back to stare at the ceiling. "I never should have reread the *Guide* last night." She looked at Genevieve over her shoulder and gave a sheepish laugh. "As I'm sure you can imagine, it put all sorts of ideas in my head."

"I'm certain it did. But I think it's far more likely that you were driven to reread the *Guide* because those ideas were already in your head—put there by Mr. Stanton."

Catherine nodded slowly. "Yes, you're right." She turned to face her friend. "What if I conceived a child?"

"As you know from the *Guide*, there are various ways to prevent that from happening." Genevieve stood and walked to stand next to Catherine. Clearly Catherine's anguish showed because Genevieve did something she rarely did—she reached out her gloved hand and touched Catherine's shoulder in a show of support and sympathy.

"I can see you are distressed, my dear, and you should not be. There is really only one decision, and I believe that in your heart you know what that is. Allowing yourself sensual pleasure does not make you less of a good mother. As the *Guide* points out, being selfish upon occasion is not a crime."

"There is no room for this man in the life I've built here."

"Perhaps not in the long term, but there could be room for the next week."

Silence stretched between them until finally Catherine said softly, "You would take him as a lover."

"Yes," Genevieve replied without hesitation. "I would not deny either of us the pleasure. I would listen to my heart and *carpe diem*! Seize the day! But based on my writings in the *Guide*, I'm sure you knew that." A sad smile touched her lips. "Every woman deserves a grand passion in her life, Catherine. It is one thing to read that such sensual pleasures exist, but to experience them . . ." She heaved a dreamy-sounding sigh. "The memories of my time with Richard will continue to warm me for the rest of my life."

Catherine's heart turned over with sympathy. "You do not have to be alone, Genevieve."

Her friend held up her hands. "These are not hands a man wants touching him."

"There is more to you than your hands. You are a beautiful, intelligent, vibrant woman."

"Thank you. But a grand affair, the taking on of a lover, is based on a strong physical attraction, and that, I'm afraid, is in the past for me. But not for you. Catherine, what is your heart is telling you?"

Catherine closed her eyes. She'd expected to listen to

an internal battle between her mind and her heart, but the yearnings of her heart drowned out any other sound—and with only two words.

She opened her eyes. "My heart says *carpe diem*."

Chapter 13

While the intimacy afforded by the dark lends itself to sensual encounters, Today's Modern Woman should not hesitate to try making love without the cover of darkness. Seeing every nuance of your lover's expressions, watching surrender overtake control, adds layers of pleasure to the lovemaking experience.

A Ladies' Guide to the Pursuit of
Personal Happiness and Intimate Fulfillment
by Charles Brightmore

Feeling in need of a brisk ride to settle her runaway thoughts, Catherine decided to stop at the stables on her return walk from Genevieve's cottage. The double oak doors were thrown open, and she stepped into the cool, shadowy interior. Dust motes danced on ribbons of sunshine streaming through the windows, and she drew in a deep breath, loving the heady scent of fresh hay, horseflesh, and leather. The murmur of masculine voices reached her ears, and her heart quickened. Was Andrew once again in the stables with Fritzborne?

She walked toward the voices, and realized the sound

was coming from round the corner—the old, rear section of the stables that had not been refurbished. As she drew closer, the voices became more distinct, and she realized that one of the voices indeed belonged to Andrew. The other belonged to Spencer.

"That's good," said Andrew, his words growing more distinct with her every step. "Keep your left hand up. Higher. Protect your face. Now jab with your right."

"I can't bloody reach you," came Spencer's breathless reply, followed by a grunt. Catherine paused and raised her brows at her son's language.

"Move your strong leg back a step. That will draw me in closer. Then, once I'm in your range, lunge forward and jab."

"Ha! I'll get you now."

"Ha! I'd like to see you try."

Catherine tiptoed forward, her slippers silent on the wood floor. When she reached the corner, she peeked around the doorway. And froze.

Andrew and Spencer appeared to be engaged in . . . fisticuffs? Neither wore their jackets or cravats, and both had rolled back their shirtsleeves to their elbows. Her jaw dropped as Andrew bounced on the balls of his feet, feinting back and forth, while Spencer, fists clenched at chin height, swung at him several times and missed. Then Andrew's hands flashed out, narrowly missing Spencer's jaw. Spencer leaned back to avoid the blow, and nearly toppled backward.

A cry of fright raced into her throat, but before she could utter it, Andrew caught her son's upper arm and steadied him. "Watch your balance, Spencer. Keep your weight forward and raise those hands to prevent—"

"What on earth is going on here?" Catherine, voice

shaking with a combination of anger and fright, stepped from the shadows and planted her hands on her hips.

Andrew froze at the sound of her outraged voice and glanced over his shoulder, hoping she would not look as upset as she sounded. Their eyes met, and his heart sank. Not only did she look angry, she appeared horrified as well.

He opened his mouth to respond, but before he could utter a word, something struck him directly under the chin with a perfectly placed blow. Instantly realizing the something was Spencer's fist, Andrew staggered back a step, got his feet tangled up, and landed squarely on his arse on the hard wood. He winced and made a mental note to fall toward the haystack next time.

"Good heavens, Spencer, have you—or rather both of you—taken leave of your senses?" came Catherine's voice from behind him. He heard her rushing forward.

Spencer shifted his stupefied gaze from his clenched fist to Andrew, then back to his fist, then to his mother, who appeared to have steam exiting her ears. He visibly swallowed, then moved toward Andrew. "I say, Mr. Stanton, I didn't mean to—"

Andrew held up one hand to stop the boy's words while he rubbed his sore jaw with the other. "Now *that* was an excellent, perfectly executed blow, and a perfect example of the second rule I taught you, which is . . . ?"

"Always take advantage of your opponent's weakness."

"Precisely. I was momentarily distracted by your mother's arrival, and the next thing I know, I'm on my arse on the floor. Very nicely done." He jumped to his feet, brushed some dust from his breeches, then with a smile, he offered Spencer his hand. "I'm proud of you."

The flush of unmistakable pleasure washing over the

boy's face, combined with the wonder and gratitude in his expression, warmed Andrew's heart in a way he hadn't experienced in a long time. "Th . . . thank you, Mr. Stanton." His smile collapsed as suddenly as it had appeared. "I didn't hurt you, did I?"

Andrew moved his jaw back and forth, then winked at the lad. "I'll survive." He then turned his attention to Catherine and smiled, pretending he did not notice her thunderous expression. "Your son is an excellent pupil."

"*Pupil?* Please do not tell me that you are teaching him to fight with his fists."

"All right, I won't tell you that."

"What *are* you doing?"

"Since you've requested that I not tell you that I'm teaching him to fight with his fists, it's going to be very difficult to answer that question."

She leveled a look on him that made him thankful he wasn't milk, as he would have curdled on the spot. She then swiveled her glance toward Spencer. "Are you all right?"

"Yes, Mum. Of course. It's Mr. Spencer who got knocked on his bottom."

"And I'm very well, thank you."

Her angry glance jumped back and forth between him and Spencer. "I'm waiting for an explanation."

"I was teaching Spencer some fundamentals of pugilism," Andrew said. "As you can see, he is a very apt pupil."

"Why on earth would you teach him something like that? Did either of you consider the risks? He could have fallen. Gotten seriously hurt. He nearly toppled backward only a moment ago."

"But I didn't, Mum," Spencer broke in. "Mr. Stanton caught me."

"And if he had not been successful?"

"But he *was*," Spencer reiterated. "He's very strong and very fast. He built this special ring for me. It helps me keep my balance. Watch." He demonstrated, then added, "The ring is surrounded by hay for a soft landing in case I should fall—which I won't, because Mr. Stanton is an excellent teacher. And as for why Mr. Stanton is teaching me . . ." he raised his chin a notch. "It's because I asked him to. It was my surprise for you."

She waved her hand in an arc that encompassed the entire room. "Well, I certainly am surprised."

"Since you know this much, you might as well know the rest, Mum."

"There's *more*?"

"I also asked Mr. Stanton to instruct me in fencing and horseback riding. We had our first riding lesson yesterday, and it went very well." He turned to Andrew. "Didn't it go very well?"

"Yes indeed," Andrew confirmed.

All the color drained from her face as she stared at Andrew. "Ride? Are you mad? What if he fell from the saddle?"

"What if *you* fell from the saddle?" Andrew countered. "Or me? Or Philip? Should none of us ride?"

A frown bunched her brows, and she turned to Spencer, taking in his glowing, hopeful expression. "Did you . . . enjoy the lesson?"

"Very much. Oh, I was nervous at first, but I caught on quickly, and my nervousness fled."

"He's an extremely bright lad, Lady Catherine."

"See there, Mum? Yesterday's riding lesson was fine, and today's pugilism lesson was perfectly safe as well," Spencer said in a rush. He shuffled forward and laid a comforting hand on her arm. "Mr. Stanton made certain of it. And don't worry. I'm not attempting to become the best pugilist in England. Just the best *I* can be. So that if anyone ever tries to hurt you, I can knock them onto their bottom, as I did Mr. Stanton."

She blinked several times. "That's very sweet, darling. And terribly chivalrous. But—"

"Please don't ask me to stop, Mum. I'm liking it very much."

"I . . . see." She drew a deep breath. "Why don't you return to the house and give me a few moments to discuss this with Mr. Stanton?"

Spencer sent a worried, hopeful look at Andrew, and Andrew gave him an encouraging nod.

"May I go to the springs instead of the house, Mum?"

"Yes, of course."

Spencer came to Andrew, and whispered, "You'll meet me for our lesson?"

Andrew nodded. He and Catherine stood in silence to the sound of Spencer's shuffling steps.

When the footfalls faded into silence, she said, "Please explain yourself. What were you thinking to encourage Spencer with this dangerous endeavor?"

Andrew took a deep breath, then related the conversation he'd had with Spencer on the afternoon they'd arrived in Little Longstone. "Spencer is entering manhood," he concluded. "He wants and needs to feel he can do some of the things other young men his age can do. He seemed so lost, floundering, and very unsure of himself. I only wanted to try to give him some measure of encouragement and confidence in himself—the same sort of encouragement I was given as a boy."

She said nothing for several seconds, and Andrew was relieved to see that she no longer appeared quite so angry. "I appreciate your kindness, Mr. Stanton—"

"Andrew."

She blushed. "Andrew. However—"

"It is not a matter of kindness, Catherine. It is a question of caring. Spencer has . . . touched my heart. He reminds me very much of someone I knew in America, and I would like to help him if I can." He reached out and clasped her hands. "You have my word that I would never do anything to place him in danger."

Her gaze searched his. "Naturally I don't think you would intentionally hurt him, but something like this . . ." Her gaze panned around the room, then returned to his. "I cannot help but worry. How can you promise he won't be hurt?"

"He—or anyone else for that matter—could suffer an injury anywhere. At any time."

"What you say is true, but let us be realistic. Because of his awkward gait, the chances of Spencer hurting himself are greater than someone who can walk normally."

"I agree, which is merely one more reason why I think these lessons in basic pugilism are a good idea. They will strengthen him. Help him gain balance. And that in turn will boost his confidence in himself. You could see how pleased he was with himself when he flattened me."

"Yes. However, I think you helped him a bit there. And please do not forget how he'd almost fallen just before that."

"Catherine, I'm not going to lie to you. He'd almost fallen a dozen times before you arrived." Her eyes widened, and her cheeks paled. "But I steadied him each time. And each time, more minutes passed before he lost his balance again. He improved rapidly, and only after one lesson. Just as he did yesterday with the riding."

"I actually tried to interest Spencer in learning to ride when he was younger. But he never wanted to try. Believing that the size of the horses frightened him, I purchased Aphrodite as a pony, but Spencer was not interested. Just as I did with venturing off the estate grounds, I finally stopped asking." Her eyes met his, and his heart performed its familiar Catherine-induced roll. "Your presence here seems to have the effect of making my son wish to expand his horizons and try new things."

"Does that upset you?"

She considered for several seconds, then said, "No, but I must admit that the cautious mother in me would have preferred that Spencer ask for lessons in backgammon rather than riding, pugilism, and fencing."

Andrew smiled. "Believe me, the boy does not need any lessons on how to play backgammon."

"But the nurturing mother in me wants my son to have as normal and full a life as possible. When I think of the added mobility learning to ride will afford him . . . I'm thrilled for him." She blew out a long breath. "I cannot allow my fears to dampen his enthusiasm and his budding independence. But even as I say that, I'll worry and be concerned for his safety. I'm entrusting his safety to you, Andrew."

He brought her hands to his mouth and touched his lips to her fingertips, enjoying the way her breath caught at the gesture. "I am honored and humbled by your faith in me, as I know how important Spencer is to you. I swear your trust is not misplaced. Now, has this matter been settled?"

"Yes, I suppose it has. But be warned: I'll be keeping my eye on you."

He smiled. "How delightful, as I relish having your eye upon me. A moment ago you said that my presence here seems to have the effect of making your son wish to expand his horizons and try new things. Does my presence perchance have the same effect on his mother?"

His heart skipped at the unmistakable flare of awareness in her eyes. "What do you mean?"

"I mean I'd like to invite you to try something new with me. I've never taken a moonlight stroll through an English country garden. Would you care to join me tonight?"

"You've a sudden yen to smell roses under the cover of darkness?"

"No. I've a long-standing yen to walk with you in a garden under the cover of darkness." He very much enjoyed the way her eyes flickered at his admission. "If we were in London, I'd invite you to Vauxhall. Since we are in Little Longstone, I am forced to improvise." He gave in to the overwhelming urge and trailed his fingertips over her satiny cheek. "Will you join me?"

She said nothing as her gaze searched his, and his heart pounded so loud he swore she had to hear it. He was asking for more than a simple walk. They both knew it. But surely she'd thought about last night's conversation. He'd thought of little else. Surely she'd reached some sort of conclusion. Yet with each passing second of silence his hopes faded, as he could see she was still wrestling with her decision.

Then, finally, she cleared her throat. "Yes, Andrew. I will join you."

He supposed that in the history of mankind sweeter words might have possibly been spoken, but he'd be damned if could imagine what those words might have been.

Catherine spent the entire evening in a mood of unprecedented heightened awareness that pushed her toward a state of near giddiness. Everything seemed sharper, clearer, all her senses fully engaged. She could not recall a time when mutton had tasted so savory, carrots more delicious, or wine more heady. With her every movement, her aqua muslin gown brushed against her uncommonly sensitive skin, skipping tingles along her nerve endings. The flickering pale tapers in the silver candelabra glowed brighter, the sound of Spencer's laughter delighted her more, and the deep timbre of Andrew's voice shivered thrills of anticipation down her spine.

Had any man ever looked so enticing? So tempting? The muted candlelight highlighted his dark good looks, casting his face in an intriguing array of shadows that lured her gaze again and again. Dressed in a dark blue jacket, snowy shirt, and fawn breeches, he looked masculine, imposing, and utterly delicious.

Every look that passed between them inflamed her, heating her skin. Every smile he gave her fluttered excitement to her heart. She knew that her upcoming moonlight stroll with Andrew was responsible for a good portion of her giddiness, but the rest of it was due to the course of action she'd mapped out for herself. She was resolute. She knew what she wanted. And after several hours of mulling over her options this afternoon, she'd finally figured out how to get it. Now she just hoped that she could stand the anticipation until she could put her plan into action.

After dinner the three of them retired to the drawing room, where she watched Andrew and Spencer play a spirited, highly competitive game of backgammon.

"This is your last roll, Mr. Stanton," Spencer chortled, rubbing his hands together with glee. "You are about to be defeated."

"Perhaps. But if I roll a double six, I win."

Spencer gave a derisive snort. "What are the chances of that?"

Andrew smiled. "One in thirty-six."

"Not very good odds."

"They could be worse."

Andrew rolled the dice onto the board. Catherine stared in amazement at the pair of sixes.

Spencer's eyes goggled, then he laughed. "Blimey. I've never seen such luck, have you, Mum?"

"No," Catherine said with a laugh. "Mr. Stanton is indeed very lucky." Her gaze shifted to Andrew, and when their eyes met, he smiled.

"Yes, I am indeed a very lucky man."

His smile wrapped around her like a warm cloak, surrounding her in an aura of pleasurable heat.

Spencer rose, then extended his hand. "Excellent job. But I'll emerge victorious when next we play."

Andrew stood and solemnly shook his hand. "I shall look forward to the challenge."

Spencer yawned, then shot Catherine a sheepish look. "I'm tired," he admitted.

"You had a busy day." She sent Andrew an arch, sideways look. "What with knocking Mr. Stanton on his bottom and all."

Spencer chuckled, then stifled another yawn. "I think I'd like to go to bed. I need to rest up for tomorrow's riding and pugilism lessons."

Catherine ignored the brick of worry that landed in her stomach at the thought of those lessons. "All right, darling. Do you want me to help you with the stairs?"

"No, thank you. I can do it myself."

Catherine forced herself to nod and smile. And accept but yet another step in her son's need for self-reliance. "Sleep well."

"I always do." He kissed Catherine's cheek, shook Andrew's hand, then quit the room, closing the door behind him with a quiet click.

Andrew's gaze met hers, and his eyes were filled with

quiet understanding. "The closer to adulthood we get," he said, "the more we want to do things for ourselves."

"I know. Deep down, I'm very proud of his emerging independence, but there's also that part of me that misses the little boy who needed me for everything."

"He'll always need you, Catherine. Not in the same way he did when he was a baby, of course, but the need for your love and support will always be there."

"Yes, I suppose that's true. And I'm glad." She smiled. "Being needed is a very nice feeling."

"It is indeed."

Something in the way he said the words made her suddenly wonder if they were still talking about Spencer. Before she could decide, he asked, "Would you like to take our stroll? Or . . ." He indicated the backgammon board with a tilt of his head. "Perhaps you'd first prefer to receive a trouncing, er, engage in a game of chance?"

She raised her brows. "With a man who has already demonstrated that he can toss double sixes at will? Thank you, but no."

He inclined his head before extending his elbow with a courtly flourish. "Then to the gardens we go."

Catherine rested her hand very properly on the crook of his elbow, knowing that if she had her way, it was the last proper gesture she would make for the remainder of the evening.

They exited the house through the French windows leading to the terrace. They walked slowly across the flagstones, and Catherine drew a deep breath, absorbing the welcome cool air on her heated skin and the comforting outdoor scents of grass, leaves, and flowers, mixed with the intriguing, subtle hint of sandalwood that belonged to Andrew. The full moon glowed in the dark sky, a gleaming pearl against black velvet, blanketing the landscape with a shimmering silvery illumination.

After walking down the curved steps, they headed toward the garden. The path branched off in several directions, but Catherine veered toward the right.

"Would you mind if we took the left fork?" Andrew asked. "There's something I want to show you."

A frown pulled down her brows at this cog in the wheel of her perfectly laid plans. "What is it?"

"You'll see when we get there."

Confound it, the man vexed her at every crossroads—literally, in this case. There was nothing to the left except a few marble statues, while to the right was the gazebo. And the gazebo was where she intended to lure him. She wanted to insist they walk to the right, indeed she wanted to *gallop* to the blasted gazebo, but in light of his polite request, she couldn't think of a way to deny him without appearing churlish. Or blurting out the truth of her plans.

"Very well," she agreed, hoping she did not sound as disgruntled as she felt. Humph. Well, she'd politely stare at whatever this thing was he wanted to show her, then turn him around. Or she could just continue him along the same path, which would eventually curve around and lead to the back of the gazebo, albeit by a more circuitous route.

Anxious to get on with things, she started down the left path, barely resisting the urge to grab his sleeve and tug him along.

"Do you normally walk so fast, Catherine?" he asked, his voice laced with amusement.

"Do you normally walk so slow?"

"Well, this *is* supposed to be a stroll. Sadly, I did not remember to bring a dictionary, and it appears we are once again in need of one. You seem to have confused the meaning of *stroll* with that of *sprint*."

"I do not require a dictionary. I am simply not a woman who likes to dawdle."

"Ah. An admirable quality," he said, slowing his steps even more. *Good Lord, snails moved more quickly than this.* "However, there are certain things that *should* be dawdled over."

"Such as?" She wasn't particularly interested, but perhaps if she kept him talking, he'd be distracted enough to move along a little faster.

"The sound of a night breeze rustling the leaves. The lingering scent of the day's blooms . . ."

She barely suppressed a sigh of impatience. Heaven help her, here he was, waxing poetic about breezes and blooms, while she grew more frustrated by the minute. Could the man not see that she was dying to be held in his arms and kissed until her knees turned to mush?

Ohhh, she inwardly fumed. What sort of miserable luck had fallen upon her to curse her with an attraction to a man who was clearly as thick as fog? And who moved no faster than a sleeping turtle?

". . . scent of a woman's neck."

That phrase yanked her from her brown study with a jerk. Scent of a woman's neck? That sounded . . . interesting. Promising. Damnation, what had she missed? Before she could ask him, he paused, then stepped around to face her. She took note of their surroundings and realized they stood in her favorite spot in the garden, a small, secluded semicircle she fondly referred to as Angel's Smile. He must have stumbled upon it accidentally, as it was hidden from the main path by tall hedges. A casual walker would pass it by unless they knew to look for it.

"This is your favorite part of the garden," he said.

Her brows shot upwards. "How did you know that?"

"Fritzborne told me."

"Indeed? I did not know you two were so . . . well acquainted."

"We shared a lengthy chat the day I arrived. We also talked quite a bit while we cleared the debris from the room in the stables where I set up the pugilist's ring, after which he offered me a glass of his whiskey. He's a good man. Drinks absolutely vile whiskey, but a good man just the same."

"You drank whiskey with my stable man?" She tried to imagine Bertrand ever doing something like that and utterly failed.

"I did. And the way that liquor tasted, I'm not sure I'd be able to repeat the task." He smiled, and his teeth gleamed white in the moonlight. "Actually, it was only the first sip that hurt. After that, my insides turned numb."

"And while you were drinking this whiskey, he just happened to mention that this is my favorite part of the garden."

"It was actually while we exercised the horses that first day. I asked him to describe your favorite part of the garden. He told me it was a place you called Angel's Smile and that it was a replica of your mother's favorite spot in *her* garden."

She nodded, slightly bemused. "Fritzborne planted the hedges for me, and I did all the flowers—mostly roses, asters, delphiniums, and lilies, as those were Mother's favorites." She looked around her, the peace she always felt in this spot infusing her. "You need to see it during the day to appreciate the beauty and serenity. The way the sun shines through those trees," she said, pointing to a copse of towering elms about twenty feet away, "bathes this little nook with a semicircle of light that looks like—"

"An angel's smile."

"Yes. Before her death, my mother and I spent many happy hours together in the gardens. When I'm here, I feel as if she's with me, smiling down at me from heaven." Feeling suddenly embarrassed by her ramblings, she said, "It's just silly whimsy."

He gently clasped her hands and entwined their fingers, a gesture that simultaneously comforted and excited her. "It's not silly, Catherine. It's important to have places that mean something to us. Places where we can go to settle our thoughts. Find peace. Relive our favorite memories. Or just enjoy a bit of quiet."

"You must have such a place of your own, to understand it so well."

"I've had many during my travels."

"Have you one in England?"

"I do." He smiled. "When next you travel to London, I'll show you my favorite bench in Hyde Park, and my favorite alcove in the British Museum."

She returned his smile and firmly ignored her inner voice, which coughed to life to remind her that she had no intention of traveling to London in the foreseeable future. "Why did you ask Fritzborne about my favorite part of the garden?"

"Because I needed to know for your surprise."

"*Another* surprise? I'm not certain how many more surprises I'm capable of experiencing today."

"Have no fear. Come."

He released her one hand, then, still holding the other in his warm grip, he led her toward the copse of elms. Curious, she looked around, but did not see anything out of the ordinary. When he stopped near the tallest tree, however, the scent of freshly dug dirt tickled her nose, and she looked down. And stilled.

There, in the pale glow of the moonlight, stretched an unfamiliar flower bed filled with a profusion of plants of various sizes surrounding the two outermost trees. She instantly recognized the familiar foliage, and her breath caught. "What is that?"

"Do you not recognize the plant? It is—"

"*Dicentra spectabilis*," she whispered. "Yes, I know."

"You said the bleeding heart was your favorite. I noticed a number of bleeding hearts scattered about your garden, but not a single large grouping."

As if in a daze, she released his hand and crouched down to run her finger gently over a delicate row of tiny, perfectly shaped red-and-white hanging blooms. "You did all this?"

"Well, I cannot take all the credit. I enlisted Fritzborne's and Spencer's help."

"They know of this?"

"Yes. Spencer helped me pick out the plants when we visited the village. Fritzborne hid them in the stables, then transported them here this afternoon. Spencer and I planted them." He chuckled. "I think keeping this a surprise nearly killed the lad."

"Yes, I imagine it did." She pulled her gaze away from the stun-inducing wonder of the flower bed and looked up at him over her shoulder. "This is why you wanted to go to the village? To purchase these?"

"Among other things, yes."

She moved to rise, and he immediately extended his hand to assist her. She slipped her hand into his, absorbing the warm, callused texture of his palm as it surrounded hers. When she once again stood facing him, she did not release his hand.

"Other things?" she repeated, her heart thumping in slow, hard beats. "Don't tell me there are more surprises."

He smiled. "All right. I won't tell you that." He brushed an errant curl from her forehead, and her hard-thumping heart skipped a beat at the intimate gesture.

"I cannot believe that the small flower shop in the village had such an abundance of plants available," she said.

"Actually they had only a few. When I told the shopkeeper I wanted more, he suggested some of the village residents might be willing to sell their plants. So Spencer and I proceeded to knock on doors." He laughed. "I think we met nearly everyone in the village in our quest for bleeding hearts."

She could only stare. "You're saying you went to the homes of people you didn't know to ask them if you could purchase plants from their gardens?"

"That sums it up very well. Everyone was quite happy to allow Spencer and me to dig up their plants for 'Lady Catherine's surprise.' "

Heavens, there had to be at least three dozen plants surrounding the elms. "You went to a great deal of trouble."

"I wouldn't call doing something for you trouble."

Her gaze drifted downward again, and at the sight of what he'd done for her, a rush of tenderness swamped her, swelling her throat with emotion, and pushing moist heat behind her eyes. Returning her gaze to his, she squeezed his hand and spoke the simple truth, "No man has ever done such a lovely, thoughtful thing for me." *And romantic*, her inner voice chimed in with a feminine sigh. *You forgot to add romantic*.

He raised their joined hands to his lips and pressed a kiss to the sensitive skin inside her wrist. "I did tell you I enjoy being first."

The feel of his mouth on her skin, the quiet words breathing heat, licked tiny trails of fire up her arm. He then lowered her hand to press it against his chest, where his heart thumped strong and fast against her palm. Almost as strong and fast as her heart was beating. Because of the way he was looking at her. How close he stood. And because of not only *what* he'd done, but the *way* he'd done it.

"The flowers are even more special because you included Spencer in your surprise," she said softly. "Thank you."

"You're welcome."

To her mortification the moisture building up behind her eyes overflowed, and a pair of tears leaked from her eyes.

His eyes widened with a look that could only be described as masculine panic. "You're crying."

He sounded so horrified and accusatory, the sob that was caught in her throat bubbled forth as a laugh. "I'm not."

"Then what do you call *this?*" He caught one tear on the tip of his finger while his other hand frantically patted his pockets, presumably for a handkerchief.

Now amused—thank goodness—she slipped her own lace hanky from her long sleeve and dabbed at her eyes.

"Are you still crying?"

"I was *not* crying."

"Again we require the dictionary." He reached out and took the handkerchief from her, then gently dabbed at her cheeks. When he finished, he tilted his head first left, then right, peering at her closely. "It appears you've stopped."

"I had not started. I'd simply . . . sprung a freakish leak of the eyeballs. Today's Modern Woman does not cry when a man brings her flowers. Heavens, if that were the case, I'd have been in a state of constant hysterics for the past fortnight."

She said the words in a teasing manner, but the instant

they left her lips, she realized that these were not just any flowers. Moreover, it was becoming alarmingly clear that the man standing in front of her was not just any man.

He handed her back her handkerchief, which she tucked up her sleeve. "Well, consider me relieved that your, er, freakish eyeball leak has corrected itself."

He did indeed look relieved, and she had to bite back a smile. Even in the aftermath of the shooting, he'd remained calm and collected. Yet the sight of feminine tears clearly undid the man, a trait she found utterly endearing.

Dear God. She simply did *not* want to find something *endearing* about him. Bad enough she already found him painfully attractive. *Speaking of which*, her inner voice interjected, *'tis well past the time to put your plan into action.*

Angel's Smile would do just as nicely as the gazebo, and she did not want to wait any longer for him to hold her. Kiss her. Which, for some reason she could not fathom, he had yet to do. She wanted to grab him by the shoulders, shake him, and demand to know what the bloody blazes he was waiting for. Well, it was simply time to take matters into her own hands.

Giving him what she hoped passed for a carefree, yet with a hint of alluring smile, she said, "Your generosity and thoughtfulness makes me feel all the more guilty about the wager we made."

"Wager?"

"Regarding you reading *A Ladies' Guide*."

His confused expression cleared. "Ah, yes. That wager. Why do you feel guilty about it?"

"When we made the wager, we'd agreed upon a time of three weeks. Since then we've mutually decided that you'll only be in Little Longstone for one week. I'm afraid that given the time constraints and the fact that it would prove nearly impossible for you to secure a copy of the *Guide* here, I think we need to discuss terms."

His expression turned thoughtful, and taking two steps backward, he leaned his back against the thick trunk of the elm behind him and studied her. "If it would be nearly impossible for me to secure a copy of the *Guide* here in Little Longstone in one week's time, I don't see how I would have been able to accomplish the task in three weeks. Or three months for that matter. Which makes me wonder if perhaps I was duped."

"Not at all. With three weeks at your disposal, you would have had sufficient time to send an order to a London bookstore and have had a copy delivered to you here. If you'd been so inclined."

"Ah. But now that I only have a week—"

"I fear that is no longer a viable option," she said, injecting just the right note of regret in her voice. However, her conscience made her ask, "If you still had the three weeks' time, would you have sent an order to London?"

"No."

It was all Catherine could do to keep her lips from curving into a triumphant smile. Perfect. He'd swallowed her bait without a hitch. Now all she had to do was reel him in.

"I thought not," she said, keeping her expression serious, "which means that—"

"Our wager is void." He nodded. "Yes, I suppose you're right."

She stared at him. "*Void?* That is not what I was going to say at all."

"Oh? What were you going to say?"

"That I was the winner."

His brows shot upward, and he folded his arms across his chest. "How did you arrive at that conclusion?"

"You just admitted that you would not have made arrangements to secure a copy of *A Ladies' Guide* from London, regardless of the length of your stay in Little Longstone. You will recall that in order for you to win the wager, you had to read the *Guide*, then engage in a discussion about it, *which* you cannot do if you do not have a copy, *which* you cannot secure without making special arrangements, *which* by your own admission you've no plan to do, *which*, even if you did plan to do, you no longer have the time to do." She finished her speech with a flourishing wave of her hand and sucked in a much-needed breath. Then she offered him her sweetest smile. "Therefore, that means I am the winner."

He remained silent for several seconds, studying her with a slightly bemused expression that delighted her. Excellent. She'd obviously thrown him off-balance. Her strategy was working brilliantly. Now for the final step . . .

"Do you concede?" she asked.

"It would appear I have little choice."

Her heart leapt in anticipation. "As I'm sure you recall, the winner is entitled to a boon of their choosing."

"Ah, yes. Now that you mention it, I do recall that." He chuckled. "So *that* is why you wanted me to concede rather than call our wager void. I suppose I'll be spending tomorrow polishing the silver."

She took one step closer to him. "No."

"Weeding the roses?"

Another step closer. "No."

"Mucking out the stalls?"

Another step. Now only an arm's length separated them. Her heart was beating so hard she felt the pounding in her ears. "No."

His watchful gaze held hers for what felt like an eternity, but was surely no more than ten seconds. Finally, he said in a husky voice, "Then perhaps you should tell me what you *do* want, Catherine."

Carpe diem, her inner voice prodded. Summoning all her courage, Catherine took one more step forward. Her body brushed against his, and his masculine scent filled her head. Encouraged by his sharp intake of breath, she placed her palms against his chest and looked directly into his eyes.

"I want you to make love to me."

Chapter 14

Today's Modern Woman should strive to gain a level of sexual expertise. The woman who is well-versed in the delights of the bedchamber can be confident that her lover will not lose interest and seek companionship elsewhere.

A Ladies' Guide to the Pursuit of Personal Happiness and Intimate Fulfillment
by Charles Brightmore

Andrew remained perfectly still, allowing his mind and body to absorb fully the stunning impact of her words and actions. Catherine standing before him, desire shimmering in her eyes, her hands splayed against his chest, her lush body leaning against his. The smoky timbre of her voice when she whispered that heart-stopping sentence. *I want you to make love to me.*

For as many times as he'd fantasized about her saying those words, nothing prepared him for the reality. His heart slapped so hard against his ribs, it wouldn't have surprised him if she'd said, *what on earth is that drumming sound?*

Yet, beneath the layers of elation, desire, want, and

need, flickered a single, tiny candle of discontent. Yes, he desperately wanted to make love to her, but he wanted a great deal more than that. Given her aversion to marriage, and her belief in the precepts put forth in *A Ladies' Guide*, one of which encouraged "women of a certain age" not to remain celibate, she clearly only wanted an affair. If he refused her, would she turn to someone else? The mere thought of her asking another man to make love to her clenched his jaw.

Not that he had any intention of refusing her.

She shifted against him, and his entire body tightened. Yes, he wanted much more from her, but for now, this was enough.

Uncertainty flickered in her eyes, and he realized that he'd remained silent too long. That she thought his silence meant he planned to refuse her. Words and feelings he'd suppressed for what felt like an eternity welled up, clogging his throat, rendering him unable to speak. But it mattered not as he was incapable of forming a coherent sentence. Only one word echoed through his mind, a mantra of all he wanted. All he'd ever wanted from the moment he'd laid eyes on her. *Catherine. Catherine. Catherine.*

She clearly read the inferno of desire he knew burned in his gaze because the uncertainty vanished from her eyes, and her lips parted. Wrapping one arm around her waist, he drew her fully against him while he ran his other hand up her back until his fingers sifted into her soft, upswept hair. He lowered his head as she rose up on her toes.

The instant their lips met, he was lost. In the sweet seductive taste of her. In the incredible feel of her pressing against him. In the delicate floral scent of her. The delicious friction of her tongue rubbing against his. The erotic sound of her moan of pleasure.

Needs and wants that had gone unanswered, unfulfilled

for so long, clawed him like sharp talons. Spreading his legs, he gathered her closer, pressing her into the V between his thighs. His erection strained against his tight breeches, and he cursed the barrier of the clothing between them. Another low moan rumbled in her throat, and she rubbed herself against him, stripping away another layer of his rapidly vanishing control.

While his lips and tongue explored all the velvety delights of her mouth, one of his hands came forward to palm her breast while his other hand slid down her back to cup her rounded bottom. She gasped, and her head fell limply back, presenting him with the delicate, vulnerable curve of her neck, a delicacy he instantly took advantage of.

Catherine strained closer, thrilling to the feel of his hard, aroused body. Closing her eyes, she clutched his broad shoulders in an effort to remain upright against the storm of sensations battering her. His lips and tongue blazed a trail of fire down her neck, fanning the flames already burning her. One strong hand kneaded her breast through the material of her gown, tightening her nipple and shooting shards of sharp want down to her womb, while his other hand massaged her buttocks with a slow, hypnotic motion that forced a long, need-filled moan from her throat. The feminine flesh between her legs felt swollen and heavy and moist, and a mounting desperation edged through her.

He lifted his head, and a groan of protest vibrated in her throat.

"Not here," he whispered, his breathing as ragged as hers. "Not like this."

Her heart tripped over itself at the naked hunger in his eyes. At the waves of desire all but emanating from him. He looked as if he wanted to devour her, and everything feminine in her thrilled at the thought.

"You deserve more than a quick grope against a tree, Catherine."

God help her, but a quick grope against the tree—indeed anything to relieve the sweet ache imprisoning her—sounded like heaven. But he was right. This was not the place.

She was about to grasp his hand and lead him toward the gazebo, when *he* grasped *her* hand, and headed in that direction.

"Come with me," he said, his voice an aroused growl. She fell into step beside him, excitement and anticipation coursing through her. "Where are we going?"

"The gazebo. It's closer than the house. And more private."

"How do you know about the gazebo?"

"I came across it while riding Aphrodite."

She was glad the darkness cloaked the satisfied grin curving her lips. Not only would they end up at the gazebo, but he would think it had been his own clever idea. Wouldn't he be pleased to discover when they arrived that the enclosed structure wasn't completely empty—it contained the supplies she'd smuggled out of the house and left there earlier this afternoon. She'd longed to bring more, to turn the space into a cozy haven, but hadn't dared risk anyone discovering her leaving the house carrying more than a basket. That would have led to questions she did not want to answer. After all, she could not very well say that she was preparing the gazebo for a tryst. And while the setting was admittedly rustic, according to *A Ladies' Guide* she'd have all she needed for a memorable night—a cozy quilt, a bottle of wine, a wedge of cheese, and . . . herself and Andrew.

They rounded a corner in the path, and the gazebo came into view. Nestled in a small clearing, the octagonal structure with its domed roof gleamed white in the moonlight, the aged, peeling paint not discernible from a distance. She'd always wanted to refurbish the gazebo, but somehow hadn't found the time.

Andrew's footsteps slowed as they approached the structure, and she gave thanks for the sturdy wooden shutters that covered the floor-to-ceiling French windows comprising the gazebo's walls, as they would provide an intimate cocoon of privacy for them.

A cloud obscured the moon, and Catherine looked down, concentrating on her feet so as not to trip over a branch or stone. Andrew's hand tightened on hers, a wordless promise that he wouldn't allow her to fall.

When they reached the door, he turned the brass knob and slowly pushed the heavy oak panel inward. "The door squeaks horribly . . ." she began, but her words trailed off into nothingness. The door did not squeak at all as it opened wider to reveal the inside of the gazebo.

Catherine gasped, and, clasping her hands to her chest, gaped in wonder. The cozy interior was gently illuminated with the flickering light from a half dozen hurricane lamps set in a wide semicircle around the perimeter of the floor. She inhaled, breathing in the delicate scent of flowers, and saw that a blanket of rose petals was strewn across the wood floor, lending beauty and fragrance to the small room.

The coverlet she'd smuggled from the house was arranged in the center of the otherwise bare room. Two enormous pillows, one maroon, the other dark blue, rested on one end of the cover. Off to the side sat a silver tray holding a bottle of wine, two goblets, a bowl of strawberries, and the wedge of cheese she'd pilfered from the kitchen.

As if in a trance, she entered the room and turned in a slow circle. A soft click echoed behind her, which she recognized as the door closing. Then she heard Andrew step up behind her. Strong arms encircled her waist from behind, gently hugging him to her. She laid her hands on top of his and drank in the seductive feel of him surrounding her, enthralled and touched by the romantic hideaway he'd created.

"When did you do this?" she asked in a hushed voice, afraid to speak too loudly lest she break the magical atmosphere.

"Just before dinner." His lips brushed her temple as he spoke, his warm breath gliding over her ear, shivering a delighted tingle down her spine. "I was very surprised—and pleased—to find the basket of items you'd obviously left. Are *you* pleased?"

Her eyes slid closed and she breathed out a lengthy, feminine sigh. Then she turned in his arms and cradled his smoothly shaven cheeks between her palms.

"You went to a great deal of time, effort, and expense to plant my favorite flowers, and to create a private, romantic place for us. Yes, Andrew. I am pleased. And touched. And flattered. I started out this evening hoping to seduce *you*, yet here I find myself thoroughly seduced."

"I started out this evening hoping to *court* you, yet here I find myself thoroughly seduced."

Heat rippled down to her toes. "We started out with different objectives, yet here we are, with the same results. Although I wonder how that can be as I've yet to try to seduce you."

He turned his head and pressed a heated kiss against her palm. "If that is so, then God help me should you put a bit of effort into it. But fear not. You've thoroughly succeeded without expending any effort."

"Indeed? How? What have I done?" Lord knows she wanted to know so that she could do it again.

With his gaze steady on hers, he clasped her hand, pressed another kiss against her palm, then touched his tongue to the spot. Her breath caught, and her eyes widened.

"That," he whispered. "The way you respond to my touch. The way you breathe in, and the heat that flares in your eyes. Very seductive. And this . . ." He drew her into his arms then leaned forward and flicked his tongue over her earlobe. A shudder ran through her. ". . . the way you tremble when you find something pleasurable. And this . . ." His lips skimmed across her jaw, before his mouth settled on hers for a soft, teasing kiss that had her lifting her face for more. ". . . the way your mouth feels against mine. The way you want more, just as I do."

He reached up and slowly pulled the pins from her hair. "The way your hair feels sifting through my fingers." Catherine felt her hair fall loose from its chignon and tumble down her back and over her shoulders. After gathering a handful of long, loose curls in his hand, he buried his face in the strands. "The scent of flowers that clings to your hair and skin. Ah, yes, then there is your skin . . ."

He brushed her hair over her shoulder, then trailed his fingertips slowly down her neck. "The pale perfection. The velvet texture. The alluring fragrance . . . that teasing hint of floral that makes me want to remain no more than an inch away from you so as not to draw a single breath that isn't scented with you." He lowered his head and brushed his mouth over the sensitive juncture where her neck and shoulder met. "Pure seduction."

Her fingers clenched against his jacket, and a low rumble of pleasure trembled in her throat. "That sound you make when you're aroused," he said, his words vibrating against her skin, "is one of the most seductive things I've ever heard."

"One of?" she asked in a breathless voice she barely recognized. "What is the *most* seductive thing you've ever heard?"

He lifted his head and stared directly into her eyes. "Your voice. Asking me to make love to you."

Warmth filled her cheeks. "I'd never said those words before."

"Just one more of the countless ways you seduce me, Catherine. You know how I like being first."

"Then you'd best prepare yourself, because I've a feeling I'm going to experience many more firsts tonight."

"As will I."

Her eyes widened slightly. "You mean you've never—?"

"No, I'm not saying I've never been with a woman, although it has been . . . a while. But I've never been with anyone I wanted this much. Or anyone whom I wanted to please more. Or anyone who pleased me so very much."

Catherine swallowed, certain that her hold on his shoulders was the only thing keeping her from slithering to the floor in a quivering heap. "I hope I please you, Andrew. I want to, but—"

He silenced her by touching his fingers to her lips. "You will, Catherine. Don't doubt it for even a second."

His expression made it clear he believed it, but a spate of self-doubt and insecurity suddenly assailed her, and before she could stop herself, she blurted out the painful truth. "I'm afraid I cannot help it. My husband found me . . . less than enthralling. He never touched me after Spencer was born. In spite of the fact that I was married for a decade and bore a child, I fear I'm woefully inexperienced." Her gaze searched his. "How can you be so sure I'll please you?"

"As I've told you, there are just some things that we *know*, Catherine. You and I are going to make beautiful love together. As for your inexperience . . ." He took one step back, then spread his arms. "Practice all you wish. Consider me at your disposal."

Catherine's heart pounded at the husky-voiced invitation, so ripe with sensual possibilities.

"Don't be shy," he said softly. "Or embarrassed. It's just us, Catherine. The only other person in this room besides you is a man who wants nothing more than to grant your every wish and to please you. Tell me how to do that. Tell me what you want."

Words from *A Ladies' Guide* popped into her mind. *Should Today's Modern Woman ever be fortunate enough to be asked "What do you want?" hopefully she will answer truthfully.*

She licked her lips, then allowed her gaze to wander slowly down, then up his long, muscular length. When their eyes again met, she spoke the simple truth. "You make me want so many things, I'm not certain where to begin."

"Why don't I start by removing my jacket?"

She watched him shrug the dark blue material from his shoulders, and suddenly she knew exactly where to begin. Stepping forward, she grasped his cuff. "I want to do it."

He stood immobile, watching her, and for the first time in her life, Catherine removed an article of clothing from a man. The simple act of slowly slipping the jacket down his arms intoxicated her. When she finished, she held the garment, still warm from his body, against her chest. Her eyes slid closed, and she bent her head to breathe him in. "You smell delicious," she murmured on a sigh. "Sandalwood mixed with something else I can't name. But it's a clean, masculine scent that belongs to you alone."

Andrew stood perfectly still, spellbound by her words and the sight of her cradling his jacket against her. God knows he'd never been more sincere than when he told her he wanted only to please her, but he didn't have a bloody prayer of surviving the rest of the night if she brought him to his knees just by holding his damn jacket.

Her curious gaze traveled again down his body, and he had to clench his hands to keep from reaching for her. "You worry about your ability to please me," he said in a tight voice, "yet you can seduce me with a single look."

Her gaze jumped back up to meet his, and he clearly read the flare of confidence that lit her eyes. After carefully setting his jacket on the floor beside her, she brushed her fingertips over his loosely knotted cravat. "I want to undress you," she whispered.

He swallowed and attempted a half smile, but wasn't at all certain he succeeded. "I'm all yours."

"I'm not certain how all these garments work."

Giving in to the overwhelming need to touch her, he traced his fingertip over her cheekbone. "Not to worry. I'll help you."

She applied herself to his cravat, and he stood in an agony of want, warring between his body's need simply to shove aside their clothing and make fierce love to her *now*, and watching, feeling the stunning miracle of her removing his clothes. The blooming confidence and wonder in her eyes as she dispensed with his cravat, then slowly unfastened his shirt. When she reached his waist, he pulled his shirt free of the confines of his breeches, then held his breath.

She slowly separated the linen, then placed her hands on his chest. Heat arrowed through him, and he pulled in a quick breath. An expression of utterly feminine delight crossed her features, and she slowly dragged her hands downward. He wanted to watch her, but his eyes slid closed of their own volition, and a growl of pure pleasure escaped him as he memorized the intense sensation of her touching him.

"Do you like that?" she whispered, her fingertips grazing his nipples.

"God, yes."

Her hands slipped down over his abdomen, and his muscles contracted. "You like that as well?"

"Yes." The word was a raw rasp. He forced his eyes open to watch her, her hands growing bolder with each pass over his skin. Everywhere she touched felt as if she'd scorched him. Need roared through him, and his erection jerked inside his tight breeches. After gliding her hands back up his chest, she pushed his shirt off his shoulders and down his arms. He pulled his hands free and dropped the garment to the floor.

She ran her hands over his bare shoulders, then down his back, and he gritted his teeth against the pleasure. "You're very strong," she said, her warm breath caressing his chest.

A shudder shook him. He felt anything but strong. His insides were shaking, and his knees were . . . gone.

She slid her arms around his waist, then stepped forward to rest her head against his chest. "Your heart is beating almost as fast as mine, Andrew."

Before he could reply, she looked up at him with solemn eyes. "I want you to undress me."

Since he wanted that more than he wanted to draw his next breath, he didn't hesitate. "Turn around."

Standing behind her, he combed his fingers through her long, lustrous chestnut locks, brushing the strands over her shoulder to expose her pale nape. Leaning forward, he pressed his lips to that soft, fragrant bit of skin that had haunted a thousand dreams and countless waking moments. A delicate shiver trembled through her, and she tilted her head to the side, an invitation he didn't even attempt to resist.

After brushing a lingering kiss to her sweet nape, he stepped back and set to work on freeing the buttons down her back. As each ivory round was freed from its loop, he was rewarded with a tantalizing peek at the thin chemise beneath. When he finally finished, he moved to stand in front of her. Her color was high, and desire shimmered from her golden brown eyes. Reaching out, he slowly pushed the garment over her shoulders. It slipped down her arms, then over her hips to land with a soft *shush* at her feet.

His avid gaze raked over her, so achingly beautiful, clad in a chemise so sheer he could see her dusky nipples through the material. Hooking his fingers under the cream-colored straps, he inched the garment down, tracking its progress as each delectable inch of her skin was revealed. When he released the straps, the chemise pooled at her feet on top of her gown.

For several seconds he stood immobile and simply drank in the sight of her, standing gracefully in the center of her discarded clothing like a single rose in full bloom rising from a priceless vase. His gaze lingered over generous, plump breasts topped with coral-hued nipples that tightened under his regard. The curve of her waist gave way to rounded hips and shapely thighs, hugging the triangle of chestnut curls nestled between her legs. Now clad in only her stockings and shoes, she robbed him of the control he'd fought so hard to keep in check. His every muscle tensed with needs that he could deny no longer. She looked ripe, luscious, and utterly delectable, and God help him, he was starving.

He extended his hand and helped her step from the yards of material surrounding her. The instant she was free, he bent his knees, scooped her into his arms, and carried her to the velvet coverlet, made softer by the bed of fresh hay he'd spread beneath it. He gently laid her down, cushioning her head on the blue pillow. After slipping off her shoes and stockings and setting them aside, he rose to remove his low, soft leather boots and breeches.

Catherine rolled onto her side, propped her head on her palm, and watched the proceedings with rapt attention. When he freed his erection from the strangulating confines of his snug breeches, he breathed a sigh of relief.

"Oh, my," she breathed, rising to her knees, her avid gaze arousing him further.

He tossed his clothing haphazardly onto the pile, then knelt on the quilt in front of her. Framing her face between his hands, he lowered his head and brushed his lips over hers. "Catherine . . ."

Everything he felt, all the love and desire burning in him, all the battles he'd waged to contain those feelings for so long were voiced in that single, heartfelt word. And the instant his lips touched hers, those battles were lost.

With a groan that bordered on pain, he pulled her against him. Each new sensation barely had time to blink in his mind before it was supplanted with another. Her body pressed against his from chest to knee. Soft breasts, aroused nipples, crushed against his chest. Her hands rippling through his hair. His palms skimming down her back to cup her buttocks, Catherine returning the favor. The weight of her breast filling his hand. Bending his head to lave her nipple with his tongue, then draw the aroused bud into his mouth. Absorbing her guttural groan of his name. Another deep, soul-searching kiss. Soft skin beneath his hands. Sleek, moist feminine flesh between her thighs, swollen with want.

She glided her fingers down the length of his erection, and he broke off their kiss to suck in a harsh breath.

"Did I hurt you?"

Unable to speak, he shook his head.

"I want to touch you, Andrew."

Gritting his teeth, he rested his forehead against hers and withstood the sweet torture of her fingers stroking him for as long as he could. But when she wrapped her fingers around his erection and gently squeezed, he grasped her wrist. His lips captured hers in a hard, passionate kiss, a frantic melding of lips and tongues. Without breaking their kiss, he lowered her onto her back on the quilt, then covered her body with his own. She spread her legs and groaned, and he bent his head to touch his tongue to the pleasure-filled sound vibrating at the base of her throat.

Propping his weight on his palms, he watched her in the flickering golden light while he slowly entered her body. A tumble of wild chestnut curls, in disarray from his exploring hands, surrounded her head. Her lips were red and moist and slightly parted, while her chest rose and fell with her rapid, shallow breaths. Her dusky nipples were damp and erect from his mouth. But it was the stark need, the acute want in her eyes that undid him.

He slowly thrust into her warm, wet velvet heat, and squeezed his eyes shut against the fierce pleasure. He wanted to go slowly, make this last, but his body, so long denied, was beyond his control. His strokes lengthened, quickened. Deeper. Harder. She met his every thrust, urging him on, her fingers digging into his shoulders. She tensed beneath him, surging her hips upward while exhaling a long, *ooohh* of pleasure. Helpless to contain his release any longer, he buried his face in the fragrant crook of her shoulder and throbbed inside her wet heat for an endless, miraculous moment that left him breathless, weak, utterly contented, and, damn near dead.

Catherine lay beneath Andrew's delicious weight—breathless, weak, utterly contented, and more alive than she'd ever felt in her entire life.

This was what all the fuss was about. *This* was what she'd been missing her entire marriage. *This* was the splendid wonder described in *A Ladies' Guide*, although nothing in the book's vivid commentary and instructions had sufficiently prepared her for such an incredible, intimate experience.

With her eyes closed, she took a moment to savor the aftermath, not wanting the stunning pleasure to end. Andrew's ragged breaths beating against her ear. His body covering hers, heated skin to heated skin. His arms still wrapped tightly around her, as if he never wanted to let her go. Her arms encircling his broad shoulders, also reluctant to release. His heartbeat pounding against her breasts. And the dazzling sensation of his body still intimately joined with hers. No, she had not known that it would be like this.

Or that he would quickly become quite so heavy.

Not that she didn't relish the feel of him on top of her, but the need to draw a deep breath was about to overtake the pleasure of him covering her like a human blanket.

Whether he sensed her need or simply possessed good timing she didn't know, but just then he stirred. After brushing a kiss against her cheek, he shifted to prop his weight on his forearms and looked down at her, his eyes dark and intense, his breathing still not quite steady. His midnight hair, mussed from her frantic fingers, spilled over his forehead. Reaching up, she brushed the strands aside, only to have them tumble out of place again.

"You look rather disheveled," she said, with a smile.

"As do you. Delightfully so." He lowered his head and kissed her. A slow, deep, intimate kiss that conveyed better than any words could have that he'd found their lovemaking as satisfying as she. A kiss that rekindled the flame he'd extinguished only moments ago.

"I'm going to want to do all that again," she whispered against his lips, trailing her fingers lightly down his spine.

"I don't know when I've heard better news. But I'm afraid I'll need a few minutes to recover first." Dropping a quick kiss onto her mouth, he eased from her body, then rolled onto his back, bringing her along.

Sprawled across his chest, Catherine watched him stuff one of the pillows beneath his head. After loosely wrapping his arms around her, his eyelids drooped.

Her brows shot upward. "Don't tell me you're tired!"

He chuckled. "All right. I won't tell you that."

"But you are!" Her voice was ripe with accusation. "How can that be? I've never felt more energetic in my entire life." She tickled her fingers down his abdomen. "I can hardly stay still."

"A fact that will greatly reduce my recovery time, I assure you."

"So you're not feeling wonderful?"

"I feel *incredibly* wonderful. But in a 'wrung-out sponge' manner, as opposed to your 'filled with vigor' manner."

"Humph. Wrung-out sponge does not sound very . . . encouraging."

A deep chuckle rumbled in his throat. "Actually, I meant it as a compliment to you."

"Indeed? I think it is time for *me* to fetch a dictionary so you can look up *compliment.* I'm certain that 'wrung-out sponge' is not given as an example."

"My darling Catherine, I am wrung out because you satisfied me so completely. So absolutely." His hands skimmed down her back. "As I've never been satisfied before."

My darling Catherine. Heavens, that sounded . . . lovely. Especially in that husky growl his voice had become. "Well, I can certainly say the same thing to you. In fact, I'm anxious to tell you about all the firsts I've experienced since I entered the gazebo. Would you like to hear about the things I've discovered?"

"I'd be delighted."

She narrowed her eyes at him. "Are you certain you won't doze off? You look suspiciously sleepy."

He dipped his chin and looked down at her with a sinful smile. "I'm not sleepy. I'm sated. I assure you that you have my full attention."

"Very well. I've never undressed a man before." She traced a series of light circles on his bare chest. "I've never seen a naked man before."

One dark brow shot upward. "Never?"

She shook her head, her chin bumping against his chest. Then she sat up and skimmed her gaze down his length. "Although I have nothing to compare you to, I think you are most likely a very well made specimen."

One corner of his lovely mouth lifted. "Thank you."

"I very much like the way your skin feels. Warm and firm." Unable to stop touching him, she rested her hand against his shoulder, then slowly dragged her palm down the center of his chest. "I've never seen, or touched hair on a man's chest. It's a bit coarse, but soft at the same time. And your muscles . . . an enthralling delight. So strong, under all that warm, firm skin." She skimmed a single fingertip slowly downward. "This ribbon of dark hair is absolutely fascinating. The way it starts at your chest, then continues downward, bisecting these lovely ripples on your stomach, then spreads again to cradle . . ." Her voice drifted off as her gaze riveted on his manhood. ". . . this part of you that so captivates me, that brought me such incredible sensations. Even at rest you are impressive." She lightly circled the tip of him with her index finger. "I've never touched a man like this before," she whispered.

He swallowed, then levered himself up onto his side, propping his weight on his forearm. His dark eyes regarded her with an unreadable expression. Reaching out, he cradled her face in his palm and brushed the pad of his thumb over her cheek. "I'm sorry your marriage was not a happy one, Catherine."

To her mortification, hot tears pushed behind her eyes. "I realized very quickly that with Bertrand I'd been denied the satisfaction that can come from an emotional bond, but until tonight, I hadn't realized what I'd missed from the physical part our union. I conceived in the first weeks of my marriage, and once my condition was confirmed, Bertrand did not approach me. And once Spencer was born . . . Bertrand never touched me again. I could count the number of times he visited my bedchamber, and none of those visits in any way resembled what you and I shared this evening. Being with Bertrand was perfunctory. Dry. Uninspiring. Hasty, cursory actions under the cover of darkness. Disappointing and frustrating in ways I didn't understand." She turned her head and pressed a kiss in his callused palm. "Being with you was . . . miraculous. Exciting. Enthralling. And very much not dry. A first in every conceivable way."

She drew a deep breath, considering her next words for several seconds before continuing. "Bertrand had lovers, you know. Several that I know about, and I'm certain many others of whom I'm not aware. I must admit that I considered such an arrangement myself on more than one occasion, when the loneliness became unbearable. When I needed to touch another person. Longed to smile at someone other than my son. Craved adult companionship."

"But you didn't take a lover?"

"No."

"Why not?"

She shrugged. "In spite of my husband's behavior, my conscience balked at the thought of breaking my marriage vows; although, if I am to be perfectly honest, my fidelity had more to do with remaining true to my own values than it did with loyalty to my husband."

"Which does not diminish your character in any way, Catherine."

"Perhaps not, but my other reasons are not quite so noble. Basically, I was afraid. I did not want to risk becoming fodder for the village gossips, and an affair in a village the size of Little Longstone would be all but impossible to conceal. I feared not only for my own reputation, but Spencer's as well."

"Caution is not an ignoble virtue, Catherine."

"I agree. Yet you can see what happened to all my caution. It was not difficult to maintain while untested. But I'd never met anyone whom I wished to take as a lover. Until now."

His eyes darkened, and a shiver of delight ran through her. Catherine's eyes slid closed, and for several heartbeats she relived the wonder of their joining. Exhaling a long, slow breath, she whispered dreamily, "Nothing we'd talked about had prepared me. When I wrote the *Guide* I didn't—"

Her words chopped off at her slip, and her eyes popped open. For one horrified second she couldn't move. Couldn't breathe. Heat rushed into her face, and her insides cramped. Then she forced out a laugh, one she prayed did not sound as nervous to him as it did to her. "*Read*," she said, willing away the blush scorching her cheeks. "I meant when I *read* the *Guide*, I thought that I knew what to expect. But I was wrong."

She forced her lips into a calm smile, but she knew her face still flamed red. Had his gaze turned suddenly watchful? Speculative? No, no surely she was just imagining it. She'd made a silly slip of the tongue. People made such errors all the time. All she needed to do was change the subject. And cease blushing.

Before she could speak, however, he said, "I'm certain you've considered that our liaison could conceive a child."

Relieved that he clearly had not attached any significance to her verbal blunder, she said, "Yes. You need not fear that. I have taken steps to ensure that I do not conceive."

"I see. And you are aware that you still run the risk of someone discovering that we are lovers."

"Of course, but surely you agree that it is greatly minimized by the fact that you reside in London and will be returning to your home in a week's time."

"In other words, you do not fear discovery as this is only a temporary arrangement."

"Yes." For reasons she refused to examine, that single word tasted most unappetizing.

Silence stretched between them, and she realized she

was holding her breath. Finally, he nodded, an obvious sign of his agreement, and for some inexplicable reason, she felt let down that he didn't argue with her. Suggest that they somehow find a way to continue their liaison beyond his weeklong visit. They couldn't, wouldn't, of course, but still . . .

Her thoughts drifted off when he sifted his fingers through her hair, eliciting a head-to-toe tingle that drove everything from her mind. "Your hair," he said softly, "your skin, they are so amazingly soft." His hand drifted over her shoulder, then down her arm. "Never in my life have I touched anything so smooth. So silky." His eyes met hers, and she stilled at the seriousness of his gaze. "I have a confession to make, Catherine."

Her heart performed a flip at his grave tone. Did he want their affair to continue beyond his visit? "I'm listening."

"I never thought I'd have the opportunity to touch you, and now that I do . . ." He cupped her breast and a wicked gleam kindled in his eyes. "Now that I do, I must confess, I cannot stop."

Her breath caught as he teased her nipple into an aching point. Splaying her hand on his thigh, she leaned forward until only a hairbreadth separated their lips.

"My darling Andrew, I don't know when I've heard better news."

Staring into the low-burning flames crackling in the grate, a slow smile curved the lone figure's lips upward. The plans were in place. All was in readiness . . .

The ticking of the mantel clock served as an irritating reminder of the passage of time. *But I shall remain patient. My quarry is in sight. I know who you are. Soon, very soon, all the wrongs will be righted.*

Chapter 15

As men tend to be forgetful creatures, Today's Modern Woman needs to make an indelible impression in her gentleman's mind so he cannot ever completely dismiss her from his thoughts. The most effective way to do this is to say or do something deliciously naughty—very discreetly, so only he is aware of it. If a man believes there is a sexual encounter in his imminent future, his attention will not wander far.

A Ladies' Guide to the Pursuit of
Personal Happiness and Intimate Fulfillment
by Charles Brightmore

Andrew prepared to exit his bedchamber the next morning, one thing uppermost in his mind: Catherine.

After a final lingering kiss, he'd reluctantly left her at her bedchamber door four hours ago. Actually four hours and eleven minutes ago, not that he was counting.

Very well, he was counting. And those four hours and eleven minutes had felt like four years. He needed to touch her. Kiss her. Hold her against him to reaffirm the miracle of last night. Making love to her had been a revelation. In his dreams, he'd touched her, loved her, countless times, but nothing had prepared him for the reality of her beneath him, looking up at him, her eyes glazed with need. His body joining with hers as he wordlessly expressed all the feelings he'd kept locked away for so long. All the things he couldn't say—yet.

He exited his bedchamber and strode down the corridor, impatience pulling at him. When he looked into her eyes this morning would he see all the magic they'd shared together reflected there? The desire to experience more of the same? Or would she have spent the last four hours and now twelve minutes deciding that last night was enough?

His lips pressed together. If she'd somehow decided that it was enough, he'd just damn well have to change her mind. She was *his*. And he intended to have her.

When he rounded the corner, he spied Milton nearing the top of the stairs.

"Mr. Stanton," the butler said in his precise tones, "I was just coming to your room. This arrived for you." He held out a silver salver bearing a sealed note.

Andrew took the missive. His stomach tensed when he noted his name scrawled in Simon Wentworth's cramped handwriting. Damn. He doubted his and Philip's steward would be writing to impart *good* news. "Did the messenger say anything?"

"Only that the note was for you and that he did not require a reply. He's already departed."

"I see. Are Lady Catherine and Spencer about?"

"Master Spencer is on his way to take the waters. Lady Catherine requested a meal in her bedchamber. Breakfast is laid out in the dining room, sir."

"Thank you. I need to read this correspondence first. I'll be down shortly."

Milton inclined his head, then headed back down the

stairs, and Andrew returned to his bedchamber. After closing the door behind him, he broke the wax seal and quickly scanned the words.

Mr. Stanton,

I am writing to inform you that someone entered the museum last night, and I'm sorry to report that considerable damage was done. The magistrate believes that when the thief—or thieves—realized there were no artifacts yet housed in the museum, he became enraged and inflicted as much damage as he could. An ax was taken to the floor and walls, and every single one of the newly installed windows was broken. The magistrate doesn't hold much hope that the scoundrel will be caught unless a witness comes forward with information. I'll set the workmen up to repair the damages—no need for you to worry on that score, but I don't have the experience to handle the investors, and I'm afraid their reactions are already not favorable. Lords Borthrasher and Kingsly were making inquiries, as well as Mrs. Warrenfield and a Mr. Carmichael. Therefore, I think it might be best if you returned to London as soon as possible. In the meanwhile, I will see about hiring on more workers. Per your instructions before you left London, I have not written to Lord Greybourne to inform him of anything regarding the museum.

Sincerely,
Simon Wentworth

Andrew blew out a long breath and raked his hand through his hair. In his mind's eye he pictured the museum's polished parquet flooring and richly paneled walls. And all those beautiful pane-glassed windows . . . Damn it to hell and back! All that work, destroyed. It made him sick inside. As did the thought of leaving Catherine, especially now. But he had no choice. And he had to tell her.

Slipping the note into his waistcoat pocket, he quietly departed his room.

Her skin still tingling from a warm bath, Catherine looked out her bedchamber window at the sun's gentle morning glow reflecting silver off the dew-laden grass. Her gaze drifted toward the garden . . . toward the path that she and Andrew had followed last night.

Her eyes drifted closed. Vivid images flashed through her mind of how they'd spent the hours until just before dawn . . . intimately exploring each other's bodies. Sharing the wine, bread, and cheese. Andrew feeding her strawberries. Laughing. Touching. Making love again, slowly, savoring every touch. Every look. Every kiss. Every stroke of his body deep inside hers.

For all the times she'd imagined being with a lover, for all the curiosity the *Guide* had planted in her mind, she'd never, not once, envisioned anything like last night. She'd always believed that one's imagination could conjure up scenarios reality could never match.

She'd been horribly mistaken in that belief.

Imagination could not experience the wonder of Andrew's lips and hands worshiping her, burning away everything, every thought, except him. The feel of her breasts crushed against his warm, naked chest. The musky scent of their lovemaking surrounding them in the gazebo's golden-lit, still air. The texture of his firm skin beneath her fingertips. And the sight of him . . .

A long, feminine sigh escaped her. Dear God, the sight of him, his strong, muscular body glistening in the flickering light, fully aroused. For her. By her. His eyes black with want. Hot with desire. Filled with a fierceness at complete odds with his gentle touch. His absorbed expression as he aroused her beyond bearing. Then the sensual, sated languor glowing in those eyes in the aftermath of their passion. His quick grin. His lovely smile. Yet behind his humor the heart-quickening heat simmering just below his surface.

Unfortunately, she suspected she was feeling more than simply heart-quickening heat for Andrew. And that was unacceptable. Disquieting. And most of all, frightening.

She wouldn't, *couldn't* allow herself to forget that this was temporary. She well knew the heartbreak associated with a permanent arrangement. And lest she forget . . .

She crossed to her wardrobe, then knelt to withdraw a small mahogany jewelry box she kept hidden in the far back corner beneath several blankets. She opened the lid and withdrew the ring inside. Rising, she stared at her diamond wedding ring resting in her palm. A flawless five carats of brilliance, surrounded by a dozen smaller stones, all equally perfect. A ring most women would covet. Sadly, she was not most women. She'd kept this painful reminder of the past so she'd never forget the emptiness that resulted from all its promises. One look at the jewel was a forceful reminder that she would not, could not allow one night of passion to cloud her common sense. Whatever these . . . feelings for Andrew were, she needed to push them aside. Forget them. They would enjoy a few more days together, then go their separate ways, leaving them both with lovely memories, but nothing more.

Satisfied that she'd put everything back into its proper

perspective, she was about to bend down to retrieve the jewelry box when a quiet knock sounded at her door. Slipping the ring into her pocket, she said, "Come in," wondering if Mary had forgotten something when she'd delivered her breakfast.

The door opened, and Andrew stepped over the threshold. Andrew, looking clean and freshly shaved, his hair neatly combed, his fawn breeches and dark blue jacket accentuating his dark good looks, cravat perfectly knotted, boots polished to a high sheen. He looked tall and broad, masculine and delicious, and, with his eyes intent upon hers, just a bit predatory and dangerous. Her heart jumped, and every nerve ending tingled with awareness.

His gaze traveled down her length, making Catherine very much aware that she wore nothing beneath the cream satin robe knotted loosely at her waist. Her skin shivered with anticipation under his leisurely regard. When their eyes finally met once again, he reached behind him and locked the door. The quiet click reverberated through her mind, and she desperately tried to recall the *Guide's* sage advice on how to greet one's lover after a night spent naked in his arms. Her common sense screamed that he shouldn't be here, that she didn't want him here. Her bedchamber was her sanctuary. Her haven. *Hers.* Unfortunately, the pounding of her heart drowned out her common sense.

He walked slowly toward her, looking very much like a sleek jungle cat stalking its prey, and her heart rate doubled at the ravenous gleam in his eyes. As she seemed suddenly incapable of movement or speech, she waited for him to stop, to smile, to say good morning, but he did none of those things. Instead, he walked right up to her, wordlessly pulled into his arms, and lowered his mouth to hers.

Oh, my. It was her last coherent thought as she simply

gave herself over to his demanding kiss. His clean scent surrounded her, as did the heat of his body. The strength of his arms. The urgent press of his thighs against hers.

She parted her lips and was rewarded with the sensual sweep of his tongue against hers. And his hands, those glorious, large, callused hands that could only be described as magical, seemed to be everywhere. Combing through her hair. Skimming down her back. Cupping her buttocks. Palming her breasts. All while his mouth devoured hers with a fierce hunger that left her breathless and starving for more. Had it only been a few hours since she'd been in his arms? Somehow it felt like years.

His arms tightened around her, and she reveled in his strength, lifting up on her toes, straining closer to him. Then he suddenly changed the pace of their frantic kiss, gentling it to a slow, deep melding of mouths and tongues that dissolved her knees. When he finally lifted his head, she wasn't certain she could recall her name.

"Good morning, Catherine," he whispered against her lips.

Catherine. Yes, of course. That is my name.

She supposed she murmured good morning, but she wasn't quite certain. He leaned forward and nuzzled his lips against the sensitive juncture where her neck met her shoulder. "You smell incredible." His warm breath sluiced over her skin, eliciting a barrage of heated shivers. "Like a flower garden."

Summoning her strength, she pointed toward the brass tub set in the corner of the room. "I just finished bathing."

He turned his head, looked toward the tub, then groaned. "Do you mean to say that if I'd arrived only minutes earlier, I'd have caught you in the bath?"

"I'm afraid so."

His teeth lightly tugged on her earlobe. "I shall have to

see about correcting my lamentable timing. Although, I don't know that my heart could have withstood the sight of you in the bath. Do you have any idea how the sight of you, simply standing there in your robe, affected me?"

She leaned backed in the circle of his arms. Surely she meant to be demure. Coy. Instead, the simple truth rushed from her lips. "Yes. Because seeing you enter my bedchamber, with desire in your eyes, affected me the same way." Warmth rushed into her cheeks at the admission. "Why are you here?"

"I needed to speak with you." He hesitated, then said, "I'm afraid I must return to London. Today. As soon as possible."

Dismay and disappointment filled her. "I see. Is something amiss?"

"A break-in and some vandalism at the museum. There was nothing there to steal, but apparently the building sustained considerable damage. I need to see how extensive the repairs will be, so I can report to Philip. I'll also need to talk to the investors, allay any fears they may have. The last thing Philip and I need is nervous investors."

She rested her palm against his cheek in a gesture of commiseration and sympathy. He looked so very grim. "How awful. I'm so sorry this has happened."

"As am I. Not only for the obvious reasons regarding the museum, but also because I have no wish to leave here. I was very much looking forward to spending the day with you and Spencer." His eyes darkened. "And the night with you."

Desire fluttered through her veins, and she swallowed before asking, "Are you . . . planning to return to Little Longstone?"

"Yes."

A breath she hadn't realized she held pushed past her lips. "When?"

"I'm hoping tomorrow."

"Please consider my stable at your disposal."

"Thank you. The journey will be quicker if I travel on horseback rather than coach. I'll do my best to arrive here by early evening, but I may be later."

"I see. Will you . . . meet me tomorrow night?"

"When and where?"

She considered for a moment. "Midnight. At the springs. I want . . ."

He cradled her face in his hands, his eyes searching hers. "Tell me what you want."

"I want you to make love to me in the warm waters."

Something that looked like fear, but surely wasn't flickered in his eyes, but it vanished so quickly she decided she must have been mistaken. He brushed a soft kiss against her mouth. "It will be my very great pleasure to grant your wish, Catherine."

His words caressed her lips, shooting want to her core. "Tomorrow might, the springs, at midnight," she murmured in a breathless whisper. Passion, desire, lust, all so new, all so long denied, swamped her. "Andrew . . . I don't want to wait until tomorrow night."

He lifted his head, and the inferno burning in his gaze singed her. "Be careful what you wish for Catherine, because you are only seconds away from—"

"Being led astray?" Stepping back from his embrace, she unknotted the sash to her robe, then shrugged the satin from her shoulders, where it fell to a soft heap at her feet.

He watched her robe slither down her body, leaving her naked. His entire body tensed, filling her with a heady sense of feminine power and satisfaction.

"Led astray?" he repeated softly, taking a step closer to her. "Hmmm. Yes, that is definitely a possibility."

"Only a possibility?" She made a *tsk*ing sound, then backed up another step, then another, until she leaned against the wall. "How . . . disappointing."

He erased the distance between them in one stride, then braced his hands on the wall on either side of her, bracketing her in. His heated gaze raked over her, a muscle ticking in his jaw, and her breath hitched.

"Is that what you want, Catherine? To be led astray?"

"I'm not certain precisely what that entails, but it sounds . . . tantalizing."

"I'd be delighted to show you."

She splayed her hands against his chest, further emboldened by the rapid pounding of his heart against her palms. Her entire body quickened in anticipation of his touch. "Excellent. I'm looking forward to a proper good-bye."

"My darling Catherine, there is nothing the least bit proper about the good-bye you're about to receive."

His mouth covered hers in a searing, devouring kiss. She slid her hands inside his jacket to stroke his back, feeling a desperate, overwhelming need to touch, to be touched everywhere at once. With a ragged groan, he deepened their kiss, his tongue plunging and stroking while he filled his hands with her aching breasts, his fingers teasing her sensitive nipples, which begged for more. His lips left her mouth, and he pressed hot, fervent kisses across her jaw, down her neck, then skimmed over her chest. His tongue laved drugging swirls around her aroused nipples before drawing each aroused bud into the velvety heat of his mouth. Catherine arched her back in a silent plea to taste more of her, and he obliged, while she tangled her fingers in his thick, silky hair

She squirmed against him, and in response he sank to

his knees, trailing openmouthed kisses along her stomach. Her muscles quivered when he tasted the indentation of her navel. She sucked in a breath, filling her head with an erotic scent she recognized as her own feminine musk, combined with Andrew's sandalwood.

"Spread your legs for me, Catherine," he demanded in a raw rasp, the words vibrating against her stomach.

Feeling as if she were burning from the inside out, she obeyed, and he rewarded her by stroking the swollen, wet folds between her thighs. A gasp, followed by a long purr of pleasure rippled in her throat, and she gripped his shoulders.

He pressed his lips to the sensitive skin just below her navel, then his lips glided lower, lower, until his tongue caressed her as his fingers just had.

Amazing, shocking sensations ripped through her. She closed her eyes and pressed her head against the wall, inflamed beyond reason as he cupped her bottom in his palms and made love to her with his mouth, worshiping, tormenting her with his lips and tongue until she thought she'd go mad from the pleasure. Her climax roared through her, flashes of all-consuming fire, dragging a harsh cry from her lips.

Her spasms had no sooner subsided than he stood and swiftly carried her to the bed, where he laid her upon the counterpane. With exquisite tremors still rippling through her, she held out her arms, silently beseeching him to come to her, desperate to feel his delicious weight, the thrust of his arousal inside her. The five seconds it required him to free his erection from his breeches seemed to her like an eternity. He loomed over her, settling himself between her splayed thighs, and entered her in one long, smooth, heart-stopping stroke.

Their gazes locked, and with every nuance of his intense expression visible in the soft sunlight filtering through the curtains, he moved slowly within her, penetrating deep, then almost withdrawing from her body, only to sink deep once again. Her hands strayed restlessly over his back, then gripped his shoulders. He quickened his strokes, and she moaned, meeting, accepting, savoring his every thrust. She arched her back, and her pleasure overtook once more. A masculine moan, sounding as if scraped from his throat, echoed in the room. He buried his head in the V of her shoulder and shuddered his release, murmuring her name over and over, like a prayer.

Breathing hard, Andrew rolled onto his side, bringing her with him, then closed his eyes and fought to regain control. Bloody hell, this woman, their lovemaking, rendered him vanquished. Vulnerable. More raw and exposed than he'd ever felt in his entire life. How would he bear it if she did not return his feelings? Didn't want him to be part of her life permanently? She cared, he could tell she did. But did she care enough?

When the world righted itself again, he leaned back and brushed her tousled hair from her flushed face. She dragged her eyes open with obvious effort, and he swallowed a groan of longing at the slumberous, languorous smolder in her golden brown depths. Surely there was something he should say to her. God knows his heart was close to bursting with all he felt for her. But he feared saying too much. Worried that if he spoke, he wouldn't stop until he told her she owned his heart. Had owned it for much longer than she knew. Would always own it. Yet he knew he wouldn't be able to contain the words much longer. Soon, she would know. And he prayed to God that telling her wouldn't cost him what they now shared. Because as miraculous as it was, having her body simply wasn't enough.

For several seconds she said nothing, just looked at him with an expression that seemed troubled. And confused. Then her expression cleared and a tiny smile lifted one corner of her lips, coaxing him to touch his lips to the spot. "Oh, my." She sighed. "I just added to my list of firsts. That was my first time being led astray. I hope it isn't my last."

"I'd be delighted to oblige you at any time, my lady. You've only to ask."

"I very much enjoyed my proper good-bye, Andrew."

He dropped a kiss on the tip of her nose. "That's because it was your *im*proper good-bye. And if you enjoyed that, I'm certain you'll like tomorrow night's proper, or rather *im*proper, hello even more."

"Oh, my. What does that mean?"

"I cannot tell you. It is a surprise." When she appeared about to argue, he said, "Do I need to fetch the dictionary?"

"No." She tilted her chin, feigning sticking her nose in the air. "However, I am therefore not going to tell you about the surprise *I* have planned."

"A surprise? For me?"

"Perhaps," she said airily.

"What is it?"

"Ha! Who requires the dictionary now?"

"How about a hint? Just a tiny one?" he asked, holding his thumb and forefinger close together.

A delightful sound that could only be described as a giggle bubbled from between her lips. "Absolutely not."

Leaning forward, he brushed his tongue over the delicate shell of her ear. "Please?"

"Ooh. Well, perhaps . . . no. Definitely not."

"Ah, a woman of strong will," he murmured, skimming his fingers lightly down the center of her spine.

"As Today's Modern Woman should be."

"However, Today's Modern Woman also knows that it is wise to make an indelible impression in her gentleman's mind so he cannot ever completely dismiss her from his thoughts. Giving me a miniscule hint regarding the nature of your surprise would surely whet my appetite and guarantee that you'd remain uppermost in my mind while I'm away."

She went perfectly still—except for her eyes, which narrowed. "What did you say?"

"That by giving me a hint—"

"Before that."

Andrew frowned and thought for several seconds. "I believe I said, 'Today's Modern Woman also knows that it is wise to make an indelible impression in her gentleman's mind so he cannot ever completely dismiss her from his thoughts.' Is that what you're referring to?"

"Yes." Her eyes narrowed further. "Where did you learn such a thing?"

"Why, from *A Ladies' Guide,* of course."

Andrew had to clench his jaw to keep a straight face at her dumbfounded expression. "How on earth would you know what was written in *A Ladies Guide*?"

"Brace yourself, my dear, but one often does learn something when one reads."

"Don't tell me you've read the *Guide*."

"Very well, I won't tell you that, but why you'd want me to lie to you is a mystery."

"You read the *Guide*?"

"Every word. Cover to cover."

"When? Where? How?"

"Such an inquisitive nature. Let me see. As to when, the night before last—before we met at the springs. As for where, in my bedchamber. And to answer how, I purchased a copy the morning we departed London. Our conversation at your father's party intrigued me, and I decided to read the tome to see what all the fuss was about. And I must confess, I was somewhat contrarily driven by the fact that you seemed so positive I would not read such drivel."

"That was your description, not mine."

"Was it? Well, I stand corrected."

"Meaning what precisely?"

"That I found the *Guide* very . . . informative. And well written."

There was no missing the smug satisfaction that fired in her eyes. "I believe I mentioned as much."

"You did. Indeed, you defended the book and the author with the sort of fierce loyalty a mother tiger normally bestows upon her cubs."

Crimson suffused her cheeks, and she averted her gaze. He brushed the pad of his thumb over the wash of brilliant color. "Surely you can understand why the book is causing such a scandal."

Her blush deepened. "Yes, but I believe the information it provides women far outweighs any trodden-upon sensibilities. Charles Brightmore should be praised for what he's done."

"Again you fiercely defend him. Almost as if you . . . knew him."

She pressed her lips together, then shifted out of his embrace. He let her go, watching her slide off the bed, then retrieve her robe, slipping her arms into the silk sleeves. After she'd tightened the sash around her waist, she turned to face him, her eyes intense with suppressed emotion.

"I defend him because God knows I wish I'd had access to the information provided by the *Guide* before I'd wed. Or at any time during the early days of my marriage. I went to my marriage bed knowing *nothing* about what to do or what to expect. I did not know women could experience pleasure during lovemaking. I had no idea lovemaking involved anything more than a few minutes in a darkened room with my nightgown rucked up to my waist. I didn't know that the warmth that began during those few minutes could, if properly tended, ignite into a blazing inferno that scorched everything in its path. I did not know I was capable of the sort of lust and hunger that I'd always associated with men. Charles Brightmore taught me all those things and more. He taught me, encouraged me, to allow myself to feel those things. And to act upon them."

"I see. You know, I've heard rumors that suggest Brightmore may in fact be a woman," he remarked casually, watching her.

"Indeed? Where did you hear that?"

He rose, and adjusted his clothing while he spoke. "Most recently at your father's birthday party. Personally, I think it's intriguing, and entirely possible. Brightmore writes with an understanding of women that I've never before encountered in a man, no matter how sophisticated or worldly." He smiled. "In case you aren't aware, women are notoriously difficult to understand, yet Brightmore clearly does not suffer from the same confusions as the rest of us poor males."

"Obviously he is well-versed in the ways of women."

"Obviously. Yet it makes one curious as to how he gained such knowledge."

"Through numerous intimacies, like the ones we've recently shared, I imagine," she said, walking forward until they almost touched. She splayed her hands on his abdomen; yet even while he welcomed her touch, he had the undeniable suspicion that she was trying to distract him. But considering she was so very distracting, he shoved the suspicion aside.

"Perhaps," he conceded. "You do realize, of course, that this now means that *I* am the winner of our wager."

She cocked a brow. "Indeed? The wager that only last night you led me to believe *I'd* won?"

"I beg to differ. As I recall, you insisted, quite emphatically, that you'd won. I, in the spirit of being a gentleman, simply did not argue with you."

He bit back a smile at her snort. "Not argue with me? Well, that is a first."

"I sensed it was the wisest course, and I very much wanted to know what boon you wished. Believe me when I say that I was delighted to discover that your wish so closely mirrored my own."

"Yet now I owe you a boon."

"I'm afraid so."

"And what do you desire?"

His fingers kneaded her supple waist. "So many things . . . it will require a great deal of thought to settle upon just one." He ran his palms down, over her hips. "What is this?" he asked, fingering a small, hard bump near her hip.

After a slight hesitation she slipped her hand into her robe's pocket and withdrew a ring, which she held up to the light. Prisms of diamond flash glittered, bouncing off the walls, floor, and ceiling, as if she'd tossed a handful of stars into the air. "My wedding ring," she said.

Unreasonable, ridiculous jealousy slapped Andrew at that physical symbol of her husband's claim upon her. He knew a fair amount about gems, yet one did not need to be an expert to see that the stones were exquisite. Forcing his voice to remain neutral, he said, "I've never seen you wear it. Why was it in your pocket?"

"I don't wear it. I was merely looking at it. When I heard the knock on my door, I slipped it into my pocket and forgot about it." She handed him the ring. "What do you think of it?"

He studied it carefully. "The stones, individually, are all beautiful, even the smaller ones. Yet, I'm surprised this is a ring you would have chosen."

"Why?"

He handed it back to her, not wanting to touch it any longer. "It just somehow doesn't seem to suit you." *Because I didn't give it to you.* "It looks a bit overwhelming for your delicate hand. But I suppose that there is no such thing as too large a jewel."

"Actually, I think there is. And while I'd wager many would think this ring lovely, I hate it. I've always hated it."

He watched her closely. "Why is that?"

"Believe it or not, I'm not overly fond of diamonds. I find them colorless and cold. Although he was aware of that, Bertrand still gave me this ring, not because he thought I would like it, but because it was the ring *he* wanted me to wear. It did not matter what I liked or wanted. Unfortunately, I was too naïve at the time he gave it to me to see it as a harbinger of things to come."

"And what had you wanted?"

"Anything other than a diamond. Emerald. Sapphire. Something with color and life. My mother used to wear an emerald brooch that I loved—it is one of my most prized possessions." She inclined her head and gazed at him curiously. "With all your travels I imagine you've collected some very interesting items. Which one do you prize the most?"

He hesitated for several seconds, then said, "I'd rather show you than tell you. I'll bring it back with me tomorrow so you may see it."

"All right."

"Catherine . . . if you dislike this ring so much, why do you keep it?" *Why were you looking at it?*

"Because it is another of my most prized possessions—but not because of its monetary value."

"Then why?"

"It's a reminder. Of what I had with Bertrand." She stared down at the ring resting in her palm. "Unhappiness. Loneliness. And what I didn't have with him. Laughter. Love. Sharing. Our union was colorless and cold, just like these stones."

He tipped up her chin until their gazes met. "Why would you want to be reminded of that?"

Something in her gaze hardened. "Because I never want to forget. I refuse to make that same mistake again. Refuse to give my life, my happiness, my care, or that of my son, over to another man again. To allow anyone to have that sort of control over me or Spencer ever again."

Andrew clearly read the resolution in her voice. Her eyes. And realized with a sinking heart that her words were a subtle warning, reiterating the fact that she did not want another marriage—the one thing he wanted more than anything.

He'd hoped, prayed, that after making love, she would have come to see that they belonged together. That there was room for him in her life. That their relationship would be nothing like her previous marriage. But the ring in her pocket was very telling. Clearly the thoughts their night together had inspired were not what he'd been hoping for.

Well, obviously he'd lost the battle. But he'd be damned if he would lose the war.

Chapter 16

Today's Modern Woman needs to maintain an air of mystery in order to keep her gentleman's interest alive. Once he knows—or thinks he knows—everything about a woman, he will consider her a "solved" puzzle and seek out a more intriguing enigma to decipher. To achieve this mysterious air, Today's Modern Woman should never allow a gentleman to be too certain of what she's thinking, or how she's feeling.

A Ladies' Guide to the Pursuit of
Personal Happiness and Intimate Fulfillment
by Charles Brightmore

Catherine entered the library, and smiled at the sight of Spencer sitting in his favorite wing chair before the fire, his nose buried in a book.

"Shakespeare?" she guessed, with a smile.

Spencer looked up and nodded. "*Hamlet*."

"Such a sad story for a lovely day."

One shoulder lifted in a shrug, and he averted his gaze, apparently finding something fascinating on the carpet—

a gesture she recognized as one that signaled something was troubling him.

She approached his chair, then leaned down to lightly kiss his still damp hair. "Did you enjoy your morning soak?"

"Yes."

"Is your leg hurting?"

"No."

"Would you like to join me for a walk in the gardens?"

"No."

"A ride in the curricle?"

"No."

"A trip to the village?"

"No."

"Accompany me on my visit with Mrs. Ralston?"

"No."

Catherine sank down to her haunches in front of him and dipped her head until she caught his eye. She clasped his hand and smiled. "Can you tell me the names of three chess pieces?"

A puzzled frown creased his brow. "Knights, bishops, and pawns. Why do you ask?"

"I wanted to hear you say something other than 'yes' or 'no,' " she teased. When he did not smile in return, she squeezed his hand. "What's troubling you, darling?"

Again his shoulder lifted. He plucked at his jacket with his free hand, and Catherine waited, forcing herself to remain silent even as she watched him struggle with whatever was weighing on his mind, knowing that he'd tell her when he was ready.

Finally, he drew a deep breath, and blurted out, "Mr. Stanton left."

Catherine's breath hitched. Ah. So *that* was the source

of his distress. Well, she could certainly understand. Andrew was most assuredly the source of all *her* disquieting, conflicting thoughts. "Yes, I know he left. He told me planned to ride by the springs to say good-bye to you. Did he find you?"

"Yes." After a few more plucks on his jacket, Spencer finally lifted his gaze and looked at her. "I wish he could have stayed here."

As do I. The thought slapped Catherine like a cold, wet rag, and she pressed her lips together, as she realized for the first time just how very much she had not wanted him to leave.

Damnation, how had he worked his way into her life, into Spencer's life, so thoroughly, in such a short period of time? She and Spencer had managed very well without any male interference for many years, and she realized with sudden unquestionable clarity that Andrew's presence in their lives threatened to disrupt the peace and serenity they enjoyed.

And with all her attention on her own dismay at his return to London, she'd failed to consider how his sudden leave-taking might affect Spencer. Clearly her son had formed a strong attachment to Andrew. If Spencer was distraught by Andrew leaving for an overnight, how would he react when Andrew left for good after a week's time? If his current expression were any indication, her son would be crushed.

"He told me about the vandalism at the museum," Spencer said, jerking her thoughts back. "Do you suppose he'll really be back tomorrow night?" he asked, his voice filled with both hope and doubt. "It sounds as if he'll have much to do in Town."

"I'm certain he'll try. But as he cannot leave London

until he puts things back to rights, don't be too disappointed if he must stay away longer."

"But I don't want to miss any of my riding or pugilism lessons. And we haven't even begun with fencing. And Mr. Stanton shouldn't miss his sw—" Spencer's words cut off as if sliced by a knife. His eyes widened, and color rushed into his face.

"Shouldn't miss his what?" Catherine asked.

"I can't say, Mum. It's a surprise."

"Hmmm. You two have devised a fair number of surprises together."

Spencer's lopsided grin broke out, and Catherine's heart smiled in response. "We've had a grand time."

"You . . . like Mr. Stanton?"

"I do, Mum. He's very . . . decent. He's a kind and patient teacher, but best of all, he doesn't treat me as if I'm made of glass. Or as if I'm a child. Or . . . defective." Before she could reassure him, his gaze turned quizzical, and he asked, "Don't you like him, Mum?"

"Er, of course." She wasn't certain that a tepid word such as *like* properly described her attraction to Andrew, but she couldn't very well tell her son that she *desired* the man. "Mr. Stanton is very . . ." *Seductive. Tempting. Delicious.* ". . . nice."

And kind, her inner voice interjected, and she could not deny it. She had only to recall how Andrew had treated Spencer and herself to know it was true.

"Do you think he could be persuaded to stay longer than one week, Mum?"

Catherine froze at the question, anticipation and panic colliding in her. Not only for her own chaotic feelings, but for Spencer's as well. "I think we need to accept that Mr. Stanton's life is in London, Spencer," she said carefully.

"Even if he were to stay on one or two days longer, which I greatly doubt he could, what with your uncle Philip not being in London, Mr. Stanton would still have to return to London."

"But he could visit us again?" Spencer persisted. "Very soon? And often?"

Catherine prayed none of her dismay showed. Good God, she'd planned that once Andrew returned to London, and their brief affair was history, their paths would rarely, if ever, need to intersect. Seeing him again "very soon" and "often" when she had no intention of resuming their affair would be . . . awkward. *Torture is more like what it would be*, her irritatingly honest inner voice corrected. She mentally stuffed a handkerchief in her inner voice's mouth to silence its unwanted musings.

"Spencer, I really don't think—"

"Perhaps we can visit Mr. Stanton in London."

Catherine simply stared, stunned. *Never* before had he made such a suggestion. After she swallowed, she said as casually as she could, "You would want to travel to London?"

Spencer pressed his lips together, then shook his head. "No," he whispered. "I . . . no." He jutted his chin out at a stubborn angle. "So we'll just have to make certain Mr. Stanton visits us. Surely he would if we *both* asked him, Mum."

Catherine patted his hand, then rose. "Perhaps," she murmured, knowing she would not extend such an invitation and hating herself for giving Spencer even that small bit of hope. The affair had to end. Permanently. Which meant that once Andrew returned to London at week's end he would make no more visits to Little Longstone.

* * *

Andrew turned in a slow circle, surveying the museum's damaged walls and floor, the empty spaces where paned glass should have glistened. His hands clenched, in a perfect match to his tight jaw, while anger pumped through him. *Bastards. By God, they'll be bruised and bloodied bastards if they are ever caught.*

"As you can see, all the broken glass has been swept away," Simon Wentworth reported. "The glazier will be here within the hour to speak with you about commissioning new windows. I've taken on six additional men to help with the floor and wall repairs, which, as you can see are extensive."

Andrew nodded, blowing out a long breath. "Extensive does not begin to describe this damage."

"I agree. The way the wood is hacked up, well, it quite gives me the shivers. Smacks of violence, if you ask me. Would hate to meet up with the fiends who did this."

Andrew's jaw tightened. *I'd love to meet up with the fiends who did this*. "How long before the repairs are completed?"

"At least eight weeks, Mr. Stanton."

Damn it to hell and back. That meant another two months of workmen's wages to be paid, two more months of paying for storage for the museum's artifacts, to say nothing of the two-month delay in opening the museum. Or the exorbitant cost of the materials. He knew exactly how much the windows, walls, and floors had cost the first time around.

"Any word from the investors?" Andrew asked.

Simon winced. "I'm afraid bad news travels quickly. Mr. Carmichael and Lords Borthrasher and Kingsly, as well as Mrs. Warrenfield, sent 'round notes requesting to see you today. The letters were rather tersely worded, I'm afraid. They await you on your desk."

Andrew banked his anger and forced himself to concentrate on the matters at hand. Obviously, Mrs. Warrenfield, Mr. Carmichael, and Lords Borthrasher and Kingsly were no longer taking the waters in Little Longstone and had returned to London. Lord Borthrasher had already made a sizable investment to which he was considering adding a significant sum, while the other three had been on the verge of handing over funds. The museum's success depended upon actually securing those monies . . .

"Answer the letters, Simon, inviting the investors to meet me here at five this evening."

"Do you think it's wise to let them see this?"

"Yes. If we don't invite them, they will come here on their own anyway, and that will reflect badly on us. They need to know precisely what happened and what steps we're taking toward repairs and ensuring this does not happen again. We don't want them to think we're trying to hide something. Investors who feel as if they are not being told the entire truth can become very nervous, and nervous investors are not something I care to heap upon the mess we're already facing."

"I'll send the notes off right away, Mr. Stanton." Simon turned, then headed toward the small office tucked away in the far corner of the room.

Andrew blew out a long breath, then removed his jacket and rolled up his sleeves. There was much work to be done, and by God, he wanted some of it completed by the time he sat down to write to Philip about this.

Catherine paced in front of Genevieve, her peach muslin gown swirling about her ankles every time she turned in the confines of her friend's cozy drawing room. "I'm glad he's gone," she said, proud of the decisive ring in her voice.

"So you've said," Genevieve murmured. "Three times in the past hour alone."

"Well, only to reiterate my point."

"Which is what precisely?"

"That I'm glad he's gone."

"Yes, that is, er, evident. However, you do realize that Mr. Stanton will be *returning* to Little Longstone. Tomorrow."

Catherine waved aside the comment. "Yes, but by then I'll have everything once again settled into perspective. I'm certain my chat with you will clear up all my . . . confusion. Then, he'll be here for only a few more days, and *poof!*" She snapped her fingers. "Back to London he'll go."

"A prospect that makes you happy?"

"Deliriously happy," Catherine agreed. "Then Spencer and I can resume our routine without interruption."

When Genevieve made no reply, Catherine glanced toward the settee. The expression of utter disbelief on her friend's face caused her footsteps to falter, and she halted. "What?"

"Catherine, has it not occurred to you that the 'interruption' Mr. Stanton has brought to your routine is a *good* thing?" Before Catherine could reply, Genevieve continued, "From everything you've told me, the man is divine. Naturally he's irritating at times, but as I've told you, *all* men are. However, all men are not the other things your Mr. Stanton is—handsome, strong, romantic, thoughtful. An accomplished and generous lover."

Heat rose in Catherine's cheeks, and Genevieve laughed. "Yes, I can tell that without your divulging any specific details, darling. The look of a well-loved woman is written all over you."

"I never said he wasn't all those things," Catherine said. "But—"

"And the friendship he's taken the time to forge with your son is clearly bolstering Spencer's confidence. Surely that must please you."

"In one way, yes, but it also represents another source of concern. I fear Spencer stands to be devastated when Andrew returns to London for good."

"And what about you, Catherine?" Genevieve asked gently, her blue eyes soft with concern. "Do you, too, stand to be devastated?"

"Certainly not," Catherine said, but somehow the words badly affected her knees to the point that she sought refuge in the wing chair opposite Genevieve. Once seated, she continued, "Today's Modern Woman is not devastated by the end of an affair."

"Darling, *any* woman would be devastated by the end of an affair if she cared deeply for her lover. I know first-hand of such heartbreaking pain, and trust me, I would not wish it upon anyone."

"Well, I run no risk of that as I do not care 'deeply' for Andrew."

"Really?"

Catherine laughed lightly. "I don't mean to imply that I don't care for him *at all*. 'Tis just that I barely know him. I'll readily admit that I desire him; however, deeper feelings that could leave one 'devastated' only develop over long periods of time. And most often between people who share common interests and backgrounds."

Genevieve nodded. "Naturally a lady of your noble lineage would share few common interests with a man of Mr. Stanton's background. Why, he's a commoner! Even worse, a *colonial* commoner."

"Precisely," Catherine said, although Genevieve's ready agreement and true words irked.

" 'Tis a blessing that your attraction to Mr. Stanton is

merely physical and that his departure for London at week's end will not affect you adversely in the slightest."

"A blessing indeed."

An exasperated sound escaped Genevieve. "Catherine, what I am about to say, I say out of love, friendship, and loyalty to you." Leaning forward, she pinned Catherine with an emotion-filled stare. "I have never, in my entire life, been forced to endure listening to a more ridiculous pile of rubbish. I'm utterly flabbergasted that I heard such idiotic notions coming from you, of all people. Not to mention lies."

Dismay, edged with stunned amazement, not to mention a dose of hurt, flooded Catherine. "I would not lie to you, Genevieve."

"It's not me, but *yourself* that you're lying to, my dear. You may say 'I'm glad he's gone' and 'I'm only engaging in a temporary affair' as many times as you wish, but even a million utterances will not make those words true. You're certainly not convincing me, and I think, if you took the time to examine your own heart, you'd realize that you can't convince yourself, either. No matter how hard we try to wish away our heart's desire, we cannot. We may choose not to act upon it, but we cannot ever fully wish it away."

Catherine opened her mouth to reply, but before she could utter a word, Genevieve pressed on. "Even if we assume for one insane moment that your feelings for Mr. Stanton fall into the lukewarm category, have you given any thought at all to his feelings for you? Because I assure you, they are anything but lukewarm."

Genevieve's words threatened to bring to the foreground emotions Catherine refused to examine. "I realize he cares for me, but he agreed that when the week is over, our affair ends as well."

There was no missing the combination of concern and annoyance emanating from Genevieve's eyes. "Darling, he more than cares for you. I could see it plainly at the duke's soiree. The way he looked at you when he knew himself observed, and even more telling, the way he looked at you when he believed himself unobserved . . ." She breathed out a long, shivery sigh. "My God. The passion, the want, the emotion in his eyes was blatant. Watching him look at you, waltz with you, I felt as if I'd walked in on an intimate tête-à-tête. You are sadly mistaken if you believe that man will simply vanish from your life in a week's time."

"I do not intend to give him a choice. He knows full well, as do you, that I've no intention of marrying again. And even if I wished to shackle myself to another husband, I certainly would not choose a man whose life is in London. I've no intention of removing Spencer from the security of our home, from the life we've created here in Little Longstone, from the healing warm springs. And if my husband and I were to live separately, lead separate lives, what is the point in marrying? Spencer and I have already suffered through such an arrangement, and once is quite enough."

Genevieve leaned back and raised her brows. "Has Mr. Stanton *asked* you to marry him?"

"Well, no, but—"

"Hinted that he *intends* to ask you?"

Catherine frowned. "No, but—"

"Perhaps you are worrying for naught. Perhaps all he wants is a long-standing affair."

"Which is unfortunate as I was, and am, only willing to engage in a *short*-lived affair."

Genevieve nodded slowly. "Yes, well perhaps that is

best. After all, a prolonged affair would entail spending more time together, which in turn could lead to those feelings that might leave one devastated when the affair ended."

"Exactly."

"Best to cut things off before there is any risk of developing a deeper attachment."

"Precisely."

"After all, except for in the biblical sense, you barely know Mr. Stanton."

"Correct."

"What do you know of his background? His family? His upbringing? His life in America?"

"Nothing," Catherine answered, relaxing a bit. Finally, this conversation was on the proper course.

Genevieve frowned. "Although . . . you were very well acquainted with Lord Bickley before he asked for your hand, were you not?"

A warning bell chimed in the back of Catherine's mind. "Our families were well acquainted, yes," she admitted.

"Indeed, I recall you mentioning that you'd known him nearly your entire life, is that not correct?"

"Yes."

"And you believed that he was a decent, kind, loving man."

Catherine frowned. "I see what you are trying to do, Genevieve, but what you are saying only serves to prove my point. Yes, when I married Bertrand—a man I'd known my entire life—I believed us well matched. I thought him kind and decent. And although I did not harbor any deep, heartrending emotion toward him, I felt respect and an affection that I was confident would bloom into an abiding love. I honestly cared for him. And look how disastrously my marriage turned out. If I'm capable of so misjudging a man I'd known for years, how could I hope to properly judge a man with whom I'm barely acquainted?"

Genevieve searched her gaze for several seconds then said, "I shall give you an honest answer to that question Catherine. Lord Bickely was cosseted and fussed over his entire privileged life. I'd wager to say that if Spencer had been born perfect, you and your viscount would have maintained a formal, friendly union, without either of you ever developing any 'deep' or 'heartrending' emotions toward one another. It was when adversity was thrown at your husband that he showed his true character."

"I wholeheartedly agree. My father has often said that how a man handles difficulties is the true test of his worth."

"And look how Mr. Stanton has handled himself since arriving in London. He has remained steadfast and loyal to your brother and their museum project. He kept a calm, cool head, protecting you and administering aid when you were hurt. He set his own concerns aside to escort you to Little Longstone to ensure your safety. He has taken the time to develop a relationship with your son. He is not a pampered aristocrat, but a man who has made himself. In the short time you've known him, you've shared more intimacies with him than you did with your husband of ten years. *That* is how you know what sort of man he is."

Catherine closed her eyes and pressed her fingertips against her temples. "Why are you saying these things? I came here hoping you'd help me see things more clearly."

"That is precisely what I am attempting to do. I believe the problem is that I am not saying the things you wish to hear."

She lowered her hands into her lap and offered a weak smile. "No, you're not."

"Because I'm your friend. Because I don't want you to make a mistake that you'll regret the rest of your life. Because not facing the truth, not listening to your heart is more damaging, more hurtful than any other pain. And I do not think you've really examined your heart in this matter, Catherine. You're afraid to do so, which, given your past, is completely understandable. Indeed, I would be frightened as well were I in your position. But you must try to put your fears aside. You were denied happiness for so long, my dear. Don't deny yourself again."

"But don't you see, I'm not denying myself! I wanted a lover, so I took one. I don't want a husband, so I won't take one. There are precisely four reasons why a woman should marry." She ticked the items off on her fingers as she said, "To increase her fortune, to better her social standing, to have a child, or if she requires someone to take care of her. As I am financially secure, am high enough in precedence, already have a child, and do not require someone to take care of me, I've absolutely no need or desire for a husband."

"There is a fifth reason for a woman to marry, darling."

"What's that?"

"Love. But since you're obviously not in love—"

"I'm not."

"Well, that's that."

"Yes, it is. I'm *happy*, Genevieve." As for examining her heart, she'd done so thoroughly enough. She'd certainly delved as deeply as she intended to.

For several seconds, Genevieve said nothing, just treated Catherine to an unreadable look. Then she smiled.

"I'm glad you're happy, darling. And very relieved that you won't be suffering a broken heart. And obviously you know what is best for you. And Spencer."

"Thank you. And yes, I do." Yet even as she said the words, Catherine had the sneaking suspicion that she'd agreed to something she should not have.

"Now tell me dear, whom do you think you'll take as your next lover?"

Catherine blinked. "I beg your pardon?"

"Your next lover. Do you think you'd prefer an older, more experienced man? Or perhaps a dashing young Brummel sort you could easily bend to your will?"

A most unpleasant sensation prowled over her skin at the thought of another man touching her. Before she could reply, Genevieve mused, "And I wonder what sort of woman will next warm Mr. Stanton's bed? I'm certain he won't be lonely for long. Heavens, you saw how the duke's nieces all but salivated at the sight of him. And London is positively littered with gorgeous, sophisticated women looking for a distraction from their daily lives. Mr. Stanton would certainly provide a lovely distraction."

Heat suffused Catherine's body. An *impossibly* unpleasant sensation prowled over her skin at the thought of another woman touching Andrew. She narrowed her eyes at Genevieve, who regarded her with the innocence of an angel. "I know what you are doing, Genevieve."

Her friend smiled. "Is it working?"

Yes. "No!" She jumped to her feet, a myriad of emotions pummeling her. Confusion. Frustration. Anguish. Fear. Jealousy. And anger. Her hands clenched, and she tried to decide if she was more angry with Genevieve for goading her, at Andrew for bringing all these unsettling feelings into her life, or at herself for allowing the situation to evolve into this.

"I don't care who his next lover might be," she fumed, anger convincing her she spoke the truth. "Nor do I know who mine will be. But I'm certain I'll find someone. Why should I be alone?"

"Why indeed?"

Genevieve's complacency only further served to fuel Catherine's ire. Determination stiffened her spine. "Exactly. I shouldn't be alone, nor do I intend to be." Reaching down, she picked up her reticule. "Thank you, Genevieve, for this chat. It has proven most . . . enlightening."

"Always glad to help, my dear."

"Now, if you'll please excuse me, there is someone I must call upon."

Something that looked like worry flickered in Genevieve's eyes, but was instantly replaced with her normal insouciance. "Of course. Shall I see you out?"

"No, thank you. I know the way."

And I know exactly where I'm going.

Andrew stood a bit apart from Mr. Carmichael, Lords Borthrasher and Kingsly, and Mrs. Warrenfield, waiting for them visually to assess the museum's damage. Finally, they turned toward him, each bearing grim expressions.

"This is dreadful," Mrs. Warrenfield murmured in her deep, raspy voice, her words partially muffled by her black veil.

"A frightful mess," Lord Borthrasher agreed, his lip curled with distaste, his cold, vulturelike stare skimming over the room.

Lord Kingsly's beady eyes narrowed, and he folded his arms over his paunch. "Never seen the likes of this."

"Looks to me like it might take even longer than the two months you've estimated to put this back to rights," Mr. Carmichael said, slowly stroking his chin, drawing Andrew's attention to the man's intricate gold ring bearing a square-cut diamond surrounded by onyx. Carmichael then clasped his hands behind his back and glared at Andrew. "Have you nothing to say, Mr. Stanton?"

Andrew's gaze encompassed the group. "I am confident that two months will be sufficient time. I've spoken with the glazier regarding new windowpanes, and additional workers have been hired on to re-lay the floor. Barring any unforeseen problems, we will be fully caught up in two months' time."

"You mean barring any *further* unforeseen disasters," Lord Kingsly said. "Have the scoundrels who did this damage been apprehended?"

"Not yet."

"And it is most likely they won't be caught," Mr. Carmichael added with a scowl. "I'm appalled at the abundance of crime I've witnessed since arriving in London only a few short weeks ago. Pickpockets and thieves abound everywhere, even in the best parts of the city. Why, it was only a matter of days ago that Lady Catherine was shot—in the supposedly safe section of Mayfair."

"The man responsible for that crime has been caught—much in thanks to your efforts, Mr. Carmichael," Andrew reminded him. "It is true that criminals exist in England, but unfortunately they are everywhere." He offered the man a half smile. "Even in America."

"A fact of which I assure you I am aware," Mr. Carmichael said in a frosty voice.

"Footpads everywhere," Lord Kingsly chimed in. "Can't trust anyone nowadays."

"I completely agree," Mr. Carmichael said, his narrowed gaze never leaving Andrew's. "Tell me, Mr. Stanton, what guarantees do we, or any of the other investors have, that something like this won't happen again?"

"Good heavens," Mrs. Warrenfield said. "*Again?*"

"Certainly possible," Lord Kingsly interjected before Andrew could reply, "especially as the perpetrators haven't been caught. Probably some sort of game to them. Recall something similar occurring a few years back to Sir Whitscour's renovations on his Surrey estate."

"I remember that," Lord Borthrasher agreed, lifting his pointed chin. "The minute Sir Whitscour set things back to rights, they were destroyed all over again. Might have a similar situation here."

"I give you my word that steps will be taken to ensure the museum suffers no further damage. We'll hire additional guards to patrol the perimeter," he said.

"All well and good," Mr. Carmichael said, "but I understand from the magistrate that the museum was already under guard, and that your man was rendered senseless by the vandals. Regardless of how many guards you might employ, they would be no match against a potential gang of evildoers." He shook his head. "I'm afraid, Mr. Stanton, that what I've seen here, coupled with what I heard last evening, convinces me that investing in your museum is not a risk I'm willing to take."

"What you heard last evening?" Andrew asked. "What are you talking about?"

"Rumors concerning the financial security—or rather lack thereof—of this museum enterprise were running rampant at the soiree I attended. As were questions regarding the authenticity of some of the relics you and Lord Greybourne claim to possess."

Andrew forced his features to remain perfectly settled while anger shot through him. "I've no idea how such vicious rumors started, but I'm surprised that you would pay heed to such ridiculous gossip, Mr. Carmichael. I assure you that the museum is in sound financial shape. I'd be happy to show you, all of you, the accounts as proof. As for the relics, they have all been authenticated by experts attached to the British Museum."

The chill did not leave Mr. Carmichael's eyes. "I do not wish to see the accounts, as this project is no longer of any interest or consequence to me. I'm only thankful that I'd yet actually to sink any funds into this folly." He turned to his companions and bowed. "You three should, of course, make your own decisions regarding this matter. Lords Avenbury and Ferrymouth, and the Duke of Kelby anxiously wait to hear what we've seen here today, and I'm guessing they will not find the report favorable."

"Easy for you to walk away, Carmichael," Lord Borthrasher grumbled. "It's too late for me. I've already handed over five hundred pounds."

"An investment that will prove profitable once—" Andrew began.

"'Fraid I'm with Carmichael on this one," Lord Kingsly said. "Greybourne's a good man, but 'tis clear his interest in the museum has waned since his marriage, and I'm not eager to throw away any money. My wife does that quite well enough already."

"I must concur with the gentlemen," Mrs. Warrenfield said, her husky voice filled with regret. "I'm truly sorry, Mr. Stanton, but as you know, my health is quite fragile. It simply would be too much for my delicate state to be constantly worrying about not receiving any return on my investment."

Andrew gritted his teeth. He could see by their expressions that no amount of cajoling on his part would change their minds—at least not today. "I see. While I understand your concerns, I assure you they are groundless. When the repairs are completed, I hope you will reconsider."

Their expressions withered any hope of that outcome. After bidding him good day, they left as a group, and Andrew dragged his hand down his face. Bloody hell. Lord Kinglsy and Mrs. Warrenfield had each hinted at investing one thousand pounds. Yet losing that wasn't nearly as crushing a blow as losing the *five thousand pounds* Mr. Carmichael had expressed interest in investing. And how many other potential investors would follow their lead and retreat? He suspected Avenbury, Ferrymouth, and Kelby would follow like sheep. He'd hoped to have some good news to relay when he wrote to Philip this evening, but unfortunately good news was proving difficult to come by.

He blew out a long sigh and raked his hands through his hair in frustration. Vandalism, harmful rumors, deserting investors—any one of these problems could spell disaster. The combination of all of them boded very poorly for the future of the museum, which in turn did not bode well for Andrew's personal finances, which were largely invested in the project. Now, more than ever, he needed the handsome reward offered to him by Lords Markingworth, Whitly, and Carweather for discovering Charles Brightmore's identity. He could only pray that the reward would not prove to be out of his reach.

Seeing that the cleaning procedures were under control, he decided it was high time he devoted some effort to the Brightmore endeavor. After telling Simon that he'd return in several hours, Andrew left the museum.

One way or another, he would find the answers he sought.

Chapter 17

Matters concerning love and affairs of the heart are very much like military campaigns. Strategy is key, with each move carefully planned so as not to fall victim to potential ambushes. If, however, in the pursuit of her intimate goals, Today's Modern Woman finds herself in a situation that reeks of failure, she should not hesitate to do what many military men have done in the past: retreat with all possible haste.

A Ladies' Guide to the Pursuit of
Personal Happiness and Intimate Fulfillment
by Charles Brightmore

Catherine strode up the neatly swept walkway leading to the modest cottage nestled cozily in the shade cast by a copse of towering elms, driven by an overwhelming combination of anger, confusion, and desperation she barely understood. Muted sounds drifted toward her from the back of the fieldstone residence including a sheep's plaintive *baa* and the quacking of several ducks.

As she raised her hand to knock, a deep voice hailed her. "Lady Catherine, hello."

She turned. Dr. Oliver walked toward her, his face wreathed in a surprised smile. Tucked under one arm, he cradled a small, snorting pig.

"A new patient, Dr. Oliver?" she asked, hoping her return smile did not appear forced.

He laughed. "No, she's payment from my last patient. I was just reassuring her not to worry—I'm not overly fond of bacon."

"I'm certain she's much relieved."

He held the baby pig at arm's length, and asked, very seriously, "Are you much relieved?"

A series of snorts met his question, and he nodded. "Glad to hear it." He nonchalantly tucked the pig back into the crook of his arm, then made Catherine a formal bow. "What brings you to my humble abode? No one is ill, I hope?"

"No, we're all very well, thank you. I'm here to make a request."

"And it will be my honor and pleasure to grant it. If you'll wait here for just a moment while I settle my little friend in the pen in the back, we can go inside."

Standing in the shade offered by one of the elms, Catherine watched him disappear behind the cottage. He reappeared less than a minute later, and she carefully observed him approach. There was no denying that Dr. Oliver was handsome. *Very* handsome. From a strictly aesthetic viewpoint, certainly far more handsome than Mr. Stanton, who, with his rugged features and crooked nose was better described as "attractive."

For the first time, she noted the breadth of the doctor's shoulders. The trimness of his waist. The length of his muscular legs outlined in his snug breeches. The smoothness of his gait. With his sun-streaked brown hair and hazel eyes, he was just the sort of man to set a female heart to flutter. The fact that her heart was not fluttering only added to her desperation and strengthened her resolve. It would flutter soon enough.

When they entered his small, but tastefully furnished drawing room, he asked, "Would you like some tea, Lady Catherine?"

"No, thank you."

He indicated the pair of brocade wing chairs flanking the marble fireplace. "If you'd care to sit—"

"I prefer to stand."

His brows shot upward in a questioning look, but he merely nodded. "Very well. How may I be of service to you?"

Now that the moment was upon her, Catherine's courage sagged. Good Lord, surely she was mad to have embarked on this errand. But then she thought of the *Guide*, of all its liberating precepts, and she stiffened her spine. *Today's Modern Woman seizes the day. Is forthright in what she wants.* And she knew what she wanted. She had a point to prove to herself, and by damn, she was determined, *desperate*, to prove it.

She raised her chin. "Kiss me."

"I beg your pardon?"

"I want you to kiss me."

He stared at her intently for what felt like an eternity, as if trying to see into her mind. When he finally moved, instead of drawing her into an embrace, he lightly clasped her shoulders and held her at arm's length. "Why do you want me to kiss you?"

Catherine barely resisted the urge to tap out her impatience against the parquet floor with her shoe. Good heavens, nothing in the *Guide* had suggested a man might ask such a question.

"Because I . . ." *want to know, need to know,* must

know if another man can make me feel the things he does . . . "because I'm curious." There. That was certainly true.

"Curious to see if you might feel something warmer toward me than merely friendship?"

"Yes."

"Well, I could easily satisfy *your* curiosity without kissing you, but only a fool would turn down such an enticing offer. And I must admit, I'm curious myself . . ."

He drew her into his arms and settled his lips upon hers. She rested her hands upon his chest and rose on her toes, a willing participant. Obviously the good doctor was well versed in the art of kissing—but he did not set her heart to fluttering. Not even a tiny bit. His lips were warm and firm, but they did not generate the fiery sensations Andrew inspired with a mere look.

Oh dear.

He lifted his head, then slowly released her. After studying her for several seconds, he stepped back and regarded her with surprise. "Rather sparkless, wouldn't you agree?"

She felt her cheeks blaze. "I'm afraid so."

"So, has your curiosity been satisfied?"

Self-recriminations rained down on Catherine, filling her with shame at using him in such an unkindly manner. Good Lord, what sort of person had she become? She wasn't certain—but she knew she didn't like herself very well.

Heat born of mortification singed her. The fact that he'd found their kiss as lacking as she clearly indicated that he did not carry a *tendre* for her at all. And she'd just thrown herself at him. Like a common trollop. She would have laughed at her own conceit if she'd been able to do so. Instead she prayed for a gaping hole miraculously to appear in the floor to swallow her. *Retreat*, her mind screamed. *Retreat!*

"I'm so sorry," she said. "I—"

"There's no need to apologize. I understand perfectly. I confess that I once kissed a woman in order to compare my reaction to another. Indeed, I believe it's a very common practice. Rather like sampling both strawberry and blueberry jam to determine which you prefer."

His good humor and understanding only served to make her feel worse. Again her mind commanded her to retreat, but before she could move, he said, "Do not look so distressed, Lady Catherine. From the moment I arrived in Little Longstone six months ago you offered me a friendship I value highly. You have invited me into your home to share meals and laughter, and except for this tiny aberration have never given me false hope that we could ever be anything more than friends—an aberration I appreciate as it satisfied my own curiosity. We are destined to be only friends." He skimmed the pad of his thumb over his lips and winked. "Better friends than most, but still only friends."

Eternally grateful that he was behaving so graciously, and that she had not humiliated herself further, she forced a smile, and said, "Thank you. I'm glad we're friends."

"As am I." He lightly tapped his jaw. "I just hope he doesn't try to break this."

"Who? Break what?"

"Andrew Stanton. And my jaw. He would not be happy should he discover I kissed you." He grinned. "But I'm confident I'd be able to talk him out of pounding me into dust. If not, well, he may be strong, but I've a few tricks of my own."

If her cheeks burned any hotter, her skin would emit

steam. She inched her way backward, toward the open doorway, everything in her straining for retreat. "I must go. Thank you for your kindness and understanding."

"My pleasure." He escorted her to the front door, and Catherine walked swiftly down the path leading toward Bickely cottage. The moment she was certain she was out of Dr. Oliver's line of vision, she pressed her hands to her burning cheeks, praying she'd not suffer an illness anytime in the near future because it would be a long while before she could face the doctor again.

Before riding on to Bickley cottage, Andrew stopped briefly in the village of Little Longstone to make some purchases. Just as he was about to enter the smithy, an odd sensation prowled through him. He turned around, his gaze panning the area. Rows of shops, several dozen pedestrians, a curricle with a man and a young girl perched upon the seat, two young ladies chatting under a blue-and-white-striped awning. No one appeared to be paying him any particular attention, yet he strongly sensed that someone was watching him. And it was the second time today he'd experienced the same sensation.

About an hour ago, while still en route from London, he'd felt the same warning tingle. He'd reined in Aphrodite, but had not seen or heard anyone. Still, the eerie feeling persisted, and even stronger than before. But who would be watching him? And why? Was it possible he was imagining it? He couldn't deny he was tired, and many thoughts occupied his mind. No doubt it was just his preoccupation run amuck. Still, he'd make certain to remain alert.

After finishing his business with the blacksmith, Andrew rode to Bickely cottage, where he spent a few minutes chatting with Fritzborne at the stables before striding quickly across the lawns toward the house, eager to see Catherine and Spencer. He'd keenly missed them, suffering a deep, echoing emptiness that had plagued him since departing Little Longstone yesterday. Returning felt like coming home—a warm feeling he hadn't experienced in more than a decade.

Late-afternoon sunshine gilded the house, making it look as if a halo surrounded the dwelling, and he quickened his pace. He'd been away for a mere thirty-six hours, yet it had felt like years. No doubt because it was actually thirty-seven hours. And twenty-two minutes. Not that he was counting.

Milton opened the door with a forbidding frown, which immediately relaxed when he saw Andrew standing at the threshold. "Ah, it is you, sir."

Andrew raised his brows and smiled. "Clearly you were expecting someone else."

"Actually, I was hoping there would be no further callers this afternoon." He cleared his throat. "Present company excluded, of course. Although, you are not a caller. You are a guest. Please come in, Mr. Stanton. Seeing *you* at the door is a welcome relief."

"Thank you." Andrew entered the foyer. His shoulders tensed as he noted the new tremendous flower arrangement. "Looks as if the Duke of Kelby has emptied his conservatory again."

A ghost of a smile whispered across Milton's thin lips. "Yes. How fortunate for us. Lords Avenbury and Ferrymouth blessedly sent smaller tributes."

"Are Lady Catherine and Spencer about?"

"They're strolling in the gardens." He heaved a sigh. "I do so hate to disturb them."

"No need to on my account."

"Not you, sir." He jerked his head toward the corridor and curled his upper lip. "*Them*."

"Them?"

"The duke and Lords Avenbury and Ferrymouth. The notes they sent with their flowers this morning indicated they wished to call, however none of them wrote that they planned to visit *today*."

"And they're all in the drawing room?"

"I'm afraid so. I kept them at bay, standing on the porch for a bit, but with all three of them, it became quite crowded. And loud. I suggested quite firmly they return another time, but they all flatly refused to go. A few moments ago they threatened to storm the gardens in search of Lady Catherine. To keep them from doing so, I reluctantly showed them into the drawing room, and I've since been plotting a way to get rid of them that does not involve coshing them all with a skillet."

"I see." Andrew thoughtfully tapped his chin. "I think I may be able to assist you, Milton."

"I'd be most grateful, sir."

"Consider it done."

Still laughing over her son's humorous imitation of a toad, Catherine and Spencer entered the house through the rear terrace doors, then made their way toward the foyer. The time spent with her son had helped Catherine settle her chaotic thoughts and form a new resolve. Her relationship with Andrew was a lovely, pleasant diversion she would enjoy for the remainder of the short time he'd remain in Little Longstone. When he returned to London, she would go on with her life, caring for Spencer, enjoying her independence, free from the encumbrances that had stifled her during her marriage. As Today's Modern

Woman should, she would look back on her affair with fond memories and wish Andrew a long, prosperous life. For, other than this brief interlude, there simply was no room for him in her life.

As she and Spencer approached the foyer, the sound of several masculine voices reached them.

"Who is that?" Catherine murmured.

They entered the foyer through the archway opposite the front door, and she halted as if she'd walked into a wall of glass. And stared.

The Duke of Kelby, Lord Avenbury, and Lord Ferrymouth stood in the foyer, each in turn shaking hands with Andrew, while Milton stood at the door with a suspiciously smug expression on his face. As if seeing this unexpected assortment of men in her foyer weren't surprising enough, it was the *condition* of the men that stunned her. The duke's right eye was nearly swollen shut and surrounded by an angry bruise. Lord Avenbury held a handkerchief that bore unmistakable streaks of blood pressed to his nose, while Lord Ferrymouth sported a bottom lip three times its normal size.

She turned to look at Spencer, who was gawking at the scene with a stunned expression she imagined mirrored her own. At that moment, Lord Avenbury turned and caught sight of her. Instead of a welcoming smile, he looked . . . frightened? He jabbed Lord Ferrymouth with his elbow, then jerked his head toward Catherine. Lord Ferrymouth's eyes widened, and he in turn nudged the duke. All three stared at her for several seconds, their countenances bearing varying degrees of what looked like alarm. Then they mumbled a jumble of unintelligible words while stepping hastily toward the door, which Milton opened with a flourish. After the gentlemen hurried from the house, Milton closed the door with a resounding bang, then brushed his hands together as if ridding them of dirt. He and Andrew exchanged satisfied gins.

Catherine cleared her throat to find her voice. "What on earth happened to the duke and Lords Avenbury and Ferrymouth?"

Both men turned toward her. Milton immediately rearranged his features into his usual inscrutable mask. Her gaze met Andrew's, and warmth suffused her. Unmistakable pleasure, along with a healthy dose of heat, flared in his eyes, filling her mind with a wealth of sensual images and tingling a shiver down her spine.

Andrew bowed at the waist. "Lovely to see you again, Lady Catherine." He shot Spencer a wink. "You, too, Spencer."

Ignoring the flutterings Andrew's presence set up in her stomach, she crossed the foyer, Spencer at her side. Before she could speak again, Spencer looked at Andrew, and asked, his voice an awed hush, "I say, did you plant those blokes facers?"

Andrew grasped his lapels, his expression turning very serious. "During the course of my duties, I'm afraid that I did."

Catherine stared. "Do not tell me that you used your fists against those gentlemen."

"Very well, I won't tell you that."

"Dear God. You *punched* them?"

"Well, it is impossible not to use one's fists while engaged in pugilism. When the gentlemen learned of my"—he coughed modestly into his hand—"stellar reputation at Gentleman Jackson's Emporium, they *insisted* upon a lesson. As they were your guests, I thought it would be rude to refuse them."

"I see. And how did they hear of your stellar reputation?"

"I told them."

A sound that could only be described as a giggle erupted from Spencer.

Catherine swallowed her own inappropriate desire to giggle. "And how, precisely, did all this come about?"

"When I arrived from London," Andrew said, "I discovered the three gentlemen in the drawing room. Quite a sight they made, all perched on the settee like a flock of fat-breasted pigeons upon a branch, glaring at each other, elbowing, vying for more room. As you were nowhere about, I offered to entertain them in your stead. During the course of our pugilism lesson, they unfortunately sustained their injuries—which are quite minor by the way." He shook his head. "Not the heartiest of fellows, I fear, although Lord Avenbury's uppercut showed some promise. After our lesson, I informed the gentlemen that I'd been giving lessons to Spencer . . . and intended to give them to you as well, Lady Catherine."

Catherine actually felt her jaw drop. "*Me?*"

"They were just as surprised, I assure you, but I told them that such lessons were necessary because of the rampant crime nowadays. After all, Today's Modern Woman must be able to defend herself, do you not agree?"

She wasn't certain if she were more amused or horrified. "I suppose, although I cannot imagine that a woman's most effective weapon would be her *fists.*"

"Precisely why the element of surprise would work so well."

"I can only surmise that the gentlemen were quite taken aback."

"My dear Lady Catherine, the way you're following this story, why it's almost as if you were in the room. Yes, they were all quite stunned. I can only hope you were not overly desirous of their company because I don't think any of them will be back."

"Indeed? And why is that?"

"Because they're all afraid of you."

Laughter bubbled in her throat, and she pressed her lips together to contain it.

"Well, I for one am glad they won't be back," Spencer said. "Pests, that what they were, all trying to impress Mum." He smiled at Andrew. "And I'm happy you've returned, Mr. Stanton."

"As am I, Spencer."

"You're back earlier than we expected," Catherine said, refusing to acknowledge how much that pleased her. "I hope that means all is well in London?"

"It means I've done everything I could for the moment."

"How bad is the damage to the museum?"

"Extensive, but the repairs are under way."

"And the investors?"

His jaw tightened, and sympathy pinched her at the sight of the weary lines surrounding his eyes. "Not pleased, as you might imagine, but I'm hopeful that their confidence will soon be restored. I've written to Philip, telling him everything. I tried to present the events in the best light possible, but obviously he'll be very concerned, which in turn will worry Meredith. And there's only one way to alleviate that." A regretful look entered his eyes, and Catherine suddenly knew what was coming next. "As much as I hate to cut my visit here short, I'm afraid I must return to London tomorrow."

"Tomorrow?" Spencer repeated, his voice ripe with the same dismay that flooded Catherine.

"Yes. But I won't depart until the afternoon, so we'll have plenty of time for our morning lessons."

"When will you come back?" Spencer asked.

Andrew's gaze flicked to Catherine, then he smiled at Spencer—a smile, Catherine noted, that seemed somewhat forced. "Your mother and I will talk about that to see if we can agree upon a date."

"But you're welcome here anytime!" Spencer said. "Isn't he, Mum?"

Catherine's breath caught at the question, and her gaze flew to Andrew, who regarded her with an unfathomable expression. She desperately did not want to offer Spencer false hope that Mr. Stanton would return, yet she simply could not force herself to say he wasn't welcome.

Heavy silence swelled for several seconds, then she said lightly, "Don't worry. Mr. Stanton and I shall discuss the matter."

"When?" Spencer persisted.

"This evening," Catherine said. *After Andrew and I make love at the springs. After we make love for the last time . . .*

"Are you feeling up to a lesson today, Spencer?" Andrew asked.

Catherine pushed aside her disquieting thoughts and watched her son's eyes light up. "Yes, I am."

"Excellent. But first, I have a surprise for you." He turned toward Catherine. "For you as well, Lady Catherine."

Her pulse quickened. She used to dislike surprises. Now, however, it seemed she liked them very much. Too much. Before she could stop herself, she asked, "What is it?"

He shook his head sadly, then made a big show of patting down his jacket. "Now *where* did I place that dictionary?" He looked at Spencer, who was trying, without success, not to smile. "Can you fathom that your mother *still* does not know the meaning of the word surprise?"

" 'Tis shocking," Spencer said.

"Indeed it is. Therefore, I suggest we go to the stables with all due haste so as to show your mother what a surprise means."

Before they took a step, however, a knock sounded at the door. Milton's eyes narrowed. "Not more suitors, I hope," he muttered. He opened the door to reveal a young footman. "I've a note for Lady Catherine," the footman announced importantly. "From Lord Greybourne."

Catherine stepped forward, and the young man handed her the missive with a flourish. With her heart thumping, Catherine quickly broke the seal and scanned the brief contents. She looked up at the anxious faces surrounding her and smiled. "The Greybourne heir has arrived—a healthy baby boy they've name William. Both mother and son are doing splendidly, although Philip claims he may never be the same again. He swears the entire process was as much an ordeal for him as it was for Meredith." Catherine looked at the ceiling. "Idiotic man."

After congratulations were said all around, Catherine briefly excused herself to pen a hasty note to Philip to send back with the footman. Then the group headed off to the stables. When they arrived, Fritzborne greeted them, a grin stretching his mouth wide. "All's well, Mr. Stanton."

"Excellent." Andrew led the way into the stables, pausing in front of the third stall, one Catherine knew was not normally used. "Before I returned to the house today, I visited the village to make several purchases. While I was there, I happened upon something that I simply could not resist."

"I thought *women* were supposed to be the renowned shoppers, yet you seem to possess little self-control when faced with any sort of shop," Catherine teased.

His gaze, avid and warm, rested on hers. "On the contrary, I possess an abundance of self-control." He paused for several seconds . . . just enough time to rush fire into her cheeks by making her aware that he referred to far more than shopping, then continued, "Although I do agree that I enjoy buying things for people I . . . care about. In this instance, however, the purchase was for me, and purely selfish. What do you think?" He opened the stall door.

In the corner, curled up on a bed of fresh hay, lay a sleeping, black-haired puppy.

"It's a dog," Spencer said, his voice filled with quiet wonder.

"It is indeed," Andrew agreed, entering the stall. He gently scooped up the small dog, and was rewarded with a contented doggie sigh. "I've wanted one ever since your uncle Philip acquired Prince, who is a very fine dog indeed. Would you like to hold him?"

Spencer, eyes wide, nodded. "Oh, yes. Please."

Andrew carefully handed over the sleepy dog. Seconds later, the puppy lifted his head and let out a tremendous, pink-tongued yawn. When he caught sight of Spencer, he immediately turned into a wiggling mass of tail-wagging canine joy, licking every bit of Spencer's chin he could reach, much to Spencer's laughing delight.

Andrew stepped closer to Catherine and said out of the corner of his mouth, "I believe my dog likes your son."

"Hmmm. And clearly my son likes your dog. But I have a sneaking suspicion you knew—"

"That they would fall in love with each other?" She felt him turn to look at her, and it required all her strength to keep her gaze fixed upon Spencer. "Yes, I admit I suspected as much."

"He's grand, Mr. Stanton," Spencer said, accepting ecstatic puppy licks to his cheeks. "Where did you get him?"

"In the village, from the blacksmith. I'd stopped to make a purchase, and he introduced me to the entire litter his dog had birthed two months ago. Six adorable little devils. It was difficult to make a choice. This fellow sort of chose me, and the feeling was mutual."

"I imagine so," Spencer murmured, burying his face in the dog's curly fur.

Unable to resist, Catherine reached out and scratched behind the adorable puppy's ears. A look of utter devotion entered the pup's black eyes. "Oh, you're a charmer, aren't you," she said with a laugh.

"What is his name?" Spencer asked.

"The blacksmith called him Shadow, and it seems to suit as the little fellow followed me all about. What do you think?"

Spencer held the puppy at arm's length and inclined his head first right, then left. Pink tongue panting, tiny ears perked, the puppy mimicked his actions, tilting his little head. They all laughed, and Catherine said, "It seems that Shadow is indeed the perfect name."

"Then Shadow it is. Now, we're heading outside, behind the stables. Spencer, would you mind carrying Shadow for me?"

Catherine couldn't help but laugh. "That is like asking a mouse if it minds eating a bit more cheese."

They walked outside together, and Andrew led them to a large blanket spread on the lawn under the shade of an elm. Catherine gazed curiously at the tarp to one side of the blanket. "What is under there?"

He smiled. "We're going to make some magic. But it's a two-man job, I'm afraid. I need someone strong to assist me." He made a great show of looking around.

"I'll help," Spencer said eagerly.

"A volunteer. Excellent. Lady Catherine, would you be so kind as to mind Shadow, so Spencer and I can proceed?" Catherine agreed, taking the puppy from Spencer.

"Just make yourself comfortable on the blanket," Andrew said, "and I'll brief my helper on his duties."

Catherine lowered herself onto the blanket and laughed at Shadow's tail-chasing antics. From the corner of her eye, she watched Andrew and Spencer speaking in muted tones, and the pleased flush that stole over Spencer's cheeks. They returned several minutes later, and with a flourish, Andrew pulled the tarp from his stash of supplies.

Catherine craned her neck and stared at the five buckets of varying sizes he'd uncovered. "What's in those?"

"Ice, salt, cream, sugar, and strawberries," he said, pointing to each one in turn. He then indicated a cloth bag with a nod of his chin. "Bowls and spoons."

"We're going to make strawberry-flavored ice, Mum!" Spencer said.

"Really?" She scooped up Shadow then walked over to have a better look. "How are we going to make that?"

"Just watch," Andrew said. "You've never eaten anything like this, I promise you."

"I had a flavored ice in London last year," Catherine said. "It was delightful."

"This will be extraordinarily delightful," Andrew promised with a smile.

Nearly an hour later, after much strenuous shaking by Andrew of an outer bucket filled with chips of ice and salt while Spencer vigorously stirred an inner bucket filled with cream, sugar, and strawberries, Andrew finally announced, "It's ready."

Spencer, his face red from his exertions, blew out a loud breath. "Thank goodness. My arms are about to drop off."

"As are mine," Andrew agreed. "But trust me, once you taste this, the pain will instantly fade."

"I feel horribly guilty," Catherine said. "While you two shook and stirred, I merely sat here and enjoyed the lovely weather."

"You were watching Shadow," Andrew reminded her, scooping heaping spoonfuls of pink stuff into porcelain bowls.

"Not a difficult task, as the imp has been sleeping for the past three-quarters of an hour." She looked down at the bundle of black fur sprawled across her lap and tried, without any success whatsoever, to stem the affection flooding her. "I believe I bored Shadow to sleep."

"Well, she who bores the dog to sleep serves the cause just as much as those who stir and shake," Andrew said, handing her a bowl and spoon. "Taste."

Catherine dipped her spoon into the creamy concoction, then lifted it to her lips. Her eyes widened with pure delight as the smooth, sweet, strawberry-flavored chill slid down her throat. "Oh, my."

Andrew laughed. After scooping out a generous portion for Spencer, then himself, they all sat upon the blanket and indulged in their treat.

"You're right, Mr. Stanton," Spencer said, "this is the most delicious thing I've ever tasted."

"Made all your arm aches disappear, I'll wager."

"Every one," Spencer agreed.

"Where did you learn to make this?" Catherine asked, savoring another delectable spoonful.

"In America. The family who owned the stables where I worked was fond of serving this to their guests." A phantom of some emotion she could not read flashed in his eyes. "Whenever they did so, their daughter would pilfer an extra bowl for me. Eventually I asked their cook how it was made."

A spurt of something that felt suspiciously like jealousy shot through her at the thought of Andrew sitting on a blanket with his employer's daughter, eating a frozen delight that she'd brought him.

"The girl who brought you the ice—what was her name?" Spencer asked, voicing the question Catherine hadn't had the courage to speak.

"Emily," Andrew said, softly, looking down into his bowl.

"Was she nice?"

"Very nice." He looked up and gave Spencer a slight smile that looked more sad than happy to Catherine. "In fact, you rather remind me of her, Spencer."

"I remind you of a *girl*?"

Andrew chuckled at his horrified expression. "Not the fact that she was a girl, but because she . . . struggled to find where she fit in. She did not feel very comfortable around people. Indeed, except for me, she had very few friends."

Spencer's brow puckered as he pondered this. Then he asked, "Are you still her friend? Do you correspond with her?"

There was no mistaking the pain that filled his eyes. "No. She died."

"Oh. I'm sorry."

"As am I."

"When did she die?"

He swallowed, then said, "About eleven years ago. Just before I left America. I bet she would be pleased that we're all enjoying this treat. And I especially wanted to make strawberry because I know it is a favorite of both of you. Who would like some more?"

"Me, please," said Spencer, holding out his bowl.

The adroit subject change had not escaped Catherine, and she wondered if there was more behind it than simply not wanting to discuss a sad subject. Andrew's pain when he'd discussed this Emily was palpable, filling her with sympathy for him. The conversation had also piqued her curiosity.

Amid many appreciative murmurs, they each enjoyed another bowl while laughing at Shadow—who'd awakened and showed a huge interest in the proceedings. "There's just enough for one more serving," Andrew said. "Since I know from experience that this is a favorite of stable masters, I wager Fritzborne would enjoy it."

"I'll bring it to him," Spencer offered.

As Catherine watched her son walk toward the stables, his uneven gait forming the familiar lump of love in her throat, she was also acutely, painfully aware that she and Andrew were alone.

She turned to look at him and stilled at the compelling, serious look in his dark eyes.

"I missed you," he said softly.

Three simple words. How did he cleave through all her hard-fought-for resolutions with three simple words? Her insides seemed to melt, and she was grateful she was sitting, for her knees felt oddly weak. As much as she hated to admit it, as much as she desperately wished she hadn't, she'd missed him, too. More than she'd believed it possible to miss a person. Much more than she'd wanted to. And certainly much more than was wise. And now, with those three simple words, she feared that all her attempts to keep her heart unencumbered were doomed to failure.

He reached out and brushed his fingers slowly back and forth over the back of her hand, sending delicious tingles up her arm. "You said earlier that I lacked self-control, and I want you to know just how very wrong you are. I cannot even begin to describe the amount of control I am exercising right now not to kiss you. Touch you."

"You are touching me," she said, her voice breathless.

"Not in the way I want to, I assure you."

Heat pooled low in her belly, and sensual images of all the seductive ways he'd touched her flashed through her mind.

"Do you still want to meet at the springs tonight, Catherine?"

"Yes." *Desperately.* "Do you?"

"Do you truly need to ask?"

"No." She could easily see the desire in his eyes. And if she didn't change the subject, she stood in danger of saying or doing something she might well regret.

"This"—she spread her hand to indicate their picnic area and the collection of buckets—"was a delightful surprise. And very thoughtful of you."

"I'm glad you enjoyed it."

"I confess I have a surprise for you as well."

"Really? What is it?"

She shot him an aggrieved look. "What are you always saying about a dictionary?"

He laughed. "*Touché*. When will my surprise be unveiled?"

"Are you always this impatient?"

His eyes darkened. "Sometimes."

Heavens, she wished she'd brought her fan to dispel the heat this man inspired. "Actually, you may have it right now." She slipped a small, flat tissue-paper-wrapped bundle secured with a bit of blue satin ribbon from the pocket of her gown and handed it to him.

Surprised pleasure flared in his eyes. "A gift?"

"It's nothing really," she said, suddenly feeling very self-conscious.

"On the contrary, it's extraordinary."

She laughed. "You haven't opened it yet."

"It doesn't matter. It's still extraordinary. How did you just happen to have this in your pocket?"

"I retrieved it from my bedchamber after I'd written my note to Philip—before I rejoined you in the foyer."

He untied the ribbon, parted the tissue paper, then lifted the white linen square. "A handkerchief. With my initials embroidered on it." Staring at the material, he gently rubbed his thumb over the dark blue, silk thread letters that had obviously been done by an inexpert hand.

"The night in the garden," she said, her words coming out in a rush, "when you showed me the bleeding hearts, you didn't have a handkerchief when you thought I was crying—not that I *was* crying, mind you—but since you didn't have one, I thought perhaps you could use this."

He said nothing for several seconds, just continued slowly to brush his thumb over the letters. Then, in a husky voice, he said, "You don't care for needlework, yet you embroidered this for me."

A self-conscious laugh escaped her. "I tried. As you can plainly see, embroidery is not my forte."

He looked up and his gaze captured hers. There was no mistaking his pleasure at her gift. "It's beautiful, Catherine. The finest gift I've ever received. Thank you."

Warmth suffused her, then quickly turned to heat when his gaze dropped to her lips. Her breath caught, anticipating the brush of his lips against hers, his luscious taste, the silken sweep of his tongue.

Shadow chose that moment to flop himself down in front of her, belly up, paws dangling, in a shameless bid to be rubbed. With a start, Catherine recalled where they were, then pried her attention away from Andrew's distracting gaze. She tickled her fingers over the pup's soft belly, much to his canine delight, while Andrew tucked his new handkerchief into his pocket. "You realize that Spencer is now going to want a dog," she said.

"Would that be so terrible?"

Catherine carefully considered before answering, then said, "As much as Spencer and I both like dogs, I've always feared having one."

"Because you thought the dog might jump on him? Knock him over?"

"Yes." She lifted her chin. "I was only trying to keep Spencer safe."

"I wasn't criticizing. Actually, when he was smaller, I think it was a prudent, wise decision. But Spencer is no longer a child."

"And a man should have a dog?"

"Yes, I think he should."

"He hasn't brought up the subject in a number of years—although I suspect that is about to change."

He clasped her hand, and she suppressed a sigh of pleasure at the feel of those callused fingers enclosing hers. "I saw the dogs who sired the litter, and neither one was large. Fritzborne mentioned that he'd be happy to have a dog stay in the stables if you didn't want the beast in the house. Said a dog would keep all those cats in line."

Catherine pondered a bit, then said, "There is no denying that Spencer is no longer a small boy. And he's careful. Strong. Such a young man certainly deserves a puppy if he wants one." She shook her head. "Everything seems to be changing, and so quickly. I swear it was only yesterday he was a babe in my arms."

"Just because something seems to happen quickly, doesn't mean it's bad, Catherine. In my experience, it usually just means those things are . . . inevitable." Before she could think up a reply, he said, "Here comes

Spencer." He withdrew his hand with clear reluctance, then reached into his waistcoat pocket and slipped out his watch. After consulting the timepiece, he looked at her with an expression that scorched her. "Seven hours and thirty-three minutes until midnight, Catherine. I pray I can last that long."

He wasn't the only one saying that particular prayer. Tonight their affair would reach its inevitable end. A bit sooner than she'd anticipated, but surely that was for the best.

Yes, surely it was.

Chapter 18

There are subtle, less obvious places on every man's and woman's body that, when touched, kissed, caressed, and stroked elicit strong and delightful sensations. For instance, the small of the back. The nape. Earlobes. The inside of the wrist and elbows. The back of the knees. The inner thighs. Today's Modern Woman should strive to discover all the deliciously sensitive spots on her lover's body, and make certain he discovers all of hers . . .

A Ladies' Guide to the Pursuit of
Personal Happiness and Intimate Fulfillment
by Charles Brightmore

Andrew walked toward the springs, trying to unravel the knotty problem that still seemed to have no solution. What to do about Catherine?

Of course, he knew what he *wanted* to do, had taken steps toward that end in London, but his every instinct warned him it was too soon to profess his love and ask for her hand. For the hundredth time he cursed the fates that necessitated his leaving tomorrow. While he'd obviously made progress, he hadn't had enough time to win her heart. To convince her to change her views on marriage. To find a way to tell her the truth about his past. Pray that that knowledge didn't turn her against him. He needed time, which he unfortunately did not have.

He also needed patience, which was becoming more and more difficult to come by. He'd wanted this woman, had loved her for what seemed like an eternity. Everything in him rebelled against taking months and months to court her slowly. He wanted her *now.*

He greatly feared that any ground he'd gained would be lost once he left here. She'd only wanted a short-term liaison. He suspected that once she returned to her normal routine, she would not be eager to issue him a return invitation to Little Longstone. Indeed, such a visit might well turn into a source of gossip. It was one thing for him to remain a few days after escorting her here so she did not have to travel from London alone. It was quite another for him to make return trips simply to visit.

As he approached the last curve on the path before arriving at the springs, the sound of a twig snapping directly behind caught his attention. His first thought was that it was Catherine, but then he caught a subtle whiff of tobacco. He tensed and turned swiftly. Unfortunately he turned a second too late. Something crashed down on the back of his head, and his world faded to black.

Catherine stood at the edge of the springs and looked down at the gently bubbling warm water, waiting for Andrew to arrive. She'd wrapped her resolve around her like a suit of armor and tightly tethered her heart to prevent any risk of its escaping its confines. For years she'd been content with her solitary existence, sharing her life with Spencer, enjoying the waters and her gardens, her friendship with Genevieve. Andrew's presence threatened to invade the safe haven she'd made here, stirring up all these confusing feelings, yearning, and desires she didn't want. She desperately needed to regain her equilibrium. After tonight, she would. Tonight belonged to her and Andrew. Tomorrow they went their separate ways. And that's the way she wanted it.

The muted sound of a twig snapping roused her, and her heart leapt in anticipation. Seconds later she heard what sounded like dull thud, followed by a low groan, then another thud.

"Andrew?" she called softly. Only silence met her. She stood on her toes and peeked over the stone outcropping that curved around the springs and peered down the darkened path. Seeing nothing but inky shadows, she listened for several seconds yet heard nothing save leaves rustling in the soft breeze. Had she imagined the sound? Or had Andrew perhaps tripped on a branch or tree root in the darkness?

"Andrew?" she called again, a bit louder this time. Silence. She cursed the fact that she hadn't brought a lantern with her, but she knew the path to the springs so well she could navigate it with her eyes closed. Besides, she had not wanted to risk anyone possibly seeing the light from the house. Had Andrew also tried to avoid discovery and been injured as a result?

She stepped from behind the rocks and walked briskly along the path. The instant she rounded the curve she saw the prone form lying on the ground.

"Andrew!" Heart in her throat, she rushed forward, praying he wasn't badly hurt. Just as she reached him, she was grabbed roughly from behind. A strong arm gripped her just below her bosom, imprisoning her arms against her side, and jerked her backward, off her feet. She managed to cry out once before the attacker clamped his other hand over her mouth.

Catherine kicked and thrashed wildly, but it was quickly obvious she was no match for this man's superior strength. He half dragged, half carried her toward the springs. And away from Andrew.

Andrew. Dear God, he must have been a victim of this brigand. Was he still alive? She redoubled her frantic efforts, twisting, kicking, but to no avail as she was dragged ever closer to the water.

Distant sounds, rising and falling like a rapid tide, permeated the thick fog dulling Andrew's mind. A vicious ache throbbed behind his eyes, and he dragged his heavy lids open with a Herculean effort. He blinked and looked up at . . . the dark sky?

It required all his strength to push himself into a sitting position, an effort that forced him to close his eyes against the nausea and sharp pains radiating from his head. He pulled in several deep breaths, trying to assimilate what had happened and why the hell his head hurt so badly. He'd been walking to the springs. To meet Catherine. A noise behind him. Then . . . someone attacking him from behind. His eyes sprang open. Catherine.

A scraping sound, followed by a muffled grunt, coming from the area near the springs caught his attention, and he forced himself to stand. He staggered a few steps and had to press his palm against a tree trunk for several seconds until the dizziness passed, and his equilibrium returned. After his vision cleared, he moved silently down the path. When he rounded the curve, the sight that met his gaze stilled everything inside him—breath, blood, heart.

Catherine, struggling mightily, was being dragged behind the tall rocks surrounding the springs by a dark-clad figure. They disappeared from sight and Andrew dashed forward. He'd taken less than a half a dozen steps when he heard Catherine cry out. Her wail was silenced by a loud splash.

Blood pounding in his ears, Andrew raced ahead. He rounded the rocks and instantly assessed the situation. The bastard was looking into the bubbling spring. Clearly he'd thrown Catherine into the water, as she was nowhere to be seen. And she hadn't surfaced . . .

With a roar of outrage, Andrew grabbed the man by collar and lifted him off his feet. Their eyes met, and a shock of recognition radiated through Andrew. "You bastard," he growled. His fist flashed, smashing into the man's nose. He then heaved him backward, against the rocks. The man's body hit with a thud. With a groan and blood running down his face, he sank.

Andrew didn't wait to see the bastard hit the ground. He jumped into the gurgling spring. Warm water closed over his head, and he fought the panic seizing him in a vise grip. His feet hit something hard and he pushed upward. His head broke the surface, and he pulled in a gasping breath as his feet settled on the bottom and warm water swirled around his chest.

He waded farther into the pool, swishing his hands under the water, his eyes frantically scanning the surface. A few feet in front of him he caught sight of what looked like a piece of dark material. He grabbed for it and tugged.

It was Catherine. Her gown. He jerked her upward, getting her head out of the water. She lolled like a limp rag in his arms.

"Catherine." His voice came out in a harsh rasp. Cradling her with one arm, the water swirling around them, he pushed the wet hair from her face. His fingers encountered a lump just above her ear, and his jaw clenched. She must have hit her head when that bastard threw her in.

"Catherine . . . please, dear God . . ." He lightly shook her and firmly patted her cheeks, willing her to breathe, unable to draw a breath himself as he stared down at her pale, wet, motionless face. He gathered her closer, squeezing her to him, whispering her name, begging her to breathe. To open her eyes.

Suddenly she coughed. Coughed again. Then gasped for breath.

"That's it," Andrew said, patting her sharply between the shoulder blades. After several more choking coughs, her eyelids fluttered open, and she gazed at him with a dazed expression. She blinked, then lifted a shaking wet hand to his cheek.

"Andrew."

That hoarse whisper was the most beautiful sound he'd ever heard. "I'm right here, Catherine."

"You were hurt. But you're all right."

He most certainly was not. In the blink of an eye he'd nearly lost everything that mattered to him.

Fear flashed in her eyes and she squirmed in his arms. "There's a man, Andrew. He grabbed me, and must have injured you."

"I know. He's—"

Andrew's gaze froze on the empty spot where he'd last seen their attacker slithering down the rock wall. In his desperate attempt to pull Catherine to safety he'd momentarily forgotten the bastard. Obviously, he'd only been stunned. He quickly scanned the area, but saw nothing.

"He's gone." Holding tight to Catherine, he waded to the edge of the spring and gently set her on the smooth rock ledge. By the time he'd exited the water, Catherine had risen to her feet.

"Can you walk?" he asked, alternating his watchful gaze from her face to their surroundings.

"Yes."

He slipped his knife from his boot, cursing himself for not gutting the bastard when he'd had the chance, but all his thoughts had been focused on getting to Catherine before it was too late. And he'd nearly been too late.

"I hurt him," Andrew whispered next to her ear, "but clearly not badly enough. I hope he's off licking his wounds and won't make another attempt tonight, but I can't be sure. We're going to walk as quickly and quietly as we can back to the house. Do not let go of my hand."

She nodded. Gripping his knife in one hand and tightly clasping Catherine's wet hand in the other, they started down the dark path. Twenty minutes later, they arrived at the house without further incident.

After locking the door behind them, Andrew lit an oil lamp and took a moment to examine the lump on her head. She winced when his fingers gently probed the tender spot, but she assured him, "I'm fine."

"All right. I want to search and secure the house." He lit another lantern, then handed it to her. "Stay close to me." He wasn't about to let her out of his sight.

"I want to check on Spencer," she said, her eyes filled with concern.

"That's first," he agreed, leading the way up the stairs.

After ascertaining that Spencer was safe, Andrew whispered, "Stay here with him. I want to check the rest of the rooms. Lock the door behind me and do not open it for anyone except me." He held out his knife. "Take this."

Her eyes widened, and she audibly swallowed. But she took the weapon, determination gleaming in her eyes.

"Be careful," she whispered.

Andrew nodded, then left the room. Once he'd heard

the lock click into place behind him, he immediately headed toward his bedchamber. After making certain no one lurked in the room, he pulled his pistol and another knife from the leather satchel in the bottom of the wardrobe.

"I'm ready for you now, you bastard." Dozens of questions buzzed through his mind, the loudest of which was *why,* but his questions would have to wait.

Slipping the knife into his boot, he carried the lantern in one hand, hefted the comforting weight of his pistol in the other, and set off to search and secure the house.

Catherine stood in Spencer's bedchamber, clutching the knife, her ears straining to pick up any foreign sound, her gaze never leaving her son's face, which was gently illuminated by the oil lamp she'd set on his desk. Her wet clothing stuck to her like an uncomfortable second skin, and she pressed her lips together to keep her teeth from chattering. She wasn't certain if the shivers racking her were more the result of being chilled or due to the shocking fright of this evening.

Spencer stirred, let out a small sigh, then settled, and Catherine squeezed her eyes shut. She'd thought the danger was over, had been convinced that the shooting in London was a random accident and not related to her connection to the *Guide* and Charles Brightmore, but clearly she was wrong. Dear God, what had she done? Guilt and self-recriminations wrapped a noose around her neck, strangling her. Andrew could easily have been killed. She could easily have drowned. And God only knows what sort of threat her actions had wrought upon her family.

She kept her silent vigil, heart pounding with every creak of the house, praying for Andrew's safety. When she finally heard a soft tapping on the door, relief wobbled her knees.

"Catherine, it's me," came Andrew's quiet voice from the corridor.

Holding her lantern aloft, she opened the door, quite certain she'd never been so relieved to see anyone in her entire life. He motioned for her join him in the corridor. After she'd done so, he quietly closed Spencer's door, then clasped her hand and led her in silence directly to her bedchamber. The instant the door closed behind them and they were ensconced in privacy, he set both their lamps on the marble hearth and drew her into his arms.

Catherine slipped her arms around his waist and rested her head against his chest, absorbing his hard, fast heartbeats against her cheek.

"The house is safe," he said softly, his words warm against her temple. "No intruders. I locked all the doors and windows. I woke Milton, briefed him on what happened, and instructed him to tell the rest of the staff in the morning." He leaned back and tipped up her chin. "I know who did this, Catherine. I saw him. Recognized him. And I swear to you, I'll find him."

"Who is it?"

"A man named Sidney Carmichael."

Catherine frowned. "He attended my father's birthday party, as well as the duke's soiree."

"Yes. He is—or rather was—one of the potential museum investors. I spoke to him just yesterday in London." His brow creased with a deep frown. "In spite of the dark, I know it was he. I just don't understand *why* he would do this. He hadn't yet handed over any funds for the museum, so he didn't stand to lose any money."

Catherine's stomach twisted. She wished she didn't have to tell him, but there was no other way. Drawing a bracing breath, she said, "I'm afraid I know why, Andrew."

His gaze sharpened, but instead of demanding an immediate explanation, he said, "I'm anxious to hear your thoughts, but first we must get you into dry clothing before you become ill. Turn around."

For the first time she noted that he'd changed into a fresh linen shirt and breeches. She turned and felt him deftly unfasten the row of buttons down her back. After he helped her slip off her damp gown and underthings, she retrieved a nightrail, robe, and slippers. While he carefully settled her wet garments over the back of a wing chair, and tended the fire which had burned too low, she quickly dressed.

After she'd tightened the robe's sash around her waist, she walked to the fireplace, taking a moment to allow the flames to chase away the last of her chills. When she was warm, she turned to him. The fire cast the room in a golden, flickering glow, gilding his features in contrasting panes of shadow and light. His eyes were serious and filled with questions as they regarded her, yet he said nothing, patiently waiting for her to speak.

Clasping her fidgety hands at her waist, she said, "I'm not certain how to tell you this, other than to simply say it. You are aware that many people are angered by the *Ladies' Guide* and that there is great interest in the author."

"Yes."

"Indeed, threats have been made against Charles Brightmore's life."

His eyes narrowed. "Threats against his life? How do you know this?"

"I overheard Lords Markingworth, Whitly, and Carweather speaking at my father's birthday party. They spoke of wanting to see Charles Brightmore dead, and of an investigator they'd hired to find him. 'Tis now clear to me that this Mr. Carmichael is the man they hired, and tonight he nearly succeeded in his mission. Again." She met his gaze. "*I* am Charles Brightmore, Andrew. I wrote the *Guide* and published it under a pseudonym."

Whatever reaction she'd expected, it wasn't this . . . unwavering calm. "I must say, you do not look very surprised."

"I confess I am not, as I had my suspicions. Your verbal slip the other night set my mind wondering. I paid Mr. Bayer a visit this morning before departing London."

"My publisher?" she asked, stunned. "But surely he did not identify me as Charles Brightmore."

"No. I knew he would not, nor did I wish to tip my hand by asking him outright. However, when I casually mentioned your name during our conversation, Mr. Bayer turned an interesting shade of pink. And when I mentioned another name, he turned positively red."

"Another name?"

"Clearly you didn't write the *Guide* alone. You couldn't have, not based on the number of 'firsts' we've shared. Someone else was involved . . . your friend Mrs. Ralston would be my guess."

Dear God. The man was too clever by half—an admirable trait, but in this case also alarming. "Since both you and Mr. Carmichael were able to ferret out Charles Brightmore's true identity, it's only a matter of time before someone else finds out and all of London knows."

"Whether Carmichael was investigating for someone else or on his own, I cannot say, but he isn't the man hired by Lords Markingworth, Whitly, and Carweather."

"What makes you say that?"

"Because *I* am the man they hired."

Catherine actually felt the blood drain from her face, and she suddenly recalled why she'd never been fond of surprises. It was because they were so damnably . . . surprising. If she'd been able, she would have laughed at the irony.

She cleared her throat to locate her voice. "Well, my confession just made your mission a great deal easier."

His brows rose. "Actually, it places me in a very awkward position. I was very much looking forward to collecting the reward they'd offered me."

"Reward? How much?"

"Five hundred pounds."

Catherine's jaw dropped. "That's a *fortune*."

"Yes, I know." He dragged his hands down his face and heaved a long sigh. "I had plans for that money." Before she could ask what sort of plans, he continued, "Of course you need not fear that I will reveal your identity."

"Thank you. But I fear the point is moot, as Mr. Carmichael clearly also knows."

Andrew's jaw tightened. "If he knows about you, it's likely he also knows about Mrs. Ralston's involvement."

Catherine pressed her hands to her cheeks as guilt slapped her. "How could I have forgotten to consider that? Genevieve is in danger as well. We must warn her."

"I agree. But you're not leaving here, and I'm not leaving you. Milton can relate tonight's happenings and warn her and her staff to be on guard. He can take a footman and Fritzborne along for protection." He squeezed her hand. "I'll return in a few minutes. Warm yourself by the fire, and—"

"Don't unlock the door until you return," she finished with a weak smile.

He returned ten minutes later, and said, "They are on their way to Mrs. Ralston's cottage."

Relief lessened a bit of Catherine's anxiety. "Thank you."

"You're welcome. Now, back to your involvement with the *Guide*—I take it the book was Mrs. Ralston's idea?"

Catherine nodded. "She told me she wished to write a book, but the crippling pain in her hands physically prevented her from being able to do so. I offered to be her hands."

Unable to remain still any longer, she began to pace in front of him. "Writing the words that Genevieve dictated, being involved, was so exhilarating. It had been years since anyone other than Spencer had needed me, and I reveled in feeling useful. And as for the content, I found it fascinating. Stimulating. And all too much of it unfamiliar. It greatly gratified me to know that I was helping to provide women with information that I wished I'd known before I married. And, I confess that I took a perverse pleasure at the thought of setting the *ton* on its hypocritical ear. I relished the thought of anonymously doling out a rebuke for the cruel way so many of them had treated Spencer."

She paused, then whirled to look directly at him. "Do you know what people I'd considered my friends whispered behind my back after Spencer was born? What my own husband said to my face?" Her hands curled into tight fists. "That there was no hope for him. That his deformity was hideous, and that no doubt his brain would be malformed as well as his foot. That he didn't deserve to inherit the title. That it would have been better if he'd *died*." Her voice broke on the last word. She didn't even realize that tears ran down her face until a drop fell on her hand.

He came to her and cradled her face between his palms, brushing her wet cheeks with his thumbs. "I'm so sorry you and Spencer had to endure such unspeakable cruelty."

"All I saw was my beautiful, sweet child," she whispered, "his eyes filled with pain that had nothing to do with his infirmity each time some other 'esteemed' member of Society rejected him."

She drew a shuddering breath. "But never in my wildest imaginings did it ever occur to me that by penning the *Guide* I would be placing myself, and therefore my son, in danger." She raised an unsteady hand and rested it against his cheek. "And you, Andrew. Obviously Mr. Carmichael meant to harm me tonight. When you got in his way, he attacked you. You might have been killed."

He turned his head to place a fervent kiss on her palm. "I have a very hard head. And clearly so does Carmichael. I thought I'd knocked him out."

"Carmichael," she repeated, frowning. "Is he not the man who identified the person who shot me?"

"Yes. A bit of a coincidence, that. And I'm not a great believer in coincidence. Based on his attacks tonight, it's clear to me that Carmichael was involved in the shooting. In order to cast suspicion elsewhere, he claimed to be a witness and identified someone else as the perpetrator. The man taken into custody has repeatedly protested his innocence."

A shudder ran through Catherine. She stepped back from him and wrapped her arms around herself. "I cannot believe that the *Guide*, scandalous as it is, would drive a person to murder. You saved my life."

"I cannot tell you how relieved I am that it worked out that way. I could very well have killed us both."

"What do you mean?"

"If that water was a few feet deeper, I'm afraid things would not have gone so well. I . . . I can't swim."

Catherine stared. "I beg your pardon?"

"I can't swim. Not a stroke. Spencer offered to teach

me. During our one lesson, it took nearly the entire time to coax me to simply *stand* in the water." He paused, then added softly, "My father drowned. I've always feared the water."

The area surrounding Catherine's heart contracted then expanded. "Yet you didn't hesitate to jump in for me."

He reached out and lightly grasped her shoulders. "My darling Catherine, have you not realized by now that I would walk through fire for you?"

Her throat swelled. Yes, he would. It was all right there in his eyes, his emotions naked for her to see. Emotions she was not prepared to see. Emotions that frightened her. Terrified her.

"I . . . don't know what to say," she murmured.

"You do not need to say anything. Just listen." Taking her hand he led her to the settee where he sat and gently tugged her hand until she settled next to him. "I have something to tell you, Catherine. Something I've agonized over telling you, but after almost losing you tonight, I simply cannot wait any longer."

Catherine stilled. Dear God, was he going to tell her he loved her? Or worse, ask her to marry him? "Andrew, I—"

"It's about my past."

She blinked. "Oh?"

A muscle ticked in his jaw, and his normally steady eyes reflected such torment and pain that her heart squeezed in sympathy. "Clearly whatever you wish to say is very difficult for you, Andrew." She laid her hand over his in what she hoped was a reassuring gesture. "Please do not distress yourself. It is not necessary for you to tell me."

His gaze shifted to her hand resting upon his. After several seconds, he shook his head, then rose to stand before her. "I wish with all my heart that it wasn't necessary, but you have a right to know. I *need* for you to know."

He seemed to brace himself, then met her gaze squarely. "When I left America eleven years ago, I did so because I'd committed a crime. I escaped the country to avoid being hanged."

"Hanged?" she repeated weakly. "What had you done?"

His gaze did not waver. "I killed a man."

If she hadn't heard the words come from his mouth, she would have suspected her hearing was afflicted. She licked her suddenly dry lips. "Was it an accident?"

"No. I deliberately shot him."

"But why? Why would you do such a thing?"

"Because he killed my wife."

Chapter 19

Today's Modern Woman must be prepared to face the unexpected. Sometimes it can be delightful, such as a surprise gift from her lover, in which case a thank-you kiss is appropriate, which in turn may well lead to more delightfully unexpected things. Occasionally, however, the unexpected proves most unwelcome, in which case her wisest course of action is to say as little as possible, then quickly extricate herself from the situation.

A Ladies' Guide to the Pursuit of Personal Happiness and Intimate Fulfillment
by Charles Brightmore

Andrew watched all the color leach from her face as she stared up at him in mute, wide-eyed shock. Memories he'd fiercely fought to keep buried for years roared to the surface. Now that he'd begun, and there was no turning back, he was desperate to finish.

He wanted to look at her, but he simply couldn't stand still. Pacing before her, he said, "My father was the stablemaster for a very wealthy, influential man, Charles Northrip. Father and I lived in rooms above the stable, and I grew up on the estate. I loved it there. Loved being with the horses. When I was sixteen, my father died, and Mr. Northrip promoted me to stablemaster."

He paused and looked at Catherine, who sat ramrod straight on the settee and regarded him through solemn eyes. The only sound in the room was the crackling of the fire and the ticking of the mantel clock. After resuming his pacing, he continued, "Mr. Northrip had only one child, a daughter named Emily who was four years my junior. I mentioned her when we made the strawberry ice."

"Yes. I remember."

"Emily was painfully shy. Awkward. Clumsy and tongue-tied. All conditions worsened by the forceful personalities of her parents. The Northrips were dismayed at their daughter's reserved ways. Emily was much more at home with horses than with people, and consequently she spent a great deal of time at the stables. Whenever her father would find her in one of the stalls or in the loft, he'd complain that he didn't know what to do with her. How had he and his wife, two gregarious, friendly people, produced such an unsociable child who preferred animals over people? He said these things as if she were deaf, and I could see how much they hurt her. Over the years, a friendship blossomed between me, my father, and Emily."

Memories he hadn't allowed himself to resurrect for years rolled through him. "I'll never forget the night my father died. I was standing in the stables, staring at his empty chair. I felt . . . gutted. And so alone. The next thing I knew, Emily was standing next to me. She slipped her little twelve-year-old hand into mine and told me not to worry. That I wasn't alone because she was my friend, and that she'd be my *best* friend, if I'd like." Nostalgia tightened his throat. "I told her that I'd like that very much. And over the next seven years the bond we'd formed strengthened. We truly were each other's best friend."

Pausing before the fireplace, he stared into the dancing flames. "Because he had no son to whom he could pass his business, Mr. Northrip was determined that Emily marry a man capable of running his enterprise, and he believed he'd found such a man in Lewis Manning, the only son of another wealthy merchant. A marriage—to say nothing of a lucrative business merger—was arranged. Emily accepted this, knowing it was her duty to marry in accordance with her father's wishes. She was actually relieved she'd finally be doing something her father approved of after disappointing him her entire life.

"But I soon learned that Lewis Manning possessed a violent temper. One night, only several days before the wedding, Emily came to me, crying, in pain from what turned out to be a cracked rib. Although there was not a mark upon her face, the rest of her—where the blows wouldn't show—was bruised where Lewis had beat her for daring to question one of his decisions. She told me then that while this was the first time he'd hurt her this badly, Lewis had lost his temper several times before and struck her. She'd told her father about those earlier instances, but he'd dismissed her concerns, saying that all men occasionally lose their tempers. After this last instance, however, Emily feared that the next time Lewis flew into a rage she might not be able to get away from him."

He pulled his gaze from the fire and looked at Catherine, who was listening with rapt attention. "My first instinct was to tear Lewis apart, but Emily begged me not to. Said I would only be imprisoned for my trouble and that Lewis wasn't worth it. I reluctantly agreed, but I was determined to protect her—from that bastard Lewis, *and* her father, who obviously cared more about the connection this marriage would make than his daughter. And the only way I could think of to do that was to marry her myself. We both knew she'd be giving up everything, as her father would be furious and surely disown her, but so be it. We left that night and eloped."

Again he could not remain still and resumed his pacing. "The next day, after settling Emily at a nearby inn, I went to see her father. I wanted to tell him about the marriage face-to-face, and let him know that further harm to Emily would not be tolerated. He was, as expected, incensed. He said he would have the marriage annulled and intended to see me charged with kidnapping and hanged. When I told him there were no grounds for an annulment, his fury doubled. Said that one way or another he'd get his daughter back, even if it meant seeing me dead. I didn't doubt for a moment that he meant what he said. I returned to the inn. Shortly afterward, as we were preparing to depart, an enraged Lewis Manning arrived. He said hateful, disgusting things about Emily, and my patience reached its limit. He informed me that he did not intend to wait for justice—he wanted to see the job done immediately, and he challenged me to a duel. I accepted despite Emily's pleas not to."

He continued on, the words coming faster now. "The Northrip's groundskeeper, Adam Harrick, was my closest friend besides Emily, and he served as my second. At the duel, unbeknownst to me, Lewis cheated by turning to fire before the full count was made. Emily, who was supposed to have remained at the inn, saw his treachery. In an attempt to warn me, she ran forward . . . and was hit by Lewis's shot."

He closed his eyes, the image of Emily crumpling to the ground, her eyes wide with shock, the midsection of her ivory gown stained crimson, indelibly carved in his mind.

"I fired, and my shot hit Lewis," he said, his voice a rough rasp. "I dropped my pistol and ran to Emily. Although she was still alive, there was no doubt her wound was fatal. I . . . I held her, trying to stop the blood, but to no avail. With her dying words she pleaded with me to escape. To leave America, go where no one could find me. She knew her father would either kill me or make certain I hanged for Lewis's death, and no doubt try to blame me for her death as well. She begged me, over and over, not to let that happen. She desperately wanted me to live, to have a full and happy life. She loved me and did not want me to die."

Fixing his gaze on Catherine, he pressed his palm against his chest, and said in a ragged whisper, "I felt her final heartbeats against my hand after I finally promised her I would do as she asked. And then she was gone."

His voice broke on the last word. Then silence hung heavy in the air as he relived the horror of that chilly day with a gutting, vivid clarity he'd forced from his mind for years. The day he'd lost everything. His home. Life as he'd known it. The sweet, gentle friend who'd been his wife.

He coughed to clear the tightness in his throat. "After saying my good-byes to Emily and making certain that Adam would see to her, I kept my promise. Several hours later, using a false name, I sailed away from America."

Dragging his hands down his face, he tipped his head back and looked at the ceiling. "For the first five years, I lived . . . recklessly, not really caring if I lived or died. It was a very dark time for me. Lonely. Bleak. Empty. I'd done what Emily had asked me to do, yet I hated myself for doing it. For running away. For all my actions that had led to her death. I felt like a coward, and that I'd compromised my honor. I actually hoped that her father would somehow find me, yet he never did.

"But one day, your brother found me—just in time to save me from the machete-wielders, a rescue I wasn't immediately grateful for, by the way. Since I had nothing better to do, I returned with Philip to his camp, and for the first time in five years I had a sense of belonging somewhere. Your brother not only saved my life, but through him, I found the will to live again. To make something of myself. He was the first real friend I'd had since leaving America, and my friendship with him changed my life. I eventually managed to bury deeply that horrifying day on the dueling field, but when that shot was fired in London, when I saw you on the floor . . ." He briefly closed his eyes. "I relived my worst nightmare."

He drew in a deep breath, feeling utterly depleted, yet lighter than he had in a decade. He turned toward Catherine. Her hands were clenched in her lap, and she stared into the fire. He desperately wanted to know what she was thinking, but forced himself to remain silent, to allow her to absorb all he'd told her. A full minute passed before she spoke.

"Does Philip know all this?"

"No. None of it. I've never told anyone before."

He wished she would look at him so he could see her expression, read her eyes. Would she look at him with disgust and shame—the same way he'd looked at himself for years? Unfortunately, he feared the fact that she steadfastly did *not* look at him told him everything.

Finally, she turned and gazed at him, her eyes solemn and bright with unshed tears. "You loved her very much."

"Yes. She was a quiet, lonely, gentle girl who'd never hurt anyone in her entire life. We'd been the best of friends for years. I would have done anything to protect her. Instead, she died protecting me."

"Why, after remaining silent all these years, did you tell me this?"

He hesitated, then asked, "Before I tell you, may I have use of a piece of vellum and a pen?"

There was no mistaking her surprise, but she rose and walked to the escritoire near the window, sliding a sheet of vellum from a slim drawer. "Here you are."

"Thank you." He sat in the delicate upholstered chair and picked up her pen. From the corner of his eye he watched her cross to the fireplace. After several minutes, he joined her there and handed her the vellum.

She looked at the markings with a confused expression. "What is this?"

"Egyptian glyphs. They spell out the reasons why I told you about my past."

"But why would you write your reason in a way that I cannot understand?"

"At your father's birthday party, you commented on Lord Nordnick's methods with regards to Lady Ophelia. You said he should recite something romantic to her in another language. This is the only other language I know."

Her startled gaze flew to his. He touched the edge of the vellum. "The first line reads *You saved my life*."

"I do not see how you can say that, as it is my fault that you were hurt tonight."

"Not tonight. Six years ago. The morning after I joined

Philip at his camp, I came upon him sitting on a blanket near the banks of the Nile, reading a letter. From his sister, he told me. He read me some amusing snippets, and I sat there listening to the words you'd written him, filled with envy for the obvious affection in which you held each other. He went on to tell me a bit about you, the fact that your marriage was unhappy, the joy you found with your son, and also about Spencer's affliction. After we returned to camp, he showed me the miniature you'd given him before he'd left England."

He briefly closed his eyes, vividly reliving that instant when he'd first laid eyes on her image. "You were so lovely. I could not fathom how your husband did not worship the ground you walked on.

"From that moment on, with every story Philip told me about you, my regard and admiration grew, and I believe I anticipated your letters to Philip even more than Philip himself. Your bravery, fortitude, and grace in the face of your marital situation and Spencer's difficulties touched me deeply and inspired me to examine my deep shame and guilt over my past and the dissolute manner in which I'd lived my life since leaving America. Your goodness, your kindness, your courage inspired me to change my life. Redeem myself. I knew that someday I would return to England with Philip, and I was determined to be a person that Lady Catherine would be proud to know. You showed me that goodness and kindness still existed, and you gave me the will to want that again. I've wanted to thank you for that for six years." He reached out and squeezed her hand. "Thank you."

Catherine's heart thumped in slow, hard beats from his words and the utter sincerity in his dark eyes. She swallowed. Her heart ached for him, for the despair he'd lived with for so long. "You're welcome. I had no idea my letters had . . . inspired you so. I'm very sorry for the pain you suffered, and I'm glad you were able to find peace within yourself."

Without wavering his gaze, he released her hand, then reached out and touched the edge of the vellum. "The second line reads *I love you*."

Catherine went perfectly still, except for her pulse, which jumped erratically. His feelings for her blazed from his eyes, without any attempt to hide them.

"My *mind* understands that my social status and past renders me not good enough for you. But my *heart* . . ." He shook his head. "My heart refuses to listen. My logic tells me I should wait, take more time to court you. But I almost lost you tonight and I simply cannot wait. Our friendship, our time together as lovers, everything we've shared, every touch, every word, has brought me more joy than I can describe. But being your lover is not enough."

He reached into his waistcoat pocket, and withdrew an item he held out to her. "I want more. I want it all. All of you. I want you to be my wife. Catherine, will you marry me?"

The bottom seemed to drop out of Catherine's stomach. She stared at the single, perfect, oval emerald set in a simple gold band resting in his callused palm. He must have purchased the gem while he was in London. Tears pushed behind her eyes. Dismay, confusion, unexpected longing all collided in her. Her emotions were a raw jumble, all vying for her attention until she simply couldn't differentiate one from the other. "You know how I feel about marriage."

"Yes. And given your experience, your reservations are understandable. But you also know how I feel about it. I told you in the carriage on our journey to Little Longstone that I wanted a wife and family. Did you think I'm the sort of man who would compromise you, then walk away?"

"Andrew, I am not a young virginal miss to be 'compromised.' I'm a grown, Modern Woman, indulging in a mutually pleasurable affair. When you said you wanted a wife, you described a paragon of perfection whom I doubt exists."

"No. I was looking right at her. You are all those things I described and so much more—a woman with flaws, who in spite of them, because of them, is the perfect woman for me. I'm asking you to reconsider your feelings on marriage. To instead consider your feelings for me." He studied her for several seconds, then said quietly, "I know you care. You never would have taken me into your bed, into your body, if you did not."

Heat stung Catherine's cheek. "I did not take you as a lover to pry a marriage proposal from you."

"I know. And there is no need to pry. I offer my proposal willingly. And with great hope that in spite of all I told you tonight, you will accept."

"When we entered into our liaison, we agreed it was only temporary."

"No, *you* insisted it was temporary. I never agreed. And even if I had, I hereby formally renege. I do not want temporary. I want forever. I want to be your husband. I want to be a father to Spencer—if he wishes me to be so. At the very least, I want to be his friend and champion." He drew a deep breath. "I've told you about my past. I've told you how I feel about you. My heart, my soul are yours. Tell me what you want to do with them."

Catherine locked her knees to steady their trembling. "You don't understand what you're asking of me, and clearly you don't know what marriage means to a woman.

It means I cease to exist. I would lose everything because it would no longer belong to me, it would belong to my husband. My husband could banish me to the country, neglect our child, sell off my personal belongings—and all legally. I've already lived through that horror. I do not require more money, or family connections. Marriage has nothing to offer me."

"Clearly we use different dictionaries, because to me, marriage means caring for one another. Loving together. Sharing laughter and helping through pain. Always knowing that there is another person standing beside you. For you."

"I must admit, your definition sounds lovely, but experience has taught me marriage is not that way. Do you honestly believe your definition is realistic?"

"I suppose that depends on *why* a person marries. If one marries for money or social position, then I agree it could prove disastrous. But if the marriage is based on love and respect, because you cannot imagine not spending every day of your life with the person who owns your heart, then yes, I believe it can be all those wonderful things." He reached for her hand. After gently placing the ring on her palm, he folded her fingers closed and nestled her fist between his hands. "Catherine, if you decide you don't want to marry me, let it be because I'm not from your social class. Because I'm a common American. Because I have a scarred past. Because you don't love me. Please don't refuse me because you think I'll take things away from you when all I want to do is give to you. Everything. Always. I want to take care of you."

"I believe I've demonstrated quite well over the past decade that I do not need a man to take care of me." A sick feeling of loss washed through her at the hurt that flared in his eyes. True, she did not want a husband, but she realized with sudden stinging clarity, neither did she want Andrew simply to disappear from her life. "Why don't we just continue on as we have?" she said, hating the note of desperation she heard in her voice.

"Having an affair?"

"Yes."

Her breath stilled while she waited for his answer. Finally, very quietly, he said, "No. I cannot do that to you. Or Spencer. Or myself. If we continue, eventually someone would discover the truth, and the gossip would only hurt you and Spencer. I've no desire to sneak around, grabbing stolen moments, and keeping my feelings hidden. I want it all, Catherine. All or . . . nothing."

The floor seemed to shift beneath her feet. There was no mistaking the resolution in his voice and eyes, and anger shot through her. "You have no right to issue such an ultimatum."

"I disagree. I believe the facts that I'm painfully in love with you and have shared your bed gives me that right."

"The fact that we shared a bed changes nothing."

"You're wrong. It changes *everything*." He squeezed her hand tighter. "Catherine, either you feel the same things I do, or you don't. Either you love me, or you don't. Either you want to spend your life with me, or you don't."

"And you expect me to give you an answer right now? All or nothing?"

"Yes."

Catherine stared at him, the pressure of the ring pressing into her palm. A myriad of conflicting emotions battered her from every direction, but she shoved the jumble aside and focused on the anger—toward him for forcing her to make a decision like this and toward herself for even hesitating. Her choice was clear. She didn't want a husband. So why was it so damnably difficult to say the one word that would send him away?

Because that word would do just that—send him away.

She moistened her dry lips. "In that case, I'm afraid it's nothing."

Several long, silent seconds passed, and she watched his expression go blank, as if he'd pulled a curtain over his feelings. A muscle jerked in his jaw, and his throat worked as she imagined him swallowing his disappointment. He slowly released her hand, and a small voice inside her cried out *No!,* but she kept her lips pressed firmly together to contain it. She slowly opened her hand and held out the ring to him. He stared at the gem for so long, she thought he would refuse to take it. And actually he did just that by finally holding out his hand, forcing her to place the ring into his palm. After she did, he quickly stepped away from her and quit the room, softly closing the door behind him without a backward glance.

Still staring at the closed door, Catherine sank onto the settee. The warmth from where his hand had held hers only seconds ago had disappeared, leaving a chill in its wake that shivered through her entire body. Her mind, her logic, told her she'd made the right choice. The eviscerating ache in her heart, however, indicated that she might have just made a terrible mistake.

Just before dawn Andrew sat on the edge of his bed, his elbows propped on his knees, hands cradling his aching head. But the dull throbbing there was nothing compared to the soul-ripping pain in his chest.

How was it possible for his heart to hurt so badly yet continue to beat? He wished he could blame the outcome of his proposal on its precipitous delivery, but he suspected that even if he'd taken months to court Catherine, in the end, she still would have refused him.

But at least then you would have had those months with her, his inner voice taunted. *Now you have . . . nothing.*

He groaned and pushed himself to his feet. Clearly he'd made a mistake forcing her to choose all or nothing, but damn it, he'd wanted her for so long, been waiting so long. Had been so hopeful that she'd come to care for him. Would realize they *belonged* together.

An image of that bastard Carmichael dragging her toward the springs flashed in his mind and his hands clenched. What had triggered such deep hatred of the *Guide* that he'd been driven to kill the author? Yes, the Today's Modern Woman premises and explicit content were scandalous—but to the point of inciting murder?

He recalled meeting Carmichael after the shooting at Lord Ravensly's birthday party. Something odd, almost familiar, had struck him about Carmichael while he'd listened to him give his account of witnessing a man running into Hyde Park after the shot was fired. And he'd experienced that same sensation at both the duke's soiree and at the museum yesterday. Philip had said Carmichael had spent time in America . . .

Andrew closed his eyes, forcing himself to recall every detail of his encounters with Carmichael, first at the parties, then at the museum—

An image flashed in Andrew's mind, of Carmichael stroking his chin, prisms of light bouncing off the square-cut diamond-and-onyx ring he wore. Recognition hit Andrew, and everything inside him froze. Carmichael had been wearing that ring at both parties as well. It wasn't the man who had inspired that flare of memory—it was the *ring*.

Andrew dragged his hands down his face, his heart pumping hard. If he hadn't relived the day Emily died, he would have missed it. He'd buried that hurt, that image so deeply . . . but there was no mistake. Carmichael's unusual diamond-and-onyx ring was identical to the one that Lewis Manning was wearing the day Andrew had shot him.

Carmichael isn't after Charles Brightmore. He's after me.

The truth struck him like a blow, and his mind reeled. Carmichael must have some connection to Lewis Manning. There was a resemblance, around the eyes, he realized as pieces rapidly clicked into place. Was Carmichael Lewis's father? Uncle? Father, most likely, Andrew decided. Which would certainly give him a motive to hate Andrew.

When Catherine was shot, Andrew had been standing next to her. The bullet had been meant for *him*. And tonight, Carmichael had planned to kill him—a plan set awry by Catherine's presence. She'd unknowingly saved his life and nearly drowned in the process.

He blew out a long breath and raked unsteady hands through his hair. Jesus. All he'd ever wanted to do was protect her, and *he* was the danger. Which meant he had to get away from her. Immediately.

After eleven years, it appeared his past had finally caught up with him. And had twice nearly killed Catherine. Well, Carmichael wouldn't get another chance.

Andrew walked swiftly to the wardrobe, pulled his leather satchel from the bottom, and quickly began shoving his belongings inside.

Don't worry, Carmichael. You'll find me. I'm going to make it very easy for you.

* * *

Catherine sat in her wing chair, staring at the grate of the fire that had burned out hours ago, the dead, gray ash a perfect reflection of her mood.

With a sound of disgust, she rose and paced. What on earth was wrong with her? She'd made the right decision, the only decision she could have made under the circumstances. All or nothing? How could she possibly have agreed to give him "all"? She couldn't have, and it was that simple. Yet in spite of that logic, she somehow still felt as if she'd been sliced in half.

Dear God, the things he'd told her. His past should have shocked her, but after hours of thought, the ordeal he'd been through only served to reinforce her sympathy and admiration for him. Yes, he'd killed a man, but a man who only seconds before had tried to kill *him.* A man who had killed his wife—a young woman he'd risked a great deal to help. Andrew had lost *everything*, and all in the name of love. Yet he clearly had not turned his back on love, on marriage, as she had. He was kind, noble, generous, thoughtful, and . . .

Oh, my, the way he'd looked at her, his heart in his eyes, all raw desire and naked emotion. She halted, and her own eyes slid closed, picturing him as clearly as if he stood before her. No one had ever looked at her like that before. And God help her, as much as she hadn't wanted it, as much as she'd tried to deny it, she wanted Andrew to look at her like that again. She simply wasn't ready to give him up as a lover.

She opened her eyes and resumed pacing, her mind racing. Surely if she put some effort into it she could convince him that his proposal was precipitous and persuade him to continue their liaison. Today's Modern Woman would not allow him simply to have the last word and walk away. No, Today's Modern Woman would use all the ammunition in her feminine arsenal to tempt, allure, entice, and seduce him around to her way of thinking.

The instant the realization hit her, it was as if the sun broke through a bank of dark clouds. Why had it taken her all night to realize something that now seemed so obvious? She roundly cursed her stubborn streak, but at least she'd come to her senses.

The sooner she began her persuasive campaign, the better. And what better way to start than issuing him an invitation to return to Little Longstone next week? Even better if she were to issue the invitation right now. In the warm intimacy of his bedchamber. While she was dressed in her nightrail and robe.

The pale light of dawn was just breaking through the windows as she left her bedchamber and hurried quietly down the corridor. When she reached his door, she tapped lightly. "Andrew?" she said softly.

Silence greeted her, and she tapped again, but still heard nothing from within. Concerned, she turned the handle and opened the door enough to peer inside. Her heart stuttered, then she slowly pushed the door wide.

The room was empty, his bed undisturbed. She scanned the room, noting with stunned dread that none of his personal items remained. As if in a trance, she crossed to the wardrobe and pulled open the oak doors. Empty.

A sharp, acute ache stole her breath. With hot moisture pushing at the backs of her eyes, she turned toward the bed, and her heart leapt at the small bundle set on the pillow. She dashed across the carpet and snatched up the note on top of the parcel. Breaking the seal, she scanned the words.

My Dearest Catherine:

I believe Carmichael is Lewis Manning's father, and that it is not you, but me whom he seeks. In my attempt to protect you from danger, I brought it right to you. Keep the doors and windows locked, and you, Spencer, and the staff remain in the house. I'll see to it that Carmichael never hurts anyone again.

I leave as a parting gift my most prized possession. Philip was going to leave these behind when we departed Egypt, so I took them. From that very first time I heard the words you'd written to Philip, I felt as if I'd been turned inside out. I fell deeply, hopelessly in love with you the moment I saw your beautiful image in his miniature. You've lived in my heart since that day. I lived off your every word for years, and I thank you for the courage and hope they brought me. Please keep the ring as a token of my gratitude and affection.

Andrew

With shaking fingers, she unwrapped the white linen, realizing with a heavy heart it was the handkerchief she'd given him. Unfolding the last piece of material she looked down. The emerald ring rested on top of a thick bundle of faded letters tied with a worn piece of leather. She instantly recognized her own handwriting.

She felt the blood drain from her face. These were the dozens of letters she'd written to Philip while he was abroad. Andrew's most prized possession.

The truth hit her like a backhanded slap, and she felt an overwhelming need to sit down. His love for her was not of a recent nature as she'd assumed. He'd been in love with her for . . . *six years*. He'd rescued these letters before leaving Egypt, keeping them with him all this time. And now had given them to her. Wrapped in the handkerchief she'd made him, leaving everything of her behind. Because she'd sent him away.

Something wet plopped onto her hand. Dazed, she stared at the tear, as another, then another, fell onto her skin. All those years she'd ached with loneliness, endured her husband's cruel neglect and rejection of her and Spencer, Andrew had been wanting her. Needing her. Loving her.

The realization, the depth of his feelings, his devotion, humbled her, enervated her, and she could almost feel the wall she'd built around herself and her heart crumbling, leaving her exposed and her feelings utterly bare. Undeniable. She could hide from them no longer. She did not simply desire Andrew. She loved him.

A sob escaped her, and she pressed her trembling lips together. With an impatient exclamation, she dashed the back of her hand over her eyes. Later. She could cry later, although she dearly hoped she would not need to. Right now she needed to figure out where Andrew had gone, think of a way to help him find Carmichael. Then tell him what a fool she'd been. And pray he'd forgive her for the hurt her fears and confusion had caused both of them.

Clutching the letters and ring to her chest, she paced to the window and stared out at the soft, golden light signaling dawn. Her gaze drifted toward the stables in the distance, and she blinked at the sight of Andrew's familiar, broad-shouldered figure approaching the wide double doors. Her heart jumped in relief. He was still here. If she hurried, she could reach the stables before he left. But with Carmichael possibly about, she needed some protection.

She dashed to her bedchamber, then dropped to her knees before her wardrobe and pulled out a worn hatbox. After opening the lid, she removed the small, pearl-handled pistol hidden beneath a pile of old gloves. She then set Andrew's letters and the ring on top and replaced the hatbox. Cursing the further delay, she hurriedly dressed, then, slipping the pistol into the pocket of her gown, left the room.

Chapter 20

Today's Modern Woman should always practice prudence and caution where matters of the heart are concerned. Sometimes, however, fate will present her with the one man who slips under her guard and turns her heart to porridge. If the gentleman should happen to feel the same way about her, she needs to recognize that for the miracle it is and not hesitate to carpe hominis*—seize the man!*

A Ladies' Guide to the Pursuit of Personal Happiness and Intimate Fulfillment
by Charles Brightmore

Andrew paused in the doorway of the stables to allow his vision to adjust to the dimness of the interior, his pistol balanced in his palm. He slowly scanned the vast interior, eyes and ears straining for anything out of the ordinary. Nothing appeared amiss, and a quick search ascertained that Carmichael wasn't hiding in one of the stalls or the loft. Fritzborne wasn't about, which concerned Andrew. Surely he'd returned from Mrs. Ralston's cottage by now.

He allowed himself another quick peek over the door

of the third stall where Shadow slept, curled up in the corner on a blanket-covered bed of hay. He'd have to make arrangements for someone to retrieve the puppy for him. And return Aphrodite. God knew he wouldn't have the strength to come back to Little Longstone again himself.

Forcing his feet to move, he walked into the tack room. After setting down his pistol on a worn bench, he was preparing to reach for Aphrodite's saddle when he heard Spencer's voice ask, "You're leaving, Mr. Stanton?"

Andrew turned swiftly. Spencer stood framed in the doorway, his eyes reflecting confusion and hurt.

Alarm rushed through Andrew. With Carmichael looking for him, the last place Andrew wanted Spencer was *here*.

Andrew approached him, his stomach tight with concern. "What are you doing here, Spencer?"

"I wanted to play with Shadow. As I left the house, I saw you entering the stables. You're leaving?" he asked again.

"I'm afraid so."

A stricken look came over Spencer's face. "Without saying good-bye?"

Guilt kicked Andrew squarely in the gut. "Only for now. And only because time is very short. I planned to write you." He quickly told him what was going on, concluding with, "As soon I've saddled Aphrodite, I'll take you back to the house. You must remain inside until Carmichael is caught. Protect your mother. Do you understand?"

Spencer nodded. "When will you come back?"

Andrew pulled in a deep breath. There was no time to say all the things he wanted to, but he couldn't do less than give Spencer the truth.

"Do you recall all those bothersome suitors who wish to court your mother?"

"Of course. We showed them not to pester Mum anymore, didn't we?"

"Yes, we did. But unfortunately I fear I've become one of the bothersome suitors."

Spencer blinked several times. "You want to court my mum?"

"I wanted to, yes, but things are not going to work out as I'd hoped."

Spencer frowned, and Andrew could almost hear the wheels turning in the young man's mind. "Why aren't things going to work out? Mum likes you, I know she does. And . . . and she enjoyed the strawberry ice very much."

"I know she likes me. But sometimes liking someone isn't enough. And in this case, it isn't enough."

His bottom lip trembled and his eyes welled with moisture. "So you're not *ever* coming back?"

God help him. How many times could his bloody heart break in one day? Andrew reached out and rested his hands on Spencer's shoulders. "I'm afraid not. But I want you to know that you are welcome to visit me in London anytime you wish."

"I am?"

"Yes. And I hope you'll seriously consider making the journey. I believe you're ready to venture outside Little Longstone. I'd show you the museum, and we could continue your pugilism lessons."

Spencer dashed the back of his hand across his eyes. "I . . . I'd like that."

"We can exchange letters if you'd like as well, although I've been told I'm an abominable speller."

"I could teach you. I'm a good speller."

"Well, it's all settled then. Except . . . would you mind

terribly looking after Shadow for me until I can send someone for him?"

"I wouldn't mind at all. Perhaps *I* can deliver him to you in London."

Andrew smiled around the lump squeezing his throat. "An excellent plan."

"Mr. Stanton . . ." He looked up at Andrew, the distress in his eyes cutting Andrew like a rusty blade. "What if people in London are . . . unkind to me?"

"I'll be standing right next to you, Spencer. If anyone is foolish enough to be unkind to you once, I promise you they will not be so foolish twice."

His words erased a bit of the worry in Spencer's eyes, but none of the sadness. And it was time to leave. Giving Spencer's shoulders a squeeze, he looked directly into his eyes. "I want you to know . . . if I had a son, I'd want him to be just like you."

Spencer's chin quivered, then a lone tear dribbled down his cheek, smiting Andrew more effectively than any weapon. He stepped forward and wrapped his arms around Andrew's waist and hugged him tight. "I wish you'd been my father," Spencer said, in a broken whisper.

Andrew squeezed his eyes shut and hugged Spencer back. He had to swallow twice to find his voice. "So do I, Spencer. So do I. But we'll always be friends."

"Always?"

"Always. If you ever need anything, you have only to ask." He patted the lad's back, then stepped back. "And now, we really must go. Why don't you get Shadow while I saddle Aphrodite?"

Spencer nodded, then walked toward the third stall. Andrew stood outside the tack room, watching him, wondering how a man could hurt so badly when he felt so bloody numb.

After the heavy wooden stall door closed silently behind Spencer, Andrew drew a deep breath and forced himself to bury this hurt, as he'd buried so many others. He turned to go back to the tack room, but had only taken a single step when Carmichael's voice said, "Stop right there."

Andrew turned and watched Carmichael emerge from the shadows, a pistol aimed directly at Andrew.

Maintaining an outward calm he was far from feeling, Andrew rapidly assessed his limited choices—choices made all the more daunting by Spencer's presence. Damn it, if anything happened to the boy . . .

He forced his gaze to remain steady on Carmichael's swollen nose and bruised cheek, and not stray to the stall Spencer had entered. Did Carmichael realize they weren't alone? If so, he had to make certain Spencer didn't reveal himself.

Andrew cleared his throat, and said loudly, "How long did you intend to *remain hidden in the stall*?"

"I wasn't in a stall," Carmichael said. "I was outside, taking care of the stable man."

Relief and fury clenched Andrew's hands—relief that Carmichael appeared oblivious to the fact they weren't alone, but fury that this bastard had gotten to Fritzborne. "Did you kill him?"

Carmichael walked slowly closer, his eyes glittering. "I'm not certain. But even if he's alive, he's of no use to you. I bound and gagged him most thoroughly."

Andrew's gaze flicked down to Carmichael's pistol, and he inwardly cursed the fact that his own weapon remained well out of his reach inside the tack room, where he'd set it down when he'd reached for the saddle. He still had his knife, but he'd have to choose his moment carefully. If he failed . . .

When approximately twenty feet separated them, Carmichael stopped. "It took you quite a while to come to the stables."

"I'd have come sooner if I'd realized you were waiting . . . Manning."

Surprise flashed in Carmichael's eyes. "So you've figured out who I am. Good. I've waited a long time for this moment. You led me on a very merry chase these past eleven years, Stanton, but now it's over. Now you will pay for killing my son."

"Your son killed my wife."

"*Your* wife? She was *never* yours. She belonged to Lewis. You stole her. Their marriage was going to unite two powerful families."

"Your son beat her."

"What of it? She was his to do with as he wished. If the girl hadn't been so stupid, she wouldn't have infuriated him so. Good God, she barely knew how to speak. Her only redeeming qualities were her family connection and enormous fortune."

Andrew's eyes narrowed, and he took a step forward. "I suggest you watch what you say about her."

"And I suggest you not move again. I'm an expert marksman."

"An expert marksman? I think not. You missed me at Lord Ravensly's birthday party by at least a foot. Your carelessness nearly killed Lady Catherine."

Andrew's jaw clenched at Carmichael's casual shrug. "One loses accuracy at greater distances, I'm afraid."

"You attempted to harm her last night as well."

"Her unexpected presence interfered with my plans."

"And the museum? Was that your own handiwork, or did you hire someone to vandalize it?"

A frigid smile curled the corners of Carmichael's lips.

"That was me. I cannot tell you the satisfaction I experienced with every hack of the ax. Every shattering windowpane. Then watching your investors abandon you. All small retributions for what you did to my family." His eyes blazed with hatred. "Lewis's marriage to the Northrip heiress would have solved all my family's financial problems. After you murdered my son, I lost everything. Northrip found out about my debts and backed out of our merger. I killed him, of course, but it yielded me nothing more than the satisfaction of ending his life. My home, my business—all gone. You deserved nothing less in return. First, losing your museum, and now, finally, after many years of searching for you, your life."

A loud gasp sounded from the doorway. Andrew turned, and his heart nearly ceased beating. Catherine stood inside the doorway, less than twenty feet away, her eyes wide with horror.

"Unless you want me to shoot Mr. Stanton, you will cease fumbling with your skirt *now*, Lady Catherine." Without taking his gaze from her, Carmichael continued, "And if you so much as move an inch, Stanton, I'll kill her. Now, hold your hands out in front of you, Lady Catherine . . . yes, just like that, and come stand near Mr. Stanton . . . no, not too close. Stop right there."

She'd halted approximately six feet away from Andrew. As he spoke to Catherine, a slight movement behind Carmichael caught Andrew's attention. Spencer, eyes wide, was peeking over the edge of the stall door directly behind Carmichael.

Their eyes met, and Andrew gave a sideways jerk of his head, praying Spencer would understand to remain out of sight. The boy's head vanished.

Andrew's mind raced. How could he get Spencer, Catherine, and himself out of this mess, alive? Carmichael stood about four feet directly in front of the stall where Spencer hid. Inspiration suddenly struck and he cleared his throat.

"You know you'll hang for this."

"On the contrary, Sidney Carmichael will simply disappear, never to be heard from again."

"I wouldn't count on that. My guess is you'll be swinging from a rope very soon." He made a *tsk*ing sound. "Yes, swinging. Just like an old stall door, just like my old friend Spencer used to do. And would probably love to do again. Right now."

He heard Catherine's sharp intake of breath, but he dared not look at her. Confusion flickered in Carmichael's eyes, then his gaze hardened. "A rather odd choice for your last words, but no matter. Your life is over." He aimed the pistol directly at Andrew's chest.

In the blink of an eye, the stall door behind Carmichael swung open, smacking him hard on the back, the momentum throwing him off-balance. Andrew raced forward. Before Carmichael could regain his balance, Andrew's fists found their marks with two hard, quick blows to Carmichael's midsection and jaw. He grunted, and the pistol slipped from his fingers, landing on the wooden floor with a thud. Andrew grabbed him by his cravat, and had just brought back his fist to deliver another blow when Carmichael's eyes rolled back, and he went limp in Andrew's grip. Andrew let go, and the man fell to the floor in a heap to reveal Catherine, chest heaving, eyes glittering with a combination of fury and triumph, holding a heavy feed pail, which bore a large dent.

"Take *that,* you bastard," she said to the fallen man.

There were a dozen things Andrew wanted to say, yet when he opened his mouth, what spilled out was, "You floored him."

"I owed him one. Are you all right?"

Andrew blinked. "Yes. You?"

"Fine. Only sorry I didn't have the opportunity to floor him twice."

Holding that dented bucket, her eyes blazing, color high, she looked magnificent—like an avenging Fury, prepared to fell any brigand who dared to cross her.

"It certainly appears you have no need for those pugilism lessons we discussed."

Spencer hurried toward them, his complexion pale, his eyes wide. "Is he dead?" he asked.

"No," Andrew said, "but thanks to your mother, he'll have a devil of a headache when he comes around."

Catherine dropped the bucket with a clang, then closed the distance between her and Spencer with two jerky steps. Hugging him fiercely, she asked, "Are you all right, darling?"

Spencer nodded. "I'm glad you weren't hurt, Mum." He looked at Andrew over Catherine's shoulder. "You, too, Mr. Stanton."

After Catherine released her son, Andrew placed a hand on Spencer's shoulder and smiled. "I'm fine, thanks to you. You saved my life. Your mother's as well."

Crimson stained Spencer's pale cheeks. "He meant to kill you. And my mum."

"Yes, he did. You were extraordinarily brave, keeping your head and remaining quiet, then acting at precisely the right moment. I'm incredibly proud of you. I'm in your debt."

Spencer's blush deepened. "I only did what you told me to do."

"And you did it brilliantly."

A smile curled Spencer's lips. "It appears we made a good team."

"Indeed we did."

Andrew jerked his head toward Carmichael. "We need to tie him up, then search for Fritzborne."

After Carmichael was securely bound and gagged, they located Fritzborne behind the stables, struggling mightily against the ropes binding him. Andrew cut through the ropes with his knife, quickly explaining what happened. Once Fritzborne was free, Andrew helped him to his feet. "Do you feel well enough to ride to summon the magistrate?"

"Nothing would give me more pleasure," Fritzborne assured him.

After he'd seen Fritzborne on his way, Andrew turned to Catherine. He folded his hands across his chest to keep from reaching for her. "Now perhaps you'd tell me why you left the house, Lady Catherine?"

"I looked out the window and saw you entering the stables. I wanted to talk to you before you . . . left." She lifted her chin. "I did not leave the house unarmed. Unfortunately, Carmichael saw my attempt to retrieve the pistol from my pocket."

"Pistol?"

"Yes. And I was prepared to use it if necessary."

"I . . . see. What did you want to talk to me about?" He searched her gaze, hoping for an indication that she'd perhaps changed her mind, but her expression gave nothing away.

"Would you mind terribly if we spoke back at the house?" Her gaze flicked to the trussed Carmichael, and a visible shudder racked her.

"Of course not. But I need to remain here until Fritzborne arrives with the magistrate. I'm certain he'll wish to talk to you and Spencer as well."

"All right." Turning to Spencer, she said, "Would you

come with me, darling? There's something I need to discuss with you."

Spencer nodded. Catherine tucked his arm beneath hers, and Andrew watched them depart, bludgeoning back the pain of knowing that after today, he'd no longer be part of their lives.

Catherine started when the knock sounded on the drawing room door. After running her hands down her peach muslin gown, then pinching her cheeks to ensure she didn't look too pale, she said, "Come in."

The door opened, and Andrew stepped over the threshold. Andrew, looking tall, solid, masculine, and darkly attractive, his ebony hair mussed as if he'd combed his fingers through the strands. Her breath hitched, and she pressed her hands to her midsection in an attempt to calm her stomach's jitterings.

"The magistrate has gone?" she asked.

"Yes. Between everything you, Spencer, Fritzborne, and I told him, Carmichael will never see the outside of a prison cell again." He slowly crossed the room, stopping with the length of the Axminster throw rug between them. "You said you wished to speak to me."

"Yes. Before Spencer and I returned to the house, we visited the gardens and shared a long talk." She turned and walked to the small cherrywood table near the window and picked up a bouquet of flowers, the stems wrapped with a red satin ribbon. When she returned, she held out the bundle, praying she did not look as nervous as she felt. "I picked these. For you."

Surprise flickered in his eyes as he took the flowers. "*Dicentra spectabilis*," he said, his voice rough.

"You remembered the Latin name."

He stared at the red-and-white flowers, and a humorless sound passed his lips. "For bleeding heart? I'm not apt to forget something so . . . descriptive." His gaze seemed to burn into her. "I remember everything, Catherine. Every look. Every word. Every smile. I remember the first time I touched you. The last time I touched you. And every touch in between."

She clenched her hands to keep them from fidgeting with her gown. "I found your note. The ring. And the letters. I . . . I'd had no idea that your feelings for me were of such a long standing."

"Is that what you wanted to talk to me about? The fact that I've loved you for years rather than months?"

"Yes. No." She shook her head. "What I mean is that I want to speak to you about *my* feelings."

His gaze sharpened. "I'm listening."

"After you left my bedchamber, I spent the rest of the night thinking, and I finally arrived at what I believed was a logical decision. I went to tell you, but you were gone. Then I read your note, saw those letters I'd written, and all my fine decisions disintegrated. I was left with only an undeniable, irrefutable realization—that I'd already made one terrible, dreadful mistake by refusing you and had been on the verge of making another. I do not wish to make any more such errors." She drew a bracing breath. "Andrew, will you marry me?"

Never in her life had she heard such a deafening silence. Her heart seemed to stall and race at the same time as he regarded her with a cautious expression. Finally, he spoke. "I beg your pardon?"

She cocked a brow in her best imitation of him. "Do you not know what *marry* means? Must I fetch a dictionary?"

"Perhaps you should, because I'd like to be certain we're speaking of the same word."

"A very wise person recently told me that marriage

means caring for one another. Loving together. Sharing laughter and helping through pain. Always knowing that there is another person standing beside you. For you." She took one step closer to him, then another. "It means I want you to be my husband. I've spoken to Spencer, and he wants you to be his father. I want to be your wife. Now do you understand?"

His throat worked, and he jerked his head in a nod. "You've left very little room for misinterpretation, although I'm not certain I understand how my note precipitated this change of heart."

"The thought of you loving me for all those years . . . it touched my heart. Opened my heart. I realized with painful clarity that if *you'd* been my husband, my feelings toward marriage would be vastly different. I realized I wished you *had* been my husband. My fears made me deny my feelings for you, but I cannot deny them any longer. I love you, Andrew."

He briefly squeezed his eyes shut. When he opened them, Catherine's breath caught at the raw emotion burning in his gaze. Reaching out, he yanked her into his arms, and kissed her, a long, deep, passionate kiss that stole the bones from her knees.

"Again," he growled against her lips. "Say it again."

"I love you, Andrew."

"Again."

She pushed her hands against his chest and frowned at him. "Not until you answer my question."

He nuzzled her neck, wreaking havoc on her ability to concentrate. "Question?"

She pushed back farther and glared at him. "Yes. Will you marry me?"

"Ah. That question. Before I answer, I want to make certain that you understand several things."

"Such as?"

"I'm afraid I am no longer available as a single entity. I now come with a dog."

One corner of her mouth twitched. "I see. I can accept those terms. What else?"

"Although I am financially secure, you should know that I will unfortunately be five hundred pounds poorer than I'd planned since I won't be able to deliver Charles Brightmore to Lord Markingham and his friends."

"As I am deeply grateful for that, I can hardly quibble about the money."

"Excellent. In order to keep Markingham or anyone else from instigating another search, I'll offer them irrefutable proof that Brightmore has escaped the country for some far-off land with no intention of returning."

"How will you come by such proof?"

"I'm a very clever fellow."

"You'll get no argument from me."

He smiled. "This morning gets better and better."

"Is there anything else I need to understand?"

"Yes. You still owe me a boon, and I shall demand payment." His eyes darkened and he pulled her closer. "In full."

A delighted shiver faced down her spine. "A truly heinous demand, but I shall concede. Anything else?"

"One more thing. I believe I'd like to follow in your literary footsteps and try my hand at penning a book. I've come up with the perfect title: *A Gentleman's Guide to Masculine Survival and Understanding Women*."

She stared at him, nonplussed. "You're jesting."

"I'm not. After our courtship, I consider myself something of an expert."

But perhaps the idea wasn't *totally* insane . . . "We'll discuss it," she said.

"Fair enough. And you might want to consider writing a sequel to the *Guide*. I'd be more than delighted to assist you with any research requirements. Now, about your proposal—the answer is a resounding yes. It would be my honor to marry you."

Catherine released a breath she hadn't realized she held. Slipping her hand into the pocket of her gown, she withdrew the emerald ring. "Will you put this on me?" she asked.

"With pleasure." Tucking his flowers under his arm, he slipped the ring on her finger. "Do you like it? Because if you don't, I'll get you a different—"

"It's perfect," she assured him, moving her hand back and forth so the facets caught the light. "It is my most prized possession."

He captured her hand and brought it to his mouth, pressing a warm kiss in her palm. A slow, devastating grin curved his lips. "I've never received flowers before. Or a marriage proposal."

Warmth and happiness suffused her, and she returned his smile. "Yes, well you know how I like to be first."

"My darling, Catherine," he said, his eyes filled with love and passion. "You always have been."